Pat Garrett had n
to a man. *Billy*
himself. *It's bet*
somebody who's willing to bring him in alive.

"Your acquaintanceship with Billy Bonney should prove to be useful in tracking him down," remarked the governor. "And there won't be any complications due to . . . old ties?"

"I'm not tied to anybody, governor," Garrett said. "I'll do the job."

LEGENDS: The Story of Pat Garrett and Billy the Kid

Other books by David Everitt:

The LEGENDS Series:
The Story of the Sundance Kid
The Story of Wyatt Earp

Raven Bravo
Rustler's Blood
Indian Territory

LEGENDS:

The Story of Pat Garrett and Billy the Kid

DAVID EVERITT

KNIGHTSBRIDGE PUBLISHING COMPANY
NEW YORK

Publisher's Note: This novel is a work of fiction. Names, characters, places, and incidents either are the product of the author's imagination or are used fictitiously, and any resemblance to actual persons living or dead, events, or locales is entirely coincidental.

Published in the United States by
Knightsbridge Publishing Company
255 East 49th Street
New York, New York 10017

ISBN: 1-877961-62-0

Designed by Stanley S. Drate/Folio Graphics

10 9 8 7 6 5 4 3 2 1

FIRST EDITION

For Ethan

FOREWORD

THE LEGEND OF PAT GARRETT AND BILLY BONNEY has been a lopsided affair. The two names of Garrett and Bonney have always been linked in the classic Western story of two gunslinging friends who find themselves on opposite sides of the law. But the emphasis has clearly been on the outlaw Bonney, a.k.a. Billy the Kid.

The number of books, articles, songs, and films devoted to Bonney is enormous. As a result, Billy the Kid may be the most famous figure in Western folklore. Pat Garrett, the man who tracked down the Kid, on the other hand, has generally been relegated to either the role of supporting player or outright villain. The real story suggests that a different balance should be struck between the two men.

As is the case with virtually every well-known outlaw in the Old West, Billy the Kid has been characterized as an American Robin Hood. Writers have claimed that he was a gallant opponent of greedy cattle barons, or that he was a champion of downtrodden Mexican-Americans, or that he was a misunderstood young man who never got a fair shake. What seems to be at the bottom of this fascination is the strange attraction that law-abiding people have to anarchic killers, an attraction that has made heroes out of not only Billy Bonney, but ruthless desperados like Jesse James and Bonnie and Clyde as well.

The fascination with Billy the Kid began during his lifetime and was fueled by sensational stories appearing in the *National Police Gazette.* The Billy the Kid phenomenon truly came into its own, however, immediately following his death. After Bonney was killed by Pat Garrett in the summer of 1881, the Kid's first biographer waited all of three weeks to come out with his version of the outlaw's exploits. This feat of instant exploitation set the pattern. The dime novel industry churned out eight Billy the Kid books in the next ten months.

At this time, Bonney was often portrayed as a senseless, cold-blooded murderer. The shift in attitude toward the gunman would come in the 1920s with the publication of Walter Noble Burns's *The Saga of Billy the Kid.*

This book concedes that Bonney killed some men in cold blood, and Burns even suggests that the Kid might have been mentally unbalanced, but the author doesn't seem to hold any of this against him. He still manages to get across the idea that Billy was a likable, high-spirited young fellow—a striking example of how little some killers had to do to win people's sympathy. Perhaps most important, Burns's entertaining, grandiose prose transformed the Kid's story into a larger-than-life tale.

A best seller, this book originated the modern Billy Bonney myth and served as the basis for the classic 1931 Western movie *Billy the Kid,* starring handsome Johnny Mack Brown as the romanticized desperado. Since then, Bonney has appeared in many cinematic forms: as the lusty hero of *The Outlaw,* Howard Hughes's notorious "sex Western"; as the whitewashed do-gooder in a series of B Westerns in the early '40s; and as a mixed-up kid, a sort of frontier rebel without a cause, in the Paul Newman vehicle *The Left-Handed Gun.* (Billy the Kid wasn't left-handed. One of many misconceptions about the legendary gunman, this particular error was based upon a famous photograph of Bonney that was often printed in reverse.) The music world has also made its contributions. Billy Joel wrote the hero-worshipping "The Ballad of Billy the Kid," and even classical composer Aaron Copland embraced the legend in his *Billy the Kid* ballet. The extent to which some people would go to capitalize on this legend is exemplified by the 1966 film *Billy the Kid vs. Dracula.*

In real life, Billy Bonney probably was not as maniacal as his early biographers claimed he was, and he was certainly not as chivalrous as the romantics have made him out to be.

Born Henry McCarty, in either New York City, Indiana, Kansas, or Missouri—depending on what source is cited—he was known as both Henry Antrim and Kid Antrim prior to adopting the William Bonney moniker. He was a petty thief and had reportedly killed a man before coming to Lincoln

County, New Mexico, around the age of seventeen. It was the Lincoln County War that set the stage for his violent, legend-making career.

Pat Garrett lived in Lincoln County at this time but played no part in the bloody local war. He didn't come to prominence until he received the call to hunt down the Kid. For his trouble, he was branded by many people as a man who betrayed his friends.

The extent of the friendship between Garrett and Bonney is not clear. Some writers have portrayed them as inseparable pals, while others suggest that the two were merely acquaintances. One thing, though, is clear. Those people who have romanticized Billy the most have tended to emphasize the friendship as well. It's easier to present the Kid in sympathetic terms if he was the victim of a two-faced villain.

While Walter Noble Burns treated Sheriff Garrett fairly in *The Saga of Billy the Kid,* other versions of the story haven't been so kind. At best, he is usually characterized as a dogged manhunter doing a dirty job. On the other hand, in the recent Billy the Kid movie, *Young Guns,* Garrett is featured in only two scenes, just long enough to make it clear that he is an arrogant, sneaky varmint. As for the historical attention that he's received, only two full biographies have been published about him. Richard O'Connor, one of the two biographers, points out that as Billy the Kid became the Western Robin Hood in the public mind, Garrett shared the fate of the Sheriff of Nottingham.

Was Garrett justified in hunting down Bonney? At Garrett's death, Theodore Roosevelt reportedly said that Pat Garrett wasn't the man who upheld law and order in New Mexico; he was the man who *introduced* law and order. Others have expressed similar opinions over the years. Leon C. Metz's 1973 biography of Garrett, in particular, put a new perspective on the Lincoln County sheriff's accomplishments, as well as his flaws. He was clearly a man faced with hard choices in the pursuit of law and order, more specifically in the pursuit of criminals who hadn't always been enemies. That is the story of Pat Garrett and Billy Bonney.

PROLOGUE

The Pursuit

The riders tramped across the sun-blasted mesquite, sitting in their saddles with shoulders stooped as if the heat were a giant invisible hand that pressed on their backs. They angled slowly across the valley toward the serrated ridge on the right where a strip of shadow promised some relief. But not for long. In another hour or two the sun would climb to the top of its arc, and the shadows would vanish. Then the real heat would begin.

At the end of the line, Sam Dobbs brought his lathered horse alongside the man riding in front of him.

"I swear we're bound to just shrivel up if he keeps leading on like this," he said. "I swear we will. This just ain't no time of day for a white man to go ridin' through this country."

José Roibal glanced briefly at him, then tipped his

head forward to let the slouch-hat brim shield his face against the sun. It occurred to Dobbs that maybe he had said something wrong. Being a Mex, José wasn't exactly a white man, Dobbs figured, and might not really understand the remark.

After some silent riding, José said simply, "He won't stop."

"And leave us all dead?" Dobbs almost whined. Darting a look up ahead, he lowered his voice to make sure he wasn't overheard. "They didn't take any of *my* damn horses. Why should I be going through hell for this?"

"You could have gone back with the others. You had the chance."

"Yeah, I sure did. And it might've been my last chance." Almost to himself, Dobbs added, "Going back by myself now'd be nearly as bad as going on, it surely would." Loosening the bandana around his neck, he squinted ahead at the tall man in the white shirt and black trousers riding point, the man's legs so ridiculously long that his boots seemed to dangle beneath his mount's belly. "Damn him," Sam Dobbs hissed through his dry throat.

"Juan Largo knows what has to be done," said José.

"Juan Largo," Dobbs repeated sarcastically. "He's a Long John all right. And a feller with no damn sense too."

"Shut up, Sam," José said mildly. "It's too hot to talk."

Dobbs cursed some more, but kept it to himself, and dropped back to ride drag once more. He felt alone and desperate with these four men.

In the ridge's shadow, the riders were spared the fierce, direct sunlight. Still, the heat lifted from the reddish brown earth and enveloped the men and animals, a lesser hardship than before, but relentless just the same.

As they reached the hills, a rifle shot whined off a rock to their side. The five horsemen, defying fatigue, wheeled their animals and spurred them to the cover of an overhanging ledge by the time the second round was fired. They dismounted in the thin cloud of dust raised by the horses' hooves. Dobbs wrestled his carbine out of its saddle boot and, backing up quickly, flattened himself against the wall of rock. José and Ramon Domingo sidestepped toward the edge of the cover, stopping just behind Jack Briscoe.

"They're up there," Briscoe said to the tall man. "I saw them fire. Shit fire, Pat, they just about picked us off, shooting down on us like that. Damn, I'd like to know where they got those damned rifles."

Pat Garrett turned away from studying the hills up ahead and looked at Briscoe. His sharply angled features were drawn into haggard lines by the exhaustion that plagued them all, but the thin lips beneath the black mustache were still pressed into a hard, dogged line. He took his time scrutinizing Briscoe. Around Fort Sumner, those gray eyes could take on a joking glint, especially during the *bailes* or times when Garrett was tending bar at Beaver Smith's saloon. Now they were ice-cold as they took stock of the fidgety man just a foot away.

"It was a wild shot they took," Pat said in a Louisiana drawl. "We still have them backing up."

"This is their country. Don't tell me them Comanches're hard pressed. They're setting us up is what they're doing."

"We got four of them," said Pat. "That means only four left. Time for you to help us finish it, Jack." He then turned away to gaze at the hills again.

Dobbs stared in consternation at Briscoe. *Him too?* he thought. Briscoe was the last one he had expected to get fed up with the hunt. Back at Fort Sumner, after getting the news of the Comanches' horse rustling, it had been Garrett and Briscoe together who had organized the posse, and when the rest of the boys had decided to turn back two days ago, it had been the two of them again who had whipped the rest into line. Dobbs now felt his mind take a hopeful turn as he calculated what Briscoe's new attitude might mean. If Briscoe was standing up to Garrett, then the two Mexes might also, and before long they would finally head back home.

More rifle fire popped along the top of the hill across from the ledge. Then a new sound rose up, a sound that made all five men in the posse freeze. It was a shrill, tortured squealing that came from somewhere on the other side of the hill. The posse stood listening to the horrible din for several moments. Then Pat Garrett led the way from the ledge at a run.

The posse scrambled to new cover behind a low hogback and turned their rifles on the hill. After a short barrage, Briscoe and Domingo took off to the right; they ran from cover to cover, moving to the side of the hill in a flanking maneuver. Dobbs and José kept up their fire, shooting at anything that seemed to move along the skyline. Garrett, meanwhile, crouched with his Winchester resting across his knees, his eyes riveted on the hill.

He moved away from the others and took a position farther up the rise on the left. Settling back into a sitting position behind a rock, he leveled the rifle to his shoulder; he braced his left elbow on his raised knee. For a long time he didn't move.

Briscoe and Domingo opened up on the right. Hidden in a depression near the top of the hill, they levered fast enough to pour a torrent of fire toward the Indian rifleman's position. For a brief moment, the Comanche raised his head as he backed away from the barrage. That was when Garrett finally moved. It was a small movement, a slight adjustment of his hands as he shifted the Winchester's muzzle an inch to the left. His first and only shot sent a .44–.40 through the back of the Indian's head.

Garrett, Dobbs, and José stayed put for the moment, listening. There was more shooting from the other side of the hill, toward the right—that would probably be Briscoe and Domingo—then there was a sudden stop. In the absence of gunfire, the terrible squealing returned, almost as loud as before.

"Time to take a look," said Pat.

No more Comanches were on the other side of the hill; just Briscoe and Domingo standing halfway down the yellow slope, gazing at the field of dead and dying horses below. The stolen animals all bled from the neck, stabbed by the remaining Comanches to lighten their load for the next leg of the chase. Some twenty horses lay there, half of them already dead.

Domingo stood nervously before the slaughter, shifting his weight from one leg to the other, darting glances at Garrett. But Briscoe didn't move at all. He stood with shoulders hunched, his right hand hanging by his side, holding the barrel of his rifle. When Garrett reached his side, he finally spoke.

"That's what the good goddamn we've been trailin' these bastards for? A pile of dead flesh?" His mouth stayed open for more words, but none came to him for the moment. He stalked away.

"This is it, Pat!" he shouted once more. "We killed enough of 'em. They're makin' a trap for us. Somewhere out there. I know they are."

Garrett glanced at the butchered horses, then turned back to Briscoe. "I'm not done yet," he said. "I guess you don't have to go any further if you don't want."

He didn't wait for an answer. Wheeling swiftly, he climbed back up the slope and headed back toward their mounts. José Roibal went with him, as did Domingo. A few moments later, Dobbs started after them, cursing for not having the nerve to ride all the way back on his own, as he knew he should. He had no doubt that Briscoe would rejoin Garrett soon enough, at least for now. Dobbs figured that later on he might be able to get the old buffalo hunter to finally draw the line; and with the Mexicans, that would make a party of four traveling across this no-man's-land back to Fort Sumner, a thought that Dobbs found comforting.

He decided his opportunity had come that night while they were camped by an arroyo.

"Seems to me, Pat," Dobbs began, "if there's a majority here for going back then it's only right that we do what they want. You have to admit there's sense to that." Out of the corner of his eye he checked Briscoe, sitting by his bedroll, staring bitterly into the night. At first there was no answer, either from Garrett or from anyone else. Then Briscoe said his piece.

"You give your word to some fat-ass rancher and you think everybody else's got to waltz right along with you, no matter what." He looked directly at Garrett. "Just what the hell do you aim to prove is what I want to know."

"I told you before," Pat growled at him, "if you don't got the sand, just up and leave whenever you want."

Briscoe stood up slowly, the moonlight picking up a cold look in his eye. "You bastard. You call me a coward again and I'll break those long legs in two and that's flat."

"Sit down and shut up, you stupid Mick."

"Now you two just ease up," Dobbs put in quickly, trying to steer things back on track. But Briscoe was already moving before the last of Dobbs's words were out.

He lashed out at Pat with a swing of his boot. Garrett flattened himself beneath the kick and rolled to the side, scrambling to his feet with his knees bent, his hands ready. When Briscoe charged at him again, the tall man sidestepped out of the way. The next time Briscoe tried it, Garrett hammered a fist to the side of the man's head. Briscoe dropped. In the next moment, though, he was up, and he ran at Garrett with arms swinging.

Pat knocked him down again.

Backing up steadily until he was halfway around the camp's perimeter, Pat kept trying to give the man some room, some chance to stop, but each time he punched him aside Briscoe was provoked even more, all of the long hunt's suffering and fear finally erupting into a mad fury. Garrett tried sidestepping again, and this time Briscoe barreled past in an attempt to tackle the tall man; he sprawled beside his saddle.

Looking up at Garrett, Briscoe's face was consumed with a dark hopelessness. He grabbed the hatchet slung from his saddle's pommel and lurched toward Pat with the blade raised high above his head.

Dobbs and the Mexicans got out of the way as Garrett sprang from the man with the hatchet. Briscoe got close enough to take one swipe, close enough for Pat to hear the blade whisper through the air. Then Garrett dove for his bedroll, took hold of the Winchester lying alongside, and with a swift working of his big hands, levered a cartridge into the chamber and fired. The .44–.40 slammed into Briscoe's chest, dead-center, and halted his forward motion, as if he were suddenly suspended diagonal to the ground, with shoulders thrust forward. The next instant he slumped in a heap, curled like a sleeping child.

Pat stood above him, rifle still in hand, for several moments before he realized that Dobbs was standing next to him.

"Damn, Pat," said Dobbs, "I thought you two were friends."

The War

All in all, there's something to be thankful for, Billy Bonney figured. When Dolan's boys had tossed those coal-oil lamps through the window, it looked like they would be flushed out in no time at all. Billy had hoped they could hold on till nightfall—that had been the only hope he had left—and now here it was close to nine o'clock and they were still inside.

The beam overhead groaned, then crackled, and as flames crept toward the middle of the rafter, it split at the far end and came crashing down. Moving quickly, Billy got out of its way by only three feet. He tried waving the smoke from his eyes and blinked rapidly to ward off the stinging sensation. Across the room, he could see McSween still hadn't moved. The lawyer stared at the blaze and pressed himself against the wall as if there were some door behind him that would allow him to escape, but he didn't really seem to be seeing the flames skittering in from the adjacent bedroom; his eyes were absolutely empty. Charley Bowdre tried to pull him along. McSween allowed himself to be moved a couple of feet before he began resisting.

Billy jumped over the fallen beam, put his rifle in his left hand, and grabbed McSween with his right. Together, he and Charley dragged the man to the next doorway. The last thing they saw before leaving the living room was Mrs. McSween's piano igniting into a sudden burst of flame. Then a gunshot whistled through a front window, and they hurried McSween along to the dining room.

Some of the men crouched by the far wall, trying to stay as far away as possible from the advancing flames. Others kneeled behind the overturned oakwood table, which served as a makeshift bulwark against the gun volleys from across the street. As smoke billowed through, a fitful chorus of coughs swept across the room.

Billy and Charley pushed McSween behind the table.

"We got us a couple more minutes, Mr. McSween," said Charley. "Do we try it now?"

McSween absently patted down the sides of his brown suit jacket and mumbled an answer, something about saving the house, but most of it was unintelligible. Nearby, Tom O'Folliard watched the broken man curiously for a moment, then turned to Billy.

"Don't look like the lawyer-man's giving too many more orders," he said between coughs.

Charley Bowdre squinted at Billy. "What do you say, Kid? Do we make a run for it?"

Billy the Kid nodded thoughtfully, then took off his hat and used his forearm to wipe the sweat off his face. A moment later, the fire's heat forced perspiration to stream down his forehead once more, as if he had never mopped it. The sweat made streaks of the soot that had blackened his face and darkened his blond hair.

"Let's give Mrs. McSween a chance," he said, the smoke turning his young voice into a dry croak. "Then we'll see."

To the side, Hendry Brown and Doc Scurlock were pumping rifle shots through the holes gouged out of the adobe wall. Billy scurried over to give them some help. He peered through the gunport and thought he saw movement by the shed to the rear. Angling the barrel of the Winchester through the hole, he fired two shots, but then dropped to the floor when a cluster of bullets thwacked against the building just inches from the hole.

When the next round hit, he could see that it must have come from the right, away from the shack. He sidled up to the gunport for another look. With his eyes stinging and watering, he managed to see a muzzle flare in the darkening hills bordering the town of Lincoln. Since this new volley was directed at another part of the house, Billy was able to keep his eyes on the sniper's position. There was no way to know who might be up there, although Billy was willing to bet even money that it was one of Dolan's bought-and-paid-for deputies, just like the one that Hendry Brown had shot out of his hillside perch on the second day of the siege.

Three days ago, Billy brooded.

For five days now they had been trapped in Mc-

Sween's house, caged up like animals, with no one to bail them out; not Chisum, not J. C. Lea, and certainly not those damned soldiers. Chisum, now *he* was a hell of a friend, the skinny old blowhard. A lot of big talk, but nothing to back it up. He had been the one pushing for this war right from the beginning, and now, Billy figured, he was sitting at home in his big old house, being waited on by his niece, and taking it easy while everybody else did his dirty work for him.

The first to fight, that was me, Billy mused. Right after Tunstall had been murdered, he had been out riding to even things up, riding for McSween and Chisum and whatever was left of Tunstall's spread. The House of Murphy had been the cock-of-the-walk back then, and it had been Billy and the rest of the Regulators who put a scare into them. *But what the hell for?* Billy now thought. *Here we are down to our last bullets and our last breath—the bastards are holding all the cards in the end.*

Billy gazed through the gunport at the rifle fire on the hill, for the moment forgetting the sweltering heat and suffocating smoke. All of a sudden, it came to him that he hated the hillside sniper—whoever the bastard might be—more than he had ever hated anyone else before. More than Brady or Morton or Baker or any of the other sons-a-bitches belonging to Murphy and Dolan. Billy poked his Winchester through the port and sighted along the barrel. He took his time trying to gauge the distance and the trajectory, but a spasm of coughing brought him up short; he pulled the weapon back inside.

When he looked through the hole again, he told himself it was pointless. He could never hit his man at such a distance in the thickening darkness. *Pat Garrett might have a shot at it,* he thought, *but not me, not at that range.* Billy had to smile at that thought, baring his buckteeth in a simple boy's grin. *Pat, that old woman,* he said to himself; *fat chance he would be throwing in with us here.*

"Billy, she's comin' in," called Charley.

The Kid moved to the kitchen at the rear of the house and saw Susan McSween crossing the backyard, walking stiffly, with arms folded, seemingly oblivious to the gunmen who, Billy knew, had to be concealed along the low adobe wall. *Well, good for them,* Billy thought, *at least they won't shoot an unarmed woman.*

When she marched into the smoky house, she stopped to dart glances from side to side, as if looking for new enemies skulking up on her blind side. Her stern face had acquired a new harshness since leaving the house an hour ago. Billy had no trouble guessing what had happened.

"He won't do a thing," she said. "Not for us anyway. That Colonel Dudley says he'll keep his troops where they are until my husband surrenders. I told him he might as well just come in here and shoot him himself."

"Well, the last I saw," said Billy, "he still has that Gatling gun ready to go on the street. There won't be much sense in trying anything in that direction."

"Where's Alex?" she said, walking onward. She found McSween where Billy had left him, still sitting behind the table. The sight of her seemed to bring some light to his eyes.

"Alex, you men have to get yourselves out of here," she told him. She knelt by his side and took hold of his hand. "They'll leave me alone, but they won't stop before they shoot the rest of you down."

McSween nodded. "Oh yes," he said, "they certainly wouldn't harm you. You're right about that." Satisfied with this thought, he fell silent again.

Susan grabbed his shoulders and shouted his name into his face. With a grim realization passing across her expression, she stopped there, seeing no point in saying anything more. But her disappointment with her husband didn't slow her down for very long. She turned to Billy.

"Can you lead these men?" she asked.

"I should. I've had enough practice at it for the last hour. We just wanted to get word from you first. Ain't that right, Mr. McSween?"

The lawyer said, "It's dark now. Can we get out, Billy?" He was getting to his feet now. Billy made sure he didn't rise above the edge of the table where he would be exposed to gunfire.

"We're going out the back, Mr. McSween. You got a gun here you can use?"

"Oh no. I can't do that. I haven't carried a gun through all of this and I'm not going to start now, now that it . . ." His voice trailed off and he began checking the other men. Most of them were looking at him and Billy.

The Kid turned to Mrs. McSween to see if she would say something to make her husband arm himself, but she remained crouched on her knees, her body slack, saying nothing. Billy shrugged. "Well, I guess you'll just have to tag along the best you can, Mr. McSween. Maybe those boys that get through can cover for you." Billy got the attention of Tom O'Folliard. "You help Hendry and Doc shoot

across the street, keep the bastards busy. After you hear us out back, it's up to you when to take your chance." He checked to see that he already had a cartridge chambered in his Winchester. "And you'll be hearing us out back. I guarantee that."

Billy moved with the rest of the men, the last of McSween's Regulators, to the rear kitchen door. He sneaked a look out of an adjacent window to see Olinger shifting to a new position behind the adobe wall. For the moment, no one fired from there, and no one else let himself be seen. An hour ago Billy had noticed Bob Beckwith's face above the wall; from the amount of shooting at the rear of the house he guessed that there were at least ten others with him.

The gauntlet he would have to run in order to get out of here alive sent a peculiar, distracted feeling through Billy. *There's no getting out of this,* he thought calmly. *Everywhere I look I'm surrounded by enemies.* "That's how it goes," he said, unaware at first that he was saying his thought out loud; then he noticed Charley squatting alongside, giving him a curious look.

Billy checked the others to see if they were ready. "Okay, fellas," he said, "let's give 'em something to remember." In the next moment, Billy charged through the doorway, followed by Charley and Harvey Morris, the clerk from McSween's law office.

Billy and Charley had their guns blasting as soon as they emerged from the house, while Morris managed to raise his pistol and thumb back the hammer before three slugs crashed through his midsection. Pivoting suddenly, Billy and Charley raced to the right, toward the gap in the adobe wall; gun muzzles spat flames, and shots pounded on all sides of the yard, some of the bullets searing above Billy, others whizzing behind him, toward the doorway where the other Regulators were making their run. Billy fired straight ahead, then swung his Winchester to the left and levered three more rounds toward the rear of the yard. He thought he saw one of his shots knock a man down. Billy kept running.

The hole in the adobe wall drew near. Triggering the last shots in their magazines, Billy and Charley reached the opening, and almost as one, sprang off their feet, vaulted through the air, and hit the ground rolling on the far side of the wall. The barrage behind them seemed to lessen as Billy scrambled to his feet, but he wasn't curious enough to look back. He bolted onward. Then the gunfire stopped, and in its place were voices, one of them high-pitched, fervent, and very familiar.

Billy glanced over his shoulder to see McSween standing in the doorway, talking loud enough to be heard across the yard. Most of the words Billy couldn't make out, but the word "surrender" was clear. Gunshots cracked, and McSween staggered, then crumpled to the ground. Watching this on the run, Billy couldn't be completely sure, but he thought he saw Beckwith fire one of the killing shots. Behind McSween, two more Regulators were gunned down.

"Charley," called Billy, suddenly coming to a stop. "I'll catch up." Without another word, he tossed his spent Winchester to his friend, pulled his Colt army revolver and spun around to creep back toward the yard.

He came within good range very quickly. By the

number of shots he had heard, he knew there must have been more than one man who had fired upon McSween, but he also knew that he would have to be satisfied with what little opportunity he had left. Against the white wall of the house, he could see Deputy Sheriff Beckwith clearly, a sturdy young man of nineteen, no older than Billy. As the deputy aimed his rifle at Hendry Brown crossing the yard, the Kid shot him twice through the side of the rib cage, then turned to run back toward the river.

He found Charley hidden behind the brush that grew on the far side of the Rio Bonito; with him were Jim French and George Coe. Before long they were joined by Hendry and Doc, and they began to walk silently along the riverbed. It would be a long hike, Billy figured, before they would reach someplace safe; for all he knew they might even have to walk all the way to Fort Sumner. He couldn't help but think about the quarterhorse he had ridden into Lincoln five days ago, a fine animal that he would now have to leave behind for some Dolan son-of-a-bitch to saddle as his own.

As the last sounds of the fighting lifted into the night air behind him, Billy told himself that there were plenty of other good horses in this country—and plenty of cattle, too. And a lot of them were owned by the wrong damned people.

THE NOMINATION

1

"If I thought he was mixed up in any rustling, I wouldn't have brought him into this," said John Chisum. His tone made the message plain: he had just concluded the argument to everyone's satisfaction.

He sat in his easy chair, with his wiry body held slightly forward, his leathery, sharp-featured face searching for any possible defiance. The first dissent from the four other men was voiced by Jim Boskett.

"I don't think you can just dismiss it all as easy as that," said Boskett, who had come to the Pecos Valley early enough to find some land for ranching that hadn't been claimed by Chisum. "There are too many stories and too many people telling them. I don't think *I* can ignore all that, even if you can."

One side of Chisum's nose arched, as if he had just smelled something disagreeable. It was a reaction he often had when somebody spoke to him in a Northeastern accent. "Haven't heard one of them stories coming from a man I liked," he said with strained patience. "Which ones're you talking about, Jim?"

"Well, for one, I heard they were in business together, one running the cows down, the other selling them. That's what I've heard."

"Some folks'll say anything, especially if they don't have the backbone to do anything else."

"You have to admit, John, he was in a good position to do that sort of thing," said Captain Lea. He took a lazy drag on his cigar and flicked its ashes into the cuspidor next to his chair before going on, confident that no one would interrupt during the long pause. "With all the men passing through that saloon, he would have gotten to know everyone he would need to know. He wouldn't be the first, John."

Already tiring of this talk, Chisum didn't bother with an answer. From outside came the clacking of a hammer being used to repair a plank on the front gallery; it was a faint sound but it carried crisply in the New Mexican autumn air. For a few moments, that was the only thing heard. Then Joe LaRue broke the silence.

"Hell, John, maybe we're just talking about a few mavericks here and there. You could allow him that much in his past, can't you?" The Lincoln storekeeper was now grinning. "When you were young enough you probably knew something about that sort of business."

This got a laugh out of Boskett, and also from Ray Purkey, the other cattleman in the room. LaRue added, "I guess all you cow barons know a thing or two about that." Now even Chisum could afford a smile.

"Okay, boys," Chisum said after another sip of his bourbon, "you came all this way to meet him, so if you're dead set on talking too much, you might as well do it to his face."

He crossed the study and swung the door open. "Bob, go ahead and bring him in," he said. A short while later, the stocky frame of Bob Olinger appeared in the open doorway just long enough for him to show Pat Garrett into the room.

Pat held himself uneasily as he stopped before five of Lincoln County's most powerful men, his long arms hanging by his side, unmoving, but looking like they were itching for something to do.

"There's a seat there for you, Pat," said Chisum with a wave of his hand.

Garrett sat in the hard-backed chair across from Chisum, and between LaRue and Purkey. *Right in the middle of things,* he thought, while trying a lopsided smile to show that he wasn't nervous. As the five pairs of eyes rested on him, he was thankful that he had found a tailor in Roswell yesterday who could alter the mail-order broadcloth suit so that it covered the entire length of him.

Chisum said, "I think you already know Joe LaRue and Jim Boskett over there. That's Ray Purkey next to you, and over there is Captain Lea."

The Captain took his introduction as a cue to get things rolling. "Mr. Garrett, you must know that a lot of people in this county are dissatisfied with Sheriff Kimball. Since the battle of Lincoln, many of us hoped there would be some order in this country, but between the *pistoleros* out to even up old scores and the rustling along the Pecos, things aren't any better than they were during the county war. Unfortunately, Kimball doesn't seem real interested in doing anything about it."

"A good tax collector is what he is," said Purkey, his broad face creasing with sarcasm, "which is about as important right now as me having a second keester."

Lea went on as if no one else had spoken. "Mr. Chisum here has been telling us that you're the man to take Kimball's place."

He stopped there, puffing his cigar, as if it were Garrett's turn to say something. Pat knew of Captain Joseph C. Lea as one of the most prominent men in the territory, a railroad tycoon with a hand in other industries as well, who could flex a lot of political muscle whenever he wanted. Pat felt adrift for the moment, not knowing what he could possibly say to such a man at this point. Finally, he answered simply, "John's talked to me about that."

"Damn right he's the one for the job," Chisum put in, taking Pat off the spot. "You all know what happened when Pat went after those Comanches a couple years back. We need a man who likes to get things done, just like he did then."

Boskett was leveling a hard-eyed stare at Garrett. "You always see a job through to the end?"

"Well, let's put it this way," said Pat, "if I see the reason for starting a job, I'll finish it." He wasn't sure these men caught on to what he was getting at, but it could wait if they didn't.

"We got some questions to ask you," said Purkey, "seeing as you've never been a lawman before. We have to know we're talking to the right man."

"I've got some questions too," Pat drawled. "For instance, this job you want somebody to take—with all the rustling I've been hearing about, it sounds like it'll be a lot of doing to drive the thieves out of the county. I'd like to know how much time I'd get to do the job. No offense, but after a month goes by, you might just bring another fella in here and tell him how you're getting fed up with me and want somebody else to take a crack at it."

Nobody answered at first. LaRue leaned forward and rested his elbows on his knees. "We want you to get the Kid, Pat. The rustling's part of it, but first there's the Kid."

This was no surprise to Pat, but he was glad it was out in the open.

"What we need to know is, are you ready to go gunning for a friend?" asked Boskett.

Garrett felt himself stiffen, unable to give an answer right away. Stalling, he ran a finger along his mustache while he put his words together.

"You got a right to ask that," he said, "but it seems to me that 'friend' is kind of a strong word in this case."

Boskett narrowed his eyes. "You saying Billy's not a friend of yours?"

"We know each other," said Pat, feeling Captain Lea's close-set eyes upon him. Although quiet now, the Captain still seemed like the most important man in the room, and Pat made sure he glanced the man's way when he continued talking. "Like I said before, I've got some questions, and one of them's got to do with Billy. Some folks're saying that going after the Kid is just a way for the Murphy-Dolan bunch to get even with an old enemy."

"Goddamn it, Pat," said Chisum, half-lifting himself out of his chair. "You think I'm doing this for Dolan? I was the one backing McSween and Tunstall. Why would I bother with that son-of-a-bitch Dolan? And how come you never told me you were thinking that before? For Christ's sake, Pat."

Lea's smooth voice kept Chisum from going any further. "Mr. Garrett, I don't think anyone still believes that the House of Murphy won the war. They beat the hell out of McSween's men in Lincoln, but Murphy was dead even before the Lincoln battle got started, and after it was over most of Dolan's money was gone. We don't have any reason to dance to Dolan's tune, Mr. Garrett."

"I heard Dolan's ready to support a sheriff who'd kill Billy. Is that right?"

"Let me tell you something, Pat." Chisum's voice was level now; bristling with determination, but under control. "If Dolan wants you to kill Billy, that's his lookout. He can tag along with us if he wants, but that doesn't change what I'm after. Billy's running wild, he's got himself a gang, and he's stealing stock. My stock and other men's, too. Lincoln County can't stand still for him any longer."

Pat concentrated on holding the cattle baron's piercing gaze, which was a challenge. Just because he physically towered over Chisum didn't exempt him from the feeling of smallness that the man could inflict on another man.

"One more thing," Pat said; he noticed Purkey sighing in exasperation, but he plowed ahead anyway. "Maybe Billy's still got some right on his side."

"Is that what Billy's telling you?" Purkey said.

Pat ignored him. "Maybe he didn't get the deal he should've gotten from the governor. Maybe he wouldn't be running wild if it wasn't for that."

"All right, Pat," said Boskett, "perhaps you *are* too close to the Kid after all. This might not be the right job for a fella like you."

"Not so fast, Jim," Lea cut in. "I like a man who thinks things through and asks questions. Mr. Garrett here seems like a thorough man. I don't think I have to tell you, Jim, that there are plenty of men who would jump at the chance to be sheriff, just so they could make a name for themselves, or maybe make a little money on the side. A little cautiousness is something I like in a case like this."

Pat kept his face blank. *If only the Captain knew how much I want to jump at this chance,* he thought. Reminded of those feelings, Pat began worrying the hat in his hands.

"And as for Mr. Garrett's being too close to the Kid," Lea continued, "well, we need a man who knows Billy Bonney. If he's going to track him down, he'll have to know where his hiding places are."

Pat checked the other men in the room. If Boskett and Purkey still had doubts about Pat Garrett they weren't showing them now, and weren't likely to as long as the Captain took a dim view of those doubts.

Joe LaRue said, "Just think of Billy as another Comanche, Pat. That's the way to see it."

"Don't rush him if he's got his reservations," said Captain Lea. "Mr. Garrett, I want you to think this over. In another month the Democratic convention is going to nominate a sheriff. I'd like to see you at that convention. In the meantime, if you have any more doubts, I think you should talk to the governor. Let him answer for himself."

"That's a damn good idea, Pat," said Chisum. "You go talk to the governor."

2

Bob Olinger was waiting by the buckboard when Garrett stepped out of the adobe ranch house. The big Buckeye Stetson was pushed to the back of his head, his gray pants tucked neatly into his boots, and the skirts of his jacket were pushed back so that he could grip his two-gun belt. He leaned against the wagon, looking at Chisum's sprawling longhouse and the peach orchard to the left as if he were surveying his own personal domain.

"I'm headed back to Lincoln," he said. "Thought I'd ride some of the way with you."

Pat wasn't sure how the route into nearby Roswell would be a good idea for a ride back to Lincoln, but he didn't say anything. For that matter, he hadn't understood why Olinger had had to accompany him to the Chisum spread in the first place.

Olinger rode alongside the buckboard on his big

gray, letting several minutes go by before saying what was on his mind.

"You going to the convention?" he asked.

"I'm thinking about it."

Olinger paused to adjust the blue bandana around his thick neck. "The man who becomes sheriff now, he could make a hell of reputation for himself."

Pat gave him a quick glance, then faced the two-horse team in front of him. Olinger wasn't going to say it, but it was still clear to Garrett: Bob thought he was entitled to the sheriff's job as much as anybody, or at least he *wanted* it as much as anybody. Pat had seen enough of the man in the Fort Sumner days to know what a fighting reputation meant to him.

"From what I hear," said Olinger, "the Kid's got himself a real hard bunch around him these days. It won't be no cakewalk bringing him in, that's for certain."

"I think you're right, Bob."

Olinger gave him a curious sidelong look. "You never did get mixed up with the Lincoln War, did you, Garrett?"

"That's right."

"Now that's something I never could figure," Olinger said. "Just about everybody chose sides and did their part. But you, you kept clear of it all. How was that, Garrett?"

"I had my own business to take care of."

"Yeah, and you know what? That's something else that's kind of funny. You not being a lawman at all, and not being a fighter in the War, and then they pick you for sheriff. Sort of funny when you think about it." Olinger spoke matter-of-factly, as though the comment really wasn't an insult.

But the tone didn't ease Pat any. His long hands held the reins tightly; he could feel the hot prickling sensation on the back of his neck. Another crack from Olinger and Pat might stop the wagon and knock the man down. In the silence that followed, though, he decided not to give Olinger a chance to prod him any further.

"Tell me something, Olinger. You haven't been a deputy for a while—what's your business now? You riding for Chisum?"

Olinger spat. "The bastard," he said.

"I didn't think a Dolan man would just jump over to the other side," Pat went on, "but you were the one to bring me to his ranch. How's that?"

"Chisum's got nothing to do with it."

"What does?" Pat said.

"Bob Beckwith," answered Olinger. "He was a friend of mine. I'm after the Kid for that."

Pat nodded, but said nothing. Olinger went along with the silence, his eyes staring blindly down the road. Finally he said, "Hell, those big cattlemen ain't about to make *me* sheriff. I know that. But if you need another gun going after Bonney, you just let me know, Garrett. You just make sure you do that thing."

Olinger didn't bother with any more talk as he rode without so much as a glance at Pat. Trying to size up the man, Garrett had trouble deciding which was more important to the big, swaggering gunman: the sheriff's job or the Kid. Without a clear idea where his own steps were about to take him, he saw no reason to ask Olinger about his motives. Those questions could wait. Olinger rode alongside the buckboard for a few more miles, saying nothing, then took off at a lope along the Rio Hondo, headed westward toward Lincoln.

Pat reached the outskirts of Roswell late in the afternoon. Bringing his buckboard to a stop in front of the two-story adobe house, he got a glimpse of little Ida running through the freshly planted oak grove that stood in rows of fragile stalks in the dry ground. She stopped long enough to wave quickly, then scampered on with one of the Mexican children who lived nearby.

At the front door, he peered in to see his wife sweeping the floor in the kitchen.

"Apolinaria," he called. "Come on out here."

Pat leaned against the door frame, idly rubbing the back of his neck, while she finished her chore; he heard the small cry of "Daddy" from the next room. Eagerness in his stride, he stepped inside to find eighteen-month-old Elizabeth sitting on the floor by the fireplace, her small, dimpled hands groping among the wooden blocks Garrett had made for her. He spoke her name, ran a hand across her light brown hair, then took her by the hand, lifted her to her feet, and walked her to the door. "Come on," he said quietly, "we're going to sit on the porch."

In the chair facing the road into town, he folded an arm around the baby's middle as she fussed for a while in his lap. She took a long time to settle, but Pat didn't mind. Just the feel of her brought a sense of homey ease to him; for the first time that day he could put Chisum's offer out of his mind.

Elizabeth swiveled to the right, then the left, to

no discernible purpose. She then turned all the way around, her pale, sightless eyes directed to the right of his face, which she now reached up to touch. Seeming satisfied, she faced the road beyond the porch and slouched against his belly. He smiled at the back of her curly head.

Apolinaria was brushing the last remnants of dust off her hands when she came out; her thick black hair, often pinned up, now hung below her shoulders; she looked serenely at Pat.

"They want me to go to Santa Fe to talk to the governor," he said. He tried to sound nonchalant.

A shine came to her dark eyes. "They must have big plans for you."

"They make it sound that way. And not just Chisum. Captain Lea too." For a few moments, he stared across the road toward the cottonwoods by the Rio Hondo and, beyond that, the red bluffs rearing above the Bottomless Lakes.

"They want me to hunt down Billy," he said.

"Can you do that, Pat?"

"I think I'd know how to find him, if that's what you mean." He could tell by her expectant look that she meant more than that. "That's why I'll talk to Governor Wallace," he added, "to find out what happened during the amnesty. I guess I can decide after that."

She said nothing for a while, as she watched the baby resting in his lap. "What do you think, Apolinaria?" he said.

"I think you'll find out what has happened to Billy in the last year. Then you'll make the right choice."

He knew that her words were meant to bolster his

confidence. She looked at him intently, her smooth-featured face showing no sign of doubt.

Apolinaria—the name was sure a mouthful. At one time, when he had first started courting her, Pat had considered calling her Polly, just to give his Anglo tongue an easier time of it, but the name didn't seem to fit the small, pretty girl. The daughter of a successful and respected New Mexican freighter, Apolinaria Gutierrez carried herself with a truly ladylike poise that seemed to demand a grand-sounding name. As it had many times before, that poise now brought Pat's worries down a notch.

When the sun moved toward the horizon after dinner, the growing darkness seemed to pull at Garrett. He stood smoking a cigar on the porch, gazing at the deepening pockets of shadows along the flat; for some reason, he felt he should be out there. Apolinaria's reassurances had had their effect, but they were dimming now, and his mind was tired of juggling his possible choices. Even the prospect of putting off the decision was wearying. The darkness seemed to promise something to him.

The hard, dry land turned into a bleak silhouette. The sight put him in mind of something he'd read, words by Robert Ingersoll that he'd committed to memory. "Life is a narrow vale between the cold and barren peaks of two eternities." Most times, Pat didn't have much difficulty in accepting barrenness and coldness in life. First, cow herding in the Panhandle, then the buffalo range on the high plains of Texas, and then the harsh country of New Mexico had seemed to tell Garrett that a man had to live with few comforts, either physical or spiritual. He wondered if his new life had lured him away from that understanding.

Reaching the butt-end of his cigar, he tossed it in a lazy loop to the packed ground. The darkness was almost complete now, and Pat started strolling away from the house. He thought it might be the old ways that were on his mind this evening, the long nights spent drinking and gambling with the Fort Sumner boys. *That's going back some,* he thought. He fetched the dun mare and brought her back to the buckboard for the ride into town.

A short time later, just short of Quincannon's saloon, he decided a couple of whiskeys would be enough to get the urge out of his system. Leaving the buckboard hitched to a tie rail, he headed toward the rectangle of light thrown out the saloon's open doorway; from inside came a murmur of voices—there weren't many customers there tonight—and an occasional gruff laugh. Pat got as far as the alley beside the low adobe building before he was stopped by the voice to his right.

"Where you going, Pat?"

Garrett turned to the alley. He had to look for a couple of moments before his eyes adjusted to the deeper darkness.

"Billy," he said, "that's a hell of a way to surprise a man."

Billy Bonney stepped closer to the street, with Charley Bowdre just a couple of feet behind. "Didn't mean to scare you to death," he said, "an old woman like you."

3

"Any special reason you're sticking to the shadows around here?" said Pat after ordering the first round of drinks.

Billy gave him a bucktoothed smile. "Now why would there be a reason for me skulking around?"

Pat shrugged as he took his glass. As casually as he could, he said, "I'd heard about some rustling along the Canadian River, over on the Panhandle side. I guess I was just wondering. Maybe somebody thought you had something to do with it."

"In the Panhandle you say? Wouldn't be New Mexico boys going that far, would it? You hear that, Charley? Taking Texas cattle and runnin' 'em through here. That's an idea, though, ain't it?"

Charley Bowdre didn't find the idea as amusing as the Kid seemed to think it was. He was too busy trying to look unconcerned as he leaned against the bar and kept his eyes moving from side to side.

Billy laughed to himself and tossed back the glass of whiskey. Garrett gave him a long look. The Kid's clothes were caked with sweat and dust, most likely meaning that he had been long-riding from somewhere, even if it wasn't Texas. Pat also noted the fuzz on Billy's upper lip, the closest thing to a full mustache that Garrett had ever seen on the Kid. *Still the light-haired boy,* Pat thought.

Billy flicked his blue eyes in Pat's direction. "How's that woman of yours? She give you a litter of babies yet?"

Coming from Billy, the crude reference to Apolinaria failed to anger Pat. It was difficult to take the young man that seriously. "We're working on it, Kid," was Pat's answer.

"I can't help it," Billy said with a smile, "I just can't help but think it's funny, you settling down like that."

"It's not so funny. That's where I was headed when I came to this country."

"It didn't look that way when I saw you going after all that whiskey and women in Fort Sumner."

Pat smiled. "I guess I kept it a pretty good secret for a while."

"Oh blue Jesus, Pat, look at Charley over there. What do you got sticking up inside you, Charley? If all you can do is just look around, why don't you just go outside and keep looking *there.*" Billy was still smiling when he said this, but Pat could see a hard glint in his eyes, meant to give Charley another, more serious message. The message understood, Charley finished his drink in a gulp and moved down the bar and out the door to the street.

"Say, Pat," Billy said in between sips of whiskey, "that deputy sheriff . . . what's his name? Meusel, isn't it? Would he still be posted in Roswell any-more?"

"He's still here. Not right now though. A couple days ago he headed out for Portales on some business." Pat got the bartender's attention for another round. Offhandedly he added, "Charley won't have to keep an eye out for him."

Billy let out a laugh. "I'll tell him that, Pat. He'll be real relieved to hear it." When he got his glass filled, he held it up in a toasting gesture. "Been a long time, Pat."

They drank to this sentiment, then took their next couple of swallows in silence. Now that Billy had brought up the subject, it seemed that the time that had passed since they had seen each other in Fort Sumner had taken away many of the things they used to talk about.

"What about you, Billy?" Pat finally said. "Who you running with these days? I heard Doc Scurlock pulled out and went to work for Maxwell. And Hendry too. He headed for Tascosa, didn't he?"

"You sure hear a lot, Pat."

"I like to keep my ears open."

"Well, your hearing's sure good. Doc up and left one day, just like you heard. Guess he was just gettin' too old. But I suppose I don't have to tell you what that's like," he added with a grin.

"And Hendry? Was he too old too? He can't be any older than you are."

Billy shrugged and stared at the backbar.

"Maybe," Pat said, "he just came to his senses, Billy."

The Kid turned slowly to him, a mean twist to the corner of his mouth. With effort, he brought the carefree look back to his face. "Hendry come to his senses? Go on, Pat. You got to know Hendry better than that." He finished his drink. "Besides, there's some new boys throwin' in with me to make up for the ones that left. Maybe they know something that old Doc and Hendry don't know."

"Maybe," said Pat.

"Maybe they know a thing or two about old Chisum and how he can abuse a man. I knew that a couple years ago. Now there are some other boys who are learnin' also."

"I remember when Chisum used to be a friend of yours."

"A long time ago, Pat. Before he left me high and dry. All that fighting I did for him for his war against Dolan, and I never got a damn thing for it. All that talk of his and not one word of it worth shit." He paused to lean closer to Pat. "And now hear him squawking. I bet you've heard it—all that bellyaching about losing beeves. Just because I want to get even like any other man in this country would. The old turncoat."

Pat couldn't help but think of riding that afternoon with the old Dolan deputy, Bob Olinger, another man who hated Chisum, perhaps as much as Billy did, but Olinger hated the Kid even more. Garrett wondered how many scores from the Lincoln County War were still to be settled, and in how many directions the shots would fly once everyone got down to business.

Glancing down the bar as Charley Bowdre headed back their way, Pat noticed a man staring at the Kid. He was a wiry young man wearing a black frock coat and an old army kossuth hat; he stood at the front of the bar, talking to a cowboy while keeping his eyes on Billy. The look of the man automatically put Pat on edge. His instincts were borne out when Charley reached Billy's side.

"That fella's talkin' about you," Charley said. "I heard him say he knows who you are. He says he aims to take you down, Billy."

Billy glanced quickly in the man's direction. "He doesn't look like anybody we ever crossed trails with."

"I don't think that's it, Billy. I think he just wants to say he killed you."

Billy now turned to give the man in the frock coat a long look. He had a friendly grin on his face. In another moment the man smiled back, not quite as friendly. Pat put a hand on Billy's arm.

"What're you thinking?"

"Oh, ease up, Pat. I figure I'd just go on over and talk to him some, see what's got him so mean. I'll find the good side to him. You'll see."

Before Garrett could say anything else, the Kid was on his way down the bar.

Garrett saw the cowboy move away as Billy started talking to the man in the frock coat. Pat stepped closer to hear what was being said.

"Is that right?" Billy said cheerfully. "You killed that man in Tularosa just because he got friendly with your gal?" He shook his head, showing that he was impressed. "Now that's what I call a human tiger. Hey, Pat, did you hear that? Come here, I want you to hear this. Pat, this here is Joe Grant, from . . . where was that again? From Kansas? Joe says he's killed as many as four men. Is that right, Joe?"

"Four in Kansas, anyway."

Pat could see that Joe Grant was just drunk enough to think he was actually being admired. At least for now. Billy could push the needling too far, and in a bar fight it would be anyone's guess who might get killed—Billy, Grant, or anybody who got in the way of a stray shot.

Pat said, "Let's go, Billy. We still got us some drinks to finish."

Billy didn't move. "Hold on, Pat. That ain't all. Did you see Joe's gun? Look at it—ivory-handled and all. You must've paid a dear price for that, Joe. Am I right?"

"Dear enough," said Grant.

"Think I can get a look at it? I don't think I ever did see a real Kansas fighter's gun before."

To Pat's surprise, Grant took the gun out of its holster after only a moment's hesitation, and handed it over. *Maybe the man's dumb enough to get flattered out of a fight after all,* Pat thought.

"Oh, I can see why you're so proud of your hardware," said Billy, as he inspected the revolver's cylinder. "And I bet you've got it fixed so it'll go off by just breathing on it. Ain't that right, Joe?"

Grant just smiled.

Billy handed the gun back. "You better take it before I shoot myself by accident," he said. He shook his shoulders in a mock display of the shivers.

Wrapping his fingers around the gun's handle, Grant brought the Colt .44 to its sheath, but then stopped there, hesitating for a while as his eyes took on a nasty glint. Pat could see that Grant was thinking slowly, either from whiskey or just natural thickheadedness, but the man was closing in on a decision. In the next moment, he swung the gun up and pointed it at Billy's face.

"Goodbye, Kid," he said. Then he cocked the revolver and squeezed the trigger. The hammer dropped on an empty chamber.

Grant's expression froze.

"You ought to be careful who looks at your gun when you only got three loads in it," said Billy. "A fella could line up the empty chambers."

Recovering from his initial surprise, Grant triggered again. Once more, an empty click was heard in the silent saloon. He was about to try the next chamber when Billy swept the gun out of his holster, aimed it point-blank at Grant's face, and blew a hole between the man's eyes.

As he watched Grant drop, Pat found himself pressed against the bar, about a foot to the side of the line of fire. It had been an automatic reaction, a move that required no thought, just as he had reached for his right hip without thinking, even though he wasn't wearing any guns.

Billy turned to him, showing Pat the revolver in his hand. "One of them new double-action guns. Sure fires fast, Pat, don't she?" Billy checked the other men in the saloon, then stepped toward the door. "Let's go, Charley. We best be saddling up about now."

4

The warmth of the morning sun brought the tangy smells of creosote and sage to the two horsemen at the top of the slope. Farther on, a sweep of bunch-grass stretching to the mesa on the horizon told them that good grazing land was finally near after a full night's riding. A mule deer stood in the distance, its head cocked to look at the two men; for several moments it was perfectly still, then it wheeled in a tight circle and bounded away.

Billy pulled the Winchester from his saddle sheath. "Come on, Charley. Let's get us some meat for breakfast."

They charged down the slope and galloped across the grass. The deer raced to the left, then cut to the right with superb agility and, taking on a frantic burst of speed, headed toward a group of low hills. Billy and Charley pushed their fagged horses for a hundred feet more before either of them felt they had a shot. Reining to a stop, they each fired once and missed. The Kid then brought down the deer with his next round.

In the hills, they butchered the animal and started a fire. Billy gave little thought to the attention that smoke would attract in these parts. If any Texans had bothered to trail them this far, he had seen no sign of them. Besides, he had other things to worry about. All that work in the Panhandle wouldn't mean a thing if he couldn't find someone ready to buy. He was considering the possibilities still open to him when he heard the slow approach of boots and hooves.

"Hello the camp," a voice rang out from the other side of a rocky shoulder. "Can we come in the rest of the way?"

Charley dropped the second chunk of meat he was about to set over the fire and pulled his revolver.

"Slow down," Billy told him. "If they wanted to throw down on us they could've done it by now." He called to the unseen visitor. "You can come on. Just make it one at a time so we can see you real good."

A moment later, a bearded man led a dun mare around the shoulder. His hard, black eyes darted from Charley to Billy, betraying his smile's attempt at friendliness.

"Obliged," he said. "That meat on the fire smells awful good. I thought you might be able to stand some help with eating it."

Billy leaned back on his elbows on the other side of the fire. "How many of you are there?" he asked.

"Just one more. All right with you if he comes in now?"

"Why the hell not? I've seen enough of you for now. Bring him in and take a load off."

The second man was shorter than the first, a light-haired, broad-shouldered man who wore a smile more convincing than his friend's. The two of them sat near the fire, their eyes planted on the broiling meat.

Billy laughed. "You're welcome to eat it raw if you want."

The light-haired man looked sheepish, while his bearded friend tried to join Billy with a laugh that sounded more like a grunt.

"You boys new to this country?" Billy asked.

"Yeah. Just come all the way from Kansas," said the man with the beard.

"That's right? I just met a fella from Kansas. Name of Joe Grant."

The bearded man gave the name some thought. "Don't know him."

"Well," said Billy, "you lost your chance to know him in New Mexico, too. Hey, Charley, that pot of coffee's ready by now. Let these boys have some."

Charley tossed tin cups to the visitors and picked up the pot. As the light-haired man held out his cup, Billy noticed something peculiar about the stranger's wrist. He saw a band of chafed and bruised skin exactly where a manacle would have been secured. Realizing what the Kid was looking at, the man suddenly pulled back the cup so that the cuff of his shirt would cover his wrist. Charley hadn't finished pouring into the cup.

"What the hell . . ." Charley snapped.

The light-haired man stared at Billy; in his eyes was a trapped and violent look. Billy checked the other stranger. He looked straight ahead at no one in particular, as if he had no idea what had just happened; he lazily adjusted his slouch hat, pulling it lower on his broad forehead. Billy thought the man might be putting his hands in motion in order to get himself ready for a grab at his sidearm.

"You boys should ease up," said Billy. "Any man on the run doesn't have any reason to be afraid of me and Charley."

Neither man replied, but Billy could still see they were drawn tight, ready for anything.

"I don't know how long you been in this country," said Billy, "but I got an idea you might've been in New Mexico longer than you let on. That manacle burn—looks to me like it's still pretty fresh, like you just come from some calaboose nearby. What I'm gettin' at, if you've been around long enough, you might've heard of me. I'm Billy Bonney. That's Charley Bowdre over there. You might've heard of him too."

The light-haired man turned to his friend, a questioning look on his face. Billy looked at the bearded man also; he was obviously the one who called the shots. A smile appeared between the mustache and beard; not much of a smile, but genuine this time.

"That'd make you Billy the Kid," he said. He shook his head. "You really *are* a kid, ain't you."

"Yes sir, that's me. And the way I figure, you knowing who I am, that'd give you a pretty good reason to stop thinking about going for your gun, wouldn't you say?"

The bearded man considered him for a moment more, then nodded and held out his cup for Charley to fill. "This is John J. Webb," he said, jerking a thumb toward his friend. "My name's Rudabaugh."

Charley stopped short, with the coffee pot poised above the cup. "Is that *Dave* Rudabaugh?"

The bearded man squinted at him. "You know me?"

"Well, I guess I *should* know you. I rode with a herd up to Dodge once." As something registered with him, he turned slowly toward Webb. "Now I think on it, I heard of a John Webb over to Dodge, too." Charley stopped again, puzzled by something. "It's the damnedest thing, but I remember a man named Webb being a lawman, ridin' with Bat Masterson, the way I recall."

This got a loud, grumbling laugh from Rudabaugh. "You remember right, boy. Old John J. was with Masterson the day I got caught for the Kinsley job. Funny thing is, he was a lawman in Las Vegas, too, when I had to break him out of the calaboose."

"That *is* pretty funny," said Billy. "But I have to tell you fellas, I'd think it was a lot funnier if I knew there wasn't any posse getting close to you."

"Don't worry about that, Kid. We lost those Las Vegas boys a long way back." When he saw the expression on Billy's face, Rudabaugh added, "You can believe me when I tell you that. You might be some kind of crackerjack *pistolero* down here, but I've ridden the trail a good long time. I know when I've got a posse off my tail."

"Whatever you say, Dave," Billy answered. He was quiet after that, studying Rudabaugh and Webb as they went to work on the first chunk of venison.

He thought about Hendry Brown and Doc Scurlock; when those two had ridden off, Billy's outfit had lost two good men. The new kid, Johnny Wilson, was a good rider and a fair shot, but he wasn't somebody Billy was liable to depend on.

And there's plenty left to do, Billy thought. *An awful lot left to do.*

Between holding off Chisum's riders and collecting what was their due, the outfit had its hands full. A couple of extra toughs just might be what was needed.

"You fellas figured out where you're headed?" Billy asked.

Rudabaugh wiped the vension juice off his beard. "Just taking it one step at a time right now."

"Riding free the way you are, maybe you'd want to keep going with us, see how we do things around here."

"We could take a look," said Rudabaugh. "We just might."

The more he thought about it, the more Billy liked the idea. A couple of older riders would know a thing or two, he figured; and by the look of him, this Rudabaugh wasn't likely to back down from trouble or ride off at the first sign of bad times coming, like that fool Hendry did.

Billy took his own share of meat, ate it quickly, and stretched out on the ground. "Best to get your sleep now," Billy said. "We'll be setting out by afternoon." The Kid closed his eyes and, within a minute, was snoring lightly.

After another day's ride, they reached Lopez's sheep ranch along a plain of stunted shrubs and tough grass to the west of Fort Sumner. Tom O'Folliard and Curly Pickett were there, helping Lopez build the mud bricks to be used for the low wall outside the adobe. Juanita, Lopez's daughter, was also there. As Billy got off his horse, he saw her standing by the house, looking at him, her slim, copper-colored face showed how pleased she was to see him. A moment later she became self-conscious and began removing the ripened chile peppers from the strings that hung along the wall.

Reaching Tom O'Folliard's side, Billy scanned the ranch. "Where's Johnny?" he asked.

"Lookin' after the herd. But I guess he won't be doin' that much longer. Where do we take 'em Billy?"

"Nowhere. Not yet anyway."

Tom gave the Kid a bewildered look; his confusion deepened when he saw the two strangers stepping closer, alongside Charley Bowdre.

"Couple of fellas we met on the trail," Billy explained. "That's John Webb and the other one there, that's Dave Rudabaugh. You probably heard of him."

"I heard," said Tom, still uneasy, "but I don't see how bringing a train robber here helps us with the Texas cattle. No offense, Rudabaugh, but we got other things to think about."

"Ease up, Tom," Billy said.

"What the hell happened at Roswell?" Tom demanded.

"He never showed. Can't say what happened. We waited for him right where he told us to meet him. We even went into town and he wasn't there neither."

"I say something scared him off," offered Charley.

Billy shrugged. "Might be. If something did scare

Pyle off, then I'm going to have to find some other way to sell the beeves."

"That's right," said Tom. "Problem is, where you going to go?"

Rudabaugh leaned against a completed portion of the mud-brick wall. "If that's the only problem you fellas have, then you don't got much to worry about."

"Now what the hell is that supposed to mean?" Tom said.

A hard gleam came to Rudabaugh's eyes as he returned Tom's look, but he didn't let the anger into his voice. "All I'm saying is, if you got to get someone to buy some stock that you don't exactly have a receipt for, you probably won't have to look for very long. There's always somebody around ready to make a slick dollar. You just got to think about it the right way."

Tom didn't find much comfort in this advice. He was about to say something to the newcomer but before he could get the words out Billy took hold of the back of his neck and pulled him a couple of inches closer.

"He's talking sense, Tom. Like he says, you just got to think about it." He patted O'Folliard's back. "You worry too much—you know that?" Billy was going to say something more, but an idea came to him, a crazy notion that made him stare vacantly beyond the adobe for a moment.

"Damn it all," he finally said, "but I think I just might have us a way."

"What're you talkin' about?" asked Tom.

"We'll just see," Billy answered with a sly smile. "I'm not saying it'll work. I'm just saying I might have a way. I got to think on it a bit more. Think it clear through."

"What I'd like to know," said Charley, "is why we got Texas cattle in the first place?"

Billy looked at him through narrowed eyes, as if Bowdre had just said something to him in a foreign language.

"I mean," Charley went on, "I thought we was supposed to be gettin' even with Chisum. The beeves we got stashed in that draw over there ain't Chisum's. Ain't got anything to do with Chisum."

Billy said, "Now you know better than that, Charley. You forgetting what we been through, with the War and all? Is that it, Charley?"

"No, I ain't forgetting."

"Okay then. So there's your answer. After all we done, this world owes us something, whether it wants to give it to us or not. And don't you forget it."

Charley stared at the ground and said nothing.

"Now you and Tom go on and show the new fellas where things are around here. Lopez, you still got some tequila hidden in that house of yours? Go on, Charley, see what he's got left. I got some thinking to do."

Billy left them and walked toward the hummock on the other side of the house. Sitting there, he brooded about Charley and Tom. *They're losing their backbone,* he thought, *that's what the problem is. If I'm not around to stand them up straight they'd just fall crying and moaning to the ground. It's been that way ever since Hendry and Doc left. That set a bad example, and now I've got to do all I can to keep things going.*

The dark thoughts lingered for a time, but as he gazed toward the distant purple hills, the gloominess suddenly gave way, as it so often did with him, leaving him sitting with a big grin on his peach-fuzzed face.

A regular little general you're becoming, he told himself. Recruiting men, trading horses and cattle, and now whipping the boys into line—a far cry from the kid of eighteen just a couple of years ago, riding for John Tunstall, just one of a large crew, barely noticed by anybody. *Life sure gets complicated being a full-grown man of twenty,* he mused.

A rustling sound to his rear distracted him. Turning, he saw Juanita snapping one of her father's laundered shirts to remove some of the creases before hanging it on the clothesline behind the adobe. He had to smile at the sight of her. True, she wasn't the one to make him forget all about Paulita, but she was still a soft, giggly girl when she was in his arms, and she made him feel as good as most girls did.

"Juanita, stop your working all the time," he called. "Come sit here a while. Come on now."

5

To look at the governor, a man would just naturally think he was a great leader. The lean face and strong profile, the deep-set eyes, the distinguished beard and mustache—Pat had no trouble imagining the man with a saber in hand, leading his troops into battle against the Confederacy. But Pat cautioned himself; he didn't want to be too impressed by Governor Lew Wallace's commanding presence. He had come to Santa Fe to get some answers, and he couldn't do that if he was awed by the man. He reminded himself that some people said the governor had been only a minor general in the War Between the States.

The governor adjusted the pince-nez on the bridge of his nose and leaned back in his chair. The stack of paper on the mahogany desk concealed part of his face from Garrett as he spoke.

"In his letter, Mr. Chisum made mention of some questions you might have. How might I be able to help you, Mr. Garrett?"

"Well, sir, it's about the deal Billy Bonney made with you. At least, I heard there was deal made, after Chapman got murdered."

"Yes, you're right. Billy and I came to an understanding."

Pat was hoping the governor would volunteer more information without prompting. For the moment, though, Wallace added nothing.

"What I'm getting at," Pat said, "has to do with the Kid getting out of the Lincoln jail." He paused there, running a finger along his paper collar. For the first time he realized how touchy this conversation might be. "The reason I'm bringing this up, sir, was that there was talk at the time that Billy wasn't getting what he deserved, what he was promised—at least that's what the rumor was. Some people even say he went bad because of that."

Lew Wallace nodded politely, showing no sign that he was taking offense. "I know that Billy was saying that at the time, but he had no reason to think so. Our understanding—or, our deal, as you put it—was simply that he would offer testimony in the Chapman case, and in exchange he would be pardoned for all past crimes. You see, when Huston Chapman was murdered, Billy was afraid he'd be blamed for it. He had been in Lincoln that night, and he had even been with the men who had committed the crime, so he was sure he would be implicated if he didn't come forward. That's what he told me when we had our meeting."

Wallace seemed satisfied with his answer. For the

next couple of moments, Pat gazed in silence out the window, across the tree-shaded plaza that bordered the Palace of the Governors. "Did the Kid have a reason for thinking he wasn't getting a square deal?"

"Not at all. He testified before the grand jury, as had been arranged, and because of his help, the prosecuting attorney was able to secure indictments against Dolan and Evans. I can't tell you what he was thinking while he was in custody, but I suppose he got nervous and decided matters weren't proceeding quickly enough." The governor shrugged. "All he had to do was remain in Lincoln a short while longer and he would have been a free man. It's really a shame he didn't trust us."

"I see," said Pat. Nothing in the governor's bland expression suggested that he might be lying, and it was easy enough to imagine Billy breaking out of jail before the amnesty had a chance to take effect. Patience was not a word to be used in describing Billy. Pat had his answer from Wallace, but he was beginning to wonder how much difference it made.

Regardless of whether Billy had been double-crossed, the image of the Kid shooting Joe Grant in the face kept coming back to Pat. His decision might have been made a little easier, now that he had gotten the governor's side of the story, but Pat realized that he had already been heading in that direction. Although Billy's shooting of Grant had clearly been self-defense, Pat had never seen killing come so easy to a man. *Billy has to be stopped,* he told himself. *It's better,* he thought, *that the job be done by somebody who's willing to bring him in alive.*

"If you don't mind," said the governor, rising from

his seat, "I would be interested in asking a few questions myself while you are here."

"Go right ahead."

Wallace sat on the corner of his desk. "Mr. Chisum tells me that your . . . your acquaintanceship with Billy Bonney should prove to be useful in tracking him down."

"It'll help."

"I am sure," Wallace said. "And there won't be any complications, complications due to . . . to old ties?"

"I'm not tied to anybody, governor. Not even to John Chisum. I'll do the job."

Wallace scrutinized him. "All right then, I suppose that's really the best answer. Just one more thing, Mr. Garrett—really just a matter of curiosity more than anything else." He stopped and looked pensively at the far wall.

"Yes, sir?"

"I understand, Mr. Garrett, you're an admirer of the writer Robert Ingersoll."

Pat felt a cold tightening along the back of his neck. "That's right, I am."

Wallace fingered the tip of his beard for a moment before answering. "I realize these are new times that we're living in, but I have to admit I still find it difficult to accept certain things. I suppose your Mr. Ingersoll would consider me an enemy. I have just completed my book," he said, gesturing to the stack of paper on his desk. "It's called *Ben Hur: A Tale of the Christ.* As you can imagine, I don't have much use for agnosticism."

"I suppose not." The answer sounded stupid to Pat, but nothing else presented itself. An apprehension was coursing through him, a reaction that caught him by surprise. He had been so intent upon asking his own questions that it had never occurred to him that this meeting might have another purpose. Perhaps the governor still wanted to make sure that Chisum's candidate was a suitable man for the job of Lincoln County sheriff. Now that Pat had finally made his decision, he was afraid that the governor would stand in his way. Ingersoll could be enough of a reason for the God-fearing old general.

The thoughts that had made Pat consider the job in the first place surged forward in his mind. Bitterly, he remembered all the failures that had somehow led him here. The buffalo-hunting venture that began too late, just as the herds were disappearing; the Fort Sumner restaurant that had lasted only a few months; the hog business with Tip McKinney that had never really gotten started. The county sheriff's job could be his chance, perhaps his last one. Bringing in Billy was important, but perhaps no more important than the house in Roswell and Pat's growing family.

The governor got up and went over to the bookcase where he removed one of the pipes from a circular rack. He continued to study Pat as he tamped tobacco into the bowl. His expression was shifting, a knowing glimmer in his eyes. "Then again," Wallace finally said, "I suppose Christian living won't have much to do with tracking a man down in this Godforsaken territory."

Pat nodded politely and said nothing.

6

They might have found a larger herd across the canyon, deeper into the Agency land, but the ten horses at the foot of the hills were too tempting to bypass. The animals grazed languidly near a spring, while a single Mescalero rider walked along the perimeter, occasionally hazing a stray horse back into the pack. Billy judged that the Indian was there to herd the animals to some other part of the reservation, but was in no mood to hurry it.

Concealed by the thick hillside timber, the Kid took his time studying the lay of the land.

"What's keeping us?" said Tom O'Folliard. "One Apache ain't going to give us much of a fight."

"Just hold on," Billy told him. "No point in throwing ourselves down there without a plan. Might as well do it right if we're going to do it at all, and never mind that there's just the one Indian."

Not getting a reply, Billy gazed again at the spring below and the trail to the right that would bring them to the Indian herder's rear. The fact was that Billy already knew how to handle the job, but he couldn't help taking some extra time, just to savor the moment. Looking at stock that he knew was about to become his own gave Billy a special pleasure; that anticipation, along with the moment when he and the boys closed in on the herd, was the best part of the job; from there on it was mostly just work, not so different from pushing stock for other men. Tom could get impatient if he wanted, but Billy wasn't about to deny himself. The extra minute or two was harmless enough, he thought. *Hell, how many other men really know how to enjoy their work the way I do?* Shifting in his saddle, Billy noticed Rudabaugh looking in his direction, his mouth curled into a half-smile. The Kid thought that the veteran Kansas tough might have known what was going through his mind.

"I'll ride point," said Billy. "Charley, you ride drag. Just follow me and take it slow. We should be able to work this with no trouble at all."

The narrow game trail opened up onto the open flat just thirty feet from the horses. When he saw the Mescalero turn away, Billy spurred his roan forward. He sprinted directly toward the Indian, who wheeled around just in time to see Billy point a double-action Colt at his stomach. The Apache stopped moving. The sudden approach, though, spooked part of the herd; three horses shied away at a lope. Before they could get far, Rudabaugh circled around to the left, Charley moved to the right, and the two of them turned the animals back.

"You don't want to pull your gun," Billy said

amiably to the herder. When this got no response, he repeated the sentence in Spanish. Although the Mescalero still said nothing, he held his empty hands out to his sides, nowhere near the pistol in his waistband. "*Bueno,*" Billy told him.

"We're ready to move 'em, Billy," Charley called from the other side of the horses.

"We'll push 'em back along this valley till we reach Cedar Creek. I'll bring up the rear. Go on, Charley. Let's move."

Rudabaugh brought his horse alongside the Kid's. "Ain't you going to take the Indian's gun away?"

Billy smiled as he considered the Apache. He spoke in Spanish again. "No real reason for that, is there, friend? You don't want to make a fuss." The Indian answered with a sharp nod.

"You see that, Rudabaugh?" Billy said as he reined his horse around. "You got to trust some people."

Rudabaugh rode beside the Kid, looking over his shoulder. "I'll trust him when he's either dead or gone."

Billy laughed.

"If you're going to keep alive," said Rudabaugh, "you ought to think the same, Kid."

"Dave, you just go ahead and show me what to do," Billy said slyly. "Whatever you do, I'll do it too."

Rudabaugh kept silent after that.

They didn't come across anyone from the Indian Agency for two miles. Even with their eyes and ears alert to any sign, they weren't aware of the two men until they were practically on top of them.

At a place where the valley narrowed, a scalloped rise on the right jutted onto their path, leaving a passage only about forty feet wide. The stolen horses had just cleared the rise when the rider and the man on the buckboard appeared around a boulder. The horseman was a Mescalero, broad and short like so many Apaches, wearing a threadbare broadcloth suit and a headband tied near the top of his weathered, bronze face. In the buckboard was a white man; he stared at Billy, then at Rudabaugh. Surprise and anger mixed on the round face, framed by black, curly hair showing beneath the derby. Billy recognized him as the Indian Agency clerk.

"You came up on us pretty fast, Morris," said Billy. "If you came up any faster we might've shot you."

Morris Bernstein checked Charley and Tom at the front of the small herd. "We were looking for these horses," he said. "We sent a man out to find them this morning."

Billy made note of the Mescalero's hands holding the reins loosely; he hadn't brought them any closer to the rifle in the saddle sheath. As for Bernstein, Billy couldn't see any gun on him, but there might have been one underneath his jacket.

"Well," said the Kid, "I guess someone was liable to find these animals sooner or later. It just turned out that it was us."

Bernstein hesitated before answering; he looked like he was bracing himself. "Don't take them, Kid. They're Agency property."

"They *used* to be Agency property," said Rudabaugh in a flat voice. "Why don't you boys just run along."

Bernstein's lips pressed together, a growing anger preventing him from turning the buckboard around.

Rudabaugh seemed to be goaded by the small show of defiance in the clerk's face.

"You got something else to say?" Rudabaugh demanded. "Or maybe you just want to run back where you came from and get some squaws to do the talkin' for you. Is that it? You just gonna let us run off your stock?"

For a moment nothing was said and no one moved. Then Billy saw the Mescalero turn slightly in the saddle. The Kid couldn't tell whether he was going for his rifle, because the Indian never had the chance to get that far. Rudabaugh pulled his revolver and shot the Indian twice in the midsection.

More gunfire cracked from the other side of the herd as Tom and Charley cut loose. They also shot the Apache. While the Mescalero spilled out of the saddle with the force of the slugs, Billy noticed Bernstein turning his way. All the shots booming around him prodded Billy's reflexes, putting his hands into motion. His vision of Bernstein seemed to lose detail, showing him nothing except an outline of a target. As soon as his double-action colt was clear, he triggered three shots in rapid succession. The clerk lurched to his feet, as if driven upward by the .41 plowing through his shoulder, then he spun to his left as the second round slammed through his chest; the third bullet knocked him into the back of the wagon.

For several moments, the only sound in the valley was the nickering of the stolen horses and the nervous stamping of their hooves as they milled around, searching for a way past the four men hazing them in place. Curiosity eventually got the better of Billy. He turned his roan, rode over to the buckboard, and reached in to pull Bernstein onto his back. Lifting the skirts of the man's jacket, he saw there was no gun on him.

"Better get moving on," said Tom as he scanned their back trail for any sign of pursuers.

Billy returned to the rear of the horses and helped Rudabaugh move them along.

"Now *there* are two fellas who won't be giving us trouble," said Rudabaugh, motioning back with his bearded head toward the two dead men. "We done it right that time. You'll see."

Rudabaugh seemed to be pretty pleased, but Billy saw no reason for being happy. He remembered Bernstein as a pretty nice fellow, the little he had known him. Especially for a Jew. Of course, he thought, there hadn't been any way to know the man didn't have a gun, but that really didn't make things much better. *If only nice folks could just stay away,* he brooded, *just keep the hell clear when there was business to be taken care of. This world is bad enough, filled with sons-of-bitches the way it is, without good people getting all mixed up with the bad.* Life could be a sad thing, Billy decided.

The sadness didn't leave Billy until they had left the new horses at Lopez's camp and were riding into Fort Sumner the next night. Crossing the plaza, Billy could hear the sound of guitars coming from Soto's house, where lamplight filled the windows and people's silhouettes could be seen inside.

"Your luck is good," Billy told Rudabaugh. "Your first night in Fort Sumner and a *baile*'s just about to start."

The prospect of dancing with the Fort Sumner senoritas took Billy's mind off the previous day's killing, but some traces of gloominess still nagged at him. He was able to put aside the last of the melancholy when he stepped into Charley Bowdre's house. Sitting with Rita, Charley's wife, was a black-haired, blue-eyed young woman in a store-bought dress. The sight of Paulita Maxwell put a big grin on Billy's face.

He took off his hat and said hello in a respectful, almost courtly manner, exactly the way he knew Paulita would want it to be done. He introduced Dave Rudabaugh, who nodded uncomfortably, then gestured to his other two friends.

"You know Tom over there, and I guess you know Charley too, or you wouldn't be here," he said, quickly dropping his formal tone and giving Paulita a wink. She smiled back. He didn't say anything more to her as he and his friends ate the meal of chili con carne that Rita Bowdre served them, only glancing at her occasionally, biding his time. Some girls, he knew, just had to be treated that way.

Once the meal was over, he noticed with satisfaction that Paulita stepped out onto the porch alone. He spit out his tobacco chaw, wiped his mouth, and strolled out after her.

Paulita leaned against one of the porch posts outside the Bowdres' home, part of a long adobe building that had once served as a hospital when Fort Sumner was a garrison. She gazed across the plaza at the Soto house, seemingly absorbed in the dance music and unaware that Billy was drawing near.

"I hoped I'd be seeing you at the *baile* a little later on," he said, "I'd sure like to have a dance with you tonight. Maybe more than one, now that I think about it."

She gave him a quizzical look, her head tilted coquettishly. "I haven't seen you in a long time, Billito. Where have you been?"

"Here and there. A young fella building up his first herd has his work cut out for him these days. I'd be here all the time if I could."

"Now that's curious. My father didn't have to leave his home all the time when he built his ranch here."

"Well, I guess in those days a man could get by without making enemies." He took a step closer and looked squarely into her eyes, taking some small pleasure in just being close to her. Her gaze wavered. Billy could see her fighting something; it was a natural curiosity, he figured, a secret interest in him and his wild ways that was struggling against well-bred sensibleness. He spoke up, before the sensibleness had a chance to win tonight's hand.

"If you come by the *baile,* it'd sure make me happy," he said, "I'll be looking for you." He smiled and stepped away from the house, headed toward the music.

For a few moments, he imagined what it would be like if she actually showed up and he danced with her enough to get her outside, behind Soto's house. The thoughts passed the time, but he didn't let them get too far along. *No sense in lathering up about something that might not happen,* he told himself. Instead, his mind turned to Celsa. Just playing the lost little boy with her was usually enough, and if her husband was away he could stay with her inside the house nearly the whole night.

He thought he could see Celsa at the *baile* through one of the Sotos' windows, but before he could go inside for a better look, he noticed a familiar face just outside the door. Being an Anglo, the stocky man naturally stood out in this town. He leaned against the house with Juan Gallegos, sharing a jug. Billy searched his memory and finally remembered seeing the man in a Lincoln saloon a few months before.

"Hey Billy," the man called.

The Kid walked over, more interested in the jug than the man's company. The name finally came to him. "How you getting by, Barney?"

"Just barely. You know the way things are."

"Well, you're doing well enough to keep your mouth from going dry." Billy gave the jug a meaningful look.

"Why don't you take a fix?" Barney Mason said, as if he hadn't been prompted. "Haven't heard much of you for a while, Billy. You been to Lincoln lately?"

"Not for a while."

Barney narrowed his eyes. "Have you heard at all?"

"Heard what?" The Kid cradled the jug in the crook of his arm so that he could tilt it to his mouth.

"Well then, I guess you haven't," said Barney. "Pat Garrett, he's getting the push for the sheriff's job. Chisum's behind him, and some others too."

Billy shrugged, then took a gulp of the tequila. "Good for Pat," he said.

"Not that kind of sheriff, Billy. The word is he's supposed to hunt you down."

The Kid stared at the man. "Who says that?"

"Just everybody who talks about it, that's all."

Billy turned to look through the window at the *baile*, now going strong, the Sotos' main room filled with people swirling to the guitar music. He took a drink from the jug, then took another. "They sure picked the right man for the job," he said, "the long-legged son-of-a-bitch."

7

They met along a bend of the Rio Hondo where a patch of cottonwood grew on the northern bank. Billy was the first to arrive. Picketing his quarter-horse by the water's edge, he sat on a rock to eat the last of his sourdough biscuits, then got up and paced, shivering as November's first cold wind blew across the high plain. Garrett rode in from the north and remained in the saddle after he stopped by Billy's side.

"Couldn't you find someplace with shelter if you wanted to see me?" said Billy. "A table in the back of a saloon wouldn't have been bad for keeping warm."

"Seemed to me," Pat said, "it might be better for both of us to stay away from that kind of place. Too many people we know in saloons in this country."

Billy nodded and offered no argument. He then

squinted at the man on the horse. "I think you better come down from there, Pat. I don't mind gettin' a sore neck looking up at you, but not that far up."

Pat smiled at him. He dismounted and left his bay loose-tied to some brush. Reaching into his jacket pocket, he took out two cigars.

"You still rolling your own these days?" he asked.

"I'm not particular. I'll roll 'em, or I'll chew a plug when it's handy. Hell, I'll even smoke one of your cigars, Pat." He kept his eyes on Garrett as he took the cigar and lit up. The grin on his face seemed strained.

"Should I be calling you Sheriff yet?" Billy asked.

"Kind of early for that, Kid. But you won't have to wait long."

"Now just listen to the old woman talk. Gettin' the nomination doesn't have to get you the election, you know."

"It just about does in this country," drawled Pat, "if you've got the Democrats' nomination."

"Is that right? Well, we'll just see, won't we. I know I'm votin' for Kimball, and I'll be telling others to do the same. There's plenty of people who'll listen to that kind of talk."

"Forget it, Kid. Kimball doesn't have the right people behind him."

Even with no names used, the allusion to those men backing Garrett was enough to get a sullen silence out of Billy. He stepped away, his agitation taking him as far as the big rock near his horse; he sat down again.

"It's a hell of a thing," Billy finally said.

Pat knew he would have to steer the conversation away from Chisum if he wanted to get Billy to talk sense. "I hear you're riding with Dave Rudabaugh these days," he said as he strolled closer to the Kid.

"Who's tellin' you?"

Pat shrugged. "Somebody."

Billy laughed. "I must be gettin' old myself if I think I can get a straight answer out of you. Okay, Pat. So somebody told you."

"It's true then?"

"We've moved down the trail some."

"That's a bad move, Billy. He's a curly wolf and he's been one a long while. A word of advice, Kid: don't plan on riding through Las Vegas with him at any time."

Billy smirked. "Why not? Dave forget to pay a hotel bill there?"

"He killed a deputy sheriff, and the people there are still boiling about it. Rudabaugh did it so he could get a fella named Webb out of jail; he's another bad one—used to be a lawman."

"Okay, Pat. The next time I go to Las Vegas, I'll go by myself."

"He's done more killing since then, hasn't he, Billy? Over to the Mescalero Agency. You were with him over there when Bernstein was murdered, weren't you?"

"Somebody was there. I don't suppose Bernstein got shot all by himself."

Pat searched the Kid's expression, looking for a sign that there might be a point to this meeting after all. Billy's untroubled front told him nothing.

"We can make this thing easy," Pat said. "You know what I mean, don't you?"

Billy looked at him with mock confusion. "I can't say that I do, Pat. What're you getting at?"

Garrett sighed in frustration. "All right, Billy. I'll make it plain. If you come in on your own, I'll make sure you get a square deal. I don't think you've done all the bad things some people say you did, and I'll do what I can so that they can't pin those things on you."

"A square deal, huh? That sounds nice. Does that mean you'll make sure the noose is real comfortable?"

Pat took a long drag on his cigar to keep himself from snapping back at him. He walked over to a cottonwood and leaned back against its trunk. "I guess there's no point in trying to convince you, but there's still one other way if the first one doesn't suit you. You could always leave this country. There's no reason you have to stay, Kid."

Billy narrowed his eyes, gave this some thought, then started to laugh. "Oh, that'd be a real fine thing. I turn tail and run—and you can tell everybody how you ran me out of the territory, and everybody can slap you on the back. You sure there's nothing else you want me to do, Pat? Maybe I should just hang *myself* and save everybody the trouble. I'll just say I did it because Pat Garrett told me I had to. That'll make Chisum *real* proud of you. He'll make you the biggest man in the territory."

"Goddamn it, Billy. Chisum's got nothing to do with it. This is just you and me talking here. Listen to what I'm telling you. Listen to some goddamned sense."

Billy got to his feet in a hurry and stepped toward the tall man. "Don't tell me what this is all about! I know what I've got to take care of, whether you understand it or not."

"You little runt," Garrett hissed. "Why the hell do you think I wanted to meet you here? Do you think I had to? I wanted to work this out."

"Yeah, so you could talk me into rolling over for you. So you could do it the easy way, like you said before."

"I didn't mean it that way, Billy, and you should know that."

"Sure I should know that. Everybody's sayin' how Pat Garrett's going to run me to earth, so I suppose that means I should know you're my best friend in the world, is that right?"

For a moment, all Pat could think of was how easy it would be to knock the piss out of the little young man; but he hadn't come here for that. He moved away from the Kid. He took a little time to settle himself.

"No, Kid, I'm not your best friend," he said. "At least, I hope I'm not, for your sake. I just thought, seeing how we had us some good times back in Fort Sumner, I owed you the chance to get out of this with something. You might even get out of it alive."

Billy cocked his head, as if peering at Pat through bad light. "You know, Pat, the last time I was in Sumner, I heard some boys figuring how to bet on us, you know, whether you'd get me or I'd get you. Seems to me now, you're not so sure what your odds are, trying to get me to walk into jail the way you are."

Pat saw no reason to say anything to that.

"I'll tell you what," Billy continued. "Maybe I'll leave this territory one of these days, but it won't be because of you. When I'm through teachin' Chisum and the other sons-of-bitches a lesson, then I won't have any reason for staying in Lincoln County. But I won't be leavin' before that."

"You and Olinger both," said Pat.

Billy's confusion was genuine this time. "You want to ride down that trail one more time?"

"I was just thinking about men who hate Chisum," Pat said. "It's kind of funny, you and Bob Olinger still on different sides when you got that much in common."

Billy tossed his cigar to the side and stared at Pat. "Is that it, Pat? You going to be riding with scum like Olinger?"

"It's all pretty simple, Billy. When the election's over, I'm going to have a job to do. If I think a fella like Olinger can help me get the job done, then . . . well, we'll just see."

Billy looked past Garrett, toward the scrubland beyond the trees. Scratching the soft, short whiskers along his jaw, he remembered the battle at the McSween house and Olinger's firing across the backyard; and also a time before that, at a stream outside Lincoln town, when he had Olinger in his sights for just a second.

"Should've killed old Bob a long time ago," he mused out loud. Billy had nothing more to say.

He turned around, headed back to his quarterhorse, and without another look at Garrett, mounted up and rode upriver, breaking into a lope when he had cleared the trees. Farther on, he rode through a shallow stretch of the Hondo to make his track hard to follow.

TRACKDOWN

8

"What are the Dedrick boys up to these days?" Pat asked Barney Mason.

"A little rustling, most likely. Some say they're pushing queer money too."

Pat turned the collar of his jacket up and stretched his long legs toward the front of the porch. "You think the Kid's getting mixed up with counterfeiters now?"

"Can't say," answered Barney. He leaned on the armrest, bringing himself a bit closer to Garrett, his face eager. "But cow stealing is something they sure got in common. I figure that's why Billy's there. I think they might be workin' on some deal with Mexican cattle."

"And Rudabaugh and Wilson—were they with him?"

"I seen 'em all, Pat."

"Any idea if they were about to pull out?"

"Don't know. The way they talked, they might be stayin' a while. Maybe takin' off from time to time, but also comin' back a lot. You could do worse than lookin' for him there."

Garrett watched Ida sitting on the low branch of a tree, holding Elizabeth on her lap. She bounced her baby sister on her knee and pointed to the branches overhead as if Elizabeth could see them, making comments on everything around her. Crumpling dried leaves in her hands, Elizabeth was oblivious to her big sister's monologue.

"What do you think?" Barney said. "Should we ride over there? Over to Dedrick's?"

"Sounds like the right idea, Barney. But other things got to get done first. I should have my warrants by tomorrow, and I still got to ride over to the longhouse this afternoon. Maybe you can help get some of the boys together in the meantime."

"Sure can," Barney said quickly. "Kind of like a deputy you mean, right, Pat?"

"Yeah, kind of like that."

Garrett thought Barney's thick body was about to spring out of the chair and bound onto his horse to get the job done. Ever since the election, he had been coming by the house with any tidbit of information that had come his way. A man that ready was bound to be useful, Pat thought.

Apolinaria's voice pierced the quiet. She appeared from the side of the house, shouting at Ida.

"What are you taking her up there for? Do you think she's a doll? Get down from there. . . . No! Not like that. Wait, I'll help you. I'll take the baby. Wait."

Before Apolinaria could reach the tree, Pat got to his feet and stepped quickly off the porch.

"Let her be, Apolinaria."

His wife turned to him, a look of complete incomprehension on her face.

"Ida'll look after her, just like she'd look after any other baby," he said.

"Pat, what are you saying? Elizabeth, she . . ." Apolinaria lowered her voice, as if keeping a secret. "She's not any other baby."

"Well, she's got to learn to be like any other. In a year or two she should be climbing that tree, and not asking Ida to help her neither. You just stay up there, Ida. If Elizabeth wants to be there, you keep her with you."

Apolinaria looked at the children, then at her husband; panic was taking the color out of her face. Pat put his arm around her and turned her back toward the house. "I got my eye on her," he said quietly. "Ida's a good girl."

Apolinaria stared straight ahead, unwilling to renew an old argument. Pat knew she understood the sense of what he was saying; only time would make her comfortable with it.

"You want me to start in?" said Barney when Pat returned to the porch. "You know, see who I can round up?"

Pat still had his eyes on the girls in the tree. He almost started to say something about Elizabeth, but checked himself, realizing how pointless it would be. What would Mason know about such things? "You go on ahead, Barney," he said. "I'll see you back in town tomorrow."

When Pat reached the heart of the Chisum spread

later that afternoon, he saw two buckboards, with teams in harness, waiting in front of the longhouse. That was one wagon more than he had expected to find, but he wasn't surprised; in the last two weeks a lot of men had come this way to parley. In Chisum's study, Pat found Captain Lea, as expected, sitting in an easy chair, clipping the end of a cigar. Standing on the other side of the room was George Kimball—the first time Pat had seen him since the election.

"Go on and say hello to him," Chisum barked. He stopped pacing just long enough to gesture at Kimball. "A winner can afford to be friendly."

"How are you, George?" Pat said.

Kimball managed to keep his moon-face placid. "Not as good as you, but I've got my prospects."

Chisum said, "Didn't know he was going to show up today, Pat, but it's good news that he did."

"Mr. Kimball has been very helpful," Captain Lea said. "Now that we have had the chance to explain the situation to him, he has shown us a great deal of cooperation."

Pat checked Kimball and noticed that the man was careful not to look at anyone. Pat tried to imagine how much arm-twisting had been necessary in order to explain things to the lame-duck sheriff.

"Since your term as sheriff doesn't officially begin until January," Lea continued, "Mr. Kimball has agreed to make you a deputy for the time being."

Pat turned to Kimball. "What kind of deputy? Will I be taking orders from you?" Kimball grimaced at the challenge in Garrett's voice, but Pat didn't allow himself to be too concerned about his ex-opponent's discomfort. There had already been too much polite discussion in the last couple of months; the time had come for some direct answers so he could get his posse on its way.

"You can pretty much call your own play," Kimball answered.

"Pat can call his own play, *period,*" snapped Chisum. "It's not just the deputy sheriff's badge we got for you, Pat. We also got a federal deputy marshal's commission to give you more jurisdiction. We got one for George too so he can lend a hand."

Pat couldn't see any sign of appreciation from Kimball for the bone that had just been thrown his way, but neither did he see any resentment. A professional officeholder, Pat supposed, had to learn to accept these things until the next position came along.

Captain Lea reached into his inside coat pocket and pulled out a folded sheet of paper. "We have also considered your recommendation from our last meeting. This letter should help you." Pat took the paper and looked it over. Some of the Captain's wording was pretty fancy, but Garrett could make out most of it. "We'll be able to back that up, Pat," said Lea. "Any member of the gang who cooperates will get leniency from the law. Perhaps, as you say, we'll be able to undermine Bonney before he has a chance to fight it out."

The letter was not what Pat was hoping for; it would have been a lot more persuasive, he figured, if it had come from the governor instead of Lea. Still, he said nothing. Any objections now would just mean another delay.

"I trust you have your first actions mapped out?" the Captain asked.

"I've got it figured," Pat answered. The look on Lea's face told him that more information was expected, but he didn't bother to continue. Instead, he turned to Chisum.

"John, I've got to talk to you."

By keeping his eyes on Chisum, Pat made it clear that he would have to speak to him alone. The cattleman stared back at him, then glanced at the other two men in the room. Captain Lea got to his feet.

"We'll wait outside, John," he said, letting only a faint hint of indignation creep into his voice. Kimball quickly followed him.

Turning toward his desk, Chisum cast a short sidelong look in Garrett's direction. "You're stepping pretty long now that you got the election behind you," he said, "telling the Captain to get the hell out of the room the way you did." He leaned against the desk and folded his arms. "I got to admit, Pat: I like it. That's the Pat Garrett I wanted to get this job done."

"There's something about the War that I got to ask you about," Pat said. "I'm going to ask it plain, John."

"That's the best way to ask it."

Pat ran a finger along his mustache, studying Chisum as he did so, preparing himself to detect any significant change in expression. "I keep hearing about you owing Billy something. Did you promise him anything when he was fighting for McSween?"

"You've heard that from Billy, haven't you?"

"I heard it from him, but I didn't give it a hell of a lot of thought until I also heard it from other folks too, from people who like him. They say that Billy's taking your stock to get even for unpaid debts. I have to know which way it is, just to settle my own mind."

"Okay, Pat, no reason you shouldn't know, because it doesn't change anything. When Billy says I promised him something, he's right—but only half-right. I told him, and I told some other boys too, that I'd make it worth his while if he stood with McSween. This was after Tunstall was murdered, when the fighting was just getting started. At the time, I didn't know if the boys working for Tunstall and McSween would let themselves get buffaloed or not. The way Murphy and Dolan had taken over Lincoln and were squeezing us out of army beef contracts, we had to keep the pressure on them. Just to make sure, I told Billy and some other boys that I'd take care of them if they kept fighting."

"You promise him money?"

"Yeah, that's right. Not an exact amount, but I said they could count on me."

"You're making it sound like Billy is all-the-way right. What's the other part of it?"

"Well, I told the boys I wanted them to fight. But what Billy did was something more than that. I wasn't about to pay for low murder, just as bad as Tunstall getting killed. When Billy and the others gunned down Sheriff Brady the way they did—that was cold-blooded, kill-crazy wildness, Pat. You heard about it. They really turned a lot of people against McSween when they ambushed Brady. Would *you* pay for that, if you were me? Well, *I* don't owe him for that. And I don't owe him for the other men he killed from ambush neither."

Pat mulled this over as he scrutinized the cattle

king's lean, scored face. "I guess you're right, John," he said. "It doesn't change anything as far as I'm concerned." *But,* he told himself, *you have to keep asking these questions, don't you.* Pat wasn't sure why.

"I guess this is it," Garrett said, stepping toward the door. "I'll be taking the men out tomorrow."

"One more thing about the job, Pat."

Garrett stopped to face Chisum again.

"With all the talk about Billy," Chisum said, "I just want to make sure we all know what else you'll have to do."

"What else is there, John?"

"Well, there's the rustling operation that Billy's a part of. Seems to be pretty well organized, and some of the other cattlemen in this valley want to make sure that you do something about it while hunting for Billy."

Pat tried to command the sudden wave of uneasiness to go away. But getting new instructions this close to the start still made him suspicious.

"I thought everyone wanted Billy caught as quickly as possible," he said. "The only way I know how to do that is go after him and nothing else."

Chisum put up his hands. "Don't get your back up, Pat. You go on and run Billy to earth any way you can. Some of the other fellas are just getting nervous about the stock they're losing, and I figured I should tell you. Between you and me, your getting the Kid is the first step in putting the fear of God into these thieves. Just round up any stolen stock you come across along the way—that'll be enough for now. We'll get to the rest of the operation as we go along."

"I'll do what I can," Pat said.

"It's not just the Pecos Valley men that're getting itchy. They're getting hurt over to Texas too. The word is, some posses from the Panhandle'll be coming this way to hunt the Kid's gang. Who knows, Pat. They might even help."

On his way out of the longhouse, Pat nodded to Lea and Kimball, and tipped his hat to Sallie Chisum, John's niece, as he walked outside. He assured himself that everything was in order; his backers weren't going to make him switch horses in midstream. After all, he had asked all the hard questions, both here and at the Palace of the Governors, and he had gotten the right answers. *These men can be trusted,* he told himself.

9

As cold as it was, Billy still had to open one of the windows. He reached over Whiskey Jim's hulking, sleeping body, pushed the window open a few inches, and savored the fresh morning smell. Moses and Joe were right to sleep out in the open, he thought. Maybe they knew Rudabaugh enough to know better. Hell, he thought, you just had to stand downwind of him for a few seconds these days to know better.

Whiskey Jim snorted, rolled onto his side, then opened his eyes, starting at the sight of someone leaning over him.

"Keep still," Billy told him. "I got no reason to kill you in your sleep."

On the other side of the room, Sam Dedrick and Johnny Wilson were stirring; Dave Rudabaugh was the last to sit up in his bunk, growling as he swung his legs over the side.

"Sweet Jesus, Dave," Billy said, "I don't mean to get persnickety, but a grown-up man's got to take a bath some time in his life. Didn't they have water up to Kansas at all?"

Wilson rubbed his eyes, smiled at Billy, and glanced at the bearded man sitting on the next bunk. Rudabaugh did nothing but glower and scratch himself.

"I swear I just about busted out cryin' last night, the stink was so bad in here," Billy said, encouraged by Wilson's lopsided grin. "I tell you what, Dave, next time we're in Fort Sumner, I'll have Maxwell fill the tub and you can go in and take a look while he's doing it. You don't have to get in the water, mind you. Just kind of stay in the same room with it for a while till you get acquainted."

Wilson slapped the mattress and hooted. The freckle-faced young man kept it up while Rudabaugh gave him a dim look.

Billy was about to make some comparisons between Rudabaugh and a long-dead bobcat he had found in the hills the other day, but something on the other side of the meadow in front of the ranch house took his mind off of conversation. It wasn't anything definite, just some movement between trees that Billy had detected out of the corner of his eye. Sidling to the edge of the window to keep himself concealed, he peered out and saw a rider trotting out into the clearing, followed by another, then a few moments later by two more. Billy was turning to fetch his gun belt when a big hand grabbed the back of his collar and wrenched him to the side. The next thing the Kid knew, Rudabaugh's face was right next to his.

"You bucktoothed little girl," the man growled. He slammed Billy against the wall and pinned him there with a hand clamped to his throat. In his other hand was a bowie knife.

"When I want to smell all pretty and dainty like a two-bit whore, I'll ask you how it's done," Rudabaugh said. "And when you're ready to become an honest-to-God man, you tell me and just maybe I'll let you know. You understand?" He brought the knife close to Billy's face. In his dark eyes was a wolfish ferocity, a fierceness that had only simmered when he had first woken but had now reached full boil. Billy felt a shortness of breath that had little to do with the hand grasping his throat. He didn't move a muscle. He was sure there was nothing left to do but die.

There was complete silence in the ranch house. Wilson, Dedrick, and Whiskey Jim all stood motionless, transfixed by Rudabaugh's fury. Some time later—Billy had no way of gauging how much time—the sound of horse hooves from outside reached the Kid's ears. Remembering what he had seen across the meadow, he was able to find his voice again.

"Riders comin' in," he rasped. "Get the hell off me."

Rudabaugh was slow to react, but the prospect of danger soon got past his anger. He blinked a couple of times, then turned to the window; he took his hand away from Billy's throat. Immediately, Billy scrambled to his bunk, grabbed his gun belt and pulled the double-action Colt from its holster. He had it aimed at Rudabaugh when the bearded outlaw faced him again.

"It's one of your boys," Rudabaugh said. "Looks like Pickett with some of the others." The sight of the revolver muzzle pointed at his belly didn't seem to faze him. The only thing that showed on his face was curiosity.

"You're not going to kill me, are you, Billy?" His tone was matter-of-fact. He shrugged. "Just got my dander up is all. You know how it is."

Billy moved slowly to the window, keeping his gun on Rudabaugh the whole time. He checked the oncoming riders to see that it was Curly Pickett leading Tom Cooper, Lee Keough, and Ellis Aker toward the house. He swung back to Rudabaugh when he heard the man move; Rudabaugh went to the door, opened it, and waved the riders in. Billy considered the man for a moment, ready to kill him, but was stymied by confusion over Rudabaugh's indifference. After some more thought, he finally slipped his gun back into its holster.

Rudabaugh shook his head. "If a man took a knife to me I'd blow his head off." He walked back to his bunk.

The boys came in laughing and pushing each other in fun; between the four of them they carried three new rifles, an overcoat, two blankets, and a sack that was filled almost to bursting.

"You come all the way from Lincoln town?" called Johnny Wilson.

"No sir," Pickett said, his lantern-jawed face beaming. "We did a sight better than that. We been over to White Oaks." Lee Keough let loose a rebel yell and Pickett joined in.

"Did you get over to Madam Varnish's place?" Wilson asked.

"Sure did, for starters anyways. Then we figured we might as well try our luck at the general mercantile. We went in and out of there as slick as could be without a body to see us. You want to try one of these Winchesters, Billy?"

The Kid stopped staring at Rudabaugh. "I wouldn't mind tryin' the feel of it," he said.

Hefting the rifle in his hands, Billy was encircled by Pickett and the others, still crowing about their haul; the high spirits got the better of the Kid's lingering fear of Rudabaugh, and he was soon able to grin again.

"Looks like you boys gave White Oaks something to talk about," he said.

"Oh, they'll talk," said Pickett. "Hell, they tried talking with their guns when we rode out of there, but it wasn't much of a conversation, you might say."

Billy narrowed his eyes. "Was that it? Just a little shooting?"

"Just a little. We didn't give 'em a chance to do much else," said Keough.

"Is that right?" said Billy. He started moving toward the front window. "Did they get up a posse after they stopped shooting at you?"

"A posse?" said Curly Pickett. "I guess you could call it that, but it was a pretty sorry bunch from what I saw of 'em before leaving 'em in the dust."

Billy looked at the trees on the right and the low hills straight ahead. "They might've been sorry, like you say, but any bunch of men is liable to be more trouble than just one. You tellin' me you lost them, Curly?"

"They couldn't catch us. They never had the chance."

"Oh yeah? Then what the hell is that dust rising above them hills?"

Pickett hurried to Billy's side. By that time, the drumming of hooves had circled to the left. The Kid craned his neck out the window to look at the left side of the house, toward the corral. On the far side, Moses Dedrick and Joe Cook were still asleep on the ground. Turning back toward the hills, Billy then saw horsemen ride into the open at a lope.

"They'll get my brother!" cried Sam Dedrick.

"Damn right they will," Billy said.

Reflexively, the Kid brought up the new Winchester, jacked the lever, but found it was not loaded. He then fired three times with his Colt; the riders were too far off for pistol fire to be effective, and all three shots went wide. Moses and Joe scrambled out of their blankets to face the first three riders in the posse; all three had their guns leveled. The two outlaws froze.

Billy ran to pick up his loaded rifle, as did the others in the house. They cut loose while the posse herded Moses and Joe back to the cover of a stand of trees. For a short time the exchange of fire was heavy, enough to shatter the house's windows and pelt the bark off the trees that shielded the posse, but the men from White Oaks had already collected two prisoners and didn't show much inclination to try for any more. They heaved Moses and Joe on spare mounts, saddled up, and tore away from the house, back through the hills toward town.

"Let's get the bastards," Sam Dedrick shouted as he ran for the door.

"You hold up there, Sam." Billy pointed his Winchester at him to make sure he got the message. "That's a fool's play."

"They've got my brother, Billy."

"That's right. And they're also ready for us. All we'd do is tire out our horses and waste a lot of ammunition chasin' after them."

"We can't just let 'em get away with this!"

"I know it, Sam. But we're going to get back at 'em the right way. We should wait till they get back to White Oaks, that's what I figure. Let 'em think they're in the clear."

"We're going to break out my brother," Sam said, hope brightening his face. "That's it, right, Billy?"

"Oh, for cryin' out Jesus, forget about your damn fool brother, will you. If he doesn't have the sense to sleep with one eye open, he deserves to get caught. And if he and Joe can't figure out how to break out of that sorry jail they have in White Oaks, then they deserve to stay arrested, too."

"Billy's right, Rudabaugh assured Sam. Dedrick didn't seem to be comforted by the thought.

"The way I figure," said the Kid, "we got to make sure the law in White Oaks doesn't get uppity. With Pat Garrett getting elected, it could be that a lot of law-dogs are figurin' to get too high and mighty."

Wilson said, "We goin' to burn down a lawman, Billy?"

"Well, I didn't see any faces too clear out there, but if it was a White Oaks posse, then it was most likely Deputy Redman that brought 'em here. Anyone ready to come along and take him down a notch?"

"You're talkin' sense now, Kid," said Rudabaugh. "I wouldn't mind seein' a law-dog kick."

"Good man," Billy told him. He liked the idea of keeping the Kansas tough itching for a fight with other men.

10

The Dedrick ranch wasn't much, just a small, slightly lopsided adobe building with a pole corral nearby that was no more than fifteen feet in diameter. The land, though, was good for grazing, especially to the rear of the adobe where patches of grama grass cured on the stem and could keep stock alive all year round. Farther back the ground broke up into a series of dry arroyos and ravines, which made the land even more useful; stolen stock could be hidden there easily.

In the gray light of dawn, the ranch house looked like an extension of the ground that surrounded it, like a pale, lifeless mound. Even the horses penned outside were still. If nothing else, Garrett figured, there shouldn't be any resistance.

Crouched behind a boulder, he turned to Barney Mason and Bob Olinger.

"Bob, you take three of the men and circle around to the back in case anyone tries running that way. Barney and me'll take the rest straight-in."

Pat watched Olinger creep away toward the rest of the posse standing by their mounts to the rear. He hadn't bothered to tell Bob which men to take with him; he didn't think it would make much difference. Excited by the bold law-and-order promises of the election campaign, many Roswell citizens had volunteered for the posse—so many, in fact, that Pat had had the luxury of picking only those he felt were the best. The problem was, he had little idea how well any of them would hold their ground in a fight or how well they would stand up to a long hunt.

Olinger took his three possemen on foot behind a hogback and, moving doubled-over, headed toward the cover of brush behind the adobe. Pat levered a cartridge into the chamber of his Winchester '73 carbine, then led Barney and the other six men around to the front. He stopped behind some creosote, forty feet away from the front door. Still there was no sound or movement from inside the ranch house. Pat judged that Olinger had had enough time to get into position. He checked his men to see that they were ready, then charged forward across the clearing.

Without losing a step, Pat kicked the door open and lunged inside, his rifle poised to fire from the hip. His eyes swept across the room. Among the clutter of gear and trash, he picked out two forms wrapped in blankets on the army cots in the corner. Both forms moved. They groped for guns left within easy reach, but stopped short at the cold sound of Garrett's voice.

"You're dead if you try it," he said.

Barney Mason bounded forward, crouched on one knee, and snapped his rifle stock to his shoulder. "Go ahead. I'll shoot your guts out. Go ahead."

The two men stared wide-eyed at Mason, then looked quickly at the guns held by the seven other possemen. Pat recognized one of the captives, the little man on the left, a small-time horse thief from Las Vegas by the name of George Davis; Pat had never seen him with the Kid, but he had noticed him once with Charley Bowdre in Fort Sumner. The other man, the broad-shouldered one with blond hair, was a stranger to Pat.

Garrett stepped over to the second man and put the Winchester muzzle in his face. "What's your name, fella?"

"Webb," the man answered quickly. "John Webb."

Pat nodded slowly, then pulled the rifle away. "So that's what you look like. Some people up to Las Vegas'd be real happy to get their hands on you."

Webb's gaze darted from Pat to the rest of the posse, both fear and calculation showing in his eyes. "You'd be Garrett, wouldn't you?" he finally said.

"That's me."

This fact seemed to buoy Webb with some desperate hope. "You're the law in Lincoln County. You got nothing to do with Las Vegas. You've got to leave me be."

"I don't think so."

"Hold on there, Garrett. I've been a lawman too, you know. I know what's what. You ain't got any jurisdiction over me. That business up to Vegas, that's all there is on me. I ain't done nothing in your bailiwick."

George Davis was getting the idea. "Me too," he blurted out. "You can't take me in for Las Vegas, Garrett."

Pat considered Davis for a moment, then smiled at him. "I didn't even know they wanted you in Las Vegas, George. I guess you can come along too."

"You don't got the badge for it," insisted Webb.

"I guess you boys don't know as much as you think you do. I'm not just working for Lincoln County; I'm a deputy U.S. marshal too. That'll give me enough to send you to Vegas or anywhere else in this territory. It'll also be enough to keep you from telling other fellas where you've seen us. You weren't figuring on telling Dave Rudabaugh, were you, John?"

Webb scowled at him. "You son-of-a-bitch. We ain't going to make it easy for you."

"And no one's going to make it easy for you neither," Pat said. "Barney, you go on out and get the irons. We'll make sure they can't move their hands too much."

Davis stared at Mason as the deputy jogged out the door; he kept looking at the doorway even after the posseman had left.

"You're ridin' with trash," Davis told Pat.

"Oh, well, I'm real sorry about that, George. I guess I should've asked you who I should've put in my posse. Maybe I should sit down right now and write a letter to the Kid and ask him who I should ride with when I run *him* down. I wouldn't want to offend him at all."

Davis's face reddened with anger, but he said nothing. Pat let the two of them stew for a while longer, then he pulled over a chair and sat down.

"What do you say, boys?" he asked. "Did the Kid ride through here?"

Pat got a snort from Davis but nothing else.

"How about you, Webb?" Pat said. "From what I hear, you've been in this country long enough to know a thing or two. Where would you say the Kid is? Does he have some kind of cattle job going on with the Dedricks?"

"Why the hell should I tell you?" answered Webb.

"For a pretty good reason. You might get a good deal from the judge if you help us. Captain Lea has given his guarantee to any member of the bunch that's wanted in Lincoln County. We probably could do something for you up to Las Vegas in San Miguel County too."

"I heard the Kid made a deal with the governor," Webb said with a smirk. "What the hell good did it do *him*?"

"Billy bollixed that deal for himself," answered Pat. "Anyway, you're not talking to the governor. You're talking to me."

Webb let out a gruff laugh. "Yeah, well, maybe I'll make my own kind of deal."

"Like the deal you made your last time in Vegas?" Pat said. "You better think again about that, John. Rudabaugh killing that man to get you out—you'd probably be in less trouble if that didn't happen."

"I was doing all right until you came along," said Webb. Then he turned to face the wall. That was his last word.

Both he and Davis kept their silence while their wrists were put in irons, but they started to make noise again when they were dragged outside to their horses. They cursed and resisted every inch of the way. A couple of the possemen started to shy away from all the ranting and tugging and spitting.

"Get them on those damned horses," Pat ordered.

One of the possemen who was hanging back, a barber named Sutton, was about to take hold of Webb's arm, but he sidestepped away and turned to Pat, his hands spread in appeal.

"Maybe we should tie 'em up, Pat. You know, tie 'em up all over and kind of throw 'em over the saddle."

"How the hell you going to tie them up if you can't even get 'em on their horses? Go on and pitch in or I'll tie *you* to the saddle."

Sutton went ahead and did his best, creeping up on Webb as if he were sneaking up on a hungry mountain lion, and between him and the other three men, managed to get the outlaw onto his horse. When Davis was also mounted, Pat tied his feet together with a rope slung beneath the horse's belly and ordered Olinger to do the same for the other prisoner. They all headed north across the clearing as Webb and Davis continued to grumble.

"An old thief like you," Webb said to Garrett's back. "I heard about all the stealin' you did with the Kid, and now there you are, so high and mighty. You're no different than me."

Pat turned in the saddle to face Webb. His face was stony. "You must be a real trusting man," he said, "if you think I'll just keep listening to that."

Webb tried to hold Pat's gaze, but soon averted his eyes. Both he and Davis were quiet for a while after that.

Olinger brought his horse next to Garrett's. His voice was low when he spoke. "If you want, I could make 'em tell where the Kid is. Just leave me alone with 'em for a while. That's all you got to do."

"Just keep in line with the rest," Pat snapped at him.

"Hell, Pat. You got any other ideas?"

"We still have a lot of rocks to look under yet. We'll take these men to Fort Sumner. Maybe we'll find more of the gang there."

Every now and then the prisoners tried to slow the posse down by reining in their horses for the purpose of making complaints or demands or two-minute speeches about the mean-spiritedness of New Mexico law enforcement. Mason and Olinger would slap their reins across the rumps of the prisoners' horses to keep these interruptions from getting out of hand; once, Davis made the mistake of bad-mouthing the deputies who had served under Murphy and Dolan during the Lincoln War and immediately felt the sting of Olinger's reins across the back of his neck. For the most part, the rest of the Roswell posse just looked on with blank expressions.

They reached the outskirts of Fort Sumner that afternoon. Pat called for everyone to stop and told Mason to bring the prisoners forward.

"You sure you boys don't want to tell us anything about Billy being here?" Pat searched their expressions for any sign that they were holding back. "Or maybe Charley Bowdre or any of the others—are they in Fort Sumner?"

Webb and Davis said nothing. Garrett couldn't decide whether he was seeing dishonesty or just plain pigheadedness in their faces.

"All right," he drawled, "we'll just have to find out for ourselves." He faced his men. "If the Kid or any of his pals are in town, you can bet they'll start shooting as soon as they see us. Better have your guns out and ready. We'll go in slow."

Pat chose barber Sutton and three other men who seemed fairly useless to stay behind with the prisoners. He led the rest of the posse at a walk toward the former army hospital, angling toward the rear of the long adobe. Just before reaching that part of the building that served as Bowdre's home, he told Mason to move ahead on foot and listen at the window. Mason returned ten minutes later with nothing good to report.

"I don't hear nothing in there," he said. "Not a damn sound."

Pat stared ahead down the length of the building as he took in this information. In his mind he charted the route he would take and the places in town that he would check. Telling his men to dismount, he led the way on foot, slipping his revolver into his coat pocket and holding it there so that he could put it to work in a hurry.

It was the first time he had been in Fort Sumner in several months, and he now found his old home to be much quieter than he had remembered—but then his memories tended to linger on *bailes* and nights in Smith's saloon, not on lazy afternoons spent sleeping it off. At Beaver Smith's corral, the posse saw no quarterhorses to indicate that the Kid might be about, and Smith himself said that Billy and some of the others had left the day before. Pat told Barney to stay with the saloonkeeper, in case the man was thinking of passing along the word that a posse was in town. Smith was an old friend, and Pat had no particular reason to think that he would do such a thing, but then Smith was a friend of Billy's too. Moving on, the posse checked Celsa Taveras's house, the blacksmith shop, the post office, and the Garcia house. Celsa said that Billy was gone, but she wouldn't say when he had left. The others wouldn't say anythng at all. They might have been quiet out of loyalty to Billy, or out of fear; Pat knew that both motives existed in Fort Sumner.

Returning to Smith's saloon, Pat found that Beaver had reconsidered and was willing to talk more about the Kid.

"You don't figure," he said, "to just go out and kill him, do you, Pat? You'll give him a fair chance and take him in alive, right?"

"That's what I'm planning."

"Because I couldn't go along with killin' Billy. That wouldn't be right." Standing by the door, the big saloonkeeper wiped his hands on his soiled apron and shifted his weight from one foot to the other.

Barney gestured to Smith. "I talked him into speaking up, Pat." He waited for some kind of commendation.

Garrett nodded, even though he wasn't convinced. He thought it was more likely that someone had seen Smith with the posseman, which worried the saloonkeeper: he could have been concerned that word might have gotten back to Billy that he was spending too much time with the sheriff's posse. If he was going to be damned in the Kid's eyes, he might as well make sure the Kid got caught.

"Where did Billy go?" Pat said.

"He was headed toward Moseby's ranch—you know, to the southeast of here. He had Rudabaugh and Wilson with him."

"Why was he going there?"

"Can't tell you, Pat. But I don't think he was just driftin'. Can't tell you what it was, but he seemed like he was riding a'purpose."

"Probably that deal with the Dedricks," offered Barney.

"Forget it," Smith said. "That's off."

"How do you know?" Pat asked.

"Well, not from the Kid, I'll tell you that. He wasn't sayin' nothing. But the other kid with him, Johnny Wilson, he was talkin' pretty good after he got a few drinks in him." Smith laughed. "I think you'll like this, Pat. He said they decided against the cattle job because they heard you were out and lookin' for them."

There wasn't much of the day left, but Garrett didn't want to spend what was left of it lazing around Fort Sumner. He told Sutton and the other there men guarding the prisoners to stay behind and keep Webb and Davis in the post office. The rest of the posse headed out to the southeast.

They were riding along the road, a little less than ten miles short of Moseby's ranch, when they spied a rider up ahead. Something about the horseman registered with Pat, but he couldn't pinpoint it at first; the man was too far off. Then he realized that he recognized the stoop of the shoulders and the broad-brimmed sombrero, its crown creased deeply from back to front. When the rider turned to see who was behind him, the sight of the long, young face confirmed Pat's suspicion that it was Tom O'Folliard. The outlaw spurred his horse and galloped away down the road.

Quickly, Pat turned in the saddle and studied the

high ground on the right. He was sure O'Folliard was headed for the Moseby ranch and that he was trying to get there in time to warn Billy. If Pat was going to cut him off, he would have to find a shortcut.

"This way," he ordered, as he reined to the right. He took his horse up the rocky slope.

11

At the first dry mountain arroyo, Pat considered doubling back. The only other time he had come this way the steep-sided pass had been clear enough for easy riding, but now it was choked from one wall to the other with mesquite. Facing the thicket, Pat calculated how long it would take to get back on the road in order to chase O'Folliard straight-on. He decided too much time would be lost that way. The mountain route, he figured, was bound to get better a little farther along.

"We're pushing through," he said, gigging his big gray forward.

"How're we going to get through *that?*" said one of the possemen to the rear. It was Milt Edwards, a Roswell freighter. Garrett stopped long enough to glance at him.

"We'll get through by not standing around talking

about it." He led on; he heard hoof falls trailing behind him.

Progress was slow, and miserable for both horses and men. The lead riders got the worst of the thorns, leaving behind them a trail of sharp, broken branches to plague the men at the rear. After a while Pat's horse stopped and refused to go on, but he spurred it forward and plowed through the wicked tangle of branches once more. He craned his neck to look ahead, searching for an end to the mesquite.

The route did not get better.

Around a bend leading to the next pass, the mesquite thinned, but only to make room for cacti that were just as punishing. When the posse finally emerged from the spiny thicket, the horses were scratched and bleeding along their flanks and bellies, the men along their legs. They now faced a jumble of sharp-edged rocks on the floor of the path angling back toward the road. Edwards and a man named Culver came to a stop. Their heads were lowered and their faces slack. There didn't seem to be any conscious decision on their part to halt; they just didn't have the will to go on anymore.

"Get your animals moving!" Pat growled.

With no strength to argue, they got themselves going again. Garrett let his horse set its own pace as it threaded its way through the field of rocks; his stomach was churning at the thought of how much time they were losing along this torturous route, but he couldn't push his horse to go any faster without running the risk of ruining a leg.

They finally reached the road to see O'Folliard loping up ahead, even farther away than he had been before. If any members of the posse felt like making a remark about the "shortcut" they had just taken, they knew better than to say it loud enough for Pat to hear. Garrett prodded his mount into a gallop. The big gray was game enough to hit its top stride, but only for a short time; from there on, it labored along as well as it could.

O'Folliard cut loose with his rifle from time to time. He fired quickly, with little aiming, but he came close enough to give the posse something to think about. Garrett and his men fired back to no effect.

The posse lost sight of O'Folliard along the jagged bottom of a mesa. An hour later, they reached the Moseby spread, as twilight softened the outline of the ranch house built in the center of the meadow. It was an adobe in the Texas style, with a dogtrot separating its two sections. Through a window in the right section Pat could see someone moving inside.

O'Folliard's horse was nowhere to be seen.

That should have been enough to tell Pat he was too late, but he had come too far not to take a closer look. For the second time that day, he split up his posse, sending a small group to guard the back and leading the rest through the front door. Inside the right-hand section, the ranch's cookhouse, were Rita Bowdre and Moseby's wife, Dolores. All the men had left.

Pat didn't waste much time questioning the two women; he knew they would tell him nothing. Stepping back outside, he circled to the rear of the house and inspected the stock in the corral. There he found two mules, obviously stolen from the Army and four horses bearing the jinglebob earmark of Chisum's herds. "At least that's something," he told himself bitterly. He had no illusions about further pursuit at this point.

Tracking at night was difficult enough with men and mounts that were rested. Battered and exhausted the way they were, his men would never make it to the end of the trail. As he walked away from the corral, Pat allowed himself to realize for the first time that it was not only his men who were dead-tired. He returned to the house and slumped against its back wall, his arms and legs limp with fatigue. The only thing that kept him awake was the evening's oncoming chill.

The early snow was driven by fierce, icy winds across the open valley. The three-quarter moon provided some illumination for the three riders traveling below the Jicarilla Mountains, but often the moonlight did nothing other than make it easier to see the snow swirling in front of their horses' noses. Just the same, Billy wasn't concerned. He had been this way enough times to trust his instincts for the proper direction.

The Kid and Rudabaugh rode with chins tucked in, their faces shielded by their upturned coat collars. After getting word about the posse from O'Folliard, Billy had sensed that the sudden nip in the air meant that bad weather was on the way, and he had talked Dolores Moseby into lending them the two overcoats in the house. He had figured that it would be wise to offer one of them to Rudabaugh, as a way of appeasing the man; that still left Johnny Wilson unprovisioned, but a couple of woolen shirts and a blanket underneath his slicker seemed to keep him warm enough to stay alive. In any case, the freckled young man wouldn't complain. He wasn't likely to let on that he couldn't keep up with the two other, more experienced long-riders.

By eleven o'clock the lights of White Oaks came into view, glistening on the blanket of snow that encircled the town. The ordeal of the harsh, numbing ride from Moseby's ranch now faded quickly from Billy's mind. Another close call, another escape, and here they were ready to do themselves some good again, with nobody to stand in their way, not Kimball or Garrett or anyone else.

The wind had disappeared by the time they reached the town, leaving only a thin, lazy snowfall, hardly enough to keep miners off the streets and away from the town's saloons and dance halls. Passing Madam Varnish's Little Casino, Billy considered stopping in for a few plays of roulette or faro, perhaps even moving on from there to one of the bordellos farther down the road. A little pleasure with business surely wouldn't hurt, he thought; but then he was troubled by the problem of Rudabaugh. Somehow he would have to give him the slip on the way to the whores so that the man's stink wouldn't scare them off. All ideas about the White Oaks high life then vanished as he neared the Exchange Bank.

Stepping up onto the boardwalk along the bank's false front, as if appearing on cue, was Deputy Sheriff James Redman, huddled inside his greatcoat, seeking the shelter of the bank's overhang.

Billy reached over to tap Rudabaugh's arm. He pointed out the lawman. "Look at the thin-blooded bastard," Billy said, smiling. "He's scurryin' around to get out of the cold, which isn't even cold anymore, and here we are, just finished ridin' through a man-sized blizzard and ready to ride out again."

Without another word, the Kid and Rudabaugh pulled out their rifles, worked the levers and opened fire. The first rounds punched through the false front and smashed the window to the deputy sheriff's rear. Johnny Wilson pitched in with the next volley as Redman dove to the boardwalk. The outlaws' arms and hands were still stiff with the cold, and more slugs went wide of the mark. Only when Redman scrambled to his feet and bolted toward the corner of the building did one of the gunmen find his aim. A .44 from Rudabaugh's carbine slammed into the lawman's hip. Redman spun with the impact of the slug, hobbled briefly on one leg, then toppled off the boardwalk into the alley beside the bank. He flattened to the ground.

Seeing that Redman was now protected by the boardwalk, Billy reined his quarterhorse to the left to get a better angle on his target. A commotion from the other end of the street, though, made him reconsider. Men were spilling out of a saloon and others came running out of another building across the way. After missing a lone man standing in the clear, Billy didn't care for his chances of fighting a mob on this night.

"We taught that law-dog something," he told the other two outlaws. "Let's ride."

Rudabaugh needed just one look at the White Oaks citizens gathering farther down the street to convince him that Billy was right. The three outlaws headed the way they had come.

Before leaving town, they passed a man stepping out of a house built onto the back of the blacksmith's shop. He held a coal-oil lamp high to throw some illumination into the street while he peered at the horsemen. In the light, Billy recognized the raw-boned man with the bushy eyebrows as Jim Carlyle. The Kid reined in his horse. With his rifle still in hand, he stared defiantly at the blacksmith and waited to see if he was going to make any trouble. The man met Billy's look, a hard cast to his deep-set eyes, but he was unarmed and unable to do anything but watch.

Rudabaugh stopped his horse a few yards ahead and called back. "What's wrong, Kid?"

"Nothing. No problem at all." Billy swung his quarterhorse about, glanced once more at Carlyle, then spurred forward to ride out with his partners.

After watching the Kid and the other two men ride past the end of the street, Carlyle walked in the opposite direction, headed toward the commotion that had roused him from bed a few minutes before. Beside the Exchange Bank, he found his friend Jim Redman lying on the ground, moaning, his blood staining the fresh snow. The other men who had been standing around gawking now turned to Carlyle, an expectant look on their faces.

12

Responsibility seemed to fall naturally on Jim Carlyle's shoulders, even though he had served as a deputy only once before. Some people in White Oaks said that he had ridden shotgun on the Deadwood stage a few years before coming to New Mexico; the story wasn't true, merely an entertaining lie invented by someone in a White Oaks saloon, but it was believed by a fair number of people because Carlyle had a certain way about him, a quiet toughness that spoke louder than any mining-town bluster. There were even some people who said that the posse that had chased the burglars to Whiskey Jim's ranch would have rounded up the whole gang if the blacksmith had been available to ride with them.

Once he had been placed in a bed and seen by a doctor, Deputy Sheriff Redman asked Carlyle to stand in for him at the head of the posse and track down the Kid and the two other shootists. The snow had stopped completely by then, and Carlyle knew that the tracks would be frozen in the ground cover until morning. He had the luxury of making sure his volunteers were well provisioned and allowing them a few hours' sleep before setting out.

Within an hour after leaving White Oaks, Carlyle believed that the northerly direction of the tracks meant that the gunmen had gone to the ranch of Whiskey Jim Greathouse. Late in the afternoon, along the slope of the Gallinas Mountains, he found that his hunch had been correct. From the crest of a rise, he could see the markings headed directly across the flat toward the corral next to Whiskey Jim's house.

Carlyle called over Dan Freese. "We're going to spread out and surround the place," he said. "You take three men and take them over there to the right, on the far side of the corral. Tell Paco to take three others and swing around to the left." When Freese turned to move away, Carlyle took hold of his sleeve. "And spread your men out. Don't give the Kid a way out."

Carlyle positioned the remaining three men along the rise and pulled out his rifle and posted himself on the right edge of the group. Lying on his front in the snow, he waited till he was sure Freese and Paco were ready. Then the blacksmith shouted toward the house below.

"Hey Kid! This is Jim Carlyle! I got a lot of boys from White Oaks here. We got you bottled up real good, Kid."

He paused to see if there would be any response.

The only thing he heard was a muffled sound of movement from inside the house.

"You try to run for it and you'll get a bellyful," Carlyle continued. "I don't know how many boys you got in there, but you can't have as many as me. You can make it easy on everybody if you throw out your guns and walk out."

Once more there was silence. Then a harsh creak broke the wintry quiet. The ranch house door inched open and a head poked out for a look around; it was a bearded face topped by a dark slouch hat. In the next moment, the head disappeared and the door thudded shut. The lamp inside was doused.

This was a challenge, Carlyle knew, and he didn't hesitate. He brought his rifle up and, levering quickly, unleashed a flurry of shots toward one of the windows. On all sides of the house, other rifles popped. The adobe sides of Whiskey Jim's place were pelted with bullets.

Whiskey Jim Greathouse crouched on the floor, sick with fear, as the posse's barrage thundered away. Not that Whiskey Jim was a coward when it came to a little shooting. In his younger days he had hunted buffalo in Texas, tangled with Comanches, and held his own against toughs in Fort Griffin town. But the law made him deeply uneasy. For four years he had operated his trading post and ranch here along the Las Vegas road without any interference. The sweet times, though, could come to an end quickly if that damned blacksmith kept the gang trapped in here.

When the gunfire faded, he crept to a window and looked at the rise facing the house, the source of

Carlyle's voice. Billy called to him from across the room.

"If you go peeking out, you better do some shooting while you're at it. Make yourself useful."

Whiskey Jim's thick body slumped below the window; he worried the collar of his woolen shirt. "You think Garrett is out there?" he said.

"If he is, we would've heard him by now," replied Billy. "You can bet on that."

Whiskey Jim nodded glumly, then moved over to the rough-hewn bar in the tavern section of the big room. He found a bottle of whiskey on one of the shelves beneath the counter. Johnny Wilson was staring at him when he finished his first gulp.

"A snort sure wouldn't hurt now," Wilson said. Whiskey Jim handed him the bottle and stared hopelessly at the dirt floor while the young outlaw hooted and shook his head like a dog at the first bite of the rotgut. The bottle was passed around.

Garrett might not be out there now, Whiskey Jim thought, but that didn't mean much. Carlyle could be a dogged son-of-a-bitch in his own right when he put his mind to it, and if he kept the siege going long enough, Garrett was likely to get word and show up to make sure things were done right. Whiskey Jim had known of Pat while on the buffalo range; he hadn't met him back then, but he knew him by reputation. That was enough to know that Garrett didn't let much stand in his way. Greathouse's business in stolen stock would get busted up for certain if Garrett came upon it while running the Kid to earth.

Another exchange of fire flared up, and Whiskey Jim figured it was time to pitch in. At least it would give him something to do. But something else occurred to him while loading up his old Spencer, an idea that just might get him out of this yet.

Crawling to Billy's side by the front window, he triggered a few shots at the muzzle flares showing clearly along the rise in the gathering darkness. He waited till the exchange of fire subsided before saying his piece.

"I got me an idea," he told Billy. "That Carlyle is a determined man, but the other fellas with him might not be so ready to drag this thing out."

Billy gave him a curious look while he reloaded. "What's your idea?" he said.

"If we can get Carlyle talkin', maybe we can make a deal with him. The way he's got us boxed in, you're going to have a hell of a time shootin' your way out—you know that, don't you?"

Billy shrugged. "Maybe."

"Well, I'm thinkin', maybe we can get him to let some of us out of here. Once those other White Oaks fellas see there's some way to get back to town and out of this cold, they'll push him to make terms with us."

"Who the hell's gonna get taken?" It was Rudabaugh's flat, deep voice. He stared at Whiskey Jim with suspicious eyes.

"That's not the point," Whiskey Jim countered. "If any of us has to get arrested, the rest of us can get them away from the posse further down the road." He turned to appeal to Billy. "It's either that or wait for more posse riders to show up. Maybe even Garrett himself."

"I wouldn't mind taking a shot at this Garrett," Rudabaugh growled.

"Not like this you wouldn't," said Billy. "Not when they got us pinned down. Whiskey Jim here is making sense. Have you got it figured any more than that, Jim?"

"Well, seems to me we got to make some kind of swap. You can send me out there and let them hold me while Carlyle comes in here to talk to you boys. I think they'll go for that. Unless," he added pointedly, "one of you three fellas would like to give yourself up instead of me."

Billy checked the other two men. Rudabaugh wasn't saying anything now; Wilson was looking at Billy, ready to go along with whatever he said.

"All right," said the Kid. "Let's give her a try."

Billy called out the window to get Carlyle's attention, then told him about the hostage swap. For a while, there was silence from the posse leader.

"Okay, Kid," Carlyle finally shouted, "but you send Greathouse out first. Then I'll come in."

Whiskey Jim smiled. "I guess he doesn't want to spend a night out in the snow either."

"That's all right with us," Billy called to the posse leader. "He's comin' out now."

Walking with Greathouse to the door, Billy clapped a hand on his back. "Don't worry, Jim. We know where to find the whiskey without you." He guided him out the door.

When Whiskey Jim was halfway to the rise, Carlyle showed himself. He still held his rifle and waited till Greathouse had come the rest of the way before he put the gun down and started walking.

Inside the ranch house, the three outlaws watched him step across the threshold in complete silence, scrutinizing the blacksmith with their weapons ready, as if waiting for him to pull a hideaway gun and start blasting. The two men with Billy were unfamiliar to Jim Carlyle; just the same, it didn't take him long to decide that the bearded man was dangerous.

Billy strolled to Carlyle's rear and slowly circled to the other side of him. The Kid shook his head and smiled: he had to admit that the blacksmith had a lot of sand to come in here by himself.

"A blacksmith who does his work as good as you," said Billy, "why couldn't you just leave the law business to other folks?"

"I might've left it to Jim Redman," Carlyle said, "but then you boys shot him. We can't let you get away with that, Kid."

"What makes you so sure we did it, Jim?"

Carlyle glanced at Rudabaugh and then Wilson before answering. "If you're so sure you didn't do it, then just come in and tell the judge."

"You're a real smart fella, ain't you?" said Rudabaugh, glaring at Carlyle.

"Dave's got a point there," the Kid added. "The way things are in this territory, a man like me can't get a square deal in court. They'd hang me first and get a verdict afterwards. And that's certain."

"I guess that's something we can parley about," Carlyle said.

Rudabaugh hefted his rifle in front of his chest. "I wouldn't mind bustin' his mouth a little, Kid. *Then* we'd get ourselves a deal from him."

Billy stepped closer to Carlyle and put his arm around his shoulders, as if he hadn't heard Rudabaugh's threat. "Why don't you sit down, Jim. This parley might take a while."

They sat Carlyle by the bar. The blacksmith made sure he kept Rudabaugh in sight.

"Greathouse was tellin' us you might settle for just taking in one or two of us," Billy said, as he pulled up a wooden chair. He put his rifle on the floor, turned the chair around and sat leaning forward on the backrest. "Which one of us you figure on taking, Jim?"

Billy could see that the posse leader was feeling the pressure. He shifted his weight in the chair—the closest he would come to squirming—and he ran his fingers through his hair, stalling until he could think of something safe to say. If he singled out any of the three outlaws, Carlyle might trigger that man into striking out at him.

"How about a drink?" Billy asked him, putting on the air of a gracious host. "You look like you could use one. Hey Johnny, go fetch us a bottle. You know where they're stashed."

The Kid smiled. *Just having a little fun,* he told himself. *After all the trouble these sheriffs and deputies have given me, I got the right to a little needling now that I got a lawman cooped up like this. Even if it's just a part-time lawman.*

Carlyle took a long gulp from the bottle and passed it back to Johnny Wilson. "I really can't say who's the one who put the bullet into Redman," the blacksmith finally said. "The best thing'd be for us all to go back and sort it out in White Oaks. What do you say, Kid? That way we can make sure we do it right."

"Interesting idea, Jim. But I got to tell you, I don't think we all want to go back with you. Me, I like you, but Rudabaugh over there, he doesn't like anybody. How about it, Dave? Are you already buildin' up a hate for Jim here?"

Rudabaugh didn't have much use for this banter and didn't bother to add anything to it. He leaned back against the bar, staring at the posse leader.

"Well," Billy went on, "I think you got the wrong idea, Dave, getting mean about this fella without knowin' him. You should've seen how Jim Carlyle fixed my horse's shoe not too long ago. He's a real craftsman. I think everybody should like him."

"Hell, I like him," said Wilson. "Your word's good enough for me, Billy."

Carlyle leaned forward, resting his elbows on his knees. "Kid, we got to figure something out. That posse out there's not going away just because you want it to. We better make a deal and get this over with."

Reminded of the predicament he was in, Billy gazed at the far wall, a sourness coursing through him. He was trapped, that was certain, but he commanded himself not to give up; something was bound to present itself. Something almost always did.

"You got an idea," he said to Carlyle, "why don't you spit it out."

"Well, I think everybody knows that all three of you were shooting at Redman. Only one of you hit him, but you were all trying, and that's a crime right there. It seems to me that a couple of you boys'd be happy if just one of you goes back to White Oaks. Isn't that right?"

Nothing was said for a while. *This blacksmith is pretty cagey,* Billy thought, *trying to get us to turn over the one that shot the deputy. Fact is, it's kind of tempting, almost tempting enough to try.*

A few moments later, though, Billy wasn't so sure how he could get away with pointing the finger at Rudabaugh. For the time being, he wasn't sure at all what he should do. He took the bottle from Wilson. He gave Rudabaugh a comradely wink, as if the two of them were sharing some secret.

"Let's think on this for a while," the Kid finally said. "Thinkin' and drinkin' is what I got in mind. Go on, Johnny, get another bottle."

For the next half hour, nothing was said about the posse or White Oaks. Billy started singing "Silver Threads Among the Gold" and tried to get the others to join in, but only managed to get Wilson to help with a couple of verses. There was talk about a bordello in Lincoln, the tequila in Fort Sumner, and gambling at the Little Casino. They were interrupted once by a shout from outside. One of the possemen demanded to know what was taking so long in there.

"Don't have kittens," the Kid shouted back. "We're just keeping your blacksmith here till we figure it all out." He then asked Johnny Wilson if he had ever known what it was like to spend time with a Mescalero squaw.

Through it all, Billy made a big show of drinking, but actually took only small sips. He kept a close watch on the others, close enough to notice that Rudabaugh and Carlyle were keeping their drinking in check as well.

"Hey Billy," Wilson said with a tongue slowed by whiskey, "maybe we should just shoot the law-dog and chuck him out the window. Hell, we're gonna have to shoot our way out of here anyway—why not start the ball right in here?"

"Is that what you think, Johnny?"

Wilson stood with shoulders slouched, directly behind Carlyle. "Hell, we rode through the blizzard to burn down some lawman . . ." To finish his thought, he made a broad, drunken gesture at the blacksmith.

Billy paid little attention to Wilson's tough talk; he was too busy keeping tabs on Rudabaugh. He didn't like the way the bearded outlaw was staring at him, as though waiting for the Kid to betray him. Billy figured it was time to try to put the man at ease, just to better the odds he was facing. The more he thought about it, the less he liked the idea of agreeing to Carlyle's terms.

"You know what?" he told the blacksmith. "Johnny might be talking sense. I heard you once rode with a posse that flushed a friend of mine out of house and home. Doc Scurlock it was. It might be that we ought to even things up for that." While looking at Carlyle, the Kid kept checking Rudabaugh out of the corner of his eye. "You just remember that, Jim. We don't got any reason to dance around with you. If you want to make a deal, you better make a good one, and I don't want to hear about one of us riding back with you to White Oaks."

A thin smile now appeared on Rudabaugh's lips. As for Carlyle, Billy could see that he was no longer nervous; the posse leader was outright afraid. There wasn't much that showed on his wind-burnished face, but the tightness of his mouth and the occasional glazing of his eyes gave him away.

"You know what," said Rudabaugh, "I got me an

idea." Before he could say what that idea was, though, a gunshot cracked outside, from somewhere along the rise to the front of the house.

Wilson practically jumped to one side. Pulling out his handgun, he shouted, "They shot Greathouse! The bastards shot Whiskey Jim!"

Carlyle didn't need to think about the consequences of Greathouse's death—or even the consequences of the outlaws' thinking that Greathouse was dead. He sprang from his chair, bolted to the front of the house, and jumped toward the window. Billy was turning around and drawing his Colt just as Carlyle left his feet. His first shot bellowed inside the adobe and drilled the blacksmith through the left leg. Carlyle smashed through the remnants of the window glass left by the exchange of gunfire earlier that evening; he flopped clumsily onto the ground outside.

The bullet in the leg didn't stop Carlyle.

Scrambling to his feet, he limped furiously across the snowy ground toward the rise. The Kid raced to the window. Against the white of the snow, Carlyle's figure stood out clearly even though it was fully dark now. Billy pumped two more .41s into his back.

Nothing more was said inside the house. All three outlaws knew what had to be done. If the posse got another chance to pin them down inside the adobe, Billy, Rudabaugh, and Wilson would never get out. They rushed out the door with their guns blasting, alternating their fire from right to left, and sprinted to the corral.

For several moments the killing of Jim Carlyle paralyzed the posse. They didn't begin firing at the escaping outlaws until the three had already run into the corral and were gathering their horses. The posse's gunshots were hurried; bullets slashed through the snow near the corral, and one killed a spare mount—a bay that had been stolen from Jim Boskett—but none came close to the three men mounting up. Billy, Wilson, and Rudabaugh galloped away from Greathouse's adobe. Finding a gap in the line of possemen to the rear, they rode through the hills, headed south.

Whiskey Jim Greathouse watched, beside the other men positioned along the rise, as the outlaws rode away. The gunshot fired by the White Oaks bootmaker a few minutes before—the one that had started everything—hadn't come close to Whiskey Jim; the bootmaker had fired at the house, thinking he had seen someone moving around outside.

The posse saddled up. Later on, most of the possemen would have second thoughts about what they had done at the Greathouse ranch, but at the time there were only feeble protests from a few of the men. And even *those* men rode away like the rest. Not knowing where the three outlaws had gone, they thought that the Kid and the other two might be swinging around to kill more of the posse. To play it safe, the men from White Oaks headed back home, leaving their blacksmith sprawled in the snow.

13

Pat was worried about some of the horses when they reached Fort Sumner. Their breathing seemed difficult and they felt warmer than they should. He hoped that Beaver Smith might be able to get them fresh animals for the next leg of the hunt.

"They've got the strangles, all right," Smith said as he inspected the posse's horses outside his saloon. "There aren't but two or three of 'em that're still healthy and they won't stay that way if you don't get 'em away from the sick ones."

"I know what to do with the horses," Pat said with strained patience. "What I need are new ones. How many can you get me?"

Smith tugged the serape tighter around his body to ward off the cold, a pained expression on his face. "I really don't know if I can spare any, Pat. If I swap what I got with you, then all I'll have is a bunch of sick animals. What'll I do then?"

"I'm not asking you to kill yourself. Just do what you can."

"I'll tell you what, Pat. I sure wouldn't mind talking about this inside where we can get a nip to warm ourselves."

Pat sent most of the posse to check on the prisoners and took Olinger along as he stepped inside the saloon with Smith. He waited till he had taken his first swallow of whiskey before asking his next question.

"Has Barney been around?"

"Yeah, he has," said Smith, settling heavily into a chair. "He rode in yesterday, as a matter of fact. Last I saw him, he was over to the Garcia house. What happened, Pat? Did he run away from your posse?"

Pat turned to Olinger. "You go on and finish your drink and then go find Barney and bring him here."

Smith was smiling. "Guess workin' regular was too much for Barney, is that it? You going to learn him something for runnin' off, Pat?"

Garrett sat across the table from Smith. "What about the horses, Beaver?"

"Seems to me you'd be better off worrying about your men than your horseflesh. Those fellas you left here to look after the prisoners—I guess you could call them a bit fidgety."

"What happened with them?"

"Well, last night there were some people in town talkin' about how the Kid was going to ride in here and bust your prisoners out. Some of 'em were scared that the Kid would think the whole town was siding with you, but that wasn't anything compared to your posse fellas. Two times they started shooting at shadows, and I don't know how many times they must've wet their pants, they were so nervous."

Pat had nothing to say to that. He poured himself another drink.

"I guess it must've been the story they heard from White Oaks," Smith went on. "A posseman doesn't like to hear about a deputy getting killed."

"Billy killed a deputy?"

"It was Jim Carlyle. He was leading a posse and had the Kid holed up. Billy shot him while Jim was a hostage."

Pat stared at the surface of the whiskey in his half-empty glass. He thought about the two days wasted hunting along the Pecos while another man had been murdered. He then thought of how much time might be wasted trying to persuade Smith to come across with fresh mounts. Pat figured the saloon-keeper was holding back because he didn't want to get tied up with Garrett's posse any more than he already had. Smith was going to keep straddling the fence between Garrett and Billy; and for now he seemed to be leaning slightly toward the Kid.

"Thanks for the whiskey," Pat told Smith as he got up to leave. He looked back to see Beaver gazing blindly at the table, unwilling to meet Garrett's eyes. Pat wondered if the man was thinking of times when they had worked this saloon together, the sort of freewheeling, happy times that should make men friends, or at least put them on the same side, for many years. *I got picked for this job,* Pat thought, *because I know all the right haunts and have all the right friends. A lot of good it's doing me.*

Garrett's next stop was the telegraph office. There

still might be another way to get new horses, he figured, and a few new men wouldn't hurt either. His wire to Lincoln was answered quickly.

Sheriff Kimball's reply stated that he and his posse had lost Bonney's trail outside White Oaks. He also said he would be able to arrive in Fort Sumner with reinforcements within two days.

Stepping out of the telegraph office, Pat considered his meager choice. If he waited for Kimball he'd be losing time, and in return all he would be gaining was the lame-duck sheriff. If he headed toward the White Oaks country right away, on the other hand, he might be strapped for men and horses and would be riding without any clear purpose. His thoughts came to a halt when he saw Olinger and Barney Mason approaching. He stood perfectly still, his insides twisting with anticipation, as he watched the two men draw near. The fact that Mason had finished his scout early might mean that he had come upon something.

"I tried asking around Ramon like you said," Barney told him, "but there wasn't hardly anyone there worth asking, Pat. So I tried pushing up to Puerto de Luna."

"Curly Pickett passes through there sometimes—you find any sign of him?" asked Pat.

"Didn't have to," Barney smiled. "On the way there, I got to talking to some boys at Augustine's place and they said they'd seen the Kid and Wilson headed toward Portales. These boys might've known something, Pat. They already knew about the White Oaks business and Carlyle and all that. I believed them."

Garrett had already decided against waiting for

Kimball. He figured there would be trouble if his old opponent was in the posse; as long as he had another month in his official term of office, Kimball wasn't likely to let Pat call the shots. In the meantime, Pat thought they could make do by using the rested horses belonging to Sutton and the other possemen on guard duty. That would mean they would have mounts for only six men, but then most of the Roswell posse was expendable anyway. As for Portales, Garrett didn't see any other possibilities. *At least we'll be on the move again,* he thought; *we might chance upon something along the way.*

Pat set out with Olinger, Mason, and three men from Roswell while there was still some light left. All the aches accumulated on the ride along the Pecos now returned in full force, while the weariness seemed to advance a notch. After a few miles, Pat's body settled into the saddle again and the aches were hardly noticeable, but the tiredness had its way with his thoughts, clearing the path for unwelcome notions.

He imagined catching up to Billy; he would run him down outside Portales, down a dry arroyo, his imagination told him. He could see himself trading shots with the Kid, but he couldn't see himself killing him. Billy would ride out of the trap with his double-action Colt blazing. Pat would line him up in the sights of his rifle, then find himself unable to pull the trigger. Billy was smiling at him, taunting him, but Pat still couldn't make the shot. He would then try to shoot the horse, miss, and watch helplessly as Billy rode away, out of the arroyo and across the plain. With a sickening sensation at the pit of his stomach, Pat would realize that he would have to start the hunt all over again. After a couple more miles of riding, these thoughts finally began to fade, and he was able to convince himself that his imagination was playing him for a fool. There wasn't any point in worrying if he could kill Billy; he was going to take him in alive.

After camping that night along the Pecos, they reached the town of Portales around noon the next day.

Mason's tip was no good.

Not only were Billy and Wilson not in town, they hadn't been there for several months. Garrett did his best to prevent himself from lashing out at Barney for his unreliable information—first the Dedrick ranch story and now Portales. He was able to keep quiet, but just barely. He reminded himself that the hunt had only just begun and that it was unreasonable to expect results right away. But other thoughts began to crowd reasonableness to the side. He imagined Chisum and Lea and the others waiting for word that the Kid had been caught. Desperation began to take hold of Garrett. Leaving his posse behind, he went to a Portales saloon and stayed long enough for a couple of whiskeys to wash away some of the frustration. From there, he rounded up his men and told them they were headed back to Fort Sumner right away. He didn't pay attention to the grumbling from the riders to his rear as he led the posse northwest out of town.

It was well into the night when they came within calling distance of Tom Wilcox's ranch house. Looking across the rolling stretch of ground to the adobe's lighted windows, Pat was able to push aside some of his hopeless thoughts. Many men passed through this ranch, he knew, and Tom might have heard some useful news. As an afterthought, it occurred to him that a cooked meal would also be a good idea.

As the posse dismounted in front of the house, two of the Roswell men moved about painfully for a while to try to get some of the saddle-soreness out of their bodies. They stared bitterly at Deputy Sheriff Garrett, then finally spoke up to his face.

"This is the end for me and Pena," said Arch O'Hara, a Roswell store clerk. "You can run around chasing nothing from here to hell and back if you want, but we're pullin' out. Ain't that right, Enrique?"

Enrique Pena nodded in agreement, but now that his time had come to speak, the little man looked almost apologetic. "We can't do any more, Pat."

Garrett stopped by the door and waited for the two men to finish.

"We're going to get us something to eat in there," said O'Hara, "then we're going to get us some sleep. And when you ride out of here you can ride without us."

Pat took in a long breath that was supposed to check his anger. "Just do me one favor," he said. "Tom's got a long table in there. Make sure you sit way the hell to the other end from me when you eat." He turned and walked inside.

Tom Wilcox had a big pot of chili heating up in the stone fireplace, and he said he could feed them all. The house wasn't small, but it wasn't quite big enough for everything cluttered inside, from the pothooks and cranes in the fireplace, to the big writing desk in the opposite corner, and the collection of broken lamps that Wilcox never seemed to get around to fixing. On a cold night like tonight, the closeness and warmth of the place was welcome. It was enough to put Pat's mind off of business, for a short while, anyway. Sitting with Mason and Olinger and ignoring the men at the other end of the table, Pat finished his first plateful, started a second, then called Wilcox over.

"Billy used to ride through here from time to time," Pat said. "You see him or any of his friends lately?"

"Wish I could help you, Pat. But they haven't been this way in a long time. I'd tell you something if I could."

For Mason and Olinger's benefit, Pat said, "Well, it looks like my luck is holding out." He meant it to be funny, but both possemen were too exhausted and hungry to do anything but shovel food into their mouths.

Pat watched Wilcox as he talked to O'Hara on the other side of the room. *Another friend to both Billy and me,* he brooded. Pat tried to decide if Wilcox was telling the truth or was just trying to play it safe like Beaver Smith had done. For the moment, he was too weary himself to weigh the two possibilities. Instead, he tried to plan his next move.

There were no leads to follow now—that much was certain—but he couldn't let himself sit around and wait for something to come along. He would at least have to make himself useful. There were still two prisoners being held in Fort Sumner, he reminded himself, and they would have to be transported up to Las Vegas for trial. He tried to force himself to work out the details of the prisoners' transfer, but the task seemed so trivial compared to the hunt for Billy and his gang.

Pat found his mind drifting, as it often did lately, to Apolinaria and the family. He smiled grimly to himself as he remembered how anxious he had been to get his posse out on the Kid's trail; right now he would settle for just being at home in Roswell. In his mind, the early wintry weather disappeared and it was warm enough again to sit on the porch and watch the girls playing in front of the house, Ida leading Elizabeth along, jabbering away, trying to get her baby sister to keep up with the games she liked to play. His smile now faded as he looked at O'Hara at the other end of the table. *Here I am,* he thought, *mooning about my family and home, while O'Hara over there thinks I'm a relentless monster.* Pat couldn't remember another time when the opinion of a weakling like O'Hara would have bothered him.

A voice outside called to the house and got permission from Wilcox to come in the rest of the way. A man of medium height wearing a buffalo coat stepped into the house a few moments later, shrugging his shoulders as if casting off the last of the night's cold. He headed straight for the fireplace.

"No night for a man to be ridin' about," he said. "Just ain't natural."

The voice was familiar. Pat turned for a better look. When the man turned his back to the fire, Garrett saw that the face had taken on a few more creases. But he had no trouble recognizing Sam Dobbs.

"Well, damn me to hell if it isn't Pat Garrett," cried Dobbs. He shook his head as unpleasant memories came back to him. "I hear you're out after Comanches again, if you get my meaning."

"I guess you could say that."

Dobbs fixed a look on Pat, an intense expression on his face that had little to do with his rambunctious manner of just a few seconds ago. Then he shook it off. He turned to the other men at the table.

"You must be his posse, huh? Now ain't that a sorry business. Me, I made that mistake once. Went out huntin' Indians with old Pat over there. Nearly died from it, the way he pushed us on and on. Yes sir, nearly died."

The faces of the three Roswell men showed that this wasn't a topic they wanted to talk about now. Dobbs shrugged in response to the silence and, when he was finished warming himself by the fire, opened his coat and sat next to Pat. He talked about how good the food looked and asked Wilcox if he could get a glass of something that would warm him up; he then turned to Pat, his voice suddenly quiet.

"Charley Bowdre says you're out lookin' for him."

Pat stared at him for a moment before answering. "You know where Charley is?"

"I just seen him. We were ridin' together a ways."

Pat waited for him to say something more.

"He wants to talk to you," Dobbs said.

"Did he say why?"

Dobbs thought this over. "He didn't say, but it looked to me like he was fretting some about getting hunted by a fella like you."

As much as he wanted to, Pat didn't ask where Bowdre was. Charley wouldn't want Pat to come to him for the talk; it would have to be someplace in between the two of them.

"You could set it up?" he asked.

"Sure, I can. Hell, I could do it tonight if you want."

"I do."

"But I'm not doing it for *you,* Pat. I just want you to know that. I'm doing it for Charley. I never thought he was too bad a fella, going back to the Fort Sumner days, and I just figured he could use a good break. He's the one I'm doing it for."

"Fine with me."

A worried look came to Dobbs's face. "He's close enough that I can get him in an hour, but I sure wouldn't mind some hot food to get me there and back if that's okay."

"You're not in my posse anymore, Sam," Pat said with a smile. "You can eat anytime you want."

The meeting was arranged to take place at a fork in the road, a few miles closer to Fort Sumner. Sitting his horse along the west edge of the main road, Pat saw Charley Bowdre ride slowly toward him, just a moving shadow among the other night shadows, then drawing close enough for Pat to see the frosted breath and the guarded look in his eyes.

"Haven't seen you for a while, Charley. Not since that time in Roswell with the Kid," Pat said.

Charley didn't answer. He looked at his hands, fumbling with the reins, as if all words had deserted him.

"Looked for you in Fort Sumner," Pat continued, "but nobody was to home."

"Yeah, I heard you been lookin' a lot of places."

Pat smiled. "Maybe you should start this thing off by telling me who told you that. Then I'll know who I shouldn't talk to anymore."

Charley disregarded the remark. "I wouldn't mind starting over again," he said.

"What do you plan on doing, Charley?"

"I know how to ranch. And I wouldn't mind doing it in this country. The wife, she's sure set on stayin' in these parts, what with her family rooted around here for so many years. I sure think I could ranch if I had the chance." He wasn't looking at Pat, but was gazing across the road; he might have been trying to imagine what a new life would be like.

"Marrying can do that to a man," Pat answered.

"But hell, Pat, I can't be doing any such thing the way things are. I was just thinking, maybe I could get myself out—you know, like that time they was holding out amnesty a year ago for those that fought in the Lincoln War."

"Why didn't you try the amnesty when you had the chance?"

"I don't know, I guess the wild life just gets in your blood. At least for a while. And besides, seein' what happened to the Kid, that didn't make the amnesty seem like such a sure thing."

"That didn't have anything to do with you," Pat said. "Billy walked away from his deal. He had his chance."

"The hell he did. He told me all about that. The way that lawyer went after him when he testified. They were making a noose for him."

Pat said nothing for a moment. He tried to keep old doubts from rearing up again. "Which lawyer are you talking about?"

"That prosecutor. That damned Rynerson. Asking Billy all those questions about killing Sheriff Brady, and there was Billy, just trying to help the county get those men who did that other murder, the Chapman fella gettin' shot in Lincoln. Billy said he knew that lawyer was tryin' to get him for the Brady killing, and then when Rynerson moved the trial to the next county, Billy just had enough. It was all too slippery. That's how Billy put it. Just too damn slippery."

Pat shifted uneasily in the saddle. "We're here to talk about you." It sounded like a feeble answer, but it was the only one that came to mind.

Charley looked down at his hands again; he shook slightly from the cold. "Well, I guess that's all in the past anyway." He faced Garrett abruptly. "Is there some way, Pat? Can I get a break? I figured, us knowing each other the way we do, from Fort Sumner and all . . ."

"You sure you're ready to shake loose?"

"Yeah, I'm sure—as long as I can get a square deal. Billy's just not the same anymore, Pat. In the War, I guess it all made sense, but now, I just can't figure it sometimes."

Pat took out the letter from Captain Lea. "Read it over, Charley. If you're ready to help us get the rest of the gang, then you'll be able to do honest work."

Charley took a few moments to study the letter. He grimaced as he handed it back.

"What's the matter, Charley?"

"It sounds all right, I guess, but I . . . I don't know, Pat. Can the Captain really make sure the law won't bother me? I know he's a big man and all, but can he stop some mean-minded lawyer or some lawman from going after me?"

Pat nodded as he thought this over. "You want more of a guarantee, right, Charley?"

"I'm stickin' my neck out just comin' here, Pat. I got to know for sure if I go any further."

Pat folded the letter and returned it to his pocket. "I'll tell you what. I'll see what I can do, I'll see if I can make it more certain for you. I know you don't belong with those other fellas in the gang—you're better than that, and I guess you know that now also. When I have an answer for you, I'll find Dobbs to bring it."

"That's good, Pat. I'd appreciate it."

"And what about you? If I try to get a square deal, what'll you do?"

"What do you mean?"

"Will you start shaking loose on your own? Just do a little less riding for Billy, that's all. If you do that, some people might be more likely to give you a guarantee."

"Okay, Pat. I'll give it a try, I suppose. I guess it can't hurt."

14

After first trying the house, Pat rode for some three miles south across the range until he saw the cattleman riding and talking to one of his hands. John Chisum sat ramrod-straight in the saddle, wearing clothes no different from any other cowboy, looking much more at home than he did in a parlor chair discussing county politics.

He nodded briefly at Pat as the deputy sheriff approached, then continued listening to his man's report on the progress of line-riding work along the spread's northern boundary. Having only a vague idea of how large Chisum's ranch was—even Chisum himself had trouble pinning down its exact perimeters—Pat judged that the northern line-riding shacks might be as far as fifty miles away.

"This snow's been hell on the beeves," Chisum told Garrett as he brought his horse to a stop. "My boys have their hands full keeping track of all the strays. Which is why," he added wryly, "Jess over here is so itchy to get back up to the line. Aren't you, Jess?"

The expression on Jess's leathery face didn't seem too enthusiastic, but he smiled at his boss just the same.

"Just be glad you don't have Sheriff Garrett as a boss," Chisum told his hand. "Then you'd know what it is to *work* for your living."

Jess gave the cattleman a short wave of his hand, then reined his horse around and rode off. Pat watched the man for a few moments, keeping the smile fixed on his face. As good-naturedly as he could, he said, "Why didn't you tell me about Rynerson double-crossing the Kid?" Despite his effort, resentment still found its way into his voice. Chisum answered the tone with a flinty-eyed stare.

"I talked to Charley Bowdre," Pat said. "He told me about Rynerson breaking the deal."

Chisum gigged his horse forward without a look back at Garrett; the cattleman didn't care whether he rode alone or not. Pat moved his big gray to the man's side.

"Is it true?" he said. If it was going to be a fight, he was ready for it now.

"Nobody calls me a liar," Chisum answered.

"Just tell me what happened. I'm not calling you anything, but I'm going to know the truth."

Chisum reined in sharply. "We all told you what you had to know. What the hell's the matter with you? You tired of being sheriff already? If you want to quit, just say so."

"What the hell went wrong with the deal?"

"Don't you try shouting me down, Pat. I swear I'll kick the guts out of you. I'm not that old that I can't take care of—" Chisum stopped himself just as the rage was about to run out of his reach. He looked away and took a couple of moments to settle himself, then faced Pat again, the last of his anger still flushing his face.

"Tell me just one thing, Pat. You been asking these questions every step of the way. We offer you a chance to make a name for yourself in this territory, and you keep asking about what was done to the Kid, making it sound like we were trying to force the job on you. Goddamn it, Pat, you already started hunting Billy. What's so damned important now about Billy's deal with the governor?"

Pat didn't know what to say at first. Although his reasons hadn't been clear to him, he had never questioned them. Slowly, they now took shape in his mind. "I guess I don't want people pointing a finger at me when the job's done," he finally answered. "I don't want them saying I went after a wronged man."

Chisum considered this for a moment, then shook his head in consternation. "If that's how you think, then I was wrong in saying you were the right man for the job."

The cattleman's voice was quiet, but for the first time that day it intimidated Pat into silence.

"Just what the goddamned hell do you think this is all about?" Chisum went on. "You want to know what happened with Rynerson? All right, I'll tell you. He went after the Kid—that's right. Bowdre told you the truth. Rynerson was working on an indictment against Billy for killing Sheriff Brady even though the deal said Billy would go free once his evidence in the Chapman case was given. Now you know, Pat."

Chisum paused, gazing across his land, as calmness came gradually to his features. "And now your next question is: Did the governor and the rest of us tell Rynerson to do that? I know I didn't. As for Governor Wallace . . . " Chisum shrugged. "I can't tell you that, but I can tell you what I think. I figure Rynerson went ahead and did it on his own hook. He probably thought he'd be a big man if he got the Kid convicted and he didn't care what the deal was. Now don't get me wrong, Pat. I'm not saying Wallace did everything that he could. Either he knew what Rynerson was doing and he didn't stop him, or he should've found out what he was doing. To tell you the truth, I think Wallace was too busy with his book-writing to really give a good goddamn one way or the other."

Pat sat stock-still, his teeth clenched tight. "I would've run out of that jail too, if I was Billy. You would've also, John."

"Pat," Chisum began, then stopped himself; he looked like he was holding down another surge of anger. "Pat, you just don't see it, do you?"

"I don't see what? I see that both Billy and me were lied to."

"Listen to me. It doesn't make a damn bit of difference if I would've run out of that jail or if you would've run out of that jail. Do you think it made any difference to the Kid, Pat? I would've told you all this before, but I didn't see why we should make it more complicated than it has to be. The fact is, Pat, that deal with the governor wasn't Billy's first chance to stop his thieving and killing, and it wasn't his last either. He could stop being an outlaw today if he wanted to. All he's got to do is leave the territory and start again somewhere else. He'd just have to change his name. Hell, he's done *that* before. He didn't become Billy Bonney until just a few years ago. If he'd leave the territory and keep honest, he'd be all right, but he isn't interested in that. He's the most famous outlaw in the territory and he wants to stay that way. The only way he's going to stop is if you make him stop."

During his ride to the ranch, Pat had rehearsed in his mind how he would give Chisum a verbal lashing if he found out that Bowdre's story was true. But now, although he still resented being lied to, the sense of what Chisum had just said kept his mouth shut.

"Now it's my turn to find something out," Chisum said. "How close're you to finding the Kid?"

Pat tried to sound optimistic. "I could be real close if I can get Bowdre to help. I talked to Captain Lea yesterday about fixing things up for Charley so he'd come over to our side. The Captain's going to see what he can do."

"Well, if that's what you're counting on, then don't count on it," Chisum snapped at him. "There's just so much we'll dance to Bowdre's tune."

"I think Charley's ready, John."

Chisum swung his horse around. "Just get the damn Kid. You hear me? I lost another bunch of horses yesterday, and Purkey says some of his cattle got run off too. If you're so damned worried about what people'll think of you, then just make sure you get this job done."

His piece said, Chisum put his horse into a trot and headed back toward the longhouse.

"You high-and-mighty son-of-a-bitch," Pat said under his breath.

Charley Bowdre tied his horse to the staircase railing and stood in the night shadow bordering the rear of the whorehouse. He looked across the back-lots for several minutes before he was satisfied that he hadn't been followed.

On the other side of the back door, the short hallway was lit by a single Rochester brass lamp hanging from a peg in the wall, leaving most of the floor's filth concealed in darkness. Charley moved down the hall to the last door on the right. Billy always used that room when he came to Lincoln town for "sportin' around," as he put it. Charley was about to knock on the door when he heard Billy's laugh coming from the front of the house.

The Kid sat at one of the two tables in the small room that doubled as vestibule and cafe. Actually, no food was ever served there, but the owner of the house, a hatchet-faced woman named Wichita Lottie, thought that the term *cafe* lent a certain air of respectability to the place. With Billy were Tom O'Folliard and Johnny Wilson and two chubby Mexican girls. The senorita on Billy's lap had on nothing but a hip bustle.

Picking up the bottle on the table, Billy waved Charley over. "Come on here and give us a hand," he said. He then glanced slyly at O'Folliard, as if sharing a joke. "I see Rudabaugh didn't feel like comin' himself. I guess a little womanly friendship got him about as nervous as a hermit expectin' company." Both O'Folliard and Wilson hooted with laughter. Billy gave the girl on his lap a squeeze. "Don't worry about Charley here, *muchacha.* He's a married man. He knows how to treat a gal. Only problem for you is he likes to *stay* married."

Charley tried, without much success, to keep his eyes off the girl in Billy's lap. "Rudabaugh told me he got the word," Charley said. He stopped himself there.

"Yeah? Go on. What'd he say?"

Charley looked meaningfully at the two whores. "Garrett knows about this place," he said.

A little slow from drink, Billy took a moment to glance at the senoritas, then got Charley's meaning. "Go on back to my room, *muchachas.* Me and the boys have got some private business to talk about here."

When the whores were out of earshot, Charley sat at the table. "You got to move the herd tomorrow morning, Billy. If you want to sell 'em fast, you got to get those beeves over to the Tularosa Valley. They'll have men there with the money."

"Tomorrow morning, huh?" Suddenly, Billy seemed a lot more sober. "That doesn't give us a whole lot of time with Rosa and Carmen back there."

"It doesn't give you any time at all, Billy."

The Kid pursed his lips and cocked his head. "Well, I guess the man's right. Let's go, boys," he told Wilson and O'Folliard. "It'll have to wait."

"Goddamn, Billy," said Wilson, "I ain't had any yet."

"Don't fret about it. There's plenty of gals between here and Sumner. We got plenty of time for that when work is done."

Charley waited out back while the others brought their horses around. They then started their mounts at a quiet walk away from the outskirts of town.

"You figuring on heading back to Sumner, Charley?" asked Billy.

"I don't have any reason not to."

"We sure could use an extra rider to push those beeves, especially one as good as you."

Charley's mind scrambled for an excuse for not going along. He had only agreed to bring the message to Billy because Rudabaugh was a hard man to say no to; and besides, carrying a message was innocent enough. But moving stolen stock was something else again.

"Come on, Charley," O'Folliard chimed in. "You got to get away from your wife sometimes."

Why do I have to think of a story? Charley asked himself. *I never made excuses before when I didn't want to throw in with Billy on something. If I start explaining myself now, he'll just get suspicious.*

"Not this time," he said as casually as he could.

"Seems to me a body should help his friends when they need him," Billy said. "Especially if he wants to keep those friends. Hell, Charley, there'll be some money for you if you do. Why the hell not?"

"You don't need me. Why don't you get Pickett?"

"I would if I could find him before morning, but I don't think I can do that. Like you say, we got to get those cows over there real fast."

Billy was smiling at him, but Charley knew him well enough to know that the Kid was going to insist on his coming. If Charley refused again, he would make Billy wonder what was behing it all. *Garrett won't know about it,* he reassured himself. *Anyway, I just said I'd* start *to get away from the Kid.*

"I guess I can put off some of Rita's home cooking for a little while longer," Charley said.

"Good man," Billy answered. "Just keep riding with us and you'll be able to start that ranch of yours in no time."

15

Eight riders came loping toward them from town along the Las Vegas Road. Pat saw that all except one of them were Mexicans, and most of them were jabbering, pointing at the prisoners in the wagon bed, and laughing. Pat brought his wagon to a stop, while the riders formed a semicircle around him. To Pat's side, Barney Mason reined in his horse and, trying to keep an eye on all the riders, slowly shifted his right hand toward the stock of his booted rifle.

The two Mexicans closest to Pat were talking in Spanish. They seemed to be talking about the Kid's gang, although they spoke too fast for Pat to keep up. He had no trouble, however, understanding what their bloodshot eyes meant. From the rear of the wagon, Garrett could hear Webb and Davis muttering, their tones uneasy.

Pat faced the one rider who looked familiar to

him, a cowboy he had met while pushing beeves for Pete Maxwell a few years ago. "You boys look pretty happy. You celebrating something, Vidal?"

"We'll get Billito for you," the man answered. "We'll get the whole gang if you want." He seemed to think that these words had somehow answered Pat's question.

"I wired the sheriff in Las Vegas to send a deputy this way," said Pat, checking the men on either side of Vidal. "Have you seen any sign of him?"

A man to the right moved his horse forward a few steps. "That's me. I am Francisco Romero. Sheriff Aguayo, he gave me the badge to help you with the prisoners. I thought we would ride out to help you bring them into town."

Garrett took a moment to study the man and took note of the even complexion and clear eyes. *At least one of them's sober,* he thought. Before he could say anything to the deputy, though, one of Romero's possemen walked his horse to the wagon bed and pulled out his rifle. He stared at the prisoners with long, Indian eyes.

"Which one of you killed the *Mejicano* in Las Vegas?"

Pat turned slowly toward the posseman, lifting his Winchester from the floorboards below the seat and placing it on his lap. "Webb didn't kill the Mexican jailer, if that's what you mean," he said mildly. "That would be Rudabaugh you're thinking of."

The posseman checked the rifle on Garrett's lap. He then smiled thinly. "If that was Rudabaugh in the wagon, would you try to stop me?"

"Mariano!" called Deputy Romero. "Back off. We're here to help Garrett. No trouble, right?"

Mariano gave the deputy a disgusted look, then shrugged his shoulders and turned his horse away. Webb shuffled forward in the wagon bed; he spoke to Pat in a harsh whisper. "Jesus Christ, Pat, you're not going to leave us with these fellas, are you?"

Garrett didn't reply; he kept his eyes on Mariano.

"I'm sorry, Sheriff Garrett," Romero said. He motioned toward Mariano and put on a pained expression. "Sheriff Aguayo wants me to help you get the prisoners from Puerto de Luna to Las Vegas and that's what I intend to do. We can take over the prisoners right now if you want."

"Well, I don't know," Pat said, stalling. Romero seemed like he might be capable, but that might not be enough. Pat scanned the faces of the other possemen. "I dismissed most of my own posse back in Fort Sumner because I figured two men'd be enough to get the job done at least as far as Puerto de Luna."

Romero narrowed his eyes, not seeming to accept Garrett's explanation.

"Besides," Pat continued, "we have to do this right. Getting better manacles on the prisoners, writing out a receipt for them—all that bothersome stuff." He smiled at Romero as if the Mexican deputy should understand how annoying these picayune details of law enforcement could be. If he did understand, Romero didn't show it; he reined his horse around in an abrupt motion and led the way along the last few miles to town.

"I knew you wouldn't let 'em have us," Webb told Garrett. "You're too good a man for that. You knew that wouldn't be right."

"Don't tell me how much you like me, John. We're only taking you as far as Puerto de Luna so I can tend to some business there. After that, we're on our way back south."

"Garrett, you can't do that." Webb's voice was strained with desperation. "You saw how that greaser looked at me. I still got ten dollars with me. You can have it if you take us to Las Vegas. One lawman to another—you got to do that for me, Garrett."

Pat stopped listening to him after that.

At Puerto de Luna, they left Webb and Davis at the blacksmith shop where fetters could be made to keep the prisoners' wrists attached to their ankles. "When you write up a receipt," Pat told Romero, "you can bring it over to me at Alejandro's store. We'll be there getting the trail off of us." Along the way, Pat and Barney found José Roibal at his small house and brought him along.

Pat told José his new plan while they got something to eat and drink at Alejandro Grzelachowski's store.

"I know the Kid's going back to Fort Sumner," he said. "I'm not sure when, but he's never been away from there too long. Problem is, I don't think I'm the one to scout around, and Barney here isn't either. A couple of Anglos like us can't slip around real well, and besides, everyone there knows we're on Billy's trail."

"You want me to go there, Juan Largo?" asked José.

"I need your help. I need a good man that the Kid doesn't know. I figured you could do that, José. There'll be some money for you if you find something."

Roibal took a sip of tequila. "I'd have to take some

time to make sure my wife and babies will be all right while I'm gone."

"You can take a day to set things right. You won't need more than that for a short trip."

A glint came to Roibal's eye. "A short trip? The last time I took a short trip with you I was gone for three weeks hunting Indians."

Pat smiled. There was no point in denying it—José knew him too well. "Don't take much more than a day," was his concession.

"I can do that," said José. "Where will you be going, Juan Largo? Are you going to Las Vegas to find the Texans?"

Pat gave him a puzzled look. "What Texans?"

"The Texas posse. They came this way last week."

"Is that the posse hired by the Panhandle cattlemen?"

"That's them. They were asking about Billy's gang. It sounds like the Kid hasn't been taking cattle just from Chisum."

"Las Vegas, you say?" said Pat, musing out loud.

Barney stopped eating long enough to say something. "You thinkin' we might be able to find some real posse riders up that way?"

Pat was about to answer when he saw the door open and a backlit figure step inside. The man didn't bother to close the door behind him, letting the cold air stream through the store. It was Mariano. He leaned against the door frame, looking lazy, and gazed curiously in Garrett's direction. He seemed drunker than before.

"You got some truck with us?" Barney challenged him. Pat shot Mason an annoyed glance.

"I came here to talk to the new sheriff," Mariano

said, paying no attention to Barney. "Romero didn't let us talk before."

A troubling thought came to Pat's mind. "Where's Romero?" he demanded.

"Don't worry," Mariano said. He took a couple of steps forward, his fingers curled around his gun belt. He wore two revolvers in tied-down holsters. "He's with the gringo prisoners. No one has done anything to them. They're not worth the trouble."

With nothing more to say to the man, Pat started eating again.

"A couple of gringos like that," Mariano went on, "anyone could have caught them. It doesn't take much of an hombre to do that."

"That's pretty big talk," said Barney. "You'd have pissed your pants if you'd been with us."

"Shut up, Barney," Pat snapped at him.

Mariano didn't seem to care much about Barney's remark. He gave him a sidelong look, then turned his long eyes back to Pat.

"I've done a lot more than either of your prisoners. You just ask around Puerto de Luna. They'll tell you. Mariano Leiva is a bad man."

"Is that right?" Pat drawled.

"Taking me wouldn't be like taking those *muchachas* you had in your wagon. You think you could do it?"

Pat watched the Mexican in silence. He had never heard of a desperado named Leiva, but then he hadn't been to Puerto de Luna for some time. It wouldn't have taken long for some would-be gun shark to make a reputation in this town.

"I don't think a gringo could arrest an hombre like

me," Mariano said, unwilling to let up. "You know that's true, right, sheriff?"

Pat sighed irritably and leaned back in his chair. "I don't have a warrant for you. You can do what you damn well please, for all I care. Just don't do it too close to me."

The Mexican smiled, exposing rotted teeth. "Another *muchacha*," he said, "like all gringos."

Something jumped inside Pat. The only thing that showed on his face was a tightening of his features, but inside, a sudden fighting rage leapt from the pit of his stomach. He held himself in check; for a moment the rage seemed to break through, but then he managed to put it under control again.

Mariano looked pleased with himself. He was drunk enough to think that the new sheriff of Lincoln County was locked into place by fear. He swaggered out of the store.

From just outside the door came a jumble of excited voices. Pat could discern five or six voices other than Mariano's. Now he understood what had made the local badman so fearless: a group of his friends had been outside the whole time, ready to back him up if need be. Speaking in Spanish, Mariano now told those friends how he had made the *muchacha* lawman back down. Pat could no longer control his anger. All the frustrations of the last two weeks' fruitless hunting cut loose at once and propelled him out of his seat and toward the door.

Once outside, Pat reached his man in three long steps. Mariano had his back turned, holding forth with his friends. Garrett slapped him once across the side of the head and sent him sprawling to the ground.

Mariano took a couple of moments to get his bearings. Then he rushed to his feet, grabbing for the gun on his right hip. Pat was ready for him. He snapped his Colt out of its holster, but he let his fury get the better of him; firing as soon as his gun cleared leather, he sent a .45 bullet into the ground, a foot in front of the Mexican badman. Mariano fired back. His shot ricocheted wildly off of the adobe wall behind the sheriff, and in that instant, Pat triggered once more. He drilled his man through the right shoulder. The round knocked Mariano back to the ground. Still with some fight in him, he groped for his left-hand gun. Just as the Mexican got the revolver loose, Pat strode toward him, lashed out with his boot and kicked the gun to the other side of the street.

Pat wheeled toward the other men outside the store. Some of them wore guns, but none of them had made any move to put the weapons into play. A couple of the onlookers now took a step back at the sight of Pat's Colt. Farther down the street, Pat saw Romero running out of the blacksmith shop, headed his way. Pat's blood was still racing, and he had no patience for staying put till the local deputy arrived. He went back into the store.

Only after downing a glassful of tequila did Pat take note of Barney Mason. The man had his rifle in his hands, as if ready to fight, but he was still near the table, nowhere near the door where he might have been able to do Pat some good. Roibal, on the other hand, was hurrying from the back of the store where he had just found a pistol; he hadn't been armed when the shooting started, but he had done all he could to change that.

Deputy Romero's eyes flared with anger and indignation when he stepped into the store. He put his hand out.

"Give me your gun," he ordered Pat.

Ignoring the local deputy, Garrett stepped to the side to get a better look through the open doorway. The men outside the store had moved away a few feet, but they hadn't dispersed.

"I have to put you under arrest," said Romero. "Give me your gun."

"I don't think so."

Romero's jaw clamped tight as he stared at Pat. "You can be the biggest man in Lincoln County, but you can't shoot a man in this county without standing trial."

"You telling me you can control those men out there?"

"That's my responsibility and I'll do it."

"Well, I don't think you can, so I'm keeping my guns, and so is my deputy here."

Barney took this as a cue. He swung his rifle toward Romero. "You want me to cut the son-of-a-bitch in two, Pat?"

"All I want you to do is go out that door with me and go to the blacksmith. Then we're getting our wagon and horses and we're taking our prisoners to Las Vegas."

"What are you talking about?" shouted Romero. "They're in my custody now!"

"We're taking them to Las Vegas for the same reason we're not giving our guns to you. We don't trust the men that make a posse around here. C'mon, Barney, let's go before those men out there figure out what the hell they're doing. Keep your rifle ready."

Romero moved back quickly to the door in an attempt to keep the two Lincoln County men from leaving. He still hadn't taken out his gun; he was going to try to stand up to them empty-handed. Pat had to give him credit for having some sand. Then he pushed him aside and led the way out.

The group outside stared at Pat and Barney but still did nothing. Mariano was sitting slumped forward on the ground, holding his right arm, careful not to meet anyone's eye. Garrett noticed that a couple of the men glanced back at the store doorway. Looking over his shoulder, Pat saw that José Roibal stood there, the pistol in his fist, making it clear that he was backing Garrett's play.

"We'll meet you back here when you're done," Pat called to him. He and Barney circled around the Puerto de Luna men, keeping them in view the whole time. No one tried to stop them.

Barney stepped closer to Pat. He spoke quietly.

"Maybe we should take one of them as a hostage," he said, indicating the men outside the store. "Sort of as insurance."

"Shut the hell up and do as I say."

16

Pat and Mason found the posse of Texans camped above the eastern section of Las Vegas, the part known as New Town. By the look of it, the Texans were preparing to set out.

"Who's the top screw here?" Pat asked the first man they reached.

Without a word, the cowboy pointed to a man some forty feet away, adjusting the cinch on a big dun. He was a square-jawed bulldog of a man, with a dark, scraggly mustache and light eyes that peered at the two approaching horsemen from beneath a flat-brimmed Stetson. He didn't pay the newcomers much attention as he moved his horse around to check the bridle.

"You heading out today?" Pat asked.

"Yeah, we are. So you can stop fretting."

Pat gave him a curious look. "Why should I fret about it one way or the other?"

"You're from New Town, aren't you? Worrying yourselves sick about a bunch of Texans hurrahing the place." Turning back to some meaningless bridle adjustment, he added, under his breath, "Guess you don't want us gettin' in the way of the gang that runs things."

Pat laughed. "Didn't take you long to figure out the way of things in New Town, did it?"

The Texan squinted at him in consternation.

"I'm not from town," Pat told him. "I'm Pat Garrett, the new sheriff of Lincoln County. I've heard we're looking for some of the same fellas."

The Texan took a while to respond. He scrutinized Pat, then sized up Mason, trying to gauge what this meeting would mean. "I've got a U.S. deputy marshal's commission in case you're wondering what gives me the right to come this-away."

"I don't doubt it," said Pat. "I'm sure those Texas cattlemen had no trouble getting some law behind you. Have you got a name too?"

"John Poe," the man said. "The Canadian River cattle owners sent me."

"All right, John. Fact is, I'm more interested in seeing how we can throw in together than in checking up on you. I need some good men. I think I'm going to be getting close to the Kid real soon, and I'll need some boys who can really stick to it—hang and rattle, like we used to say in Texas."

"That where you're from?"

"I've been through there. Did some cowboying there, just like you did, I suspect."

Poe nodded. "We were on our way to the White

Oaks country. I know the Kid's been giving them some trouble there, so I figured that'd be the way."

"No offense, but you'd be wasting you time."

Poe cocked his head. "You can go ahead and tell me something I don't know if you want."

"George Kimball's already been through there and he lost the trail. Billy won't be there anymore. You can bet on him not staying anywhere too long."

"Well, I was figuring, if things're as cold in White Oaks as you say, we'd go through the mountains and head up the Pecos, cut his trail somewhere along the line."

"That'd take you up to Fort Sumner, which is good, but you'd be getting there too slow."

"Fort Sumner," said Poe, "that'd be the place?"

Pat was about to give him an answer that would make it seem like he was certain; he caught himself in time. He had no reason to try to bluff this man, even if Poe could be bluffed, and the Texan's iron eyes told him that it wouldn't be likely anyway.

"I'm banking on the Kid going there sooner or later," he finally said. "If he's got any home, it's Fort Sumner, and I figure the chances are good that he'll wind up there after shaking a posse the way he did in White Oaks."

Poe left his horse alone now and sat on a nearby rock, clasping and reclasping his hands several times before settling on a grip. "I've done my share of trackin' in Texas," he said, "but I can't say I'm an expert in *this* country."

"But the men who're paying you are going to expect you to find the gang just the same," Pat said, as if completing Poe's thought.

The Texas marshal took out the makings and

started to roll. "Tell me what you got in mind, Garrett."

"I need men—I told you that before—but everybody's got to know what to expect. Billy's already killed one deputy, and he killed a sheriff during the Lincoln War. You think you got the men who'll be ready to ride and fight till the job's done?"

"There's a couple I could count on right this second." The Texan paused to give it some thought. "As for the others, I'd have to put it to 'em to make sure."

Pat looked down at Poe from the back of his horse and noted the way the man looked back at him, as if he weren't looking up at all, as if they were staring at each other straight-on. Pat had a hunch about this Texan.

Pat said, "Those men that'd be ready right off—you'd be one of them, right?"

The corner of Poe's mouth curled into a trace of a smile. "I didn't come all this way to make a damn jackass of myself."

"Glad to hear *someone* doesn't want to make a jackass of himself," said Pat.

"One thing I'd like to ask you before anything else, Garrett. If I'm riding down to Lincoln County with you, I wouldn't mind having a deputy sheriff's badge. Just to make sure I'm doing this right."

"I'll see what I can do, John."

"I'd still be paid by the Canadian River cattlemen—I wouldn't need money from Lincoln County."

Pat grinned. "I don't think I'll have any trouble at all getting that badge for you."

Poe got to his feet and put up his hand to shake

on it. "Doesn't seem like you got any time to waste," he said. "Might as well put it to the boys right now."

Garrett held the handshake an extra moment to keep the Texas marshal from walking off just yet. "One more thing about this country, John. There's plenty of folks who'll get word to the Kid if they happen to hear anything. Better not tell your boys exactly what we got in mind, just in case."

When he rounded up his men, some thirteen in all, John Poe told them he planned to ride with Sheriff Garrett to retrieve some stolen Texas stock below Puerto de Luna. He gave it to them pretty strong:

"The Kid hasn't gone this far to give up anything without a fight, so you can be damn sure we'll have to shoot our way to the cattle, and if we don't kill off the gang then, we'll also have to shoot our way out to get the beeves back to Texas." He went on to talk about all the hard riding ahead of them and the vicious weather that might be waiting for them. By the time he was done, five of his men were still ready to ride: Lon Chambers, Jim East, Poker Tom Emory, Bob Williams, and a Mexican named Luis Bozeman who was mostly known as the Animal. Pat thought the moniker was a good recommendation for the job.

While they got ready for the ride to Puerto de Luna, Pat toyed with the idea of telling Barney Mason to go his own way; the man's useless information and useless feistiness had soured Pat on him. But when the time came to saddle up, Garrett said nothing to the posseman. He told himself that another Lincoln County man, besides himself, could be useful now that the posse was composed primarily of Texans. He also found he was reluctant to dismiss a man who had stuck with him when others had given up.

The posse moved south along the Pecos that afternoon. Pat took some satisfaction in the range-toughened faces that surrounded him. These were the kind of men he had known ten years before when he had first gone west. Growing up on a Louisiana plantation had done little to prepare him for the harsh life on the Texas cattle range, but the cowboys there had set the proper iron-willed example for young Garrett. Looking at the raw-boned men who traveled with him now, he felt he had found the posse that would help him get the job done, once and for all. His new confidence rode with him for several miles in the invigorating December cold before the doubts set in again. Too much had gone wrong already.

17

"The Kid, I hope I don't run into him," said José Roibal. "I hear he likes to shoot *Mejicanos* just to watch them kick."

George Mullin stared at him across the table, stunned that anyone would say such a thing. He then blinked his whiskey-heavy eyelids several times, recovered the sense of humor he took so much pride in, and unleashed a laugh that bellowed through the saloon.

"The Kid shootin' Mexicans! Now who the hell told you that, Juan?"

"José," Roibal corrected him.

Mullin waved the correction aside as something of no concern. "Let me tell you something about the Kid. Him and the Mexicans—they're as close as peas in a pod. Everywhere he goes, he's got some Mex filly just waitin' to take him in, ready to do anything she can for him. The Kid's got a way about him, you can bet on that. And the Mex men, they like him too." The features on one side of George's face bunched together in what José had come to assume was a sly expression. "And it don't matter hardly at all if the Kid's studdin' the man's wife. The fella just goes along helpin' the Kid like he was his best friend. I wouldn't mind having a little of what the Kid's eatin', you catch my meaning?" He reached across the table to punch Roibal's shoulder for emphasis and let out another big laugh.

Taking a drink of whiskey, José decided to try the same tack once again. There was no sense in getting too clever with a slob like this.

"I guess I'm just not used to being near a killer like the Kid," he said. "I guess I should stay away from the *baile* if I want to steer clear of him."

"Go wherever you damn please. Billy won't bother you. I'll tell you, there's a sight more Anglos who should be worryin' about the Kid than Mexicans. He's got a bunch of them on his list that he figures to finish before he's through, and he don't care how high up they are, neither. Of course," he added with strained modesty, "some of us Anglos're the best friends Billy's got, and he knows it. He knows where he can come for help. That's because there's still some of us that know the Kid for the right fella that he is."

"Isn't he afraid to stay around here by himself? I hear the law's getting close to him."

Mullin inspected the empty bottle and called to the saloonkeeper. "We're gettin' dry here, Beaver. Fetch us another one."

For the first time that evening, José was impressed

by the fat livery driver sitting across from him. Mullin had already taken care of half a bottle when José had strolled into the saloon a half hour ago and now Mullin was ready to attack another—and was still sitting upright.

As Beaver Smith put down the new bottle, Mullin picked up the conversation without missing a beat. "Don't worry about the Kid. He's smart enough to keep his boys around him. He knows Garrett's coming for him. Hell," he said, lowering his voice and glancing furtively to either side, "he even knows what Garrett is up to right now. The sheriff went up to Las Vegas with Barney Mason to deliver a couple of boys that got caught. Billy knows that Garrett's on his way back this very minute, but he also knows he's only got that trash Mason with him, so how much you think Garrett's gonna do, shorthanded like that?"

"Sounds like Billy knows just about everything that goes on in this territory."

"Well, he knows it when he gets it from them who've got the right information." Mullin made a broad gesture to indicate himself. "Just happened I heard about Garrett and Mason when I was drivin' a team up to Puerto de Luna. I heard the sheriff had to get on his knees and beg for his life to get out of there just a few days ago. I'd surely like to see him come here and try to beg his way out of a fight with Billy."

Mullin's laugh erupted again, and José laughed with him.

When he finally extricated himself from Mullin's company, José Roibal ambled around to the back of the saloon, letting the night keep him inconspicuous as he checked Smith's corral. Six horses stood saddled there. From what Mullin had told him, José was ready to guess that those animals were the mounts that the Kid and his gang kept ready for a getaway. That much of Mullin's story was borne out. But José couldn't convince himself to stop his scouting there. For all he knew, the saddled horses could belong to some other outlaws—Lincoln County certainly didn't suffer from a shortage of them. And as for Mullin's other stories, any sensible man would have his doubts about the livery driver's reliability. Juan Largo had trusted José enough to ask him to do something, and he was going to do the job as thoroughly as he could.

He crossed Fort Sumner's plaza, gravitating naturally toward the guitar music coming from one of the houses. José had never met Billy Bonney, nor any of his gang, so he would have no way of recognizing any of them on sight. But then, that was why Juan Largo had sent him: Roibal wouldn't be recognized either. His idea was to mix with the people in this town until the Kid was clearly identified by someone else.

One of the things he knew about Billy the Kid was that he liked to kick up his heels and flirt with the Mexican girls. José kept walking toward the music.

He hovered on the fringes of the *baile* for some time, but knew he would draw suspicion if he continued to do nothing more than that. He had no trouble finding a girl who would dance a fandango with him, and when the dance was done, he talked with her for a while and managed to work in his explanation for being in Fort Sumner; then he drifted off to watch once again.

Around nine o'clock he spotted four young Anglos walking toward the dance. He couldn't see any guns on them, but that didn't mean they weren't carrying.

The Kid was proud of his letter. In fact, he was so proud of the way it was coming out that he stuck with it to the end, even though the *baile* music was starting and was tempting enough to make his mind struggle with the words.

Rita Bowdre fussed around the table, clearing the last of the dishes, wiping the tabletop, and ordering Billy to move one chair over when he got in her way. He couldn't very well complain. Not only had she fed him, but she also had lent him the vial of ink and the steel pen point. A genuine pen-and-ink letter he was writing; he didn't have to scratch it out with a dull wooden pencil this time. Billy figured it was the implements that were inspiring him to write such a forceful case for himself.

"Who the hell you writing to?" Rudabaugh demanded from his seat by the window.

"Oh, just an old friend of mine," replied Billy. He smiled meaningfully at Charley Bowdre stretched out on the bed.

Rudabaugh shook his head, picked his teeth, and spat on the floor. Rita's chubby face turned red with fury. For a second there, Billy thought she was going to charge over to the bearded hardcase and beat him to death with a wooden ladle. But she managed to control herself.

O'Folliard, Pickett, and Wilson rushed into the room from the plaza, their entrance sudden enough to make Rudabaugh pull out his pistol and cock the hammer. Tom O'Folliard, the first one in, jumped back at least a foot when he heard the gun click.

"Goddamn it to hell, Dave!" he shouted. "Why you always got to throw down on a body when he just moves a little fast?"

Rudabaugh's mouth twitched a couple of times before he spoke. "Maybe I should just shoot you once to keep you from askin' that fool question anymore."

"Ease up, Dave," Billy put in. "The boys're just natural happy about something. Anyone can see that just lookin' at 'em. Of course," he added, turning to Tom, "a fella could learn to be a little more careful." He smiled as he brought up his left hand from beneath the table, already holding his double-action revolver. "A suspicious nature can get contagious these days."

"Okay, Billy," said Wilson, glancing at Rudabaugh, "we'll mind ourselves."

Tom O'Folliard stepped toward the table. "We just wanted to tell you about the *baile* is all. Garcia's got things going early and fast this time. And Paulita, she's there too, Billy."

"I'll be coming," Billy said. "I got some business first. Almost done, though."

Tom knew enough not to question this kind of business; he just found a place to sit on the floor and waited. When he was done with his letter, Billy slapped the steel pen on the tabletop, pushed himself away a bit, and cocked his head to look at his work, as if gazing at a painting.

"You going to read it out loud?" Tom asked.

"Ought to, I think," said Billy. "I wrote it to the governor, may he rest in hell sometime soon." The rest of the men watched Billy closely as he picked up the paper; all of them except Rudabaugh, who continued to stare sullenly out the window.

"This is it," Billy began. "To the Governor of the Territory of New Mexico: You have by now most likely heard the news about the murder of Jim Carlyle and how the country is out to get me for this crime. It seems that just about everything that happens in this country is laid at my door. This is no exception. If you want justice done, look somewhere else than me. First, it was the White Oaks posse that opened fire during the truce that started everything. And then it was the posse that shot the killing bullet when Jim tried escaping. I think you can see that there would be more peace in this country if dishonest posses would leave me alone.

"You may have heard also that Sheriff Garrett took some stock from the Moseby ranch. Garrett says the stock was stolen but I know that it belonged to the Dedrick brothers at the time and they had a bill of sale to prove it.

"Bad work like this has pushed me more than I was pushed before. It does not do anything to help the peace in the territory. I am ready to leave this country behind me if the law here will let me put my outfit together and not push me. If the law keeps on in this work then I will go to war like I have done before.

"Yours Truly, William Bonney."

There was silence for several moments. This pleased Billy. He knew the others were impressed and were still thinking how strong the letter was. His words stretched a thing or two, he conceded, especially the part about Carlyle, but the letter made it clear that he was up against men who wouldn't let him live, and that, after all, was the truth.

"That's real fine writin'," said Johnny Wilson.

"It'll tell him what's what in this country," Billy said, "that's for certain."

Tom was puzzling over something. "You mean to say we're really leavin' the territory, Billy? I didn't know that."

"I've been mulling it over some, and I was thinkin' it might make sense, what with Pat Garrett beating the bushes for us up and down the Pecos. But I'm not about to do it if they don't make way for me. If I'm going to have to fight my way out of New Mexico, then I'd just as soon stay here and fight it out to the end."

Tom gave this some more thought. "I never figured we'd leave the territory."

Billy folded the letter, placed it on the table, and got to his feet. "Well, don't get all twisted up about it, Tom. We got us some girls and dancin' before we do anything else. Let's get to it." Halfway to the door, he stopped to face Bowdre.

"You comin', Charley?"

Bowdre didn't move from the bed. "I'll be stayin' a while."

Billy noticed a glance pass between Bowdre and his wife. Smiling, he realized that he and the boys hadn't left the husband and wife alone since coming to Fort Sumner. As a favor to them, he convinced Rudabaugh to sit outside, since he obviously wasn't going with them to the *baile.*

They found someone with a jug along the way and were pretty loosened up by the time they reached the Garcia house. Standing inside the door, Billy started to tap his foot to the music as he scanned the people dancing. Before he could find what he was looking for, a voice called to him from a group standing along the left wall.

"Billito," the woman called. "Billito."

Standing there, talking to her brother Pete, was Paulita Maxwell, dressed up in a skirt and blouse of bright colors, the prettiest girl in the room, as far as Billy could see. But the Kid stopped himself from going to her.

Something had caught his eye as he had turned toward Paulita's voice, something that had triggered an instinctive caution. He now turned back to check. Through the window to his left, he saw a man looking at him. He was of average height, solid build, and common Mexican features—everything about him was uninteresting except for the fact that Billy didn't know him. Just as Billy's eyes rested on him, the stranger turned to walk away. There was nothing hurried about his movements, which either meant that he had no reason to be afraid or he was making sure that he appeared that way.

Billy nodded and smiled at Paulita to tell her that he would be coming to her soon, then gestured for Tom to step aside with him.

"See that fella walking across the plaza?" he told O'Folliard. "Somebody better talk to him. He's a stranger and he was looking my way. Take Curly with you. Don't make trouble if you don't have to, but don't let a son-of-a-bitch get away."

José Roibal continued to move at a leisurely pace while his limbs itched to take him across the plaza at a run so that he could saddle up and be gone from here. He didn't know why he had stared at the Kid for so long. He should have turned away as soon as the light-haired young man responded to the name Billito; but curiosity had kept him looking; he had wanted to get a good look at Billy the Kid.

He told himself there was no reason to assume that the Kid was suspicious, especially if he continued to act in an unsuspicious manner. The maddening thing, though, was not knowing what was going on behind his back. For a moment, José wished Juan Largo had sent him out to hunt Indians instead of asking him to come to Fort Sumner.

He reached his horse without hearing any sound of pursuing footsteps—for all that was worth. Between the music and the feet stomping on Garcia's wood floor, a man could sneak up on Roibal without his knowing. Resisting the temptation to glance over his shoulder, he swung into the saddle and rode away from the plaza at a walk.

He traveled west and found a spot where fording the Pecos was easy. He didn't hear the two riders until he had reached the far bank.

Looking back, he saw the two horsemen splashing across the shallow bed, the moonlight glinting off the water's spray. Without seeing them too clearly, José knew they were two of the men who had been with the Kid. He fought the urge to break into a gallop. Everything he had accomplished tonight would be lost if he betrayed himself now. He turned his horse and waited.

The two riders stopped beside him, not bothering with words for quite a while. They looked José over. The one on the left was lean-faced, with a boyish attempt at a beard on his chin; the other one had dark, curly hair and was heavier-set than his friend.

"You don't mind talkin' some, do you?" the lean-faced one finally said.

José put on an indifferent expression. He didn't want to seem eager to please.

"Some folks in town were just wonderin' who you were," the Kid's friend continued. "There's been some thievin' around here and some people just tend to get suspicious when a stranger comes through."

"I'm no thief," said José.

"That right? You come to Fort Sumner for any special reason?"

"Looking for strays. I was herding sheep just north of here and some of them got away. I thought they'd be near the town."

The curly-haired rider now spoke. "I never met a sheepherder who didn't stink—and this one doesn't stink much. You smell sheep on him, Tom?"

His friend Tom sniffed loudly. "No, he don't stink much at all. Isn't that kind of funny, friend? You smellin' so good?"

José shrugged. "When I didn't find any strays, I went into town and took a bath at Smith's saloon. I don't get to take a town bath too much."

The two gang members glanced at each other, then turned back to José; they look stymied.

"You sure got a lot of answers," said Tom.

"You ask a lot of questions."

The curly-haired one let out a frustrated sigh. Then he pulled out his revolver. "There's one way to make sure he doesn't talk to nobody."

"You hold on, Curly," snapped Tom. "We don't

need any killin'. That'd just make trouble for everybody, especially if there's no need for it."

Curly didn't fire, but he didn't holster the gun either.

"I don't know about you," Tom said, "but I'd rather be at the *baile* anyway. I think even *you* can find yourself a gal tonight."

Curly kept staring at José. Roibal inched his right hand toward the pocket that held his pistol.

"Hell," Tom said, "these Mexicans don't do anything but push sheep anyway. You know that." Not bothering to wait anymore, he reined his horse around and walked it toward the water's edge. He stopped there to look back. Only now did Curly put his gun away. He headed toward his friend.

Still acting like a man with no reason to be afraid, José didn't move until he saw the two riders reach the other side of the river. He then turned his horse and started north, moving at an easy walk. A few minutes later, he allowed himself to lift his animal to a lope. He rode hard for a mile before his nerves stopped rattling.

18

The cold was so penetrating that some of the Texans chose to dismount and lead their horses in order to stamp some circulation back into their feet. Through that frigid last leg of the journey, Pat still didn't hear any grumbling from his new posse; the Texans were still driving themselves as relentlessly as he was, after sixty miles of forced riding in less than two days.

A stop at a ranch along the Pecos gave them a few hours' rest, then they pushed on at first light and reached Puerto de Luna by nine o'clock that morning. Riding through town, Pat noticed a few familiar faces along the road, faces he had seen when brushing past the Mexican posse the last time he had come this way. The Puerto de Luna men now watched him and his posse with curiosity and a hint of apprehension; a couple of them held an angry look in their dark eyes, but there was no show of defiance or Dutch courage this time.

Pat found José Roibal in Alejandro's store.

The Mexican was sitting at the table, rolling a cigarette; a revolver lay on the tabletop within easy reach, in case any members of the Puerto de Luna posse still held a grudge against Roibal for having sided with the gringo deputy sheriff a few days before. Pat's first impulse was to hurry over to José and ask what he had found in Fort Sumner. But something told him that he might jinx himself by being too eager. He called in John Poe, then told Alejandro to bring over a bottle before taking a seat opposite Roibal. As it turned out, Pat didn't have to ask for the news from Fort Sumner. The satisfied look on José's face told him that the scout had been a success.

José told the deputy sheriff and his Texas posseman about George Mullin and about seeing someone called Billito at the *baile.*

"The Kid was there with four of his friends," José said after Pat had poured him some whiskey. "At least that's how many I saw there. Whether he's still there now . . ." He put up his hands in a questioning gesture. "He was ready to ride out fast if he had to. I can't tell you if he's taken off already."

"If he's gone," said Pat, "he might've gone someplace nearby. He's got plenty of places to hole up around there." His voice was ringing with anticipation. For the first time since the hunt had begun, he was confident that he was on the right trail.

John Poe said, "We can get my boys moving in a couple of hours. They won't like it much, but they won't kick if they know they're getting close."

Pat leaned back in his chair, holding his glass of whiskey halfway to his mouth. He stayed that way for several moments. "I don't think they have to," he finally said. "They can rest longer. Till tonight anyway."

Pat noticed an incredulous José raise an eyebrow. He smiled back at him. "As long as Billy thinks I've only got Barney with me, like you say he does, he'll be cocky enough to stay close to Fort Sumner. He'll figure he's got a chance to either shoot me or make me run if I try going through there." He paused, gazing off, examining his idea some more. "Yeah, that's what he'll think," he concluded out loud.

"Well, the boys won't fight against some more rest," said Poe.

"They'll *need* the rest. If we get close to Billy, then that's when the real work begins."

José reached for the bottle by Pat's elbow. "I'll ride with you, Juan Largo," he said. "If you're that sure, I want to be there."

They set out shortly after dark, as rested as they'd been for two days, and started their nightlong ride. Just before midnight, the wind rushed across the valley with a sudden icy force, lashing the backs of the men and horses. Before long, the wind carried a thick flurry of snow across the road. The animals plodded along for an hour through the storm, a snowfall that thinned after a while to fool the posse into thinking that the end was near, when in fact it was only retrenching for a second wave as intense as the storm's first blast. Huddled inside his greatcoat, with his hat pulled low, Pat told himself that the snowfall was a blessing. Billy wasn't likely to give up the comforts of Fort Sumner on a night like this.

The town's adobes could be seen in dim outline as the posse reached Fort Sumner's outskirts just before first light, an hour after the snowfall had finally ended. Pat gave the order to make camp a half-mile north of the plaza.

Before the town had a chance to rouse itself, Pat wanted to take a look around; he took only Barney Mason with hm to make sure that his Texas posse would remain a secret. They went directly to Beaver Smith's corral, where they hoped to find the saddled horses that José had seen a couple of days before. The mounts were no longer there.

"Seems like old Beaver just can't be helping the Kid when we want him to," said Barney.

"This time," Pat answered, "we should give Beaver one more chance to help *us*. One real good chance."

Finding the back door unlatched, Pat and Barney moved into the room where Smith slept. They stood just inside the threshold for several minutes to give themselves a chance to thaw out and to let their eyes adjust to the inside's deeper darkness. When shapes began to take more definite shape, Pat stepped over to the bed, took hold of Beaver Smith's shoulder, and yanked him onto his back.

Smith let out a series of gasps and moans as he rose painfully from a whiskey sleep. Fear finally emerged from his confusion, and he tried to scramble away. Pat grabbed him with both hands. He lifted the man to his feet.

"Just an old friend, Beaver," Pat drawled. "Come on, let's get you sitting down. Barney, go find a lamp and fire it up so we can all see each other."

Smith's frantic agitation began to fall away as he got his bearings, but when Barney lit the lamp by the bed, Pat could see that the saloonkeeper's fear still lingered. Sitting on the stool that Pat pushed under him, Smith scratched at his nightshirt and glanced quickly from the deputy sheriff to Mason.

"What the hell you tryin' to do?" Beaver growled, attempting to sound indignant.

"I thought it was time for us to talk again," said Pat. "Time for us to talk the way old friends are supposed to."

Smith looked up at the tall man standing above him, trying to divine something in Pat's angular, half-lit features. He started when he heard Mason moving behind him. Barney looked back at him with a smug grin as he leaned back against the wall, his rifle held loosely by his side.

"Christ almighty," cried Smith. "Pat, what the hell is this?"

"I've waltzed around with you a couple of times already, Beaver. I let it slide before because I didn't think you could do me much good anyway. But this time—I got a feeling I'm real close, and I can't let you get away with it anymore."

Real indignation now pushed aside some of Beaver's uneasiness. "Goddman you, Pat. I've told you all I can tell you. You wearin' a badge doesn't give you a right to bust me out of bed like that. You don't do that to old friends."

A searing impulse shot through Pat's mind, and in the next instant, he kicked the stool out from underneath Smith. The saloonkeeper thudded to the floor. Bending over, Pat put his face next to Beaver's.

"That's right—old friends! A fella doesn't keep an old friend from doing what he was elected to do. And that's what you're doing, *friend.* And if you keep it up, you're going to make it easy for Billy to kill me. Now what the hell kind of friend is that! Billy's killed two lawmen already. You aim to help him murder me too? Is that it?"

Sprawled on the floor, Beaver watched Pat through narrowed eyes, fury turning his face red. He now pushed himself to his feet.

"You goin' to tell me about friends!" he shouted. "What the hell about a man who hunts down his old pals? What the hell about that?"

"You got it wrong, Beaver. Billy and his gang are running wild. They'd have to be stopped, whether I'm the one doing it or somebody else. Billy's the one who's the outlaw. Not me."

At these words, Smith give him a nasty, sarcastic look. He let out a harsh laugh. The next moment, Pat grabbed him by the shirtfront, hauled him across the floor, and slammed him against the wall. He had his fist up for several moments before he convinced himself not to hit the man. Smith stared at him, motionless, not daring to make any move that would trigger a beating. He had seen Garrett batter a cowboy senseless a few years ago because the man had called Pat a liar. Despite the cold, Smith started to sweat.

"You can think any damn thing you want about me," Pat said. "It doesn't matter anymore. All you got to know is that you're going to tell me what's going on around here. I figure Billy's either in town or he's close by, and I'm going to take charge of this town until something happens. So don't think you're going to slip away from me. If I have to, I'll get a warrant to arrest you for buying stolen cattle.

Whatever it is, I'll do what I have to do to find out where Billy is. You understand me?"

Smith nodded his head, then said, "Goddman you, Pat."

"Try telling me something else, Beaver. Is Billy in town?"

"Not anymore. He was around for a while, but he left just last night. You didn't have to push me around to find that out."

"Did he have his boys with him?"

"They all left together. None of them are here."

Barney stepped closer, bringing his rifle up. "The same story, Pat. Every time we talk to this bastard he says Billy just left. I say he's still here."

Pat never took his eyes off Smith. "Don't think so," he said. "He's telling me the truth. But he can tell me more. Isn't that right, Beaver?"

"What the hell else you want to know?"

"I won't bother asking you where Billy went, because he probably wouldn't have told you that. But you can tell me what else is going on. You still buying cattle from Billy?"

"Damn it to hell, Pat, I don't do that kind of thing. I gave that up."

Pat's mouth twisted into a crooked smile. "Okay, Beaver. Who *are* you buying stock from?"

"Nothing to tell of. Just bought some milch cows from Dan Dedrick this week. That's all."

"From Dedrick? That means Dedrick probably got them from Billy. Either that or he stole them himself. Could the Kid be with the Dedrick boys, those that are still out of jail?"

"How the hell am I going to know that? Like you said, the Kid wouldn't tell me."

Pat nodded, then moved away from the saloon-keeper. "I believe you, Beaver—you being such a good friend and all."

"We're wasting our time with him," said Barney, pointing with his rifle at Smith.

"Not really," said Pat. "We know the Kid's not in town, so he must be somewhere just outside it. That tells us something."

"You real sure about that?"

Pat didn't want to answer that. "Barney, go get Poe and the rest. I want them in town before it's light, before anyone can see them. We'll all stay here and keep Beaver company. That's how you're going to help us this time, Beaver, by keeping my men out of sight."

19

The posse had been asleep for only two hours when Barney Mason ran through the back door of Smith's place. He shook Pat awake.

"The Kid's in town," he said. He spoke in a hoarse whisper, as if no one else in the room was entitled to know. Pat rose quickly from his pallet, stopping when he reached a sitting position; he was disoriented, unable to place his surroundings for several moments. Staring at the empty bottles standing in the corner, he remembered that he was in Smith's back room, and after glancing at the other possemen asleep on the floor, it came back to him that Barney had left earlier to sleep at his father-in-law's house along the plaza.

"The Kid's in town," Barney repeated, as he gave Pat's shoulder another shake.

Garrett got his tongue unlimbered. "In town? What're you talking about?"

"I just heard he's been here all the time. Over to a deserted house south of the plaza. Some of his boys're with him."

Lurching to his feet, Pat picked up his gun belt and strapped it on. By this time, other possemen were awake. Poe was staring at Garrett and Mason, and so was the Animal. As he put on his greatcoat, Pat said to them, "Barney got word about the Kid." Before he could say anything more, and before he moved any closer to the door, a new wave of alertness made him stop short. He turned slowly to Mason. *This is another lead from Barney,* he told himself, *and probably no better than any of his others.*

Pat stood there wavering for some time. He wanted to lie down again and pretend he hadn't heard anything, but he couldn't bring himself to dismiss any possibility, even if the information came from Mason.

He wasn't willing to expose his posse on such a long shot, and took only Poe with him. If the lead turned out to be accurate, he could always send Poe back to bring along the others. Mason led them around the plaza in the early light, moving as inconspicuously as possible. Pat told himself that Barney couldn't be wrong every time; sooner or later he was bound to hit upon something true. This thought helped to keep Pat from feeling foolish, until they reached the deserted, broken-down adobe—which was *still* deserted.

Pat didn't say anything to Barney, but he leveled a hard stare at him, curious to see if the man would show any sign of embarrassment. Having trouble meeting Pat's gaze, Barney walked to the near corner of the house and looked around at the other side, presumably to check if Billy might be hiding just a few feet away. After shuffling about a bit, he spat onto the snow-covered ground and said, "Damn him," referring either to his information source or the Kid. Pat wasn't sure. He didn't bother to find out.

He returned to Smith's saloon with Poe and stretched out on his pallet to get some extra sleep. But his mind became crowded with visions of the town stirring outside, of people starting to pass through the plaza. He soon left his posse sleeping and headed outside again. He liked the idea of proceeding on his own.

Keeping himself concealed alongside the old army hospital, he watched the people in the plaza, either crossing the open ground or stopping to talk to one another, never staying in one spot too long in the early morning chill. Pat watched for half an hour, not exactly sure what he was looking for but still convinced that there would be something useful here. Restlessness then got the better of him, and he struck upon a new tack.

He headed toward the south side of plaza, where the Maxwell home occupied the former officers' quarters. Pete Maxwell had known both Billy and Pat well in the old days, and Pat wasn't sure where the man's sympathies would lie. He liked to think he could trust his former employer, but he also had heard that Billy was sweet on Pete's sister, Paulita, which might make the Kid part of the family. Garrett sneaked in a back way; if Pete could be used as a spy, Pat didn't want people to know he had been spending time with the new county sheriff.

Pete Maxwell stood by the fire in the front room; he was a small man, whose thick trunk and limbs made him look like someone with a tall body that had been compressed. His dark, bearded face was turned to someone standing next to him, a lean man in a frayed black suit, his hat in his hands. Pat recognized the melancholy-looking man from his cowboy days along the Pecos, a good hand named J. W. Bell. Still unnoticed by either man in the room, Garrett stood in the doorway, trying to decide if he should let Bell see him. Searching his memory, Pat couldn't recall any connection between J. W. and Billy.

Pat stepped into the room.

Startled, Maxwell and Bell turned quickly in his direction, then eased up when they recognized the tall intruder.

"Sorry to sneak up on you," Pat said, "but there's some people who shouldn't know I'm around."

"You didn't miss the Kid by much," said Maxwell, "but you're a little late, Pat."

Garrett tried to decide if he had heard some satisfaction in Pete's tone. "I'm not planning on being late anymore," he said. Still looking at Pete, he tilted his head meaningfully toward Bell. Pete got the message.

"Why don't you come back later," he told Bell. "Maybe I can do something for you."

Bell nodded in understanding. "Sure thing, Pete." When Bell was halfway to the door, Garrett stopped him.

"I got to ask you something," Pat said. "I figure on

keeping my head down for a while around here. Will you give me your word you won't tell anybody about me?"

"Whatever you say, Pat." His sad brown eyes now brightened with hope. "If you need help, Pat, you just let me know. Okay?"

Garrett looked curiously at him, not sure what to make of this offer. He was sure, however, that he could count on the man keeping quiet.

When he was alone with Maxwell, Pat went over to the fire to warm his hands.

Maxwell said, "It's a cold business tracking a man these days, eh Pat?" Realizing his words could be taken more than one way, he quickly added, "In this weather, I mean."

Pat darted a sharp glance at the man. "You see much of Billy when he was here?"

"He came to the house once."

There was a brusqueness to Maxwell's answer that intrigued Pat. Moving away from the fire, he took a seat in an overstuffed chair; for a few moments he sat silently, just watching Pete.

The Fort Sumner rancher poked absently at the fire for a while, then picked up a green log and placed it in the back of the hearth to help throw the heat out into the room.

When he had first come to this country, Garrett had found it difficult to imagine Pete as the son of Lucien Maxwell, a man Pat had heard of even in Texas, the trapper and friend of Kit Carson who had become the biggest landowner in New Mexico. The stumpy, unimpressive Pete didn't seem to have an inherited mark of greatness about him, but Garrett had come to learn that the man could be shrewd and determined when he had to be.

"You have any idea why Billy left town?" Pat asked to break the silence.

"I think he probably figured he was pushing his luck by staying in one place for too long. I know I would if I was him."

"Did he tell you that?"

"He didn't tell me," said Pete. "He told my sister."

Pat heard the edge return to Maxwell's voice. The picture was getting clearer.

"Billy's seeing a lot of Paulita, isn't he?" Pat said.

Maxwell nodded and paced away from the hearth. Not about to let the matter slide, Garrett pressed the point.

"I wouldn't figure Billy to be the marrying kind. Would you, Pete?"

Pete shook his head in silence for a moment. "She doesn't know what she's doing. I thought she had good sense, but she's showing less and less of it the more she sees the Kid."

"She wouldn't run off with Billy, would she? That would be a pretty long step, even if she's not thinking straight."

"I wish to hell I knew what she'll do." Bitterly, he added, "I wish to hell I knew what she's already done."

Watching Maxwell pace, Pat told himself he shouldn't take pleasure in the man's worries, but he couldn't help feel reassured. Finally, Billy had worn out his welcome with one of his friends; that meant another man on Pat's side.

"Billy's nearby, right, Pete?"

Maxwell stopped moving. He stared at Pat, then

nodded. "I think he is. The way Paulita's acting, I think she expects to be seeing him soon." He rubbed his thick hands together, and his eyes fixed on something across the room while he brooded some more. "What is she thinking? That's what I'd like to know. Billy spends half his time with her and the other half of his time with a married woman. Everyone seems to know except her."

Having no good reply to that, Pat let some time pass in silence; then he tried to get the man back to business. "I'm ready to take Billy," he said. "If I can cross his trail, I think I can trap him. You might be able to help me, Pete."

Maxwell laughed dryly. "Well, you picked a good time to do it, what with the reward they're holding out."

"There's a reward?" Pat said.

"I just read it in a newspaper from Santa Fe yesterday. I guess they're getting itchy to get this over with, so the governor's offering a five-hundred-dollar reward for Billy. You're catching up at the right time, Pat."

Pat's thoughts drifted ahead to what life would be like after the Kid's capture. Both a reputation and money—he wouldn't be scrounging around anymore. He would be a man of substance—finally—with the opportunities to provide for a family that would grow into a new Garrett clan, as reputable as the plantation Garretts had once been in Louisiana. But with these thoughts came new worries. The reward wasn't necessarily his for the taking. If somebody stumbled onto the Kid and got the drop on him, then that man would be the one to make the claim in Garrett's place.

Pat got out of the soft chair. "You know you shouldn't be telling anyone about me," he told Maxwell. "I'm going to see if there's anything else for me to find out in town."

On his way out the back door, Garrett found J. W. Bell standing by the picket fence, alternately swinging his arms and clapping his gloved hands to fend off the cold. He watched Pat approach with a forlorn-looking smile.

"You can go back and finish talking to Pete if you want," said Garrett.

"Yeah, well, I suppose I should, even if it won't amount to hardly nothing at all. I just figured Pete might have some work I could handle to get me through the winter."

Pat now understood J. W.'s eagerness when he had offered to help before. The man was down on his luck.

"I guess it takes a certain kind of man to start himself in business," Bell continued, with a self-effacing laugh. "And it just might not be my kind. I figured on freighting between here and Las Vegas, and just about lost my shirt and pants and everything else in just a few months. Damned if I can understand the why of it all. I figured there had to be enough goods moving up to the railhead for there to be room for another fella in the deal. I'll be damned if I can figure it."

Pat's own experiences made it easy for him to understand Bell's problems, but he was too consumed with new problems to respond to what the man had said. Instead, he considered the fortunate timing of Bell's visit to Fort Sumner. Here was a good man with an innocent explanation for being in town.

"Maybe you *can* help me, J. W.," he said. Bell looked at him keenly. "I need somebody to help me keep an eye on the plaza in case any of Billy's amigos pass through. Somebody's got to know where he is. I could probably get you some pay as a deputy or a special officer if you're interested."

"I sure wouldn't mind doing that, Pat. Anything Pete would get me wouldn't be anything more than charity, I know that. It'd make me feel a whole lot better doing something useful."

"It'd make us both feel better."

Pat told him to walk across the plaza and snoop around the far side, while he kept an eye open along the old officers' quarters. Moving along the back of the Maxwell house, Pat turned at the corner to head toward the porch that looked upon the center of town. When he reached the front edge of the building, some movement to his left brought him up short and made him flatten against the adobe, his right hand reaching for his pocket. His hand was inside the pocket and wrapped around the handle of his Colt before he stopped himself.

Standing before Garrett, even more startled than he was, was Damaso Lopez, a sheepherder who worked a spread outside of town. Garrett took his hand out of his pocket.

"Who's staying with you and Juanita at your camp these days?" said Pat. "Anybody I should know about?"

Lopez hesitated. In that moment, Pat pulled him over to the side of Maxwell's house.

20

The wagon jounced harshly along the frozen road. Damaso Lopez flicked the reins across the backs of his two mules to get them to move faster, but the animals had already settled on their gait and didn't seem to think that the driver had any say in the matter. Turning in the wagon seat, Lopez checked his back trail, the network of premature wrinkles on his face deepening with anxiety. Fort Sumner could still be seen in the middle distance, but no one rode between town and the sheepherder's wagon. Lopez couldn't account for his good fortune. Why was no one following? And why had he been allowed to leave town in the first place? He was convinced that someone would ride out of town at any moment to bring him back, but still he found himself alone on the road. God was smiling on him today, he decided.

The tall gringo with the killer's mustache had

always made Lopez uneasy—even when the man laughed there seemed to be something grim about him—and when he had collared the sheepherder next to the Maxwell house, Lopez was sure he would be locked up. His friendship with Billito was well known; that could easily be considered a crime in itself by a man like Garrett, Lopez had figured. But then Juan Largo had let him go. All that Lopez had said was that he needed to bring supplies back to his ranch, and the gringo had let him leave town. Not about to press his luck, Lopez now prodded the mules again to pick up the pace; once more he had to satisfy himself with their steady, plodding progress.

By early afternoon he reached the tableland that he often used for grazing his herd. The land was blanketed with snow, and the leaden sky promised more snow to come. Lopez was able to forget about Garrett as his mind turned to the business of getting his ranch through the winter, but the sight of two men herding milch cows along the road up ahead reminded him of the run-in at Fort Sumner. The two men were Sam Dedrick and José Valdez, good friends of the Kid.

When Lopez stopped his wagon alongside the cow herd, there was some small talk for a while. Dedrick was cursing Beaver Smith for asking them to bring in the herd on a day when snow was on the way—flakes had already started to dance through the air—but Lopez couldn't keep his mind on what the man was saying. All he could think of was Garrett's warning.

"You're not going to tell Billy you saw me," the

deputy sheriff had said, "because if you do I'm going to make you sorry for it."

Lopez had already decided that he wouldn't send word to Billy; he was awed enough by Juan Largo to want to stay out of trouble. His daughter Juanita would berate him mercilessly if she ever found out he didn't do something to help her Billito, but, he told himself, she was too young and headstrong to understand such things. The problem Lopez now faced, though, was that Dedrick and Valdez presented a convenient way to change his mind.

Since he hadn't known where Billy was hiding, it had been easy for Lopez to steer clear of this business; he couldn't have helped Billy if he had wanted to. Dedrick and Valdez, on the other hand, were likely to know where the Kid was. If he told these two cowmen to pass along a message, Lopez would be defying Garrett; if he kept quiet, there was the chance Billy might find out, putting Lopez in just as much danger.

"How did things look in Sumner?" Dedrick asked the sheepherder. "Is it all right for Billy and the rest to head back?"

"Could be," said Lopez, stalling. His mind calculated as fast as it could. If Billy got caught, Lopez would have nothing to fear from him. But would the Kid *stay* caught? Hadn't he escaped from the McSween house during the Lincoln siege? And from the posse outside White Oaks? Some said there was no trap that he couldn't get out of.

Now that he was well out of Garrett's reach, Lopez decided that the odds had shifted.

"Can you find Billy?" he asked

Sam Dedrick narrowed his eyes. "I might."

"Juan Largo is already in the town. He stopped me and tried to get me to lead him to Billy." Lopez shrugged, a gesture of offhanded modesty. "I wouldn't help him. I hear he's got Mason with him, but not much more than that."

"Is that right?" said Dedrick. "Just might be we'll be running into the Kid. That could be real useful, Damaso."

A look passed between Dedrick and Valdez. After that, they had no more interest in talking to the sheepherder. Lopez watched them herding away their cows a couple of minutes later, a feeling of satisfaction beginning to grow inside him. It had been a difficult choice, but he was certain now that he had done the right thing—and Garrett be damned. After all, the way Billy had been acting the last few months, he just might marry Juanita one of these days. For the first time, that possibility struck Lopez as something desirable. A *pistolero* like Billy would be a good man to have in the family if there was any more shooting trouble in the county.

In the gathering snow, the road to Fort Sumner became less distinct; in one moment it was a well-marked trail cutting through the crust of snow cover, pitted here and there by the muddy remnants of hoofprints left by earlier travelers; only a few minutes later, though, nothing was visible except a slightly depressed strip of white bisecting the larger whiteness. Letting the lead cow set the pace, Dedrick stared at the hills along the left.

He searched for a familiar pass.

The snowfall clouded his vision, but soon it dissipated, allowing him to see a sharply cut ridge that told him he had gone too far. He gigged his horse so that he could reach José Valdez's side.

"We can stash 'em back there," he said, pointing over his shoulder.

Valdez nodded in understanding and spurred his horse forward to turn the lead cow.

Billy was tired of poker. Playing his last hand—a pair of nines that lost to O'Folliard's three kings—he swung a leg over the bench to turn himself away from the game. He held his arms out to his sides and stretched them backward to put some feeling back in his limbs.

"Shouldn't quit now," said Joe Brazil as he gathered the cards for the next play. "Not when you're losin'."

"And in another half hour I'll be winnin' again, and then I'll lose and then win again." Billy made a sour face. "Now's as good a time as any."

Brazil shot him a curious glance, then shuffled the deck and dealt to O'Folliard, Wilson, and Bowdre sitting on the other side of the long table.

Billy got up and went to the window. Outside, the snow still fell, not as heavily as before, but still enough to make a man think twice about leaving a warm ranch house for a twelve-mile night ride. The Kid called over his shoulder.

"Tom, don't you know enough to keep your wagon from going to pieces?"

Tom Wilcox looked up from the old lamp he was fixing at his writing desk. He kept his face blank. "Sorry about that, Kid. Things just slip by me sometimes."

"Yeah, well, with a good wagon, we'd be able to

chance it on a drive tonight instead of lolligaggin' around here, pesterin' you all night long. You'd think a fella could keep a wagon, for cryin' out loud." Billy turned his peevish scowl back to the window. Wilcox and Brazil exchanged a look that they tried to conceal from the others.

Billy listened to the cards flicked across the table for a while, then let out a long sigh. *A hell of a way for you to treat a friend,* he admonished himself. He stepped back toward the center of the room, a careless look on his face. "Not your fault, Tom," he said. "I've just been thinkin' on too many things lately. Gets me kind of twisted up sometimes. I'm real sorry."

From the hearth came Rudabaugh's voice. "You need something to do is all," he said, swiveling on the stool so he faced the Kid. "Why don't you write the governor and tell him to send us a good wagon. He can send the wagon to you when he sends back an answer to all your other letters."

The man's mustache and beard didn't conceal the nasty smirk, but Billy wasn't about to let it bother him. He grinned at Rudabaugh.

"Yeah, that would be something, though, wouldn't it," he said. "Maybe I should be asking the old bastard for ranching equipment instead of justice. I'd be more likely to get the one thing instead of the other."

Curly Pickett grinned along with him and so did O'Folliard, none of which disturbed Rudabaugh's smirk. He still thought he had put a dent in the Kid.

Noticing Wilcox's stepson reading in the corner, Billy struck upon a notion. He moved quickly to the fourteen-year-old boy, jerked the dog-eared dime novel out of his hands, and pulled him toward the table. "C'mon, Pablo, there's no sense in readin' that damn thing. Don't you know it's not good for you?" He stopped to squint at the title. "*Bob Woolf, the Border Ruffian*—you don't want to read a pack of lies like that. Come here and we'll show you what real livin' is."

Pablo let himself be seated on the bench, while Billy sat next to him, his arm around the boy's shoulders. The Kid turned to Brazil. "Start a new hand, Joe, and deal Pablo in. You ever play real poker, Pablo?"

The boy's thin face was flushed; Billy was moving too quickly for him. "Guess not," he managed to mumble after a while.

"Well," said Billy, beaming, "about time you learned. I was playin' in gambling halls when I was your age, and I was just a jump and a holler away from tryin' my first cathouse too. C'mon, Joe, deal 'em up."

Brazil was looking past Billy. The Kid turned to see that Brazil was looking at his partner, Wilcox, who was no longer at his desk; he stood in the center of the room, his eyes riveted on Billy.

"Just leave the boy alone," said Wilcox.

The intensity of the man's voice caught Billy by surprise. He turned to O'Folliard and Bowdre and checked their faces, as if their expressions would tell him if he had heard right; then he pulled a comical face. "Excuse me all to hell, Tom. I guess I can't do nothing right tonight. Go on, Pablo, you heard your daddy."

Billy watched the boy move away from the table, then tossed back Pablo's book. "Sorry about that, boy. I guess you little fellas start a little later these days."

A call from outside took the Kid's mind off Wilcox's persnickety ways. Peering out the door, he could see Sam Dedrick, sitting his horse some thirty feet away, wrapped inside his slicker and looking miserable even though the snow had stopped.

Once inside, Dedrick took some time to take the chill off, which gave Billy his opening.

"You bust open any jails lately, Sam?" This got a laugh out of Pickett and O'Folliard. Sam Dedrick squirmed under the gang's gaze. He muttered "No" and hoped nothing more would be made of it.

"Now that's funny," Billy went on, clasping his hands behind his head as he leaned back on the bench. "The way you were talkin', I figured you'd be the biggest jail-cracker in the territory by now."

Dedrick laughed weakly. Billy didn't let up.

"And your brother Moses—he's still in that White Oaks jail, right? With you bustin' in from the outside and him makin' a break from the inside at the same time." He turned to O'Folliard. "I guess the whole family's a bunch of living terrors, ain't they?"

Dedrick tried to busy himself with inspecting what was cooking on the hearth, hating himself for what he had said to the Kid the last time he had seen him.

"If you ain't man enough to throw in with me when I break out Moses," he had said, "then I'll just have to show you up all by myself."

He had been shut out of the Kid's business since them, left to shift for himself. *But,* he reminded himself, *that'll be different now.*

When the laughter finally started to fade, Dedrick

told Billy about the sheepherder's story from Fort Sumner. There was no response from Billy or anyone else in the gang for a few moments. Dedrick stood awkwardly, waiting, a nervous tic showing at the left corner of his mouth.

The first to speak was Rudabaugh. "If it's just one or two fellas that Garrett's got with him, then we could take care of him lickety-split."

"Yeah," said Billy, "*if* he's still got only a couple of boys with him by the time we pull into Fort Sumner." He thought back to the Mexican, the stranger he had seen in town a few nights ago. Billy was becoming less and less sure of the man's innocent story.

"Hell, Kid," said Rudabaugh, "we're plannin' on hauling that wagonload of beef to town anyway. Might as well kill us a lawman while we're at it. Put everything in order."

"You don't jump Pat Garrett just like that. Ain't I right, Charley?"

Bowdre made a point of keeping his hands still, flat on the tabletop, to show that he really wasn't nervous. "Garrett's a cagey one," he said.

"And O'Folliard can tell you the same," Billy told Rudabaugh. "I'm not sayin' we turn tail and run. I just want to make certain."

Sam Dedrick saw his moment. "I took care of that, Billy," he said. "I sent Valdez into town, you know, to kind of look around. He'll find out for certain what Garrett's up to."

Billy nodded thoughtfully. "That's pretty good, Sam. Matter of fact, it's almost good enough."

Dedrick's smile froze as he tried to cover his disappointment.

"Problem is, Sam, when Valdez gets back here, we won't have anybody left in town, in case something else happens."

Tom O'Folliard let out a laugh. "Garrett's not the only cagey one in this country. Not at all."

"What else could I do?" said Dedrick, sounding desperate.

Billy looked around the room, ignoring Dedrick's question as he pondered the problem. His eyes soon rested on Pablo, sitting next to his stepfather.

"Now if we had us a body to go see Valdez," Billy said, "we could get the word back, and then Valdez could kind of keep guard until we send somebody else. You see what I mean?" The Kid seemed to be directing the question at Wilcox.

"How about it, Tom?" Billy continued after a moment's pause. "The snow's stopped, and a strong young boy like Pablo can ride to town real easy. It'd be a good thing to help the boy grow up some." He laughed. "And it sure wouldn't hurt us neither if he did it. I don't think any of these fellas here'd want to show their faces in town all by themselves if old Pat is around."

21

J. W. couldn't help but notice him. In the early morning hush, the man was one of only two other people in the plaza, and there was something familiar about the low, broad build and the hint of a swagger to his walk. Stepping away from the Maxwell porch and moving quickly along the edge of the square, J. W. Bell caught up to him just before he could reach Smith's saloon.

"Don't think she'll be open," J. W. said to get the man's attention. He jerked a thumb toward the saloon. "Old Beaver ain't about to be up much before noon."

The man turned to him, an annoyed look on his wide, dusky face. J. W. saw that he had been right about the man's identity. In the next moment he saw movement through a saloon window. He turned the man away from Garrett's concealed posse.

Putting an arm around the man's shoulders, Bell managed to put some cheerfulness in his melancholy eyes. "I just knew it was you, Valdez. Clear from the other side of the plaza I could tell. You're lookin' for a little tequila to get you up and at 'em, right? I know where there's a bottle just waitin' for us."

José Valdez nodded and bared some teeth in a strained smile. J. W. could see the Mexican was doing all he could to keep from glancing back at Smith's place.

"Just stick with me," Bell said. "It's just over there by Bowdre's house. Good thing I saw you, eh Valdez? I sure do hate to drink by myself, especially after a long ride to get someplace."

"I'm pretty thirsty, you bet," answered Valdez, trying to match Bell's carefree mood. By the time they reached the porch of the old adobe hospital, he had started telling J. W. about his long cow drive and how he was looking forward to the next Fort Sumner dance. They came to a sudden stop when Pat Garrett stepped out of the shadow of the doorway.

Valdez jerked himself free of the arm Bell had wrapped around his shoulders and even lunged a few steps away before he realized there was no point in running. He stood with knees bent, his arms held away from his body, his eyes darting back and forth between the two gringos. Now that the Mexican was still, Pat stepped over to him, reached inside one of the man's pockets and then the other, and took out Valdez's pistol. He looked down at the short man.

"It's bad weather to be riding into town without a good reason," he said. "What's *your* reason, José?"

"I have business here."

"Saw him over to Smith's place," said J. W. "I think he might've been snoopin' around."

"Is that right?" Pat asked the Mexican. "Who'd you talk to before J. W. found you? Who told you to look at the saloon?"

"Nobody tell me. I have to talk to Smith. I have to tell him about cows. We had to find a place for them until the weather gets better."

"I can tell Smith *for* you," Pat offered. "All right? Now you can leave town and get back to your stock, right, José?"

Valdez looked at Bell, then at Pat, trying to figure what sort of game they were playing. "All right, you tell Smith. That's good." He put on an innocent expression to tell Garrett that they trusted each other. Pat let him take one shuffling step away before he spoke.

"Where did you come across Lopez?" he asked matter-of-factly.

Valdez stopped, his mouth frozen for a moment. Pat sensed that the Mexican was about to spit out a denial but then thought twice about it.

"I saw him drive his wagon," Valdez said after giving it some more consideration, "but far off. He was coming from town, yes?"

Pat nodded, a grim smile on his lips. "Yeah, he was coming from town. I let him go so he could talk to people."

Pat studied the Mexican's reaction, searching for some sign that his plan had worked. He had figured that Lopez wouldn't have been able to resist talking if he came across the right man, and Valdez could have been that man. But still Pat wasn't certain. He thought he saw something flash across Valdez's black eyes, some fear that he might have been trapped, but the look quickly vanished as the Mexican got hold of himself again. Pat wasn't quite ready to bet on it.

"What do you think, J. W.?" he said. "You think we should get José here something to eat? Something to make up for dragging him around like this for no good reason."

Bell caught on to the deputy sheriff's meaning. "I could get him something over to Pete's," he said. "And I could keep him company too if you want."

"Yeah, that'd be a real good idea."

Valdez didn't bother to resist when Bell took his arm and turned him toward Maxwell's house. Before they got too far, though, a series of yelps reached them from the plaza.

Diagonally across the square, Barney Mason was holding onto a skinny teenaged boy, wrestling to get a grip with his second hand as the boy squirmed and tugged. The boy was able to throw Mason off balance for a second, and in that moment bolted away, but Barney recovered quickly, clamped two hands on the back of the boy's jacket and threw him to the ground. Pouncing on him, Barney grabbed the boy by the collar and twisted an arm back. He pushed him across the snowy ground.

Pat reached them as they neared the porch.

"Who's this?" he demanded.

Barney had to tug his captive back into line before answering. "Wilcox's boy. Caught him askin' questions. Over by the church."

"Let him go," Pat ordered.

Mason gave him a bewildered look, then backed

off from the boy. The teenager skittered away from Barney, his eyes wide with fear.

"Keep still, boy," said Pat. "Who are you? Would you be Pablo?" Garrett didn't sound sure of his guess. The boy jerked his head up and down to tell him he was right. Pat could see he wasn't going to get any answers from him as long as he was scared.

"You've grown some since the last time I saw you. I was at your father's place just a little while ago, but I didn't see you there."

Still breathing hard from his fight with Barney, Pablo took a few moments to settle himself before answering. "I was at the camp. With Joe."

Pat nodded. "Then you really *are* grown. Out doing a man's work these days, are you?"

"Yeah. I guess so." The chance to answer some harmless questions seemed to take some of the agitation out of the boy.

"That what you're doing here today?" Pat asked. "Doing something for your father? Something for the ranch?"

"Askin' questions he was," cut in Barney. "Heard him askin' where you were, Pat."

Garrett gave him a tired look. "Find something to do, Barney."

Mason didn't move at first. He stood with his mouth twitching, ready to say more about the boy, but then he kicked a clump of snow and stalked off.

Pat took the boy with him to the south side of the plaza, walking in silence to give Pablo more time to calm down. By Pete Maxwell's house he stopped and told the boy to take a seat on the bench next to the near adobe wall; Pat kept Valdez and Bell in sight as the two men continued to stand outside the Bowdre home. Garrett was pleased that J. W. had decided to stay put for now until the business with the Wilcox boy was settled.

"What were you trying to find out?" Pat finally said.

Pablo rested his elbows on his knees and stared at the ground. "I was supposed to find Valdez." Pat could hardly hear him.

"And what about me? Barney said you were asking questions about me."

"They told me to find out for myself, to check up on what Valdez told me."

Pat smiled. "Billy doesn't like to take chances when it comes to some things, does he?"

Pablo glanced unhappily at the deputy sheriff, then averted his eyes once more.

"I know your father's been a friend to the Kid," said Pat, "but I also know he sticks to the straight and narrow. Him and Brazil both. Is he behind your coming here, or was it just the Kid?"

"Well, Poppa, he said it was all right for me to go, but . . . I don't know. I don't think he wanted me to."

Pat sat next to the boy and made sure the next thing he said had a man-to-man tone. "Having the Kid roosting at his place like that, I guess that kind of puts your father in a spot. As long as Billy's got his gang with him, there's not much he can do, no matter how much he wants to do the right thing—and your father's a man that can take care of himself. Make no mistake about that. He might be looking for a way out of this, that's what I figure. What do you think, Pablo?"

The boy answered eagerly. "Oh, I don't think he

really likes Billy, not really. Billy just kind of moved in on us, eatin' our food, usin' our shelter and such. No one asked him to."

Pat took a long breath to keep his excitement at bay, to make sure he took his time and handled this right. "What made the Kid think of sending you here, Pablo?"

"Am I going to get locked up?" the boy said, finally facing the deputy sheriff. "Am I going to get arrested?"

"Don't worry, Pablo. Just tell me what you know and we'll figure this out together. Why did Billy send you here?"

"Well, because of Sam Dedrick. He came by and told us how some sheepherder passed the word about you. Sam said he sent Valdez to town to keep an eye on things, and Billy wanted me to bring word back from Valdez."

Pat looked at Valdez standing under the hospital overhang with Bell; he felt like he should congratulate himself for sending Lopez to spread the word, but a wave of caution told him not to get too far ahead of himself. Gazing at Valdez, Pat felt a new plan taking shape in his mind.

He placed a reassuring hand on Pablo's shoulder. "You've done the right thing telling me all this," he said. "Now I just want you to answer me one more thing. I want you to think about this before you answer. All right, Pablo?"

The teenager nodded.

Pat said, "Would your father do something to help if I could figure out a way?"

Pablo didn't have to mull this over very long. "Yes, I think he would."

"Okay, Pablo." Garrett stood up. "Come along with me."

When they reached Valdez, Pat asked, "Do you know how to write, José?"

22

Billy read the note three times, his face solemn, his eyes narrowed; he might have been searching for some sinister meaning in the words, or simply trying to decipher the rough pencil scrawl. His last reading done, he studied Pablo, the messenger. The boy stood before him, his hands stuffed in his jacket pockets, the flexing of his fingers showing through the fabric. He looked uneasy, but then, Billy told himself, he always did when he was around the Kid.

"Goddamn it, Billy," O'Folliard called from the other side of the room. "What does it say?"

The Kid didn't seem to hear him as he walked over to Sam Dedrick sitting at Wilcox's table. "You know Valdez's hand?" he asked.

"Well, yeah, Billy. I guess I should."

Billy spread the paper on the table. "Then look at this."

Dedrick pushed his plate aside and wiped his mouth with his sleeve. Feeling the importance of his task, he picked up the paper by the edges as if it were a delicate, yellowed document that might crumple in his hands. He held the note close to his eyes. His mouth silently formed the words as he scrutinized the few sentences.

"Well, what about it?" the Kid demanded.

The meaning of the words distracted Dedrick from the style of the handwriting. "Billy," he said, "it says here that—"

"I know what the hell it says. Just tell me if Valdez wrote it."

"Well, hell, yeah—it looks like it. I haven't seen but a couple notes he wrote down, but this sure looks like it's him."

Dedrick's face almost slammed onto the tabletop when Billy slapped him on the back. The Kid let out a long, ear-piercing hoot.

"Goddamn it to hell and back!" he hollered. "We got us an open road now."

"What's it say?" O'Folliard cried.

"Valdez says here that Pat left Fort Sumner this morning. He says the old woman took Barney and a Mexican and took off for Roswell to try to get reinforcements. Fort Sumner is all ours, boys."

O'Folliard, Pickett, and Wilson whooped and slapped Brazil on the back and all started jabbering at once.

"Garrett knew we'd come shootin' for him!" shouted O'Folliard.

"The *hell* kind of manhunter he is," put in Pickett, "takin' off with his tail between his legs like that. We would've really whupped him, right, Billy?"

The carousing even infected Charley Bowdre. He got up from his seat at the table, a smile growing across his face, loosening the tightly wound expression he had worn for the last two days. For now, he stopped worrying about his deal with Garrett, and instead remembered the full-tilt hell-raising when he had ridden with Billy and the other Regulators—not so very long ago, he realized.

Charley came around the table to reach the Kid's side. "We goin' to take that load of beef into town now, Billy? Maybe kick things up some?"

Billy gave him a sidelong, inquisitive look, then his eyes brightened with a sly glint. "The beef! The hell with freightin' a wagon around. Smith can wait for his shipment now." He flashed a bucktoothed smile at the rest of the gang. "It's time for us to be ridin' light and fast. I say we go into town and celebrate Pat showin' the white feather, and then maybe we should just ride out and run him down."

"We can burn him down!" cried O'Folliard. "Yes sirree, we surely can."

The gang started to round up their gear, leaving Pablo standing alone in the middle of the room. He now backed away, keeping his eyes on Billy and the rest, trying to keep his hands from fidgeting. Finally he found himself by his stepfather's side. Wilcox paid no attention to the boy; he sat by the hearth, watching the outlaws closely, as if waiting for them to steal everything he had for their ride to Fort Sumner. When Dave Rudabaugh, sitting nearby, finally got up to join the others, Wilcox felt his stepson press a folded sheet of paper in his hand.

The look on Pablo's face told Wilcox that he would have to be careful. As nonchalantly as he could, he stood up and wandered over to his desk, feigning interest in the lamp he had left there that he had been tinkering with earlier that afternoon. He was able to turn his back to the gang and hide the letter as he read.

> Tom:
> I have given this letter to your boy so you can know the real facts. I am still in Fort Sumner and I have a good posse of 9 men with me. We are sticking to it until the end. Your boy says you would help if you had a good chance. I will stand by you if you do help.
>
> Patrick F. Garrett

Wilcox stayed at his desk for several more minutes to follow through on his lamp-tinkering deception. When Billy told his boys to get out and saddle up, the rancher felt he could then move to the other side of the room without stirring up suspicion. At the table, he passed the note to Brazil without a word, and then walked to the window to look at the gang start their horses. Billy took the point, with O'Folliard and Pickett close behind, the riders' shapes growing darker in the late afternoon light as they moved at an easy lope toward the road.

Pat sent his possemen one at a time across the plaza.

In the early darkness, the sporadic procession of Texans attracted little attention; some townspeople cast curious glances at the Anglos walking through the mostly Mexican town, but Pat didn't see any indication of alarm. The last to cross were José Roibal and Luis the Animal, who stopped to talk to two *Mejicanas* who had been scurrying through the cold from one warm adobe to another. Roibal later assured Pat that they had only been doing what was natural to avoid appearing suspicious. He conceded, though, that the Animal would have dragged one of the young women off if José hadn't stopped him.

Inside the Bowdre home, Charley's wife, Rita, looked from one posseman to another, demanding an explanation for the intrusion. Poe and Mason tried to settle her, to little effect, until Garrett finally got back from a last look around the plaza.

"Juan Largo, you can't stay here," she rattled at him in Spanish. "I won't have my husband's enemies in my house. You have to go. I'll make you go."

Pat ignored the smiles appearing on the faces of a couple of Texans and, taking the Mexican woman's fleshy arm, steered her to a far corner. She tore her arm out of his grip when they came to a stop.

"You're going to kill your friends," she spat at him. "You're dirt. You can't use my house to kill my Charley."

Pat grabbed her by both arms this time and pulled her halfway off her feet so that her face was closer to his. "Quiet," he hissed back at her in Spanish. "You have to listen." She fought against his hold and spoke so rapidly that Garrett could only make out some of the words. "Quiet!" he yelled, shaking her until she stopped.

"When was the last time you spoke to Charley?" he asked once they both had had a chance to calm themselves.

"Why do you want to know?"

"Because I'm trying *not* to kill him—that's why. We're supposed to make a deal and I have to know what he's up to. Did he tell you he was trying to get away from the gang?"

Her expression froze. Now that her anger served no purpose, she was thrown off balance. Pat could see the answer to his question in her face.

He said, "Maybe he didn't tell you anything because he wasn't sure if he could make the deal. I'm trying to get word from Captain Lea, but I don't know what'll happen. That's why I want to know if he's still with Billy. Was he with him here in Fort Sumner?"

The confusion in her expression was beginning to give way to a cold fear. "I don't know . . . I mean, he was here with Billy, yes—but I don't know if he is still with him."

"Did he leave here with the Kid?"

"You mean yesterday . . . two days ago?" The fear was making it harder for her to think straight. Garrett lowered his voice to try to soothe her.

"Billy and the others left here two days ago, Rita. Did Charley go with him then?"

"Yes, he went with him." She seemed somewhat comforted by her ability to get the facts straight.

Pat's mouth twisted reflexively into a grimace. He shook his head bitterly. "Why did he go with him, Rita? He didn't have to."

"He was afraid you were coming. I think they all were. Charley thought you'd get him with all the others."

Pat now felt he was absorbing some of her fear, a clammy, sickening dread that rolled and twisted in his stomach. "I told him he'd have to start moving away from Billy. Maybe he's got enough sense not to come back here with him. I really hope so, Rita."

It took a couple of moments for these words to register with her, then she glanced wide-eyed at the hard-looking men on the other side of the room. Still holding her, Pat could feel her body curling tightly inside. He knew what had to be done.

Calling over Roibal, Pat told him to take Charley's wife over to the Maxwell home and to make sure that Pete kept her out of the way. Rita said nothing while Pat gave his man the instructions, and she moved silently and obediently when Roibal took her out of the house. Walking onto the porch outside, she managed one more hateful glance at Garrett.

The possemen had laid out blankets on the floor where they continued the low-stakes poker playing that had whiled away the hours in Smith's saloon. Pat sent Jim East to stand guard at the eastern end of the plaza, the direction from which anyone would come if they were riding from the Wilcox ranch. Kneeling by one of the blankets, Pat watched one of the games, unable to focus on the play. He heard John Poe's voice at his side.

"You think there's any chance they'll stay at this Wilcox place?"

Pat gave him a blank look, not sure what the Texas marshal was getting at.

"I mean," said Poe, "maybe they'll just stay put. Maybe we'll have to go out and get 'em."

"I don't think so," Pat said quickly.

"How long do we wait for him here? You know, in case they head in some other direction?"

"Like what direction?" Garrett snapped at him.

"Well, like Roswell. The note said you were going that way. Maybe the Kid wants to cut you off."

Pat held himself back from snapping again. He

tried to tame his doubts, the second thoughts that the Texan was prodding with his questions. After a while, Garrett finally answered, "I don't think the Kid would do that."

Poe nodded and left it alone.

He has to come here, Garrett insisted to himself. *Billy thinks he's made me run and he's going to celebrate before he does anything else. That's what he's going to do, all right. I'm going to have the Kid by Christmas.*

Pat moved away from the game to change the course of his thoughts. Through the window, he saw two Mexicans standing under an overhang across the way. Except for an occasional passerby, those men were the only people in the plaza—and the night was too cold for anybody to be lazing about outside, Pat thought.

"Barney," he called. "Those two Mexicans over there—they've been hanging around too long. Take Chambers with you and bring them over to Maxwell's. Nobody's sending word out of town tonight. And Barney," he added when the two men headed for the door, "just take them over to Maxwell's. Don't make a range war out of it."

Pat stood watch by the window until Mason and Chambers had taken the Mexicans out of the plaza; he took some comfort in the fact that Barney was able to do something right. *Some time tonight,* Pat thought, *I might have to depend on every man in this posse.*

An hour later, he sent John Poe out to take East's place as sentry.

Pat tried a few hands of poker but didn't have the patience for it, or for conversation either, and decided to stretch out on the bed as a way of clearing his mind. The worry that Billy wouldn't come to town soon faded, only to be replaced by memories that were even more unwelcome. For the first time that night, the inside of Bowdre's house reminded him of old times: sitting at the table eating Rita's food, surrounded by boisterous talk; sharing a jug on the porch when it had been too hot to stay indoors. Sometimes he had been with Tom O'Folliard, sometimes with Tip McKinney, and sometimes with the Kid. He hadn't come here very often, but Rita was always a good hostess, even if she could get a little bossy at times. And there always seemed to be less to think about back then.

At first troubling, these memories began to make a comfortable fit in his mind after a while, and they soon lost some of their crispness until they were just a string of pictures that slid back and forth. Before long, Pat eased into sleep.

John Poe's voice woke him, making him jump off the bed.

"Somebody coming!" Poe said from the open doorway.

23

The snow cover along the road was a dull, milky white in the moonshine. The pale light seemed to carry with it an icy stillness, broken only by the clacking of the horse's hooves, as the seven men rode westward at a steady walk. At first the riders had been noisy as they had sung half-remembered verses of barroom songs, had told tall stories, and had traded friendly abuse; but after a couple of miles they gradually gave in to the country's quiet.

The closer they got to town, the heavier the silence weighed on Billy. All he could think of were the warm comforts of Wilcox's ranch that they had left behind. He couldn't shake the feeling that he had been a fool to leave; the excitement of Fort Sumner meant nothing, and his high spirits at the beginning of this ride were hard to understand now.

Not willing to let the sourness remain without a

fight, he turned to Tom O'Folliard riding beside him at the front of the line. "You thinking about Maria? Is that what's keeping you so quiet?"

Lulled by the ride, Tom was slow to react. When he faced Billy, he smiled sheepishly and shook his head. "Yeah, I guess so. Off and on."

"Well, I'd think more of her than that, the way some of the *muchachos* in town would take her behind the house if they had half a chance. You better be thinking about keeping her away from them."

Tom nodded, but didn't seem interested in saying anything more about it. Billy decided there was no point in even trying to be good company tonight.

"Are you still thinkin' we might leave this country?" Tom said a moment later.

"Don't see why the hell we should now," the Kid answered. "Not when we got Pat on the run the way we do."

"Yeah, no sense now." Tom seemed in better spirits as he gazed absently ahead. "Wouldn't want to leave Maria behind just now. Rita says she's going to put a word in for me, so I can be sure Maria'd be mine. I figure on spending Christmas with her if I can."

Billy looked strangely at him. He had never heard Tom talk like that, and he wasn't sure he liked it. Here they were with work still ahead of them, and Tom was mooning about a family holiday. For his part, Billy hadn't given much thought to Christmas in a long time. The last good Christmas that he could remember had been almost ten years ago, in Silver City, not too long before his mother died. At least it hadn't been as bad as most. To the good, his stepfather hadn't been there that time, and there had been enough food on the table, and the house hadn't been too cold. *Not so bad really,* Billy thought, *but I'll be damned if I'll sit around wondering if Paulita will have me over for Christmas dinner.*

"Well, I guess I can't worry about such things now," Tom said. "After we burn down Garrett, I can have all the time I want to think about Maria. Right, Kid?"

Billy turned back to O'Folliard; his eyes became glassy as he stared at his friend without really seeing him. The Kid should have been comforted by Tom's words—after all, the old boy was getting back on track—but a sensation seemed to come out of nowhere to suddenly grip him, keeping him from talking, or even moving.

I'm not going to see Paulita again, he thought.

"Something wrong, Billy?"

The Kid made himself focus on Tom.

"No, nothing's wrong," he said, finding his mouth dry. "Just ridin' like this at night—sometimes it can spook a man if he's not careful."

Tom squinted at him, not sure what Billy was talking about, then suddenly turned to look the other way, as if checking whether there might be a ghost riding next to them. Not seeing a ghost seemed to make it harder for him to understand the Kid's meaning.

Billy had stopped paying attention to his friend. He could feel the blood pumping through his neck, and he was finding it difficult to keep his breathing even. He had no idea where the feeling had come from, but he knew he would have to get away from riding point. He wasn't going to be the first one to ride into town.

"I sure could use a chaw," he told Tom after clearing his throat.

O'Folliard reached into his pocket. "Think I got a twist to spare, Kid. Here you go. Just enough for the two of us."

Billy reached for the tobacco, then feigned second thoughts. "I don't know, Tom. A special night like tonight, with Garrett on the run, I guess I got a hankering for a plug of Winesap. I think Johnny's still got some of the genuine stuff from White Oaks." He grinned at Tom and swung his horse around.

Passing Pickett, Rudabaugh, Dedrick, and Bowdre, he finally brought his horse alongside Johnny Wilson, riding drag. As it turned out, Johnny had a plug of Star of Virginia, not Winesap, but it served Billy just as well. With the tobacco tucked inside his cheek, he rode in silence, undisturbed now by the quiet night, watching the other riders rock in the saddle up ahead. The panic was fading quickly. Billy had to laugh at himself: some men just let a bad idea drag them down for days on end while a quick-thinking man like himself could snap out of it just like that. Billy thought it was funny, and just a little bit sad too, for the moody, slower-thinking fellows.

He considered telling the others about the spooky feeling he had just had, but decided against it. He figured the feeling had just been a wild notion, and besides, they had already come this far. Saying something now just might be bad luck, he thought. For all his doubts about the premonition, though, he stayed at the rear of the line.

A handful of lit windows shone as pinpoints in the dark as Fort Sumner came into view.

"Take Poker Tom and Bozeman with you," Pat told Mason as he guided him out the door. "They might try coming in along the back. If they do, make sure you know it's them before you cut loose. We'll be around to pitch in as soon as we hear shooting. Go on, get moving."

Pat watched Mason and the two other possemen jog around to the other side of the old hospital. When he saw them go around the corner and out of view, Garrett waved Bell out onto the porch. He put a hand on the man's shoulder and spoke quietly, a haltered intensity putting an edge on his voice.

"I need somebody to keep Barney in line. You think you can do it?"

J. W. glanced over his shoulder at the route Barney had taken, then turned back to Garrett, his face pensive. "Well, I guess I could if you tell me you're making me the ramrod."

"You're the one. You sit on him till you're damn sure it's the gang coming in. You got your rifle inside?"

"I got an old Winchester carbine."

"Then load it up."

Pat looked eastward, past the end of the plaza, but the riders were still too far off to be seen. *No one's got any business riding in here tonight except Billy,* he reassured himself. Starting to pace, he walked past Roibal, Poe, East, and Chambers, all crouched against the front of the house. Williams now stepped out the Bowdre door, his rifle in his hands, moving toward a night shadow by the window. The man was looking Pat's way. Sensing something, Garrett turned to see that Poe and East were also staring at him, a curious look on their faces. Pat was about to ask what they were gawking at, but then realized it was his pacing that the Texans' expressions were questioning. Any movement on the porch, no matter how shadowy it was under the overhang, was bound to attract attention. Pat moved over to the open doorway and stayed there.

While his body remained still, his mind continued to race. Studying the porch, he judged that it was too narrow to conceal more than three or four men; he figured if he made the right play he wouldn't need more than that. He motioned Williams over.

"I want a couple more men to back Mason up," Pat whispered. "Take East with you."

The two Texans moved quickly, their boots making only the slightest scraping sound across the porch's plank floor. When that noise disappeared, another, fainter sound rose dimly in the other direction, the rhythmic fall of hooves.

Now that the time had come, the possemen took their positions without speaking. Pat moved to the left of the door, pressing himself against the wall, while John Poe crept to a spot just a couple of feet away. José Roibal posted himself a foot inside the doorway; Lon Chambers squatted farther along the base of the house.

As they reached the edge of the plaza, the riders were outlined clearly by the snow-reflected moonlight. Angling for better cover, Garrett positioned himself behind a harness hanging from the porch roof. He counted seven of them, but couldn't see any faces clearly; one thing was certain, though: they were headed toward the Bowdre house.

Pat slipped the glove off his trigger hand to give himself a bitter grip. The palm of the hand was beaded with sweat that had somehow defied the cold. Gazing at the riders coming closer, he suddenly had the impression that the plaza was a box, much smaller than he had ever thought it was before, and sealed on all sides by adobe and impenetrable night. He was pressed as flat as he could against the front of the old hospital, reflexively catching his breath. The riders moved at an infuriating, languid gait, and managed to avoid the few patches of window light slanting across the square.

The lead horseman reached the porch with his face still masked by shadow.

The others were strung loosely behind as the point rider brought his mount right up to the porch railing. Pat's eyes raked across the band of men. He strained to find Billy's face. He then fixed his gaze on the fifth man in line, trying desperately to see if the hunched figure belonged to Charley Bowdre.

He was suddenly aware of Poe's coiled presence beside him, and he realized there would be no more time for looking. Just then, the lead horse poked its head under the overhang, just a few feet away, nickering softly, mist curling from its nostrils. Behind the horse's head, Pat saw Tom O'Folliard's face.

Garrett swung his rifle around. "Put 'em up!" he shouted.

There was only an instant's hesitation, then O'Folliard stabbed his hand into his pocket and pulled out a gun.

Pat's Winchester roared. John Poe fired a second later. O'Folliard wrenched back, screamed, then drooped lazily forward, his face almost nuzzling his horse's neck. The animal bucked and plunged away as gunfire pounded from both sides of the porch.

The second rider's horse lurched forward, and the flare from the rider's pistol lit the gunman's face. It was Curly Pickett. The outlaw's shot cracked harmlessly through the porch roof. Pickett battled his spooked horse while trying to line up his revolver at Garrett. Pat turned his way, levered the Winchester, and was about to fire when the flash from Poe's gun cut across his field of vision. Pat knew his shot was wide as soon as he squeezed the trigger, but the howl Pickett let loose made it sound like he was already half-dead. Reining wildly, the outlaw bounded to the far side of the plaza, then veered toward an alley between two houses.

Chambers and Roibal were firing quickly, but the outlaws were already on the move. At first the horses milled frantically, then steadied just long enough for two of the outlaws to cut loose and drive Roibal back away from the doorway. In that second's respite, they wheeled their mounts around and charged back the way they had come. Chambers put a slug through the side of a big bay in the middle of the group. The rider, though, never let up. After the animal faltered with the bullet's impact, the bearded rider dug in his spurs, beat the animal's flank with his gauntleted hand, and pressed the horse into a gallop, just behind his comrades.

Pickett showed himself briefly just beyond the church as he galloped in a northeasterly direction. By this time Mason, Bell, and the others had reached the plaza and now opened up on the fugitive. But Pickett loped out of range, still howling, his voice trailing off into the night.

Across the plaza, a lone set of hoof falls punctuated the hush that followed the final gunshots. Facing the source of the sound, Pat saw Tom O'Folliard, still slumped on the back of his horse, the animal weaving from one side to the other. O'Folliard managed to get a firmer grip on the reins and moved them slightly; the horse ambled back toward the old hospital.

Pat didn't leave the porch, and neither did Roibal or Chambers. In the square, the rest of the posse held their guns on the passing rider, following at a distance until the outlaw came to a stop in front of the Bowdre home. Pat took one step forward and stopped there. He still couldn't see the man's face clearly.

"Put up your hands, Tom."

At first the only response he got was a series of rasps, then O'Folliard brought his head up a couple of inches. "I can't," he said.

A Winchester was levered in the plaza. "You heard him," cried Barney. "Throw up those hands or we'll shoot."

"Back off," Pat shouted.

Tom's horse moved on its own, walking tentatively to the side, then coming a few feet closer to the porch, seeming to be unmindful of the limp form on its back.

"Don't shoot, Pat," O'Folliard wheezed. "I'm killed."

Garrett stepped off the porch, his rifle leveled, and stopped a few feet short of the rider, staring at the man for a couple of moments before he was sure he could move in the rest of the way. With Roibal's help, he pulled O'Folliard out of the saddle. He reached for Tom's right hand to find the man's revolver was cocked.

24

The young outlaw groaned miserably as he was placed on Bowdre's table. He cut the sound short; his face creased with effort to withstand the pain. "Oh God," Tom finally blurted out.

Unbuttoning O'Folliard's coat, Pat could see two wounds in the man's torso, one just below the heart and the other on the right side of the stomach. Barney let out a low whistle.

"Looks like both you boys made 'em count," he said, gesturing to Garrett and Poe. Neither man answered. For a while, there was no sound in the room except O'Folliard's ragged breathing and the shuffling of wood in the hearth as Animal Bozeman and Lon Chambers stoked the fire. Although the rest of the posse had preferred to stay outside while the outlaw died, Bozeman and Chambers couldn't see any reason to do without the fire on this cold night.

Pat sat in a chair next to the table, trying to decide if there was any point in talking to O'Folliard. Tom grimaced and stiffened through another wave of pain. When it subsided somewhat, he said, "Put me out of my misery, Pat. As a friend."

Some of the fighting adrenaline, triggered by the shootout, still coursed through Garrett. He spoke quickly, before he could give his words any thought. "You're my friend? A couple of minutes ago you threw down on me. You were going to shoot me on sight, weren't you?"

Tom groaned again and pressed his lips together until they were white in a desperate attempt to steel himself. Pat's anger sickened and seemed to turn on himself for lashing out at a man in his last moments.

"You've killed me," O'Folliard said.

Barney spoke up before Garrett could. "Take your medicine, old boy. Take your medicine."

Pat had nothing more to say to Mason. He just got up, strode over to him and, dragging him to the door, heaved him out onto the porch. Sprawling out into the plaza, Barney rolled onto his feet and glared at Garrett. Pat waited long enough to make sure the man wasn't going to come at him.

Tom's head was turning from side to side when Pat returned to the table. "I'm not goin' to die, am I? I'm not goin' to die?"

Pat sat down again, his mind groping for something to say; then finally he put his hand on top of O'Folliard's. "You haven't got much time, Tom," he said quietly.

"You're not goin' to let him shoot me, are you?"

Garrett exchanged a puzzled look with Poe, then realized Tom must be talking about Barney. "He's not here anymore," he said. "You'll go when it's your time if that's what you want. But you should try to set things straight before then, Tom. That'd be the thing to do."

Pat couldn't imagine the outlaw going to heaven or hell when he died; he couldn't say whether the man's soul would be going anywhere at all. But in the final moments, he figured, Tom would go easier if he settled up.

Tom's eyes held a terrible glassy look for several minutes. In gradual steps, the fear began to give way as some sense of grim resolve found a foothold.

"Tip McKinney," he finally rasped. "Tell Tip for me."

Pat leaned closer. "What about Tip?"

"He can tell my grandma about me. In Texas." O'Folliard's head lolled to one side and his expression loosened. "Tip's a good old Texas boy."

"I can't tell Tip," Pat said. "He left a while back, Tom, went back home to Texas. We'll have to get word to your grandma some other way."

Tom nodded, looking pleased for some reason, until the pain returned. When O'Folliard had himself under control again, Pat said, "I'll get word to your grandma, Tom. You can count on that. But meanwhile you can tell me just one thing. I've got to make sure that it was Billy you were riding with tonight."

"You caught up to him all right," Tom said. "He was riding back there with Johnny and Charley. The lucky bastard said he needed a chaw." Tom stopped to scrutinize Garrett, as if he had never seen him before, then one corner of his mouth twisted convulsively, a movement that might have been a smile. "I guess you got me pretty square, Pat, seeing as how I was figuring to shoot you myself. You were right about that, Pat. For a second there I thought I was goin' to be the one to beat the Kid to it, what with him hangin' back. I had a good look at you there for just the one second."

Pat let him be quiet after that. Any more settling up would have to be done by Tom on his own. The fire in the hearth was going strong by then, crackling and popping behind Garrett's back, throwing a shifting orange light across the table and the far wall's cracked adobe. John Poe found another chair and pulled it over to the opposite side of the table. He sat there with his hat in his hands, an empty look in his eye, a look that said he knew there was nothing left to do for now but wait.

After Tom died a half hour later, Poe walked with Garrett onto the porch where Bell and East waited. People had collected in the square, but they showed no interest in coming close to the gringo possemen, apparently content to rehash mangled stories about the shootout at the old hospital from the other side of the plaza.

Footsteps to the right turned Pat around. Barney stood a few yards away, half-hidden in the moon shadow cast by the overhang.

"You can ride on without me," he growled. "I'm through gettin' pushed around."

For a moment Pat toyed with the idea of making Barney a liar by pushing him off the porch. *Then* he'd be through pushing the runt around. Instead, Pat just shrugged and looked away, across the moon-bright plaza. *He's done something right after all,* Pat thought. *He's saved me the trouble of firing him.*

The rest of the gang kept glancing at Billy. Once they had galloped clear of Fort Sumner, it soon became clear that Garrett wasn't behind them, at least for now, but that didn't mean the long-legged bastard wasn't figuring on pursuit. The question was how he planned to do it, and if he had any more tricks up his sleeve. Billy would be the one to make a good guess; he knew the man better than any of the others. But Billy wasn't talking.

Even Rudabaugh looked to the Kid for some word about what they should do. When he wasn't lashing his half-dead horse onward, the bearded outlaw kept an eye on Billy, but all he could see was Billy's blank, almost frozen expression as he pressed his mount for all it was worth, so unlike the brash, upstart ways that Rudabaugh had come to expect from the Kid.

All of the horses began to struggle before long, and the pace had to slacken. To make up for lack of speed, the Kid led the way into the hills, along a trail that would be more difficult to follow. The easterly direction made it seem like they were headed back to the Wilcox ranch, but still Billy offered no clue as to what they would do once they reached that place.

By the time they left the hill trail behind, Sam Dedrick was no longer with them. He had been riding drag and apparently had dropped back further to take another trail on his own, thinking he would be safer without the gang's company. "Sam's lit out," Bowdre said to the others, but no one said anything else about it. None of them thought it mattered, and most of them thought they were now better off.

Rudabaugh's horse staggered to the ground while moving down a slope. The outlaw shot the animal where it fell and climbed onto the back of Bowdre's horse for the last leg of the ride to the Wilcox spread.

Stopping among the hills that overlooked the ranch, Billy turned his horse to face the others and finally had his say.

"We're not going in just yet," he said. His face was red with windburn, which made him look flaming mad. "The old woman could've slipped around on us and gotten to Wilcox's first, or he might be comin' along real soon. Either way, we've got to be somewhere that'll let us cut loose at him if he comes out into the open. Those rocks up there—we can camp up there and keep an eye on the ranch and the road comin' in."

"After that?" said Rudabaugh. "What do we do after we freeze our balls up here all night?"

"We'll figure that out when we see it's okay to go to the ranch house. And if we can't go there, then we'll figure that out too. You'll just wait till we know something more, Rudabaugh. You can't figure Garrett too many steps ahead. I'm the one that knows that and you'll just have to live with it."

Rudabaugh should have knocked the Kid out of his saddle for talking to him like that—that's what Rudabaugh told himself—but he found himself anchored in place behind Bowdre's saddle. This was a new strength he was seeing in Billy, not the usual devil-may-care damn foolishness. Rudabaugh wasn't one to tolerate someone carrying on with him in high-handed ways, but he had to admit he was impressed by the boy's gumption.

Hidden along the rocky crest, the men picketed their mounts and split into groups of two; Bowdre and Wilson to keep an eye on the house, Billy and Rudabaugh to watch the road. The Kid said that one in each pair should rest while the other acted as lookout.

"Get some sleep if you want," Billy told Rudabaugh. "I'll take the first guard."

"I'll get around to sleepin' when I'm ready," Rudabaugh said.

"Suit yourself," answered the Kid. He sat with his back to a slab of rock so that he could see the road between two boulders just below the crest. Easing down across from him, Rudabaugh took out the makings and began rolling a Bull Durham cigarette, not bothering to ask Billy if he cared to roll one for himself. Billy wasn't offended; he just figured the Kansas man was in one of his usual dark, solitary moods—which was why the Kid was surprised when Rudabaugh started to talk.

"This Garrett," he said, "he seems like some kind of tough *buscadero* after all."

"After all?" said Billy. "I knew he was a rough customer all along. You just didn't take my word for it, Rudabaugh." He looked toward the road and shook his head. "*After all,*" he repeated wryly.

"You think Wilcox and his partner knew about this? About Garrett still being in Fort Sumner and waiting for us?"

"I don't know. I've been thinkin' on it but it just doesn't come clear. The boy, Pablo, he'd have to have been the one to trick us, but I don't think he's got the sand for it. A scared kid like that—hell, if I was as skittish as he is, I'd be dead a long time ago. I don't know, Dave. I don't think they were really in on it. I figure Pat just made himself scarce, and maybe had somebody to tell him when he could slip back into town and set the trap. That's what I think. Old Pat Garrett could've done that, sure."

Rudabaugh lit the cigarette and blew out a long trail of smoke, his eyes narrowed, seeming to be lost in thought. If someone else had blown smoke at him like that, Billy would've thought the man was taunting him, trying to make him beg for some tobacco. But Rudabaugh was different. *He's too mean to even know I'd want some,* thought Billy.

"How much do you really know this Garrett?" Rudabaugh finally said. "Were you real good friends?"

"We knew each other," answered Billy. He then let out a dry laugh. "We sure used to be better friends than we are now, I'll tell you that."

"Didn't you rustle with him? That's what Pickett told me. He said you two were sort of in business together."

"Yeah, *sort of,* that's right. I guess that's the whole damn problem, going back to the old days."

Billy let it stand at that. Suddenly fatigue had caught up with him, and all he wanted to do was sit against the rock and look at the road. But he could feel Rudabaugh's eyes still on him.

"That don't tell me a whole lot, Kid."

"Any reason I should tell you anything more? You figurin' on writing a stor 'or the *Police Gazette* or some such?"

"No, but I do figure on stayin' alive, and right now

that means keepin' Garrett from killing me. I kind of like to know something about a law-dog that's tryin' to run me down. John J. Webb, he was a lawman in Dodge when we first crossed trails, then we started workin' the same side. Never hurts to know how much a man can bend, you know what I mean?"

"Well, I guess you might as well know," said Billy. "It was back in Fort Sumner when I first got friendly with Pat. Matter of fact, it was at Charley Bowdre's house that I met him, right where he shot Tom tonight. Kind of a funny thing when you think on it a while. Anyway, he was a pretty high-livin' fella back then, not a bad fella to be around when the *bailes* got started—you might not believe it, him being such a son-of-a-bitch now, but it's true. As for me, I wasn't doing much in those days, just picking up a few stray cows here and there, just like anybody else, but the more I thought on it, the less I could see why I had to keep killin' myself with work while some big cattlemen could just sit around and work up a sweat countin' the money. One time I talked to Pat about that. He was kind of on the lookout for some fast money—hell, with all the times he went broke with all his damn businesses, he *had* to find some way to make his way in this world."

"He went in on some rustling with you," Rudabaugh said.

"He sure did, the long-legged bastard. I was going to rope in the beeves and he was going to buy 'em and then sell 'em to somebody else so he could make a nice profit. It was just the cattle business, plain and simple, that's how he put it. But then he backed out. Right after our first deal he just up and decided he had enough. It was the damnedest thing.

It wasn't like we had just made scads of money and we could retire and leave it at that. He just said he was through."

"Somebody was tumbling to him. These go-between fellas always get squeamish in a hurry."

"Not that I know of, no sir. All he said was that he was fixing to make some kind of respectable man out of himself, and he was a damn fool to get mixed up in such things with me. That's what he said, the old woman." Billy stared off, remembering, then leaned his head back and laughed, long and loud. He cut himself off, putting a hand up to his mouth and looking sheepish, as though he'd get in trouble for laughing too loud.

"Then you know what that old woman did?" Billy went on, finding it hard to stifle another laugh. "He started up a hog business with this fella Tip McKinney, and got himself run over by one of the damn hogs. Nearly got killed by that hog, he was so busted up. That's when Apolinaria took him in. That's his wife, you know, except she wasn't his wife back then. She took him in and nursed him back onto his feet, and I guess the old woman figured he had to marry her for it." Billy shook his head, a rueful smile on his lips. "That was the end of old Pat. He's been nothing but a sour-faced, long-legged bastard ever since."

25

Charley Bowdre saw the man poke his head out of the haystack, look one way, then the other, and creep out into the open. The man moved doubled-over, sticking to the night shadows as much as possible, as he headed toward the corral and then angled toward the ranch house. At the window, he peered in and kept looking for a long time. Whatever he might have seen inside couldn't have disturbed him much because he now walked straight-up as he ambled about the place, still on the lookout.

Charley had seen a light in the ranch house window when he first started his watch a half hour ago and thought he saw some movement inside as well. Soon the light had gone out. There had been nothing else to see. No sign of guards posted around the house, no extra horses to be accounted for—no sign of Garrett. The man from the haystack was suspicious, but he certainly didn't look like a posseman.

The man, spooked by something, now hurried back to the haystack and crouched along its side. His eyes adjusting to the distance, Bowdre was able to make out some details of the man's face. Charley smiled.

The prowler was Curly Pickett.

Charley called Billy over and pointed out their friend hiding below.

"He found his way here after all," said the Kid, "the screaming scared rabbit. Well, if Pat was around he would've hauled Curly in by now. Okay, boys. Go get your horses. Looks like we can get out of the cold for a while."

Once they were within shouting distance, they had to call out to Pickett to make sure he didn't take a shot at them. Even so, he watched them approach with his Colt leveled and ready, and his shivering wasn't caused solely by the cold. When the riders' faces were clear to him, Curly finally moved away from the haystack, managing to force a cocky smile.

"Didn't think you boys would make it," he said, "takin' that bad way out of town the way you did."

"And you found a good way, did you?" said Billy. "Funny how you didn't let us know which way we should go at the time. The way you were screamin' your head off it was real hard understanding what you were tryin' to tell us."

Pickett didn't even have to take a moment to come up with an answer. "Well, yeah, I guess you can say I was kind of spooked. And why the hell not? I knew I shot that damned Garrett and that meant everyone in his posse was going to go shootin' at me to make it even. I got him, Billy—did you know that? I'm sure of it. That's why the whole damn posse was after me."

"Oh yeah? Then how come Dave here got his horse shot if everyone was shooting at you? Or maybe *you* shot Dave's horse right after you finished killing Garrett."

"I got a good shot at the long-legged bastard. I swear it."

Billy spat and neck-reined his horse toward the ranch house. "Shut the hell up, Curly. Just get in the house. We got some plannin' to do."

Inside, the lamp was lit again, and Wilcox, Pablo, and Brazil were all up. Wilcox had a rifle in his hands when the gang stepped in.

"What're you fidgety about, Tom?" Billy said. "You afraid Garrett was coming? Or were you just afraid it'd be me again?"

The harshness of Billy's voice made Charley take a long look at Wilcox. It hadn't occurred to him before that the rancher might have been in cahoots with Garrett, and the fact that he hadn't even considered the possibility made him uneasy. His mind was so bollixed up these days that he didn't notice the things that any man running from the law should immediately pick up.

Wilcox stared at the Kid with an expression that seemed genuinely offended. "What the hell kind of thing is that to say to me, Billy?"

"O'Folliard got shot up. Maybe killed," Billy answered. "As soon as we got to Fort Sumner, Garrett was waiting for us. I just thought you might've known something about that."

"How the hell would I have known that? For Christ's sake, Billy, that's just plain stupid. I got a mind to shove you boys out of here and send you packing. You can't talk to me like that."

Billy sat at the table, rubbing his arms to get some of the chill out of his bones. "You can't blame me, Tom. O'Folliard was a good friend and I had to put it up to you, just to see what you'd do." He studied Wilcox some more to reassure himself, then his mouth puckered into a grimace and he waved one of his hands. "Goddamn it, I didn't think you knew about it. I just had to make some noise. Put the damned rifle down. We're all friends here, aren't we?"

"Sure, Billy, that's what *I* thought. That's what Brazil thought too, me and him both."

"I said put the damned rifle down. Go on and get us blankets so we can get some sleep. It's not a whole lot warmer in here than it is outside, you know."

While Wilcox went for the blankets, Bowdre noticed Pablo sitting hunched-over on his bunk, a serape wrapped tightly around his slim shoulders. His eyes darted nervously from one outlaw to the other, as if his life depended on knowing where each one of them was at all times. Feeling sorry for the boy, Charley went over to sit next to him.

"We won't be stayin' long this time," he told Pablo. "Just long enough to figure something out and then we'll be gone before there can be any trouble." He watched the boy to see if there was any hint of relief in his eyes. Only a faint smile appeared on Pablo's face.

"Billy won't be havin' much time to be funnin' you while we're here," Charley added.

"Okay," Pablo said, nodding his head. He sounded like he felt he just had to reply in some way.

Charley noticed the Kid talking to Rudabaugh at the table. Their voices were too low to be heard, but the way they talked was enough to tell Bowdre something. It looked like they were working on a plan, and that in itself seemed peculiar. Charley knew what Billy thought of the Kansas tough: Rudabaugh was a good man to back up a play, but he wasn't about to become one of the boys, the way Charley and O'Folliard had become during the Lincoln War, and the way Johnny Wilson had become the last few months. But here was Billy talking to the man like they were fast partners, as if the Kid didn't want to make a move without hearing what Rudabaugh had to say. *It wasn't so long ago,* Bowdre thought, *when Billy would ask me what I thought of a thing before he'd go ahead and do it.* Charley told himself not to be envious of the bearded outlaw—after all, Charley was supposed to be pulling away from the gang—but he couldn't help feeling that something was slipping away from him.

"We got a job for you," Billy said when Wilcox walked back to the table. "Seeing as you're such a good friend of ours, we figured you wouldn't mind ridin' over to Fort Sumner and takin' a look around. We're not sure if Garrett has gone after us yet or what the hell he's got in his head. We figured you could do that for us, Tom."

Putting the blankets on the table, Wilcox gave Billy a blank look, hesitating slightly. "It's a hell of a night to be traipsin' around, isn't it? Can I wait till morning?"

"Now why would you want to do that, Tom? Think of all the time we'd lose. You don't think Pat would laze around just because it's kind of cold out, do you?"

"No, I suppose not," Wilcox conceded. He wiped his hands on his pants, as if the blankets had made them filthy. "And I guess I could stand the ride well enough if I had to."

"Sure you could, a big, strappin' man like you."

"It'd be a whole lot better," put in Rudabaugh, "than sendin' your boy out again." He glanced at Pablo with some meaning he wasn't about to explain, then he smiled at Wilcox.

After Wilcox had pulled on his greatcoat and his gauntlets, Billy stepped over to him and draped an arm around the man's shoulders. "Like Dave there says, it's better than your boy going out." He guided the rancher toward the door, giving the man's shoulder a friendly squeeze. "And just think, if you run into any trouble, Pablo'll be with us and we can take care of him. Any trouble at all, we'll take care of the boy. Go on, Tom, you do right by us now, okay?"

Charley was at Billy's side as soon as Wilcox was out the door. "You're not really going to do anything to Pablo, are you, Kid? You were just bluffin' Tom, just making sure he got the message. That's all you were gettin' at, right?"

Billy cocked his head back, as if he needed to move back a bit in order to see Bowdre clearly. "Charley, you must be God-awful fagged to be thinkin' like that. What would I want to hurt the boy for? Go on and get some sleep and stop worryin'.

Hell, just look at Pablo over there, he doesn't need you worryin' about him." Billy laughed and slapped Charley on the back. "He's worried enough for all of us."

Charley had a dumb smile on his face as he watched Billy walk over to Rudabaugh at the table. He decided he had gotten a good enough answer; even if he had thought there was something false about Billy's words, he wouldn't have been able to hold onto his doubts for very long. Too many other worries were filling his mind.

Once he had made his pallet on the floor, he lay there listening to the shifting bodies and steady breathing that told him the other men were falling asleep. He looked at Rudabaugh keeping watch, silhouetted bleakly in the window; Charley couldn't shake the idea that he was to take the bearded outlaw's place as sentry in another two hours. As weary as he was, Charley knew he had no chance of going to sleep.

There has to be some way to slip out of here. He kept telling himself that, but no convincing ideas came to him. *Maybe,* he thought, *I can say that I'll go fetch Wilcox if he takes too long in coming back.*

Not very likely, he then decided. *Billy's not about to send out a second man if he thinks the first one isn't going to be able to make it. But then, maybe I can go out on a scout, find out if Garrett's somewhere near. Billy knows I can cover this ground as good as anybody. I might have a chance at that, but hell, I can't even talk about it until tomorrow, after we give Wilcox a chance to get back.*

Charley cursed himself for being a damn fool, for leaving Fort Sumner with Billy and the rest. He had been worried that Pat would catch up to him if he stayed in town; after all, Garrett might have heard about his running the stolen cattle to the Tularosa Valley, and if the deal with Captain Lea had already gone sour, then Charley would have been really up against it. All of this had made sense at the time—even Rita had told him to leave, to play it safe. Now Charley knew that anything would have been better than holing up with the gang as Garrett closed in.

Sifting through all his worries, Bowdre was finally able to extract a comforting thought. Garrett might catch up to them, and they might have to fight their way out, but his being with Billy might be his best insurance of all. He had made it out of the burning building in Lincoln by sticking with the Kid, and there had been scrapes before and since in which Billy somehow had managed to lead the way clear. *Just keep close to Billy,* Charley thought. *Until something else comes along, that's your best bet.*

26

"They've got my boy there, Pat. I don't know what they'll do to him if they find out I came here to talk to you. Especially that Rudabaugh—I swear I don't know what he'll do, and I don't know if the Kid can hold him back." Grasping the whiskey glass in both hands, Wilcox slouched over the table, the last of the icicles on his beard melting into beads of water that dripped onto his greatcoat. Pat saw that the man's glass was empty. He told Beaver Smith to bring over a bottle.

"You don't have to help us out if you don't think you can," Pat said to Wilcox. He had trouble putting some conviction into the words. He just felt it had to be said.

"Damned if I'll back down," Wilcox shot back. "The Kid comes around like he owns the damn place, putting us in a bad spot, threatening us. I don't need a friend like that." Wilcox stopped as doubt flickered once again in his eyes. He took another swallow of whiskey.

Pat said, "We'll just have to play it so the Kid won't know. For Pablo's sake."

Not seeming to hear Pat, Wilcox dropped his gaze to the table and dragged his glass from one side to the other. "You think Billy would really hurt the boy? You think it's come to that?"

Pat lifted a shoulder to say he didn't know. "Seems to me we shouldn't give him the chance. Or Rudabaugh either. We catch them, you won't have to worry about it."

Wilcox sat perfectly still and waited. He wanted Pat to explain how it would be done. Garrett figured the man was already half-convinced.

"I don't want to fight Billy at your house," Garrett said. "He's on the lookout for me there, and I don't want to get Pablo and your partner caught in the crossfire. All I need is somebody to tell me when he leaves. I want you to go back, Tom, and let me know as soon as the gang is on their way. Can you do that?"

Wilcox's face was blank, but Pat could see that he was thinking it through. "I can do it if they keep believing I'm on their side," he said.

"Tell them I'm still in town. I've got a few men with me, and I want to get back to Roswell, but I'm afraid to ride out of here because I think Billy might have set up an ambush. Tell Billy his best bet is to stay away from town."

"The way he was talking, he's going to want more persuading before he thinks I'm on the square."

"All right," Pat said, thinking of some information

Wilcox could pass along, something that wouldn't hurt the posse. "Tell him about Valdez," he finally said. "Yeah, that's it. Tell him we got him arrested and that he shouldn't trust any message coming from him. The Kid'll like that."

Wilcox nodded, running the plan through his head. "That might do it, Pat. I sure hope to hell it does."

"Tell it to him the right way and it *will* do it. Take some time to rest up before you head out. By the time you get back there you'll know how to say it. You'll see." Pat turned to Smith. "Beaver, get him a warm bath. He's got some cold riding to get out of his bones and some more ahead of him. And Beaver," he added when the saloonkeeper walked heavily toward the tub in the back room. "Better find somebody else other than Billy to buy cows from after this. Maybe I can find somebody who'll do business with you. You know, as a favor to an old friend."

Smith threw him a bitter scowl; he pressed his lips together to keep himself from answering, then trudged off to the back room. Garrett knew it was meanspirited to kick the man when he was down, even though it was true that Beaver bought stolen beef, but he couldn't deny himself the pleasure of needling an old friend who had turned away from him. Billy would be caught soon, probably within a couple of days, Pat figured, and he could afford to be a little cocky. *I got it coming,* he told himself.

When he was left alone at the table, Pat considered the most likely hideouts Billy would ride to once he left the Wilcox ranch. As the whiskey loosened his thoughts, he imagined the different places and the approaches that would keep his posse concealed until they were close enough to strike. Involuntarily, he also saw Billy's face, his lips drawn back in a bucktoothed grimace, just above the double-action Colt. The revolver would be smoking and pointed at Garrett as he moved in on the hideout.

Pushing himself away from the table, Pat walked out onto the plaza to clear his mind.

Now late in the morning, the sunlight was about as warm as it was likely to get that day, and people were going outside to take care of chores. An old woman pushed a cart filled with firewood toward the houses on the west side of town, while a freighter in a thick beaver coat drove a wagon past pedestrians and children throwing snowballs toward the northbound road. Pat had already talked to the man and was confident that he had no interest in getting word to the Kid once he left Fort Sumner. Crossing the square, on his way to pass the time with his posse outside the Bowdre house, Pat heard a steady, rasping sound and turned to see two Mexicans digging a grave for Tom O'Folliard in the old military cemetary.

A hint of thaw had been in the air all day, but only now did Billy see any sign that it might actually arrive. Along the trail through the hills, the snow began to soften and its melting crust glistened in the slanting sunlight. For all that, though, Billy still wasn't counting on a true respite from the cold. In a couple of hours, night would come and with it a new wave of harsh weather, possibly as bad as the others that had crossed this country in the last few weeks. *At least,* Billy figured, *we should've reached shelter by then.*

The hoof falls directly behind him quickened and drew closer until Dave Rudabaugh brought his horse alongside. The Kansas man looked to their rear, faced forward, then looked back again; his lips were pressed into a thin line that twitched slightly at the right corner.

"You goin' to tell me what the hell's eatin' you, Dave? Or are you just goin' to fuss yourself to death?"

Rudabaugh squinted at the trail ahead in an effort to put the Kid's impudence out of mind. "We can turn back. You know that, Kid, don't you? There's no sense in runnin' if we don't have to."

"We're doing the right thing."

"That's what you say. But we won't have to run anymore if we just kill the bastard."

Billy sighed heavily, frustrated. "You just can't let a thing lie, can you, Dave? I told you this here isn't the time to make a fight with Garrett. He's killed one of us and he's got his blood up. There'll be a better time. There's got to be."

"But Wilcox said all Garrett wants to do is go back to Roswell." Rudabaugh glanced back at the rest of the gang, looking furtive, as if he thought a spy might be among them. "Comin' this far away like we have, that can be a decoy, make him think we're runnin. We can double back now and slip up on him if we do it right."

"Sure, Garrett wants to run back to Roswell," said Billy. "Maybe that's what he wanted to do yesterday, but I'm not betting on him staying that way. I got us a place to hole up until we know for certain what he's up to. Then we'll start to figure."

Rudabaugh unleashed a stream of brown tobacco

juice that sailed into the snowbank on the right. "Shit," he said, his voice mild; he was getting too weary of this argument to work up much emotion. He rode alongside Billy in silence until the trail narrowed and he had to fall back into a single file again.

"Good idea, though," Billy called back to him. "Even if it isn't the right idea for now."

Oughtn't to let him get too discouraged and mean, the Kid thought. *Dave's an ornery son-of-a-bitch, but it's better to be caught* with *him than without him. After all, that idea of his to make Pablo a hostage while his old man went out to scout was pretty smart. And with O'Folliard gone, there aren't too many amigos left to really talk to.*

Billy looked back at the line of four riders behind him. Except for Charley Bowdre, all of the old boys from the War were gone, and there was no telling how long Charley would be staying. The Kid had seen the way Bowdre looked at the road back to Fort Sumner when they left the Wilcox ranch last night. Charley hadn't known that anyone was noticing, but Billy could see the homesick look on his face. There was no telling when he might light out and leave the gang for good, and that would leave just Billy to carry on with the new men.

Looking at it that way, the Kid couldn't help appreciating having Rudabaugh around. Sure, the Kansas tough had nearly cut him open back at Greathouse's place, but that, after all, was water under the bridge. *A good leader of men has to look to the future,* Billy told himself, feeling just a little proud of his open-mindedness.

Just after dark they reached a stone house fronting

a string of low, snow-spotted hills. Chased by a freezing wind, the men rode as quickly as they could around the dry arroyo to get to the front doorway. The door itself had been missing for a couple of years, but the house's walls were well chinked and kept out most of the wind, and the house had some spare room once the five men were inside. Billy brought his horse inside to keep it warm, and so did Rudabaugh.

Throughout the night, Billy found he couldn't stay asleep for very long. Several times his deep sleep would suddenly vanish and he would find himself lying on his back with his eyes wide open. He would try to put his finger on what was troubling him, but the only thing he was aware of was a vague sense of discomfort, compounded by snatches of dreams that made no sense and that he could only remember for a few seconds at a time.

He woke at first light with his limbs feeling heavy, yearning for more rest. Sitting up on the house's dirt floor, he wrapped his arms around his uplifted knees and glowered straight ahead, in no mood to speak to Wilson or Bowdre stirring themselves at his side.

I've been running too long, he brooded

The thought settled him as it seemed to crystallize all the fuzzy, troubling notions that had plagued him through the night. *I may be a grown-up man,* he thought, *but I'm a young one too, and I'm entitled to some fancy-free living, something other than dodging posses every which way I turn.* It occurred to Billy that he might be right in leaving the territory after all. Down in Old Mexico would be plenty of tequila and friendly senoritas, and nothing to do but laze around. He still had some money left from the last herd he had sold at Tularosa. That could last him a long time down south.

Looking at the other men in the stone house, he wondered if he should bother telling them what he was thinking or whether he should just pick up and leave. That was the whole problem: talking over every little detail with his men, making sure every little thing was done just right, thinking for five men instead of just one. As if to gall him, the thought came to him that only the horses inside the house had been fed the night before. *Damn it,* he told himself, *if I don't tell them to do right by the animals outside, these boys'd probably just end up afoot and stranded.*

"Charley," he called. "Take out the damn nose bag and feed those animals outside. That's your horse out there, you know. You'd think I was the only one that had ever worked in the saddle around here."

Bowdre rubbed his eyes, glowered at the Kid, then got up without a word to do as he was told.

Billy shook his head.

Maybe I'll just set out on my own and the hell with all of them, he thought. Billy then tried to put a halter on his irritation. There was no sense in jumping to any decision just yet. This stone house was a good hiding place, one that Pat wouldn't know about, and the Kid could just wait for a while until the right idea came to him. He knew he would figure it out if he just gave it some time. *One thing I know,* he told himself, *I'll take Rudabaugh with me to*

Mexico if I take anybody. At least there's one fella who knows enough to come in out of the rain.

Just then, a shout and some gunshots outside blasted the morning stillness; first one lone shot, then a volley of three or four.

27

The Kid doesn't know as much as he thinks he does.

That's what Pat thought when he saw the trail veer to the left, headed toward a pass through the hills. Just a few miles from the Wilcox ranch, he led the posse through the darkness over the westward route to a place where the tracks disappeared along a sloping ledge of rock. The snow had melted and drained off, leaving the stony surface bare. Pat judged that the gang had followed this untrackable stretch for as long as they could to throw him off the scent, but still Garrett had no doubt where the outlaws had gone.

When Wilcox had returned to Fort Sumner with word that the gang had left the ranch, Pat had settled on a few places as the Kid's most likely destinations. None of those guesses turned out to be right; the direction of the trail convinced Pat that he should have been thinking of Stinking Springs all along.

Pat had heard of the place only once before. It had been soon after coming to Lincoln County, when he had been desperate and foolish enough to get tangled in Billy's rustling schemes. After that first deal he had decided to pull out, but not before Tom O'Folliard had told him about the deserted house where the next cattle purchase would take place. Skirting the ledge of rock, Pat now led his posse down a slope toward a sweep of tableland, a more direct route to the house at Stinking Springs. *The Kid's cagey,* he told himself, *but he doesn't know how much* I *know.*

The dry arroyo in front of the stone house provided an ideal hiding place; moving along this gully in the last hour before dawn, Pat was able to bring four of his men within forty feet of the open doorway. John Poe took the rest of the posse to the hills in back.

The night's cold made Pat's teeth chatter as he waited for first light to give him a clear view of the house. Beside him, Bell, Roibal, Bozeman, and Chambers were pressed against the arroyo bank to shield themselves from the wind. Pat tried not to curse the frigid air blowing across the valley; since they were downwind of the house, the wind was something to be counted in their favor, no matter how brutal it was.

When the man carrying the nose bag stepped out of the house, the early morning's shivering misery was suddenly left behind, replaced by a swift exchange of actions. Pat felt his own movements were awkward and much too slow at first. His joints still creaky from the freezing temperature, he flopped clumsily onto his belly as the man came out into the open, and then he wrestled with his Winchester to swing it into firing position. The sound must have caught the outlaw's attention because he turned away from the horse he was about to feed and faced the arroyo. Pat sensed the alarm in the man's movements; he shouted before the outlaw could do anything else.

"Put up your hands! Now!"

What happened next was pure instinct on both sides. The man in front of the house pulled a gun from his coat pocket and pointed it at the first target that presented itself. In a flash of heightened sensation, Pat was aware, for just an instant, that the outlaw's pistol was aimed at J. W. Bell, who had raised himself above the rim of the arroyo to Garrett's left. In the next instant, Pat's right hand jacked the lever of his rifle and squeezed the trigger, working the lever once more as the first shot roared. He immediately fired a second round at his man, and other shots boomed to either side of him, a pounding chorus that echoed off the hills on the far side of the house. It wasn't until the outlaw crumpled, then staggered back, that Pat realized he had just killed Charley Bowdre.

Pat lay stock-still against the bank as he watched Charley stumble back through the doorway. Each of Bowdre's limbs seemed to follow its own command, his body wobbling out of control as if it were performing a spastic dance. He collapsed into the darkness of the house's interior while muzzles spat flames through the doorway and window.

The barrage was answered by a new volley from

the rest of the posse, but Garrett's hands didn't move to trigger another round. Reflexively, he slumped down the bank a few inches until most of his body was well protected; only his hat, his forehead, and his eyes remained above the arroyo's lip. As he stared at the house's empty doorway, his glimpse of Charley's contorted face stayed with him, an image that was cast into harsh relief by the feelings that surged through him. Another face came to mind, but Garrett did everything he could to will it away. There was still too much to be done. There was no time to let memories prey upon him.

A voice called from the house. It sounded like Billy.

"Charley wants to come out, Pat! He's shot up bad and he doesn't want to die in here!"

Pat hesitated. Bell and Chambers turned to him with questioning looks.

"Is he up to something?" asked Chambers.

Suddenly, Pat was tired of trying to outguess the Kid. He shouted to the house. "Send him on out, Billy!"

Charley appeared in the doorway, his legs unsteady, propped up from behind by the Kid. Billy stooped to pick up the revolver Bowdre had dropped at the threshold and pressed it into his friend's right hand. He spoke quietly to Charley, too quietly for Pat to hear.

"You still got a full chamber," the Kid said, "and you can still walk. Go on and get some of the sons-of-bitches that murdered you before you go."

Charley nodded, a gesture that might have meant agreement, or might have been simply a semiconscious movement of a dying man. Billy shoved him forward, and Charley plodded toward the arroyo.

At the sight of the revolver in the outlaw's hand, all of Pat's men brought their rifles to their shoulders. For a moment, Charley brought his gun hand up, managing to raise it a few inches, but then his arm went slack and the revolver hung by his side. He lost his balance. He was able to right himself, propelling himself forward at a headlong, uncontrolled pace until he planted his feet with a new assurance, just a few feet short of the arroyo. In that moment he seemed to train his eyes on Garrett. His right knee then buckled, he staggered forward and then slumped to his side. He looked up at Pat, gesturing to the stone house.

"I should've . . ." he rasped. "I wish . . ." His mouth couldn't form any more words, but his eyes were still riveted on Pat's face.

Slowly, Garrett pulled him into the arroyo.

Going to his saddle, he took out a blanket, stretched it at the foot of the bank, and laid Bowdre on top of it. He saw that Charley was already dead.

The outlaws opened up again and the posse fired back to keep them pinned down. At the new outburst of fire, Garrett pulled himself away from the dead young man to resume his position at the top of the bank. Before he could fire his first shot, he noticed that the reins of one of the horses tied outside the house started to move. He then saw what had made them move. A hand poked out of the window, grabbed the reins and tugged on them. This time the hand succeeded in pulling the reins clear of the projecting rafter where they had been tied. The horse was led toward the doorway.

This maneuver got Pat's mind back on track. Knowing that there were five outlaws in the party, he figured that there had to be two horses inside in addition to the three mounts tied to the rafters. With Charley gone, that meant that the gang could make a mounted getaway if they could get a third horse inside, assuming that two of the outlaws doubled up. Pat pressed the stock of his Winchester to his shoulder.

His first thought was to shoot the reins out of the outlaw's hand, but he didn't have a clear angle, and the target was moving too much for such a precise shot. As the horse neared the doorway, another idea occurred to him. He set his sights and waited till the animal had poked its head inside. Then he fired. The horse went down, wedging itself in the doorway as it hit the ground. Anyone trying to get over that blockade would have to slow down so much that he would make himself an easy target.

Without pausing, Pat then swung his rifle toward the other two horses. He took deliberate aim and shot the reins of one animal, shifted the rifle and cut the other reins as well. The two horses wandered away, oblivious to the gunfire and curses from the stone house.

Rudabaugh decided it was all Wilson's fault. After being pinned down by the posse for three hours, he was desperate to lash out at anything. "What the hell were you doing?" he shouted at Wilson. "All you had to do was get the damn horse inside. I swear I never saw a body take his own sweet time about something like that. I swear I never did."

Johnny Wilson was slumped on the floor with his back to the wall, resting his head in his hands. He muttered something in reply, but no one could hear what it was. Wilson then moved his right hand in a quick, jerky motion, and Billy, sitting just a few feet from him, thought he saw him wipe away a tear. Billy picked up a rusty spur off the floor and threw it against the far wall as hard as he could. Sometimes Johnny made him sick to his stomach. It made him even sicker to realize that there was no point in railing at the damn fool.

"Johnny's not to blame," he told Rudabaugh. "It's that son-of-a-bitch Garrett—he's the goddamned problem. You just can't shake the bastard. Doesn't make any damn difference how fast you bring the horse in, the bastard's going to shoot him down every time. Damn, he doesn't miss much." Billy slammed his back against the wall. To give his hands something to do, he checked the chamber of his double-action Colt, then realized how stupid the action was. *What difference does it make how many bullets we got if we end up starving to death?* he thought.

His eyes rested on Pickett sitting across from him. The man's face was white, his eyes wide open; he kept rubbing his right wrist for no particular reason. Billy could see it was up to him to raise the spirits around here.

"Look at it this way, boys," he said, "with that dead horseflesh in the door like that, we can't hardly smell Rudabaugh anymore."

Even as he let out the last of these words, the Kid realized how pitiful his attempt at humor was. He stared at the window above him as an oppressive silence gripped the room. Bleak as things were, a lot more was needed to keep his men going than a tired joke.

"I'm God-awful hungry," said Pickett. "I'm so hungry it hurts, I swear it hurts all inside."

The silence resumed for several more moments, then Rudabaugh lurched to his feet, levered his rifle, and unleashed a flurry of shots out the window. The return fire made him plunge back to the dirt floor, shouting at the top of his lungs:

"You son-of-a-bitch bastards! I'll kill every last one of you! You bastards!"

The explosion seemed to do him some good; at least it quieted him down as he slouched against the wall, cradling his rifle, gazing with glassy eyes across the room. Billy was grateful for the silence now. Somehow the hunger seemed easier to bear when it was quiet.

Someone shouted from the arroyo out front.

"How you boys doing in there?"

Billy tilted his head toward the window; he had no desire to move any more than that. "Not so bad, Pat," he answered. "I'd feel a whole lot better though if you'd just stand up so I could take a shot at you."

"I'm not feeling real obliging today, Kid. Sorry. But if you boys want anything just let me know."

"Well, if we had some wood we might be willing to cook us some horsemeat. Providing you don't shoot us through the door while we cut off a chunk."

"Don't start eating horse now, Kid. There's plenty of game out around here. Why don't you come on out and take a look?"

"You're a real funny bastard, Pat."

"Okay, Kid, suit yourself. Just the same, anything you want out there, you just let me know. You remember that."

Rudabaugh grumbled for a while, not distinctly

enough to be understood, but his ferocious tone make it clear he was talking about Garrett. He became quiet again when the faint odor of a campfire drifted into the house, traveling with the wind from the hills in back.

The old woman's just keeping himself warm, Billy told himself, desperate to believe this explanation and to keep his other theory at bay. But it was no good. A few minutes later, the smell of roasting meat reached the house to confirm his worst suspicion. *The long-legged bastard can't blast us out of here,* the Kid thought, *so he's going to lure us out instead.*

It didn't take long for Billy to realize that the tactic was going to work. If they stayed where they were, sooner or later they would die of hunger. There was no other possibility.

Before announcing to the others what they would have to do, he reassured himself that Pat would make sure he got a proper trial. That meant he still had time.

"We ain't done fightin' yet," was Rudabaugh's response after the Kid spoke up. Billy gave him a long exasperated look.

"Pat isn't stupid enough to send himself in as a hostage," he said. "You got any other plans, Dave? Maybe you figure on stepping out into a line of Winchesters."

Rudabaugh looked resigned after that, his stomach obviously speaking louder than his instinct to fight. He even gave Billy a dirty white handkerchief to wave out the window.

"Decided to take up your offer," shouted the Kid. "We wouldn't mind some of that meat."

"Come on out, Kid. We've got some waiting for you."

Meeting Garrett by the arroyo, with his guns left inside the house, Billy managed to put on a smile as he looked up at the lawman.

"We got to put the irons on you boys before we can let you eat," said Pat. "You understand, right, Kid?"

"Just doin' your job, I know."

"I'm glad to hear you won't be giving us any trouble." Billy hadn't said any such thing, but now he knew there wouldn't even be any point in trying to make trouble; Pat wasn't going to stand for it and that's all there was to it.

"I sure hope you'll be taking us to Lincoln for trial," said Billy, as J. W. Bell clasped a manacle onto his left wrist.

"We won't," answered Pat. "It's Santa Fe we'll be going to. That make any difference, Kid?"

Billy shrugged. "Just that Lincoln was such a nice place to break out of the last time I was in jail there."

The second manacle was put on his right wrist. Billy held out his hands as far apart as they would go—only a foot—and gazed at the restraint as if it were some piece of work he had requested. *Maybe I was wrong giving up just yet,* he mused. *Then again, maybe I wasn't.*

It was night when the possemen rode back into Fort Sumner plaza. Only a few townspeople were in the square, but many more came out when word was spread about Garrett's captives. Passing the onlookers, Pat led the way to Pete Maxwell's place, then he left his men and prisoners behind. He would have to take care of the next part of the job on his own.

Rita Bowdre was just opening her door to see what was the cause of the commotion when Garrett brought the wagon to a stop alongside the porch. They held each other's gaze for a long time. For his part, Pat knew that he was staring because he had no idea what to say. He judged that Rita's eyes never left his face because she was reluctant to look at what was in the wagon bed.

There was none of the anguish that Pat had expected to see in her face. Neither was there any of the fury that she had shown him a couple of days before. Her chubby face seemed lifeless.

Pat swung down from the seat and walked to the rear of the wagon. In the wagon bed, Charley lay on his back with his legs splayed. A sense of tidiness made Pat bring the two legs together in a more dignified pose.

His eyes ran across the bloodstained coat and the muddy chaps, and he finally thought of something to say. He took some coins from his vest pocket.

"There's enough money here to buy a new suit of clothes for the burying," he said. "It'll pay for the funeral too." He looked up only when he reached the last of his words, and saw that Rita was closer, standing now with one foot in the plaza. Her frozen mask was betrayed by a searing look in her black eyes. Pat felt like a clumsy idiot.

Moving quickly, he placed the money on the wagon bed and started walking away. He thought he could hear Rita step away from the porch, toward the wagon; he wasn't sure if he had actually heard her steps above his own, but he seemed to sense her movement. In the next moment, her wail pierced the air from one end of the plaza to the other.

At Maxwell's place, Pat told his men to get the prisoners saddled. "We're starting for Santa Fe right now," he said.

BACKTRACK

28

In the end Billy got his wish and wound up back in Lincoln. The route he took, though, was long and roundabout, and the experience was bitter.

All the way to Santa Fe, Billy kept his eyes peeled for a chance to escape, but trying to get away from Garrett was an exercise in futility. After being delivered to the federal marshal, Billy didn't have Garrett to worry about anymore, and he and Rudabaugh wasted no time in taking advantage of the new situation; they immediately attempted to dig their way out of the Santa Fe jail with spoons and bedsprings. Rudabaugh came up with the idea of hiding the unearthed dirt under their bedding, which seemed like a good idea to the Kid, but it wasn't enough in itself to fool the guards. They watched the prisoners like hungry hawks and thought the blanket in the corner looked suspicious. It appeared to be carelessly thrown there, but one of the guards lifted it to find the hole underneath. After that, Billy couldn't sneeze without finding a delegation of jailers peering in through the doorway.

The Kid's next best hope was the court. Although his first trial was heartening, he soon learned that the judges were no better than Chisum and Wallace and all the other sons-of-bitches in this world.

First he faced a murder charge in the federal court in Santa Fe for the killing of Buckshot Roberts on the Mescalero reservation. Billy took a dim view of that. *A mighty peculiar thing to bring up now,* he thought, *seeing as we dusted old Buckshot a long while ago, and hell, it was during the War, wasn't it? What the hell were we supposed to do to Roberts with a war going on—kiss the ugly bastard?* But then, he figured, *that just goes to show how they're all so petty and set against me, dredging up such things as Buckshot Roberts the way they are.*

Petty or not, the charge didn't stand up because witnesses were hard to find. But any hope planted in Billy by this trial was then destroyed when he was taken by a federal deputy marshal to the territorial court in Mesilla, where he was tried for the murder of Sheriff Brady. *More old business,* he brooded. *There's just no end to the mean-mindedness of the powerful men in this territory.*

Billy had to listen to a string of witnesses describing how he had shot Brady from behind an adobe wall, witnesses that Billy had known back in happier days before the Lincoln War got started. Billy's depression deepened. The simple truth that he had shot the man was established by the first one or two witnesses, but then he had to hear it driven into the ground over and over again. And to listen to them, you'd never know that four other boys were with him that day; maybe they didn't do as much as the Kid, but they were there. But then, that just showed how hopeless it all was.

The Kid knew the cards were stacked against him, and he felt no surprise, nor sadness, nor much of anything at all, when Judge Bristol sentenced him to hang by the neck until dead. May 13, 1881—that was to be the day, less than a month off. And the place would be Lincoln town, his old stomping grounds, and his last ground of any kind by the look of it.

If things could get worse, Billy was sure he had no idea how—until the day came for his transfer from Mesilla. The two men who arrived to take him to Lincoln were Deputy Sheriff J. W. Bell—whom Billy had no feelings about one way or the other—and Bob Olinger, sporting a badge that said he was a deputy U.S. marshal. That was something different.

The Kid and Olinger said nothing to each other until they were well out of town, but the look that passed between them when they first came face to face bristled with hatred. Billy had known him for the son-of-a-bitch that he was even before the Lincoln War had started, based on the stories that had made the rounds about the man's bullying ways as town marshal of Seven Rivers. Olinger's shotgunning of Billy's friend Frank McNab during the War just confirmed what everybody had said about him.

As they rode away from Mesilla, Bob Olinger brought his horse alongside the wagon that held Billy. He looked to one side, then the other, as if there might be something of interest nearby other than the Kid. Matter-of-factly, he said, "A scrawny little neck like yours, most likely your head'll pop clean off your shoulders when you hit the end of that rope. That'll sure be something to see, Kid. It surely will."

Billy knew better than to expect anything different the rest of the way to Lincoln.

"I still can't figure you givin' Olinger the job, Pat. I know you're supposed to make sure I hang—I understand that—but did you have to make my last days a living misery like this?" Billy paused as J. W. Bell dealt him his fifth card. Still adjusting to the weights of the new manacles on his wrists, the Kid fumbled with the cards a bit before he managed to fan them. "I know horse thieves who wouldn't drink at the same bar as a man like Olinger, and don't you tell me you don't know what kind of bastard he is. You know him from Fort Sumner the same as me."

Pat's face was set into hard angles that showed nothing as he leaned back in his chair, studied his cards, and glanced across the table at the Kid. J. W. Bell looked nervously at the two men. He couldn't fathom how they could talk and play cards together, after all that had happened, and he kept waiting for some eruption between the two of them. For the most part he kept quiet, as if too many words from him might somehow push the trigger.

"Hanging you isn't my doing," Garrett said. "That was the court's decision, Billy. You know that."

The Kid smirked at him.

"And it also wasn't me that killed Sheriff Brady or Roberts or Morton or any of the others," Pat continued. "Didn't you know it'd catch up to you, Kid?"

"There was a reason for all of them, all of those killings."

Pat studied Billy for a moment, then asked J. W. for two cards.

"Brady needed killing," the Kid said. "He was as crooked as they come—everybody knew that. And he was behind Tunstall getting murdered. That's fact."

"You shot a sheriff in the back, Billy. And you boys had Buckshot Roberts outnumbered when you took him."

"He was huntin' bounty. He pushed it on me."

"And Bernstein—what about him?"

"He couldn't stay out of something that wasn't his concern," Billy said.

Garrett sighed tiredly and shook his head. With all the cards and bets in place, the time had come to play the hands. Bell folded, and the Kid's pairs of kings and fives beat Pat's pair of sevens.

"You know, Kid," Garrett said, "if they didn't get a conviction on Brady, they wouldn't have stopped there. There was still Jim Carlyle, and don't tell me he forgot to mind his own business. He was deputized. His business was bringing you in."

Billy took in the pile of matchsticks that substituted for chips. For a moment his eyes stayed fixed on the tabletop. "There's more to it than that," he said. Pat waited, but the Kid didn't say what else there was to it.

"I suppose," Billy said after the next hand was dealt, "that old Bob Olinger has done his share of killing, eh Pat?"

"I guess he has, Kid. But he knew when to stop."

"You're hiring scum," Billy snapped at him. "It's

as simple as that." Turning to Bell, he added, "No offense, J. W. It's not you I'm talking about, you know that. It's that damned Olinger that Pat here thinks is such a fine lawman."

Glancing at Pat, Bell kept his mouth shut.

"I didn't say he was a good lawman," said Garrett, "or any kind of lawman at all. I just figured he'd be a man who'd make damn sure you didn't get away, Billy. I don't want to have to hunt you down a second time."

The subject of Olinger kept Billy's eyes blazing for several more moments, then he managed to get the better of his hatred and put his mind back on his hand. He accepted a card from Pat, rearranged his hand, and looked up smiling. "Kind of insulted, Pat, the way you're talking about not wanting to hunt me again. We could have us a hell of a time the second time around. It'd be a hell of a ball, it surely would."

"I'll pass," Garrett said, placing his cards face-down on the table. He took his watch from his vest pocket and checked the time. "And I'm out too. Got some sheriff business to tend to."

Billy said, "You'll be coming back for the hanging?"

Pat stopped, halfway out of his chair, then stepped away from the table. "Will you be wanting me to see it, Billy?"

Billy pursed his lips, tilted his head, and gave Garrett a long, considering look. "I don't know, Pat. I hear a hanged man shits all over himself. I don't guess I need more people watching than has to be."

Pat wanted desperately to get of there, but found himself rooted to the floor. There was something he should say—he knew it—but for the life of him he couldn't think of what it could be. Billy sat looking at him, a grin on his face, a smile that Pat could not understand. With nothing else to do, he waved to the Kid and walked out the door.

The silence in the room was broken a couple of minutes later when J. W. asked if Billy wanted to play another hand, head-to-head.

"No," said the Kid, serious now, "I don't think so." He fingered the cards left in front of him and idly pushed them around. Slipping off his hat, J. W. ran his finger along the inside band to fill in some of the time.

"You just want to sit for a while?" J. W. asked. "Is that it?"

Billy nodded his head slowly. "Yeah. Yeah, I guess I do."

His leg shackles clanging with each step, Billy crossed the big room to the corner window where he had left the rocking chair. He sat there watching the street below. His manacled hands rested in his lap. Standing by his side, J. W. finished rolling a cigarette, then handed Billy the makings to roll one for himself.

The brilliant spring sunshine outside dried the street's top layer into a bed of dust, churned up by a passing wagon loaded with freight.

"He'll be headed for Fort Stanton, I'd expect," said Bell, pointing down at the wagon. "That'll be the business for me, soon as I get everything straightened away."

"You'll be tryin' it again, will you, J. W.?" Billy's eyes never left the street.

"Sooner or later I surely will. The wife, she sure

likes an enterprising man, she does." He was about to say more, but then realized he was talking about what he'd do after the hanging. The Kid never complained about that kind of talk, but J. W. figured it had to pain him. He turned his sad-dog look away from Billy and headed back to the table.

The Kid continued to gaze at the street.

Perhaps the worst thing of all for him was being cooped up in this particular building to await his execution. The old Murphy & Dolan store, of all places. Not so long ago—the War can't be that far back, Billy thought—this place had been the headquarters for his enemies. At one time Billy had dreamed of bursting in here with guns blazing to kill the last of the sons-of-bitches that were eluding him. Now it was the last shelter he would ever have.

After Murphy had died and Dolan had left the country, Lincoln County had taken over the two-story structure for public use. In the room next to Billy's was Garrett's office, and beyond that, on the other side of the hall, was the room for the other prisoners, the ones that didn't warrant any special treatment. Looking out the second-floor window of Murphy's old bedroom, Billy decided, as he usually did, that there was something awful about this view, something terrible but fascinating at the same time.

Down there, just a bit farther up the street, was the adobe wall where he had hidden, waiting for Sheriff Brady to walk into his sights. Just a little beyond that was another set of memories—the charred remains of the McSween house. Fighting the good fight was supposed to mean something in this world, but Billy and the boys had fought the best fight possible, and what had they gotten for their trouble? A curse on their heads, the Kid thought.

What puzzled him the most was that people only remembered him for gunplay and death in this town. While those memories continued to weave in and out of his mind, they never seemed to last very long. Mostly he remembered the mischief, the small trouble with Tom O'Folliard and Charley Bowdre when he had first come to this country. Other times, he remembered, they had lived as high and easy as any young cowboys could, drinking and singing in the saloons, looking for the girls called soiled doves along the back streets. Nobody remembered the happy young fellow who had been ready to be anyone's friend if they treated him right. *Could it really be only three years ago?* he mused. *Just three years ago when Chisum gave me my first steady work in this country?*

Heavy bootsteps entered the room, and Billy's insides froze. He didn't move, didn't bother to turn around. He knew who had come in, and looking the man's way would just start things that much sooner. They would start soon enough.

Bob Olinger eased his thick body onto the windowsill, just a couple of feet from Billy's chair. Working methodically, he broke open the 12-gauge American Arms shotgun, pulled out one of the loads, and checked the inside of the casing. He smiled at Billy, then went through the motions with the load from the second barrel. He finished the procedure by snapping the weapon closed with a loud click.

"All there, Billy," he said. "Eighteen buckshot in each barrel."

"Now that sure as shit eases my mind," said Billy.

Olinger's smile didn't let up, but iron went into his eyes. "Just want to make sure you don't figure on running, Kid. These two loads cutting through your back'll just make a goddamned mess of you. You wouldn't want any of your girlfriends seein' you looking like a chewed-up old doll, would you?"

Billy didn't say anything. He wasn't sure whether it was fear or fury that was making him shake.

"Not to mention all them folks that'd be disappointed, not getting to see you dangle," Olinger went on. "I figure Bob Beckwith's folks'd be here to see that. I know your murderin' Bob will rest easier with *me* after I get to see you choke to death. Or maybe your neck'll just break. Which will it be, do you think?"

"For Christ's sake," called J. W. Bell from the table. "He knows what's comin'. Leave off already."

Olinger got to his feet, turning slightly to face Bell, careful to place the shotgun's twin muzzles in the Kid's face. "Just makin' sure the Kid here gets the message. Hell, there ain't that much time left to make certain he gets the whole idea."

Sauntering a few feet to the right, he came to the calender nailed to the wall, the adobe room's only form of decoration. "And damned if I forgot to cross today off," he said. He took a stubby pencil from his pocket and marked a neat X over today's date. "How about that, Kid? Just two weeks and three days left. Sure hope you don't get a back full of buckshot before then."

29

Pat had to wait on the longhouse porch. When Jim Boskett and Ray Purkey arrived, he watched them step inside without bothering to knock, and then he had to wait some more. He could hear the muted voices from inside as his pacing brought him to the east end of the gallery where the study overlooked the orchard. The words were not intelligible, but just knowing that something was being said made him snap the cigar out of his mouth before it was halfway smoked and fling it to the dirt. *They think I'm just some hired hand,* he thought, *with nothing to do but cool my heels. The almighty bastards.*

By the time Chisum's niece asked him to come in, he was in no mood to dance around.

The whole bunch was there: Lea, Boskett, LaRue, Purkey, and the man himself, Chisum. Pat took a few steps into the study and, ignoring the others, faced Chisum sitting on the other side of the room.

"No one's answered my letters to Santa Fe, John," Pat said. "You gotten any word?"

Garrett was ready for the withering look that the cattleman shot his way; he didn't allow it to get under his skin.

"The way you've been making me wait out there," Pat went on, "I figured you didn't have much time for me today, so I thought I'd get things out of the way real quick."

Chisum darted an irritated look at Boskett and Purkey. It occurred to Pat that John might not have been the reason for the long wait.

"You made your point," Chisum told Pat. Glancing again at Boskett and Purkey, he added, "Maybe next time some fellas'll realize they shouldn't waste the time of the county sheriff—or anybody else's time either. Go ahead, Pat. Take a seat and let's start all over again."

"We came here to get some things said, John, and that's just what we did," said Purkey. "Whether we make somebody wait or not, it doesn't make any damn difference. It had to be done."

"John, I didn't see *you* rushing Garrett in here," put in Boskett, the beard on his square face jutting out in a show of indignation.

Before Chisum could answer, Captain Lea spoke up to settle the issue. "None of that matters now. We're here to take care of county business, so let's get to it and forget everything else."

As usual, the Captain's voice brought order, but it didn't stop the others from rankling in silence. When he thought they had stewed long enough, Pat tried again. "What about Santa Fe, John? I still haven't gotten any word about the reward. I thought you—or maybe somebody else here—I thought you might know something that I don't."

"Don't worry about it," said Chisum. "It's just the change in governors. Now that Ritch has taken over for Wallace, there's got to be some motions to go through first."

"It must be a lot of motions."

Boskett said, "We didn't come here to talk about rewards. That's not our concern now."

"Well, it sure as hell is my concern," said Garrett. "I've done the job for you. For you and the governor and a lot of other people. All I want is what was promised."

Chisum was quick to put up both hands in a conciliatory gesture. "Hold on, Pat. We're going to do what we can. That's *my* promise, and you know you can count on *that.*"

"And my promise too," said Captain Lea. "All Boskett was trying to say was that, while you've already done a big job in getting the Kid, there's still a lot left to do. The time has come to take a hard look at what that is."

Pat nodded, but found he wasn't able to agree with the man out loud. All those newspaper articles describing him as a great lawman weren't going to help him provide for his family. And he still felt these men owed him something more than a promise when it came to settling the reward business. As caution began to overcome his anger, he reminded himself to watch his step. If he drove too hard, he wouldn't have any powerful friends left to help him.

"What this is all about," said Joe LaRue, "is the

rustling ring around here. I may not be a cattleman, but I know there's still trouble on the range, even with the Kid in jail."

"Can't exactly say it's as bad as it was," Chisum said, "but the rustlers are still nippin' away at us, and they sure as hell seem organized. We figure the Kid left some friends behind who're still carrying on."

"It's not Pickett or Wilson," Pat answered. "They were both arraigned a couple days ago for passing some of that counterfeit money that the Dedrick boys were pushing. They're still in the Santa Fe jail, the last I heard."

"And the same goes for Rudabaugh," said Boskett. "So who does that leave?"

"Don't count Rudabaugh out. He's free again," Pat said.

"Free? What the hell happened?"

"They took him to Las Vegas to try him for that jailer murder. I tried to tell them it'd be trouble if they did, but they went ahead anyway. Sure enough, he busted out. Just yesterday."

"Damn," Boskett said. Purkey and Chisum said the same thing.

"What have you done about all this?" asked the Captain.

"Well, like you say, this thing is still organized, and it's still swinging through the Panhandle too. That means I can still use a couple of the boys from my Texas posse. I got two of them snooping around right now."

Boskett let out a loud, nasty laugh. "Garrett, don't you hear right? The Captain asked what *you* been doing about it. All you're telling us is what some damn Texans are doing. And one thing's for sure, whatever it is they're doing, it's not stopping these rustlers. Not with my herds, or John's, or Ray's, or plenty of other ranchers. Your job didn't end with running down the Kid, you know."

Pat glared at him. He could have told Boskett more about how he was going after the cow thieves, but pride kept him from making a defense that he felt wasn't needed.

"And there's also the matter of taxes." Captain Lea's voice was as smooth as ever, but now there was a brusqueness to it as well. "Now that your official term as sheriff is under way, the collection of taxes is, naturally, part of your duties, and I have to admit, there doesn't seem to have been very much progress in that area. Of course, my information might be incorrect, but I am told that that is the case."

Pat sat perfectly still, his muscles drawn tight. He didn't mind the Captain's bringing up taxes, but when he said things like "I have to admit" and "my information might be incorrect," Pat felt like storming out of the room. *The two-faced bastard,* Pat thought, *acting like he doesn't want to throw this in my face. He's been chomping at the bit to say this ever since I walked into the room.*

Pat shot a glance at Chisum to see the cattle baron leaning toward him, about to say something to keep Garrett quiet. Pat spoke while he had the chance.

"I'll tell you what," he said, "while I'm rounding up Rudabaugh and all the rustlers between here and the Panhandle, I'll make sure they all pay their taxes on the way to jail. Then I guess everybody'll be happy."

"Goddamn it, Pat—" began Chisum.

"Maybe," Pat went on, "you'd all be happier if Kimball was sheriff again. He collected taxes like nobody's business. Maybe that's what you really want now that I've done the real work."

"Mr. Garrett!" Captain Lea roared, his face suddenly turning red. "If that's what you think, maybe you should resign and let somebody else take over! Somebody who doesn't mind doing the job that's expected of him! Maybe that's what *you'd* like!"

Never having seen Lea lose his temper, Pat was completely unprepared for the man's rage, such a fiery, unsettling contrast to the Captain's usual placid manner. Just the same, it didn't take long for Garrett's own anger to rise back to the surface. He had always made a point of never letting anyone talk to him like that, and he was now a breath away from getting up and walking out and telling them all to go to hell. But that was a young man's reaction, the response of someone without a home or a family, with no reason to consider second thoughts.

Someone like Billy, he thought bitterly.

Pat remained seated and said nothing, just as everyone else in the room did. Boskett and Purkey, though, unlike the others, were relishing the silence. They stared at Garrett, their faint smiles badly concealed. Pat began to imagine what these two cattlemen had said while he had been waiting on the porch. They must have torn him to pieces, telling the others how Pat Garrett was resting on his laurels, fixing to coast through the rest of his term while the real business of being sheriff lay ahead. Pat wasn't sure why they were so determined to cut him down to size, but he guessed they just wanted a sheriff who'd jump at every command. They had had their doubts about him from the beginning; now they wouldn't let up until he buckled under.

He met their stares, slowly shifting from one man to the other.

Getting to his feet, Chisum circled around to the back of his chair, where he began to pace. "All right, Captain, you had your say, and maybe Pat here was asking for it. But damn it all, look who the hell we're talkin' about here. Pat here's the man who's going to hang the Kid, which is something nobody else was able to do. You got to admit that, for Christ's sake."

Pat's eyes now left Boskett and Purkey. *I'm not hanging Billy,* he thought. *Why the hell did he have to say that?*

Chisum said, "Pat's done the right thing for us. It seems to me we ought to be doing the right thing for him too."

Captain Lea pulled on the lapels of his coat as if the action might restore his composure. "You're right, John. Of course. But," he added, just barely glancing at Pat, "I didn't come here to listen to back talk. From anybody."

"I know," said Chisum, "and Pat's real sorry about that. And for once, Pat, let me do your talkin' for you." The cattle baron forced a smile. "You're sorry and that's all there is to it, right?"

Joe LaRue laughed, and the Captain smiled along with him. Chisum forged ahead before any more arguing could spring up.

"I'm sure you got your own ideas about chasin' these rustlers," he told Pat, "but maybe it'll help to get some more information. Boskett's got some word that he wants to pass along to you. Maybe we can get something accomplished here other than yelling at each other. Go on, Jim. Tell him about it."

Boskett met Chisum's sharp look, then turned slowly back to Garrett. "That's right," he said. "It's something that one of my hands saw." He paused to study Pat, as if still convincing himself to be civil. "My man was trailing some stolen stock, and he followed them as far as the White Oaks country, just to the south of the town. He said he thought the cattle were probably hidden somewhere around there."

"There you go, Pat," Chisum put in. "Maybe that'll point you down the right trail a little faster."

"One of my men's in White Oaks," Pat said. He paused to swallow, to get the last of the sour taste out of his mouth. "I'll go talk to him about it."

"Now that's something," said Chisum. "I don't know if anybody else's got more to say, but it seems to me Pat might as well be heading White Oaks way as soon as he can." He glanced at the other men in the room. "That'd probably make everybody feel better. Right, fellas?"

Stepping out of the house a few minutes later, Pat went to the edge of the porch and stopped. He looked across the range and took in long breaths, trying to figure how much damage he had done to himself with his temper and his harsh tongue. The voices from the study could still reach him. He strolled away, toward the west end of the longhouse. He started thinking of Apolinaria and what she would say to make sense of all this.

Before long he heard a pair of boots behind him, stepping out of the house onto the gallery planks. He didn't turn to look. He imagined it might be

Chisum, coming to say he had smoothed things over and now everybody was satisfied again with their sheriff. *Wishful thinking,* he told himself. When the bootsteps drew near, he saw that it was Jim Boskett who had come to see him.

The man's face didn't show any of the resentment of before. Instead he seemed simply tired, and just a bit sheepish.

"We put a lot on you in there," he said. "I guess I think I've got to bully a man sometimes to get what I want from him." Boskett finished the statement with a shrug of the shoulders. Pat thought it might have been an apologetic gesture, but he wasn't going to say anything until he was certain.

Boskett was looking away, toward Sallie Chisum's garden, when he added, "You did a hell of a job getting the Kid—I don't think I ever got around to saying that. I guess I just want to tell you I'll do anything I can to help you do the rest."

"Is that right?"

"Goddamn it, Garrett, I said I'm going to help." Boskett stopped himself there. His face tightened as he strained to pull in his temper. "All right, Garrett," he finally said. "I guess it seems like a big switch after that meeting. It's just that running a ranch around here isn't as easy as it used to be—and it was never easy. It feels like I have to fight and claw for everything I get." He gave Pat a sidelong look, then shook his head. "I suppose I've got as much trouble holding my tongue as you do."

Finally letting up, Pat smiled at him. "You're right about that, Jim."

Boskett leaned against the upright, content to say nothing for a while, letting the quiet put some distance between them and the angry words they had exchanged this afternoon.

"Just one other thing," he said a while later. "That hand of mine, the one that trailed the stolen cattle, he heard something about the rustlers around White Oaks."

Pat faced him squarely as he took two cigars out of his vest pocket and handed one to the cattleman. "Did he hear any names?" he asked.

"No, not that. But it's something you might need to know," Boskett said. "The word around White Oaks was that the rustlers were real stirred up about your catching the Kid. They're saying they won't be taken alive."

Pat nodded as he gave this some thought. "Thanks for telling me. I'll keep that in mind."

"The same thing with Rudabaugh," Boskett said. "If I was you, I wouldn't be taking any chances with these outlaws. If they're so determined to die by the gun, you should be willing to oblige them. No one would blame you."

30

The shotgun was snapped shut to end the routine.

"You know, Kid," Olinger said, "I got other casings filled too, and all of them eighteen buckshot. Just want you to know in case you think you can get out of the way of the first two loads—which isn't likely," he added, grinning.

Billy sat at the table, shuffling the cards just to give himself something to do. As long as he could keep himself busy—even if it was only staring out the window—he could steer his mind away from Olinger. The last couple of days he had gotten so good at it that he now barely heard the man. The problem, though, was that he could still feel the thick-set deputy marshal's presence; just being in the same room with Olinger sent a sick, heavy feeling through his limbs.

"You ever kill a man with a shotgun?" Olinger asked.

Billy's teeth pressed tightly together and his hands stopped fiddling with the cards. Olinger's question changed things. If the Kid didn't answer, the deputy marshal would shout the question in his ear until Billy couldn't ignore him anymore. The only thing to do was say something noncommittal, just to appease him; without resistance, Olinger's taunting was liable to slow down. Billy was simply going to say, "No, don't think I have, Bob," but something snapped inside him before he could get those words out.

"Never used a shotgun on a man, never liked 'em," he said instead. "But when I think on it, I sure wish I had that shotgun of yours when I killed Bob Beckwith. I would've liked to have cut the bastard in two."

Billy kept his eyes on the tabletop as he spoke and didn't bother to glance at Olinger when he was finished. The next thing he knew he was hurtling out of the chair. His shoulder thudded against the hardwood floor, and he flopped on his back, too stunned to move for the moment. He saw Olinger standing above him, his boot still lodged between the legs of the chair he had just upended; his face was mottled with rage and his eyes were crazy. Swinging his foot, he sent the chair sailing across the room, and then charged Billy, crouched swiftly by his side, and banged the shotgun muzzles into the Kid's forehead. Billy's head snapped back to the floor.

"You little shit," Olinger shouted, "I'll blow your head open right now!"

Staring at the two muzzles held half a foot from

his face, Billy was still, a sense of resignation holding him in place.

But not for long.

Suddenly, all he wanted to do was to rail at Olinger at the top of his lungs, to say everything that had to be said, now that his last chance to speak had come. Before he could say anything, though, J. W. Bell lurched into view and wrenched the shotgun aside.

"Goddamn it, Bob! Stop!" he said.

Olinger fought against Bell's hold, but J. W. had him off balance and yanked the big man onto his side. For a moment, the two deputies were locked into a test of strength over the gun, a sort of arm-wrestling match in which each man prevented the other from gaining any ground. After a few moments, the bunched features around Olinger's mouth began to loosen and a saner look finally came to his eyes. He eased away from Bell, who snatched the shotgun away.

"I told you to leave off!" Bell said. "Now get the hell out of here, Bob."

Olinger gave the Kid a dim, heavy-lidded look, then slowly got back on his feet. Moving his hands up and down, he rubbed them along the sides of his legs while he continued to glower at Billy.

"It's time to take the other prisoners to lunch," J. W. said. "You take 'em. Go on, Bob. Take 'em and get the hell out of here. Go on."

Olinger didn't seem to hear him. He raised a hand and pointed a thick index finger at Billy. "Just two more weeks, Kid. Two more weeks and you dangle." Turning quickly, he stalked out of the room.

J. W. asked, "You okay, Billy?"

The Kid pushed himself up to a sitting position

and checked to see that the muzzles hadn't cut his forehead. "Yeah. Okay, J. W. I'm okay."

While Bell put the shotgun in the sheriff's office, the Kid got up and walked across the room, feeling no relief at this reprieve, only a sense of not quite being here in this room in the old Murphy & Dolan building. He paced aimlessly for a while, the empty room echoing the sound of his leg shackles, then he wandered toward the window in the corner. Not bothering to sit in the rocking chair this time, he stood with his forehead resting against the glass, looking at the street below without seeing anything. Only when he heard Olinger take the other prisoners down the hall did his mind start to clear.

Below the second-story porch outside the window he could hear Gauss, the German caretaker, hammering a new slat into place, one of the few signs of activity along a street made lazy by the strong mid-day sun. From the side of the Murphy & Dolan building came walking hoof falls. This got Billy's attention. He moved to one side of the window to get a better view of the entrance to the yard that bordered the building. The next moment he saw a man leading his horse from that yard to the street, a short man whose dusty cowboy clothes were distinguished only by a bright green bandana tied loosely around his neck.

"I can get Gauss to bring us up some food if you want." The closeness of the voice surprised Billy. He turned to see Bell standing behind his right shoulder.

Billy gave his guard's question some thought, as he always did when the subject of food was brought up. Questions of when he would eat were just about the only decisions the Kid was allowed to make these days, and he preferred to savor these few choices.

Smacking his lips, he finally turned to J. W. and said, "Just as soon wait a bit if it's all the same to you."

"I'm in no hurry. Just tell me when."

"Would like to go out back, though," Billy said. "Old Bob came pretty close to shakin' something loose, if you know what I mean."

"Yeah," Bell smiled. "Yeah, I guess I do."

Restricted to mincing steps by the leg shackles, Billy shuffled along behind J. W. as the guard led the way through Garrett's office and down the hall to the staircase. The Kid had to go down the stairs sideways, one step at a time, hopping across the square landing before taking the second flight down to the back door. On the other side of the rear corral, Bell took off the wrist manacles, and Billy shut himself inside the outhouse.

Sitting down, Billy waited for some sound to tell him whether J. W. would stay close or pace around the building. He then heard Bell starting to whistle "My Bonnie Lies Over the Ocean." Billy judged that he was whistling loud enough to prevent him from hearing anything.

Billy found the bump in the ground and started digging. He didn't have to work long before finding the burlap sack; inside it was a single-action Colt with five rimfire cartridges in its cylinder.

After waiting a convincing amount of time, Billy stuck the gun in his waistband, pulled his shirttails loose to conceal it, and stepped outside.

"When Pat gets back, I'll talk to him about Olinger," J. W. said as they walked back around the corral.

Preoccupied with his thoughts, the deputy hadn't bothered to replace the wrist manacles. "Pat wouldn't have any truck with that kind of thing if he was here, you know that, Kid, don't you?"

"If you say so."

"You know I'm right. If he knew how loco Olinger was getting, he wouldn't keep him here. I'm sure of it."

"Yeah, I guess so," said Billy. "As a matter of fact, I keep thinking how good the old woman is treating me. I guess I'm just too damn lucky."

"Aw, Kid," J. W. began, then thought better of it. He figured he wouldn't feel much different if he were in Billy's shoes.

At the rear of the building, Bell held the door open for the Kid, allowing Billy to get ahead of him. He couldn't understand why Billy was hurrying up the stairs, shuffling his manacled feet as fast as he could, skittering across the landing and then keeping up the pace for the next flight up. He then thought of the surplus arms room at the top of stairs.

"Hey Billy," he called as he charged up the steps. When he reached the landing he stopped short.

The Kid hadn't reached the top of the stairs yet, and hadn't had the chance to reach the gun room, but there he stood a few steps above Bell with a single-action Colt leveled and cocked.

"We can settle this nice and easy," said the Kid. "Just take out your gun and put it on the floor. That's all you got to do, J. W." All the color in Bell's face was gone. The Kid had come to know J. W. enough to sense that it wasn't just fear of dying that he now saw in the deputy's expression; the man was also shaken by the realization that he had failed to do his job. Billy didn't like that.

"No one'll blame you," the Kid tried. "You're too nice a fella to have to die for Garrett and Chisum."

He waited for an answer, either by word or action, but J. W. didn't say anything and he didn't move. Billy could see the struggle of thoughts in the man's eyes as they remained fixed on the Kid's face. A moment later, Billy wasn't surprised at all when the deputy turned to run.

The gun was unfamiliar to Billy, and he was also out of practice, so he pulled the trigger more quickly than he had to. The Colt bucked high, and the bullet thwacked into the adobe wall above J. W.'s head. But the Kid cocked and triggered rapidly and got off the second round just as the first boom faded. Bell was an instant away from rounding the corner and racing out of view when the slug tore through the left side of his rib cage and knocked him sideways across the bottom flight of stairs.

Billy stood motionless, listening for any sign that the deputy could still move. All he could hear was J. W. rasping for breath, which didn't mean much: he could die quickly or, perhaps, he could find the strength in a few moments to pull out his revolver. The Kid considered the time it would take to hobble down the stairs and finish the man off; then he considered how loud the gunshots must have sounded in the street.

He turned around and struggled against the shackles up to the second floor.

His first thought was to go to the arms room, then something stopped him. In his mind he pictured a sequence of events, some of which might be happening now, others that could happen very soon. These pictures flashed through Billy's mind in a couple of seconds. He then changed direction once more and ran in haltered steps down the hall, toward the front of the building.

In the sheriff's office he found the shotgun propped up in the corner. He took it with him to the corner window of Murphy's old bedroom, where he looked out at the people, roused by the gunfire, stepping into the street below. Billy smiled.

Coming at a run from Wortley's Restaurant across the street was Bob Olinger.

The Kid hobbled over to the side window as the deputy reached the adjacent yard; Billy thumbed back one of the hammers and brought the stock of the shotgun to his shoulder.

"Hello Bob," the Kid called.

Olinger stopped directly below the window and looked up, his revolver still in its holster. Over the shotgun's twin barrels, Billy watched the man's jaw drop.

"The Kid's killed Bell!" shouted someone. Billy glanced to the side to see that it was Gauss, facing the big deputy marshal from the rear of the yard.

"And by God he's killed me too," said Olinger.

Billy fired one of the loads. The eighteen buckshot threw Olinger back into the street, where he staggered senselessly for a moment, then crumpled to the ground. His chest was riddled from one side to the other; a chunk of his shoulder was missing and so was part of his face.

Wasting no time, Billy shuffled out of the room and onto the second-story porch for a better angle.

Then he fired the second load and watched Olinger's body jounce with the impact.

The Kid slammed the shotgun across the porch railing and kept swinging the weapon until it broke. He threw what was left of it at Olinger's motionless form. "Try followin' me with that damn gun now!" he yelled.

The sound of footsteps approaching the front corner of the building got Billy's attention, and for the first time since spotting Olinger, he became aware of the other people in the street. For now, the citizens of Lincoln weren't willing to get too close, the nearest of them at the edge of the road outside Wortley's Restaurant. Turning to the near corner of the Murphy & Dolan building, Billy saw whose footsteps he had heard just a few moments before. Gauss peered around the corner at Olinger's body and glanced apprehensively up at the second-story porch.

"Go get me something that'll knock off these shackles," Billy told the German. Gauss didn't wait to be told twice. He scurried to the back of the building. While waiting for the caretaker, the Kid hobbled to the arms room, rammed the locked door open, and found a good Winchester and cartridges. He loaded the rifle on the second-story porch where he could keep an eye on the street. Still nobody seemed interested in approaching the county building, and none of the distant onlookers had even bothered to put guns in their hands. *Damn yellowbellies,* the Kid thought. *Probably the same spineless bastards that watched McSween's house burn down without raising a finger.*

Gauss brought him a prospector's pickaxe. Billy

told him to break off the right shackle, but took the pickaxe away after the first swing when he saw how the man's hands shook.

"I'll do it myself," he said. "Just get me a horse."

While Billy hacked away, the people of Lincoln receded to homes and stores, and watched the outlaw through windows. In Wortley's Restaurant, the proprietor and one of the customers managed to keep Olinger's abandoned prisoners at bay, and told themselves they were performing enough of their civic duty. People in other parts of the town promised themselves that they would send word of the escape as soon as the Kid was gone. For half an hour that was all they did. In that time, Billy managed to break off one of the shackles but couldn't get anywhere with the other. Hearing a horse approach from the back of the building, he tied the loose chain to his belt and moved downstairs to the street.

With Gauss's help he was able to swing his shackled boot over the saddle. For a few moments, he sat the horse without moving, gazing idly at the faces that were framed in windows on either side of the street.

"Bell's dead, huh?" he asked Gauss. When the caretaker nodded, Billy shook his head. "Someday it's got to end," he said sadly, then gigged the horse forward.

Two teenaged boys moved tentatively out onto the boardwalk fronting the hotel, just ahead to the Kid's right. Seeing the wide-eyed looks on the boys' faces, a notion came to Billy as he drew alongside. He stopped the horse just a few feet from the teenagers, boys who were only a few years younger than he but, in his mind, separated from him by a lifetime of bad luck. He gave them a long considering look, then held out his right hand.

"You boys want to shake the hand of Billy the Kid?" he said. "Don't expect you'll be having another chance."

The boys looked at each other, not sure what to make of this offer at first, then they each took a turn shaking the Kid's hand.

31

Deputy Sheriff John Poe was sitting with Garrett in the First Nugget saloon when the Mexican boy brought in the letter. Poe had been telling his boss about the rustlers reportedly seen at the Dedrick ranch, but now there was no chance of anything further being said on the subject.

Once Poe had the chance to read the letter himself, Garrett took it back to look it over once more. The sheriff's eyes seemed to scan the note's three sentences over and over again, as if the man hoped the words might suddenly rearrange themselves into some other meaning. Finally, Garrett put the letter on the table. Knowing what he himself would have needed under the circumstances, Poe reached for the bottle and poured more whiskey into Garrett's glass. Pat didn't touch it.

To break the silence, Poe said, "You think the Kid's on his way to Old Mexico?"

Garrett took a moment to focus on his Texas deputy. "He will be if he's got any sense," he said. The clipped manner Garrett used to answer his deputy didn't make Poe want to pursue the point.

Garrett fumbled for a cigar in his vest pocket. Getting up, he went to the saloon's false-front window and lit the cigar while staring out at the outskirts of White Oaks.

For several minutes the only sounds in the dirt-floor saloon were the rumbling voices of the three miners at the bar. Poe drank the whiskey that Garrett had left behind. He wondered how long he would have to wait. He had witnessed one of Pat Garrett's brooding silences before, after they had loaded Charley Bowdre's body onto the wagon at Stinking Springs, and that had lasted a good part of the ride back to Fort Sumner. The difference here, though, was that there was no time to be wasted. For that reason, Poe couldn't help but think there was something else preying upon Garrett other than the realization that he would have to chase the Kid all over again. The sheriff of Lincoln County didn't strike Poe as a man who would stand around feeling sorry for himself if he could be mustering a posse and hitting the trail instead.

Poe began thinking of his own leads about the White Oaks rustlers, leads that weren't being followed while he sat at this table. Then he thought of how long his investigation would be put off, now that he would have to ride in the posse chasing the Kid. Finishing the last of the whiskey in the glass, he got up and walked over to Garrett.

"I figure we can get to Lincoln by early tonight," he said. "Maybe even get as far as Roswell if you think that's a better bet. You want me to fetch the horses?"

Poe was already stepping toward the door when Garrett said, "Don't bother."

"Pat, we got to be riding—now. The Kid's already got a day's jump on us."

"That's right. But you can stay here."

Poe squinted at him, bewildered.

"You stay here and follow your leads," Garrett said. "For all we know the Kid'll look up the fellas you were telling me about. I can raise a posse in Roswell. Not in Lincoln," he added, almost to himself. He turned to look out the window again. "Lincoln already had its chance to do something about the Kid."

Poe could see the sense of the sheriff's plan and didn't waste any more time talking about it. He got his horse out of the corral at the back of the saloon, saddled it, and rode back to the street to head out of town. He planned on talking to some placer miners on Baxter Mountain who had passed by the Dedrick ranch last week. When Poe passed the First Nugget saloon, he saw Garrett through the window, still standing there, smoking his cigar.

Two nights later, Pat's bad dreams began.

The dream started with Pat and his posse camped in the middle of Fort Sumner plaza. Freezing rain gave way to blistering sunshine, which in turn gave way to rain once more. Through it all, however, the wind blasted across the camp.

The faces of the possemen kept shifting. At first

they were men Pat had known from the buffalo range, then they were members of his posses that had tracked the Kid. All of them tried to keep their gear from flying away in the wind, but none of their efforts was worth the trouble. Just the same, they never seemed to lose all the gear as more seemed to appear whenever Pat turned to look at another part of the camp. Pat called to the people standing along the edge of plaza, to no effect. The wind always carried his voice in the wrong direction.

Some of the details of the dream would change from one night's sleep to the next as Garrett led his new Roswell posse in pursuit of Billy's escape route, first riding to Fort Stanton, then traveling south through the Mescalero Reservation. Some of the faces in the dream would change, and sometimes the buildings along Fort Sumner plaza would look like places in Santa Fe or Las Vegas, but always there would be the sense of something closing in. And each time Garrett, in the dream, would be surprised when he turned to see the horseman bearing down on him, the hooves about to trample him. At the last second, just before waking up, Pat would see that it was Jack Briscoe in the saddle, a huge gash in his neck, as if he had been mutilated with his own hatchet that night three years ago when they were chasing Comanches.

After Pat returned to Roswell and dismissed his posse, there was nothing he cared to remember about the pointless chase back and forth across the Pecos Valley. Everyone he talked to was either too scared or too ignorant to give him any useful information about the Kid, and none of the tracks his posse followed led to anything. He wanted to forget the whole disastrous ride, but most of all he wanted to forget the dream that had come to him each night.

For two weeks he stayed at home in Roswell, occasionally sending out Lon Chambers or José Roibal to check up on stories that came his way about the Kid being seen in Las Tablas or Ruidoso. But nothing came of these scouts, and Pat did little else to pursue the Kid.

When he went into town he could see the curious, furtive looks he got from people as he passed them in his buckboard. He knew they must be talking about him behind his back, saying that he had given up, that he was taking the county's salary and not doing the job, that he was afraid to go after the Kid. Pat also knew that if he asked any able-bodied men in town to ride with him to follow a new lead, they would find some excuse to back off. The men he had recruited immediately after the Kid's escape had been reluctant from the start and were eager to get away from him when the ride was done. They were even less willing to help now. *They were ready to do anything for me when the Kid was in jail,* he brooded.

The people on the streets of Roswell weren't the only ones to notice the sheriff's inactivity. Roswell's leading citizen was also well informed. Captain Lea sent one of his men to the Garrett house with the message that he wanted to see Pat.

"There's nothing for me to tell him," Pat responded.

"The Captain wants to see you," the messenger repeated. He didn't seem to think that anything more needed to be said.

"When I've got some information about the Kid, I'll come tell him about it."

Pat didn't hear from Lea after that, but three days later, the man himself, Chisum, rode up to the house in his buckboard. He was all smiles with Apolinaria and the children when he was ushered inside, but his lean face turned rock-hard when he was alone with Pat in the main room.

"What the hell're you up to?" the cattle baron demanded.

"I'm handling things my way, John."

Chisum looked at him as if Pat had suddenly sprouted horns. "And just what the hell kind of way is that?" he said. "You looking for the Kid in your fireplace? What the hell are you doing?"

Garrett paced in front of the sofa, clasping and reclasping his hands behind his back. "I took a posse out as soon as I got word. You know that, John."

"And you didn't find him," Chisum barked, taking a step closer to Pat. "That your idea of hunting a man—taking one crack at it, then giving up?"

Pat couldn't meet the man's gaze. "I also sent men out. They didn't find anything either. That's the whole point."

"It is? Then maybe you can explain it to me because I sure as hell don't know what that point is."

Pat finally stopped moving. He faced Chisum. "Either Billy's gone to Old Mexico or he's still hiding somewhere in the territory. If he's left the country then I can't get at him. And if he's still riding the owlhoot trail around here, then he'll be on the move as soon as he hears I'm coming for him. There's plenty of people who'll help him, you've got to know that."

"They were helping him before, but you managed to run him down just the same. What's the damn difference now?"

"I'll tell you what the difference is. Before I caught Billy there were still some people who'd help *me* too. Now I wouldn't count on it. Billy's got too many new scores to settle after being in jail and facing a hanging. Even if he doesn't plan to get even, people think he will. I saw Tom Wilcox last week. He came sneaking here in the middle of the night. He doesn't live at his ranch anymore, John. Both him and Brazil are on the dodge these days, certain that the Kid'll catch up to them if they stay in one place too long. They're certain Billy'll kill them for helping me find him. Wilcox even has his boy staying with folks up to Santa Fe so he won't be seen around here."

Chisum sat on the sofa, much of the anger gone now, but dissatisfaction still showing in his eyes. "You're talking about giving up, aren't you, Pat?"

"No, I'm not. All I'm saying is I can't head out after Billy unless I'm damn sure I know where he is. I have to know I can slip up on him. If I just ride out of here asking a lot of questions, he'll get skittish and run. I'd just be chasing my own tail, John. Can't you see that?"

Chisum rubbed his forehead and pulled the hand slowly down the side of his face. "It's getting so that I almost believe you, Pat. But we can't leave it there. I've been losing more stock since the Kid got loose, and I'm not the only one. You can't just sit here talking about playing it cagey when that's going on."

"What the hell you want me to do? Go off on

another wild goose chase just to make it look like I'm doing something?"

"I'm talking about getting off your butt," Chisum snapped, getting back to his feet. "Just do something!"

Finding themselves back where they had started, the two men argued and yelled until they stopped listening to each other at all. They shouted at the same time, each trying to shout louder than the other until Apolinaria came into the room to tell them they were waking up the baby. "Quiet, the both of you," she scolded them, as if talking to two troublesome boys. Pat and Chisum glared at each other, then the cattle baron wheeled, shot Garrett a furious glance, and marched out of the house.

Pat was unwilling to concede that anything Chisum had said was right, but the cattle baron's words stayed with him, goading him, making him repeat his own arguments to himself as he tended to his small herd of cattle and the struggling orchard beside the house. Just to set his own lingering doubts aside, he spent the next day in and around town, trying to recruit another man to scout for him. He already had Roibal in Puerto de Luna and Chambers outside Tularosa, and he figured it wouldn't hurt to have a man in Fort Stanton as well. At least Chisum or any of the others couldn't say he wasn't doing his job.

Pat didn't nurture any high hopes that he would find an ally in Roswell who was both willing and capable—he had been down this trail before—so he wasn't disappointed with what he found. The best response would be, "Sure would like to help, Pat, but. . . ." Then would come the excuses: inventory had to be taken, corral fences had to be mended, freight had to be readied for the trip up to Santa Fe. The only ones who seemed genuinely interested were either too young or too old for the work.

Satisfied that he had at least proven his ideas about civic spirit in the area, Pat stopped at Quincannon's saloon before riding home that evening. He felt his pointless work that day had earned him at least that much. Standing at the far end of the bar was a short man wearing a duster caked with pieces of the range from outside town. It was Tip McKinney. Pat had heard that his old friend had returned recently from Uvalde, but he hadn't looked him up; he hadn't been sure how Tip had reacted to the killing of O'Folliard, his friend from the Fort Sumner days.

Tip McKinney turned in Garrett's direction just as the sheriff reached the other end of the bar. The man's gaze was steely, but soon he began to nod his head slowly, as if just realizing something; then he waved Pat over.

The first mention of Tom O'Folliard came after several minutes of small talk about Tip's new ranch; the subject came up during a long pause that seemed to give them only one choice for conversation. "Got your letter in Uvalde," Tip finally said. "If you're still wonderin', I passed the word along to Tom's grandma."

Pat nodded but said nothing. Once more, Tip was the one to interrupt the silence.

"I think I know how it was when you shot him," he said. "I also think I know what it means to face down these rustlers. You hear about Bob Edwards?"

"I heard he was coming this way."

"Well, he came. I found Bob with some beeves that weren't his, just north of my spread it was. I tell you, he just about shot my head off before I managed to dust him." Tip's high forehead was creased with thought for a moment, then he took hold of the bottle and refilled both their glasses.

"Bob wasn't so different from Tom really," he continued. "It's a damn shame about old Tom getting killed, but then from what I hear, it was a damn shame about Jim Carlyle too. I used to know Jim real good, as good as I knew Tom."

Pat was beginning to think this trip to town wasn't completely foolish. "You see any other rustling near your place?" he asked.

"Some signs of it, maybe not at my spread, but at others around here. But these boys can pass through without hardly anybody noticing."

"That's for certain."

"I did hear something, though, about a fella named Lee Keough. You ever hear of him, Pat?"

"Heard the name, but that's all."

"I thought maybe you'd know more, seein' as he says he's with the Kid's new bunch. Anyhow, that's what he told one of my hands. He said he'd just seen the Kid, and Billy was talkin' about how he was going to leave the country, kind of as a ruse, to make you think he was gone for good. Then he was going to come back and burn you down."

Pat did his best to appear unconcerned, to look like the flinty *buscadero* everyone had said he was a couple of months ago, while the Kid was still in jail.

When his drink was finished, Pat considered asking Tip to snoop around Fort Stanton, but then thought better of it. If the Kid really had left for Old

Mexico, Fort Stanton would be a waste. Pat figured he was still better off waiting.

Late that night, Apolinaria woke to the baby's crying and reflexively got out of bed. She moved sluggishly for the first few steps, then more quickly as the crying continued. She reached the baby's room calling to her little girl to assure her that her mother was there, then she gasped and lurched to the side when she saw the man holding Elizabeth and walking her across the room.

In her half-conscious state, Apolinaria hadn't noticed that Pat's side of bed was empty when she left their room. Even if she had been aware that he wasn't sleeping with her, however, the sight of him in the baby's room would have surprised her. As much as he tried to look after the children the few times he was home, Pat was not one to be found comforting a baby in the middle of the night.

He was wearing his trousers but was shirtless and shoeless; his greatcoat was draped over his shoulders, and it was against the coat's soft shoulder that the baby's head rested. In the dark room, his long, cloaked figure looked ghostly.

When she had recovered enough, Apolinaria walked over to her husband and put her hands up to Elizabeth. "Pat, give her to me," she said sharply. Never having seen him comfort the baby at night, she didn't quite trust him. Pat obliged her without a word. Only after she had quieted the baby and started to hear her regular, sleeping breathing did Apolinaria stop to consider why her husband was up and about at this time. She turned to see him standing in the doorway, barely discernible in a deep pocket of shadow. By the time she had put Elizabeth back in the crib, Pat was no longer in the room.

She found him leaning against an upright on the porch.

He was staring at the craggy silhouette of the hills on the horizon. Apolinaria stood beside him for several minutes, not bothering to ask him any questions; not that she wasn't curious about his behavior—she just knew the time wasn't right. There had been other times when she had noticed him getting out of bed in the middle of the night, and each time she had become more concerned, but he would have to give some indication that he wanted to talk about it before she would say anything. Otherwise, she would get nothing from him.

The chill in the night air made her press herself to his side for warmth. Pat lifted his arm and enclosed her inside the greatcoat. Huddled against his bare chest, she could feel the shallowness of his breathing.

"I guess I should've known from the start," he said, "that I'd have to keep killing friends until it's all over."

32

The stranger put Billy on edge as soon as the man stepped into the hotel lobby from the rooms in back. He was a dark-haired man with a full beard and mustache, dressed in tailored nankeen pants, a brown sack coat, and a wide-brimmed planter's hat. Everything about him was well groomed, but Billy detected a fierceness also, held in check, yet still discernible in the gaunt lines of his high cheekbones and the deep-set gimlet eyes.

The Kid put out a hand, stopping Lee Keough just as he was about to step from the porch into the lobby.

"Have you seen that fella in town before?" he asked.

Keough followed Billy's gaze and focused on the bearded man talking to W. S. Moore, the hotel proprietor, by the registration desk. Absently adjusting the bright green bandana around his neck, he took his time in studying the man.

"Not familiar," Keough finally said. "He's a new boy all right."

Billy shuffled nonchalantly to the side of the door to keep himself inconspicuous. Keough's word was good enough for him. The Kid had only been in Hot Springs for two days, but Lee had been here for a week, and he was a good one for keeping track.

The stranger's appearance at this time was troubling. Hot Springs was to be the Kid's last stop on his northbound ride away from Lincoln; he was confident now that no more posses were after him, and tomorrow he was going to send Lee Keough southward to set up horse relays for his ride to Old Mexico. But if this stranger was hunting bounty, he had come to town just in time to cause some serious problems.

"I'll tell you what, Lee," Billy said, "why don't you kind of waltz in there and make some talk with Moore. That'll give you a chance to start talking to the stranger. Try to see what he's up to."

Keough's young moon-face brightened at the chance to do something for the Kid. The short cowboy stepped inside and sauntered over to the desk.

Taking out the makings, Billy peered through the door to watch Keough strike up a conversation with Moore. The bearded man in the fine clothes glanced from Keough to Moore—the slant of the man's eyebrows made it seem like he was scowling—then he leaned back against the desk to face the lobby, appearing to be lost in thought. But not for long. As hoped, Moore brought him into the conversation.

The talk went on for several minutes, much longer

than Billy thought it should have. What the hell was Lee doing? The Kid was starting to get a bad feeling about this situation, and the feeling quickly got worse when he saw Moore's long face turn in his direction. Billy took a step back, but before he could take himself out of view, he saw something that nearly made his fingers drop his tobacco and paper.

Moore pointed at him, while at the same time saying something to the bearded man.

Billy froze. He considered running but decided it was too late for that. He also considered pulling the new double-action Colt he had bought in Anton Chico last week, but something told him to hold up, to see what would happen next.

What happened was that Keough turned toward him with a puzzled look on his face, then he shrugged, and walked back to Billy's side.

"Moore says you and the new fella should have lunch together." Lee spoke the words as if he had no idea what they meant. "The fella says his name is Mr. Howard, and he got real interested when Moore said you were Billy Bonney. I don't know, Billy. Moore seems to think it's a good idea."

The Kid took a long breath and reassembled the tobacco and paper so that he could roll it into shape. He looked at Moore standing behind the desk. The man waved him in, smiling.

"Well, Moore's a friend, so I guess we got to trust him," Billy said. "What the hell, we were going to have lunch anyway."

Moore made the introductions face-to-face and, looking slyly from one man to the other, took Billy and Mr. Howard by the elbow and guided them into the dining room.

At a corner table, Billy sat across from Mr. Howard, the man's shoulders thrown back, his hands placed flat in front of him; Moore and Keough sat to either side. The Kid took his time lighting his cigarette, waiting for someone else to make some sense of this.

"I have heard a lot about you, Mr. Bonney," said Mr. Howard. "I reckon everybody has by now."

"That right?" replied Billy. "What've you heard?" He glanced at Moore to see that he still wore a smile.

"Mostly I have read about you in the newspapers, which isn't much to say. They print nothing but lies, especially in Missouri where I come from. I'm sure your true story is different."

"You're right about that." This somber, stiff-backed man was getting Billy nervous. He exchanged a look with Keough, then grinned to show them all he really didn't care. "How come you've been readin' so much about me, Mr. Howard? What I mean is, how come a Missouri man makes a point of knowing about me—and then comes all the way to Hot Springs?"

For a brief moment, a corner of Mr. Howard's mouth turned up in something that looked like it might have been a smile. Getting impatient, Billy turned to Moore.

"There some reason why we're all sittin' at this table?" he demanded. The Kid now noticed the bulge in Mr. Howard's coat, just beneath the left armpit. Under the table, Billy had his hand next to his Colt.

"Sorry, Kid," the hotel owner said. "Just havin' a little fun. You remember me tellin' you about how I knew Jesse James and some of his boys back when I was growing up in Missouri? Well . . ." He ended the sentence by tilting his head toward Mr. Howard.

At first Billy sat perfectly still, no trace of his bluffing grin left on his face, then he was about to laugh it off as some kind of joke. He thought better of it as he studied the man before him and recalled pictures he had seen in newspapers.

Mr. Howard said, "I figured, as long as I know who you are, you're entitled to know the same about me. Someone like you would know why a thing like this should be kept quiet."

"Well, goddamn," said Keough.

Mr. Howard flicked a displeased glance in Keough's direction.

Now Billy started to laugh. He had been right about this "Mr. Howard" right from the start: he *was* a dangerous man—for some people, anyway. "Yeah, well, I guess I'd know enough to keep quiet, Jesse. The news just got here about that holdup of the Rock Island train over to Missouri. Yes sir, I'd expect New Mexico would be a fine place for you to go to after that."

"Just my point," Jesse James said. "Whatever you read in the newspapers about that, it's a pack of lies by a bunch of poltroons. That conductor was alive when we left that train and there's plenty of people who'll swear by it."

"I believe it," Billy said with a straight face. From what he had heard, James had only put about three or four slugs into the man's back and shot him clean off the train.

Jesse James's fierce eyes were still riveted on Billy, unrelenting and hard as glass. The Kid couldn't decide whether the Missouri raider knew Billy had been unconvinced by the conductor story.

"That escape of yours," James said, "that was pretty lucky, coming so close to the hanging."

The Kid bristled at this. "Lucky! It was more than that. When you got friends to get you a gun when you need it—I don't call that luck."

There was only a slight change in James's expression, a dilation of the pupils that made his eyes darker. "I guess you're right, Billy. God can look kindly on a man who won't buckle under to the liars that think they can run this country."

Billy stared at this notorious border bandit, fascinated by his strange righteousness, so different from the raw wildness he had found in most men running wide of the law. Minna Moore came over to the table with an apron fastened around her plump figure; when she asked what they'd have, her husband told her to bring the day's special for the four of them. During this distraction, Billy took the opportunity to size up the Missouri badman in silence.

"What I was trying to tell you," Jesse said, "was that you're lucky to get away any time you let these sons-of-bitches take you in. The court will cheat you and make sure you get the worst of it—that is, if you're not mobbed and lynched before they can carry out their crooked sentence. Better off to make sure they never catch you at all, Billy. I learned that a long time ago."

"Garrett's going to have his work cut out for him trying to find me this time," the Kid answered. "Make no mistake about that."

"Sheriff Garrett," Jesse mused out loud. "Sounds like him and his deputies are no better than those damn Pinkertons that've been dogging my brother and me all these years."

"Well, those Pinkertons can't be much worse. Garrett surely loves to chase people more than anything else, it seems to me."

"Maybe so," Jesse said, leaning back in his chair. He stopped looking at Billy; he gazed through the air above the Kid's head. "But you can only run from these dogs so far. Soon as you stop fighting the good fight, you make less of a man of yourself—in front of friends and family." A thought seemed to lead him away, but soon Jesse was able to pull himself back. "I'll be heading back home myself soon enough. There are too many good people back in Missouri who know the truth about how my brother and me got pushed into all this. They expect something of me, and you know what, Billy? They got a right to expect that."

Moore managed to steer the conversation to smaller talk, and by the time the food was served, Billy and Jesse were passing the time talking horses and guns. Billy was about to bring up the subject of women, as he would naturally have done with any other man, but he sensed that it wouldn't sit right with the solemn Missouri raider. Throughout the meal, no matter what subject was bandied about the table, Jesse's words about fighting the good fight stayed in Billy's mind.

When lunch was finished, Billy was explaining that his double-action Colt was as reliable as any single-action gun, such as Jesse's Smith & Wesson. James got up abruptly, for no reason that Billy could see. His action may have been sudden, but his manner was still polite. He shook Billy's hand, wished him the best of luck, and did the same with Keough, who continued to stare at the man as if he had just realized who he was. For the second time since sitting at the corner table, Keough said, "Well, goddamn."

Still holding the young man's hand, Jesse lowered his head to look at him from beneath his brow. "Running wild doesn't give a man call to swear with the Lord's name," he said. "Best make sure you got Him on your side any way you can, son."

Jesse James left the dining room, pulling on the lapels of his brown sack coat, and headed toward the rooms in back. Billy had no doubt that he had just seen the last of the man in Hot Springs.

To wash down the meal, Billy and Keough went to Chavez's saloon on the outskirts of town, a place owned by a friend who would let the Kid know if any law was getting close. Whatever had tied Keough's tongue during the meal with Jesse James had been sprung by now, and he talked a steady, excited stream.

"Wait till I tell Aker and Rudabaugh about this," he said. "They'll think I'm lyin' for sure, but I won't be, goddamn it. He was sitting right there with us at the table. That Rock Island train job he pulled—I heard they took thirty thousand dollars. Maybe more. You hear that too, Billy?"

The Kid nodded as he settled into a chair at the rear table in the saloon. He thought his silence might slow Keough down, but the young man kept talking just the same, not saying much of anything, just finding new ways to say he had just met the great Jesse James and was about to bust wide open, he felt so honored. His next questions to the Kid were answered with grunts, and still he didn't get the hint.

After a while, Billy managed to interrupt him long enough to tell him that the horses needed looking after. "Just to make sure they're ready for your ride tomorrow," Billy said. Keough looked longingly at the bottle of whiskey that Chavez placed on the table, but he wasn't about to refuse to do something requested by the Kid.

Billy poured himself a drink and, settling back in his chair, did his best to put picayune things out of his mind.

A notion had been nibbling at the back of his head ever since they left Moore's hotel, an idea that was too unformed to make itself clear, but was persistent and tantalizing. It had remained just beyond reach on the way to Chavez's place, and under the barrage of Keough's senseless chatter it seemed to recede further until Billy was sure it would vanish if he didn't do something to call it back. Once Keough was gone, the quiet allowed the notion to creep back into partial view. By the time Billy finished his first drink, he could see that he had been right in taking the time to gather his thoughts. A new understanding of what he had to do seemed to take shape.

It came to Billy as he watched Chavez behind the bar, wheeling his low-built, heavy frame from one end of the unvarnished counter to the other in order to serve his afternoon customers. No one else in the saloon was in focus. Only Chavez mattered, a man who had helped the Kid here in Hot Springs, giving him a place to sleep in the saloon's back room, and keeping his eyes peeled for any newcomers who might mean trouble. Billy realized he had come to take these favors for granted, and there had been many of them on his way here: Damaso Lopez, who had let him stay overnight at his sheep ranch outside Fort Sumner on his way from Lincoln; Sam Dedrick, who had gotten him a fresh mount when his stolen horse went lame outside Portales; even Lee Keough, for all his damn-fool chatter—when Rudabaugh had backed off from bringing the revolver to Lincoln for the escape, Lee had stepped forward to get the job done. Billy could see now that he hadn't given much thought to all these loyal friends.

And that's a hell of a thing, he thought.

Jesse's words about friends and family came back to him; those words had triggered all these ideas, Billy now realized. He didn't have any family here in New Mexico, but he had plenty of friends, and he figured he could pay them back by standing up for them, fighting the good fight against all the fine-haired sons-of-bitches that made trouble in this territory. *That's what they want me to do,* he told himself, *even if they don't come out and say it. Lopez, Celsa, Chavez, Paulita—all of them.*

Billy leaned forward across the tabletop, his weight on his elbows, feeling a sudden urge to spring out of his chair and do something, but not knowing what. He was consumed with a sense of purpose that he hadn't felt since the Lincoln War.

Some time later, Keough returned to the table and sidled next to Billy, not bothering to sit with him. His gaze moved from one side of the saloon to the other.

"We might have us some trouble," he whispered.

Billy took a moment to leave his thoughts behind

and concentrate on what his friend had just told him. "See someone?" he said.

"That fella over there," Keough answered, nodding almost inperceptibly toward a table by the front window. Two cowboys sat there. "The long drink of water, the one with the gray mustache. I've seen him before. He works for Tip McKinney."

Billy studied the sinewy man as the McKinney hand talked to the cowboy sitting next to him.

"He's got a right to work for Tip if he wants," the Kid said.

"That's not all of it, Billy. I seen him keeping an eye on you. There—look. He just did it again, lookin' your way."

Billy met the man's look and held it until the McKinney hand turned back to his friend. "I suppose that could mean something," he said, "if he's got some bad ideas instead of just plain natural curiosity."

"He's trouble," Keough insisted. "I came across him just a while back, over to a cow camp along Salt Creek. His name's Brock, I think. He was askin' questions about you. Seemed real interested to know where you might be." Keough didn't mention that the man named Brock had become interested in talking about the Kid only after Keough had started shooting his mouth off about how well he knew Billy.

The whiskey had started to do its work, and Billy was reluctant to be on the move just yet, but he knew he couldn't take any chances. "I guess you might as well leave here a day early," he told Keough, "and I might as well go with you."

While the McKinney man was looking out the

window, Billy and Keough slipped away from the table, moved into the back room, and left the saloon through a rear door. Billy waited in the back lot until Keough fetched their mounts—a saddle horse and a spare for each of them—then they rode east out of town. Billy turned in the saddle to see that no one was behind them.

Keough said, "Guess it won't hurt to ride into Old Mexico a little early, eh Kid?"

"Don't suppose it would," said Billy. "Except we're not going there anymore."

As he was about to poke some Winesap chewing tobacco inside his cheek, Keough stopped with his mouth open and his hand an inch away from his lips. Billy glanced at his partner's face and laughed.

"You heard right, Lee. No more Old Mexico for me. We're stayin' close for a while. I can't say how long, but I'm in no hurry."

"What happened, Billy?"

"Everything's changed—that's all," the Kid grinned. "A full-grown man's got to show people a thing or two in this life."

Keough's hand holding the tobacco was still poised in front of his face; he squinted at Billy, then remembered himself and stashed the Winesap in his mouth.

They rode in silence for a while, until something occurred to the Kid, something he should have thought of before. He laughed to himself, shook his head and lightly slapped the side of his head, as if to admonish himself.

"Damn it all, Lee, I'm just not thinking straight. That's for certain. If a man's going to make a stand, he can't put it off till the next day, now, can he?"

Billy turned his horse, handed Keough the reins of his spare mount and, starting back toward town, called over his shoulder, "You wait here. I won't be but a minute or two."

"Okay, Billy," said Keough, his eyes wide and uncomprehending as he watched the Kid ride back at a lope.

Riding up to the mouth of the alley beside Chavez's saloon, Billy looked both ways along the street and, seeing nothing, pushed on toward the center of town.

He didn't have to look for long.

In front of Moore's Old Adobe Hotel, the McKinney hand named Brock was mounting up. He reined the horse around as he hit the saddle and found himself face to face with Billy the Kid, sitting his horse in the middle of the street. For a moment, Brock was absolutely still, staring at the Kid, then he quickly swung his horse to the left. Before the McKinney man could do anything else with his hands, Billy pulled his double-action Colt; it bucked three times and hammered three .41 rounds into Brock's trunk. Brock spilled from the saddle, dangling by the left boot still caught in its stirrup as his horse pounded down the street.

The nearby Hot Springs citizens were slow to react, and Billy was off and galloping down a side street before anyone even thought of stopping him. Sweeping past Chavez's place, he rode hard across the open country, with Keough in sight in the middle distance.

Jesse thinks he's something over to Missouri, Billy mused. *Wait till he hears what goes on in New Mexico.*

33

The box canyon along the slope of the Gallinas Mountains was filled with stolen cattle, just as John Poe had said it would be. Riding along the perimeter, Garrett and Poe made sure no sentries had been posted, then moved down to the floor of the canyon to inspect the stock.

Some of the cattle bore Chisum's jinglebob ear brand, while the rest had been taken from three smaller ranches. Pat estimated about fifty head in all. At the canyon entrance, John Poe turned back two of the beeves that had wandered off, then moved back to the sheriff's side.

"Think I saw some tracks over there," he said. "They looked fresh. Headed back toward the road, as far as I could tell."

"Any idea how many?" Pat asked.

"Some cow tracks were muddying it up, but I'd

say probably two or three riders. Couldn't be much more than that."

Pat nodded as he surveyed the herd once more. He then checked the sun, now on its downward arc. "I guess these beeves'll keep. Let's see where the trail takes us."

John Poe showed him the markings that led out of the canyon; the tracks curled around an outcropping of rock and sloped up to a series of jagged ridges where an occasional juniper groped with gnarled branches across a rocky shelf. Traveling now in the last hours of light, they pressed their horses so that they might reach the trail's end before nightfall.

The hard riding brought dull aches to Pat's joints, a feeling that was welcome, proof that he was finally doing something after a month of biding his time at home. He had been sitting on his porch, lazing after a lunch of Apolinaria's *sopapillas,* when he saw the black mare carrying Poe's bulldog frame toward the house. At first, he had felt a vague sense of annoyance that his deputy was no longer at his post in White Oaks, and also some trepidation that the Texan might bring news that would require action. The habit of home life had lulled him that much. But the determination that Poe showed when he told Garrett his story soon got the better of him.

"Not just one man told me about it," Poe had said, "it was two fellas. One was a placer miner up in the hills. He told me about some long-rider who came to his camp, name of Aker he said it was. He was looking to swap horses. He said he was riding alone, but the miner saw him join up with a herd after he left. The other fella I spoke to was a freighter who saw the herd on its way to the box canyon. We move fast, Pat, we could catch 'em before they sell off the beef."

Garrett had been slow to react, but Poe didn't let him dawdle. "You know as well as I do what people're saying about you, Pat. You go out and round up a couple of cow thieves, they'll have to put a halter on all that bad-mouthing."

Riding now in the fading afternoon light, Garrett found satisfaction in being in the hunt again. He was doing the right thing, thanks to John Poe, whether they found the White Oaks rustlers or not.

Within an hour they reached the main road to town, bordered by yucca plants, their stalks now in full bloom. The tracks turned away from White Oaks and kept heading north, past the remains of Whiskey Jim Greathouse's ranch. Garrett and Poe rode on, coming across no one else on the road, and at dusk, they brought their mounts to a stop within sight of a squat adobe building. *If we really are on the trail of rustlers,* Pat thought, *then the tracks have ended in the right place.*

The adobe had been built four years ago by a speculator who had believed a stage line to Santa Fe would be run along this route. When the stage line didn't materialize, the would-be station was abandoned, and the speculator moved on to the next territory. Since then, the building housed squatters passing through the area who hoped to cash in on the nearby gold strike. The last squatter was a man named Spangler. After Whiskey Jim's ranch house was destroyed in a fire—a fire set by angry White Oaks citizens, Pat had heard—Spangler took over Whiskey Jim's trade in bad whiskey and stolen horses, and just about anything else his customers wanted.

Garrett and Poe tied their mounts at the front of the adobe, alongside four other saddled horses. Pat inspected the animals, but there was nothing familiar about them.

"Got any ideas on how to do this?" Poe asked the sheriff.

"There can't be too many in there," Garrett said. "And I don't figure they're expecting anybody as long as they've been listening to all those stories about how scared I am." Pat stared at the doorway, his mouth twisted into a bitter smile. "I say we just go straight-in. Turn over the rock and see what crawls out. That all right with you?"

"Good enough," said Poe. "But if you don't mind, I think I'll take my carbine with me."

To make sure they didn't tip their hand by looking too well armed, Pat stepped inside with just his holstered Colt.

On the left, a bar had been made of an oakwood plank laid across two barrels. Some badly made shelves, filled with a few folded blankets, a coil of rope, and two bridles, gave the other side of the room the appearance of a trading post. In the middle of it all was a table at which sat two men. Pat didn't recognize either of them.

From the other side of the makeshift bar, a stocky man watched through narrow eyes as Garrett and Poe approached. He wasn't squinting; his puffy eyelids just didn't leave much of an opening for his eyes to peer through. His hand scratched the grimy flannel of the shirt that covered his stomach as he sized up the two strangers. Garrett was sure this was

Spangler; the man was ugly enough to fit the description.

John Poe stood with his back to the bar and his eyes on the two men at the table while Garrett spoke to the proprietor.

"I'm looking to buy some beef," Pat drawled. "Thought maybe you could help. I'll buy it on the hoof if I can."

Spangler pressed his thick lips together in a peevish scowl. "I don't sell beef," he said with a slight German accent.

"Well, I guess you wouldn't lie to me, but I'm willing to guess you might know someone who'd sell. Someone who'd sell without asking a lot of questions—if you know what I mean."

"I don't know what you're getting at. Tell me more."

"Well, it's really simple. You see, I need to know who's selling stolen stock because I'm Pat Garrett, sheriff of Lincoln County." At that moment, he looked quickly to his rear.

The two young cowboys sitting at the table wore the same expression: they both stared at Pat with alarm shining in their eyes. But it was the one on the right that commanded Pat's attention. The moon-faced kid shoved his chair back to make room for a grab at his holster. He barely moved his right hand before John Poe had his carbine aimed at him. The cowboy became as still as his companion.

"Spangler," Pat said, "I think you better come out from behind there. That's it, come on. Come out where we can see you real good."

The thick-bodied German was slow to start, but then he stepped toward the end of the makeshift bar, hesitated next to an open crate—Pat thought he might have a gun in there—and moved on to the center of the room.

"Don't bother to sit down," Pat told him. "There's just the one extra chair at that table, and I think I'll take it myself. You just stay next to the deputy there."

After getting the two cowboys to put their revolvers on the floor, Pat moved the extra chair so that he could sit facing both of them.

"We know about the cattle in the box canyon," Pat told them. "We followed the trail back here, and now we also know you don't much like sheriffs. I'm telling you this just in case you figure on telling me you don't know anything about stealing cows."

Pat saw calculation pass swiftly across the eyes of the cowboy on the left, the short, hatchet-faced one. The rustler darted a look at his friend, then said, "I just met this fella here. I swear."

Garrett almost felt like laughing. The other cowboy, the one who had tried for his gun, wasn't so amused. He glared at his friend as if he hoped his look could cut him in two. He took a while to say something.

"This bastard's name is Ellis Aker," he said slowly, "and he knows as much about stealing cows as I do, sheriff."

Aker stared at the tabletop with glazed eyes.

"From what I hear," Pat said, "the rustlers around here know an awful lot about stealing. I hear they even go as far as the Panhandle, just like the Kid used to do. They find some cattle over there and bring it back over the territorial line. Is that right, Ellis?"

Aker shrugged. He didn't look at Garrett and he wasn't about to talk to him either.

"What about you?" Pat said to the other cowboy. "You introduced me to your friend here. Now why don't you tell me who the hell you are?"

"I'm Keough," the moon-faced kid said.

"Are you as stupid as your partner, or do you know something about the way things're done around here?"

Keough looked up suddenly, his face flushed with defiance. "What if I do know something about the Panhandle? That don't have nothin' to do with you."

"It's got something to do with my deputy," Pat said. "He comes from the Panhandle, and he's carrying a deputy U.S. marshal badge along with being my deputy sheriff."

Pat could see Keough trying not to look at the Texan with the carbine, but the rustler couldn't help himself.

John Poe said, "I hear they're *still* losing Panhandle cattle to New Mexico, and they're pushing me real hard to bring a thief back. Real hard."

"The hell with you," Keough said.

"That's no way to talk," answered Garrett. "You're already caught and we're going to put you on trial for something, somewhere. It might help if you were on trial around here instead of in Texas. Those Texas boys might not be as friendly as we are."

Keough shot a glance at his partner, but Aker wouldn't look his way. He sat hunched over, rocking slightly back and forth, his eyes empty.

"You see," Pat went on, "we're trying to find out things about the way beeves get stolen. We know some of the cattle comes from the Panhandle, and we also know that you've got an organized way to get rid of the cattle. That's something you could help us with, Keough. You too, Aker."

There was no answer.

"I got a feeling you're still working the way the Kid taught you. Is that it? Did Billy set things up?" Pat looked from one sullen face to the other. "Is Billy back in it with you?"

When he finally spoke, Ellis Aker blurted out the words, his voice sounding thin, strained with desperation. Half-rising out of his chair, he said, "Keough sells the beeves. He takes care of it. I ain't goin' to jail for him. I ain't the one that knows the Kid."

Before Garrett could do anything to prevent it, Keough lunged out of his seat and backhanded Aker across the face. Aker tumbled back over his chair. In the next instant, the hand Keough hadn't used to hit his partner was holding a gun, a Remington Elliot hideaway pistol.

Pat swept his Colt out of its holster and lurched out of his chair. Keough had his gun pointed at Aker sprawled on the floor, but he quickly swung it toward Garrett when the sheriff reached his feet. The little gun popped, sending a .22 past Garrett's ear. Pat fired and drilled Keough through the collarbone and then fired again. The second .44–.40 plowed through the young cowboy's forehead. Keough's head snapped back, and for a moment he stared at the ceiling, a puzzled look in his eyes. His hideaway gun fired once into the dirt floor before he collapsed.

Before Keough hit the ground, Pat wheeled to his right to see Spangler lumbering around the bar toward the open crate. John Poe was a couple of steps behind him. As the German pulled the pistol out of the crate, Poe rammed the stock of his carbine into the back of the man's neck. That was when Aker bolted.

He didn't bother to pick his revolver up off the floor. His arms flailed and he barely stayed on his feet as he scrambled for the door. Pat shoved his chair aside and raced after him. He reached the door in time to see Aker grabbing the reins of his horse.

Then Pat heard the back door open.

At the first creak of hinges, Garrett pounded to a stop and dove to the side. He hit the floor, twisting his body so that he could look at the rear of the roadhouse. Through the open back door a small room had been revealed, just big enough for a bed and some space to walk around it. Standing in the doorway was Dave Rudabaugh. He wore only his pants, and clutched a revolver in his right fist. Hovering behind him was a small Mexican woman wrapped in a blanket.

Rudabaugh's gun was cocked and leveled before Pat could swing his own revolver around. A carbine shot then boomed through the adobe.

John Poe had reacted quickly and had fired just as quickly, too fast to take good aim. He didn't hit the center of his target, but he put a bullet through Rudabaugh's forearm, just missing the bone. The outlaw's gun dropped. For a moment, Rudabaugh was stunned, motionless. Then he bounded back into the small room. Pat forgot about Aker.

The Mexican woman got in Pat's way as he charged through the doorway. She might have been blocking him, or just might have happened to be in the wrong spot because the room was so small. Garrett shoved her onto the bed. Rudabaugh was already climbing out the window. Throwing himself across the room, Pat grabbed the outlaw's boot. The top of Rudabaugh's body plunged to the ground outside while Pat brought the leg down on the windowsill and applied some pressure, just enough to let Rudabaugh know that he could break his leg. Rudabaugh was suddenly very still. Pat didn't give him a chance to think of some way out of the hold. He grabbed the outlaw's waistband, hauled him back inside and pressed his Colt to the man's throat.

"Stay on the damn bed," he barked over his shoulder at the Mexican woman. Then he slammed Rudabaugh against the wall.

"Where's the Kid?" Pat said.

"I don't know, Garrett."

Pat pressed the muzzle of the Colt up against the underside of the outlaw's jaw. "Don't shit me. If anybody knows, you do. What're you boys up to? Is he in Mexico? Where the hell is he? Talk, goddamn it. Where is he?"

Rudabaugh's bearded face darkened with fury. "I don't know! And I don't give a shit where he is! I don't know where the goddamn hell he is!"

The Kansas tough's anger stopped Garrett short.

He figured a man on the run would be rattled if he had been caught in this way. And Rudabaugh's rage didn't seem like a bluff. Slowly, Pat pulled the Colt away from the outlaw's jaw. He took a couple of moments to settle himself as a bitter realization came to him.

"He's left the territory, hasn't he?" Pat said.

"You're asking the wrong fella. The one who could've told you is that fool kid Keough, but you fixed it so he won't tell you anything. He's seen

Billy, but he's been keepin' it to himself, like he was something special and nobody else deserved to know."

Pat gave him a skeptical look. "You telling me you didn't hunt up the Kid when you escaped from the Las Vegas jail?"

"I put out the word, sure. I let some fellas know I was ready to get back in business with the Kid, but I never crossed his trail. I heard he didn't want to have any truck with me. He figures he got caught with me, so now I'm bad luck. The little pissant."

Garrett studied the man's glowering expression. He couldn't help but believe the outlaw. His resentment against Billy sounded genuine.

"I did hear one thing, though," Rudabaugh said. His yellow teeth were bared in a smile. "Keough did say one thing about Billy being up to Hot Springs. He said the Kid murdered a man for just looking at him the wrong way, some fella working for Tip McKinney. Now that's really something, eh Garrett? Shooting as quick as he is, I'd say Billy's getting ready for you."

At first, Pat answered him with silence. Finally he said, "One of Tip's boys?"

"That's what I heard."

Pat felt something move inside him, something giving way. Before now, he had thought Billy had gone as far as he could, but now Pat was sure he had been wrong. The longer the Kid was out there, the more senseless his killings would become.

Pat focused on Rudabaugh's face again and saw the outlaw staring quizzically, wondering what was leading the lawman's thoughts astray. Pat forced his mind back to the business at hand. There was one last tack he wanted to try with Rudabaugh, just in case the outlaw wasn't telling the truth about the Kid.

"All right, Rudabaugh. I guess you don't have anything to tell me. And I won't even bother asking you about what kind of rustling you been doing around here these days. It doesn't matter. All I got to do is get you back to the Las Vegas jail. Let's go. Get on your feet. We'll see if we can find someone to look after that arm of yours along the way."

Rudabaugh did as he was told, but by the time he stood up, a new expression had taken over his face. The outlaw bravado was gone. Fear was taking its place.

Pat pulled him across the room. "I said, let's go. What the hell's the matter with you?"

Rudabaugh came to a dead stop just before the door, as if his feet were bolted to the ground. "Don't do it, Garrett."

Pat didn't answer. He just feigned a bewildered look.

"Damn it, Garrett, you know what I'm talking about. Why the hell do you think I busted out of that jail?"

"I kind of thought you preferred to be on the outside."

"They were going to lynch me there! And that's what they'll do if you take me back there! All those Mexes in town, all they care about was that it was a Mex jailer I killed when I got Webb out of their calaboose last year."

Pat rubbed his jaw, as if this was something that hadn't occurred to him. "You could be in a tough spot up there," he said. Then he pulled Rudabaugh toward the door.

"Damn it, Garrett. What do you want? Let's work it out. Just don't take me back to Las Vegas. For Christ's sake, Garrett."

Pat stopped pulling him once they reached the doorway. "All right, Rudabaugh. How about telling me what you really know about the Kid."

"I told you everything, damn it."

Garrett pulled on his arm. "Well, maybe you can break out of the jail before anything happens."

"I won't be able to. They won't give me the chance. They'll get me the first night—I know it. Garrett . . . wait! Stop! Wait a minute, I can tell you something. Hold on, I got something for you."

Pat stopped. "Is that right? What would it be?"

"Just give me your word. What will you do for me?"

"Well, if I like what you tell me, I can make arrangements for you to go to Santa Fe instead. But you haven't told me anything yet."

"All right. All right. I'll tell you. It's about the rustling. I can tell you who's buying most of the cattle. It's the fella that Billy made a deal with. I can tell you that." Rudabaugh stopped to see the sheriff's reaction.

Pat said, "That just might be good enough, Dave."

34

One of the ranch hands showed Garrett to the bedroom that doubled as an office. In the far corner was a massive walnut desk, its varnished side casting a dull sheen as it was struck by the morning light slanting through the window. Pat got no greeting from the man at the desk. Not bothering to turn and take a look at his visitor, the rancher merely raised a hand to tell Pat that he shouldn't be interrupted. He dipped his pen into a vial of ink and continued writing.

By the time the man was finished, the ranch hand who had escorted Pat was long gone, which was all to the good as far as Garrett was concerned. He closed the door and stepped closer to the desk. Jim Boskett turned toward him, still saying nothing, letting out only an impatient sigh. He didn't like to be disturbed this early in the morning.

"I found Rudabaugh and a couple of his boys over to White Oaks," Pat said.

There was the slightest shifting of Boskett's gaze a moment after Garrett had spoken—at least Pat thought there might have been. Then the rancher shook his head in irritation. "For crying out blue Jesus," he said, "if you've got some reason for coming here, then tell me. I've got my morning desk work to do." Boskett's grating manner made Garrett forget any fancy notions he had had about getting the man to reveal himself.

"You told me to be ready for gunplay when I went up against the White Oaks rustlers," said Pat. "That's because you wanted me to kill them if I caught up to them. In case they decided to tell me something. That's right, isn't it?"

Boskett's eyebrows lowered and met in a single line as his irritation deepened. It seemed to be the only way he knew how to react.

"Before you try to shout me down," Pat went on, "let me tell you I got the story from Rudabaugh. I didn't kill him, Boskett, so he's still around to testify if he thinks it'll be worth his while. It won't take much to make him think that. He'll do just about anything to stay away from Las Vegas."

Boskett kept his square jaw firm, his expression stoic, but he gripped his pen so hard that his knuckles turned white. "I suppose," he began, "you think that I'll listen—" His voice stopped abruptly.

He sat stock-still for a few moments, then his head swiveled in a quick, tight movement, first to the left, then back to its original position. His eyes seemed to alternately glaze over and sharpen their focus.

Sensing that the time had come to ease up, Garrett walked over to a chair halfway across the room from the desk and took a seat. He took off his hat and rolled it through his hands while watching Boskett.

"I closed that door," Pat finally said, "to make sure we'd be alone. How about your wife, Boskett? Would she be the kind to eavesdrop?"

"No."

Pat's stomach soured as he watched Boskett keep his back erect, trying to appear as if he really weren't dropping down a notch. Garrett was surprised at the feeling. He had thought he might take pleasure in this.

"What happened, Boskett? Why did you want me to kill them? Did the deal go bad?"

Boskett let out a laugh that sounded unnaturally loud. "It didn't go bad for them. Not for them, that's for sure. They just started to get greedy, which wasn't so good for me."

"Who was it? Rudabaugh?"

"No, I don't think so. Although he would've gotten around to it himself, I'm sure. It was that damn kid Keough. He got real full of himself after you caught Bonney. Thought he was the one to call the tune after that. He told me he'd let it be known about me unless I started to pay a better price for the beeves." Boskett let out a long breath and looked off, consternation creasing his face. "The damn greedy runt. He probably ruined it for all of us. He should've just let it ride the way Billy and me had set it up."

Pat saw no reason to dig any further. Boskett was moving on his own steam now. A while later, the rancher turned to face Garrett. He started up again once he had a chance to read the sheriff's expression.

"It all made sense, Pat. At the beginning, anyway. I was really losing to the rustlers—that part was really true when I got behind Chisum and the Captain to make you sheriff. But it all seemed to move so slowly, and something came along that seemed like it could push things along a lot quicker. Damn, Pat, you know what it was like before Chisum really got rolling? I was a real cock of the walk around this valley. Then Chisum kind of took over, and then a couple of years ago the rustlers really went to work. When Bonney sent word he wanted to talk about solving my rustling problem, I figured it couldn't hurt to listen. I guess he knew I didn't much like Chisum—hell, I guess Billy figures everybody hates the man. And he said the money I'd make by working with his gang would make me the top dog again." Boskett stopped and stared at the pen in his hand as if he hadn't known it was there before. He placed the pen back on the desk, then flexed his fingers, cramped now from the way he had been holding tight.

"I don't have to tell anyone about this," Pat said. "Chisum doesn't have to know you've been stealing from him if you just leave the county. We can leave it like that. Just leave and there won't be an arrest."

Pat didn't expect Boskett to bust out crying in gratitude, but he did think he was making a generous offer. In any case, he didn't count on getting laughed at.

"Is that what you're thinking?" Boskett said through the last of his bitter laugh. "You're going to save me, eh Garrett? You're going to lord it over me. Is that it?"

Pat stared at him in disbelief.

"It doesn't end here," Boskett said. "No sir." He got to his feet and started striding back and forth in front of his desk. "No matter what's happened, I'm not getting pushed around by my own hired gun. You think you can pull more weight in this county than me? You really think that?"

Suddenly Boskett was no longer a broken man. Pat couldn't decide if the rancher had snapped and was unable to realize the predicament he was in, or if this harangue was just a last, desperate bluff. Pat didn't spend much time wondering about it. Soon he was too furious to do anything but lash back.

"I could put you in irons, you bastard. I don't care if you can buy a judge and a jury and the whole damn courthouse. I could drag you through the streets of Mesilla, shackled like an animal. Maybe *that'd* kick some of the stuffings out of you."

The smirk on Boskett's face made Pat want to throw him through the window. Finding himself on his feet—he didn't know when he had gotten out of the chair—Pat held himself tightly together to keep himself from uncoiling.

Boskett stepped away, scratching his beard, and kept pacing for several moments before he faced Pat again.

"All right, Garrett. You're a big man in this county—I admit it. Does that make you feel better? Now maybe we can talk business."

"And what the hell does that mean?"

"What it means is, no matter how much you hate

me, I can make it worth your while to keep this quiet—and let me stay right here while you're at it."

Pat couldn't think of anything to say at first. The man's gall stupefied him. He started to laugh. "A bribe? Is that what you're getting at? Are you that stupid that you think I would go along with that?"

"I think you're calling the wrong man stupid, Garrett. I'm pretty damn sure you can't be bought once you're on a man's trail. Not with money, anyway. And you should be smart enough to know I wouldn't try that. But I think you can be bought with information. I know you'd do just about anything to find out where the Kid is."

Pat almost asked Boskett to repeat what he had just said; he wasn't sure for a moment that he had heard right. Then he moved back to the chair and sat down, staring at the rancher.

It hadn't occurred to him that Boskett could help him track Billy. He had already come to the conclusion that the Kid must have taken off for Old Mexico—after all, what else would make sense? A doubt now crept into his mind.

"Now wait a minute," he told Boskett. "If you're just going to tell me what town in Old Mexico the Kid went to, that's not going to be worth anything."

"Oh, for Christ's sake, I know that. But it *is* worth something if he's on this side of the border, isn't it? Worth enough to keep you quiet about me, I'd say."

"Yeah, it would be. If you're not lying."

"Now you're really being stupid, Garrett. I know enough not to try that with you. Billy didn't light out for Mexico, and that's the truth. I saw him just a few days ago. Hell, Garrett, he didn't even leave the county. He's back in Fort Sumner, right back where the two of you got started."

Garrett sat puzzling about this for a while, but then decided it didn't matter if it didn't make any damn sense. He left the room without another word.

35

The roadrunner streaked through an opening in the patch of shrubs and snapped its long beak around the sidewinder, just behind the head, before the snake had the chance to turn and strike. The snake's rattle chattered fitfully as the roadrunner jerked it from side to side, raising a cloud of dust all around. In another few moments the dust cleared, and the bird tore out the snake's insides.

Sitting on a hummock some fifty yards away, Billy watched the roadrunner do its work. He finished cleaning his Colt and rested it on his thigh, thinking it was a shame that the bird had beat him to the punch. Billy liked rattlesnake meat and had been thinking it would have made a welcome change from Juanita's cooking. But his disappointment only flickered for a short while, then was gone. *Too hot today to be bothered,* he thought.

When the roadrunner moved off, Billy considered taking a shot at it, but then figured it wouldn't even make good practice. Aiming at anything that fast, that far away, with a handgun, would be pointless. Instead, he looked around him and picked out a creosote bush that had two spindly branches rising above the others. He loaded the Colt's chambers and fired twice, snapping the shots and hitting nothing. Flexing his grip on the handle, he was more deliberate on his next shot and sent a .41 through the branch on the right. *Got to take that extra moment,* he told himself, *if you figure on getting things done.*

From the other side of the hummock came the sound of running feet. Billy turned to see Juanita Lopez headed his way, her face constricted with fear. When she saw that Billy was alone, she became angry.

"Just practicing, Juanita," Billy said. "When it's real, it'll probably sound different. I'm not sure how. But different some way."

The impulse in Juanita to say something almost won out, but in the end she just blurted out "Billito," spitting out the name with the last of her anger. Then she marched back to the ranch house. Billy had to smile as he watched her storm off. It was just like Juanita, peevish and quiet all the time because he wasn't paying enough attention to her, but running to him at the first sound of gunfire, afraid that something had happened to him.

Just to give himself something to do, Billy got up and started walking toward the house. Across the flat scrubland he saw Damaso Lopez riding in from his sheep herd. Billy leaned against the low adobe wall and waited.

When Lopez reined in his horse at the Kid's side, the sheepherder looked quizzically from one side of the ranch house to the other. Billy laughed.

"It was just practice," the Kid said. "Just trimmin' one of your shrubs back there."

Lopez nodded and smiled weakly. "Good, Billy," he said. For a few moments, the only sound was the clattering of pots from inside the house, where Juanita was making lunch with more noise than was needed. *Better talk to her,* Billy thought. *Better not let her get too mad.*

"The boy and me," said Lopez, "we could use some help with the sheep. Why don't you go back with me?"

Billy pursed his lips and cocked his head as he gave this some thought. "Just might do that, Damaso. I just might be along after awhile. But I got some thinking to do first. I got a feeling something's got to be done if I'm to make things right and I just have to sit and figure it for a while."

Damaso Lopez had no trouble understanding the Kid's message. It was time for him to get away from his own house and leave Billy alone. As he reined around, he glanced apprehensively through the house's open door at his daughter working inside. More and more these days he was troubled by the idea of leaving the Kid alone with Juanita. He wasn't so sure this young gringo who did no work would make a good son-in-law, no matter how good a protector he would be.

Billy's own thoughts had nothing to do with Juanita. He continued to sit on the adobe wall, running a hand over its rough surface. He couldn't help but remember the time Charley Bowdre and Tom O'Folliard had spent helping Lopez build this wall. The memories made him sad and frustrated. Billy had come back this way to make his stand and to do right by his friends, both the living and, especially, the dead, but he saw now that he still wasn't on the right track. And that was the saddest part of all.

Sorting through his memory, the Kid tried to piece together the thoughts that had run through his head on the way down here. It had only been a week ago, but the time spent here at Lopez's place had been so empty, it seemed much longer ago than that.

He had thought that just his being in this area would be some kind of victory; every day spent here, right in Garrett's backyard, would be another slap in the old woman's face. But, the Kid realized now, doing nothing was draining him. And the prospects for something happening were slim. Some cattle business would be just the thing he needed, but he still hadn't gotten word from Keough about the recruits for their next raid against Chisum. And there was nothing from Boskett either. If they took any Chisum cattle, they'd need to sell them fast, and they couldn't do that unless Boskett told them where the deal would take place.

You just can't depend on some fellas, Billy decided. *You depend on too many people, you'll end up nowhere—or on some pitiful little sheep ranch, which was close to the same thing.*

It occurred to Billy that maybe what had to be done was to make Garrett come to him. He could put out the word where he could be found, and then pick his spot to gun Pat down.

Billy liked that idea.

Of course, the Lopez ranch was no place for getting

the word out. Fort Sumner town—that would be the place. With all his friends around, Billy knew he could find the right man to pass along the information to Garrett, and just as important, he'd be surrounded by people who would let him know when any trouble was coming his way. *I'd like to see old Pat slip into town while I'm around,* he told himself. *You won't get away with it this time, friend. No sir.*

The more Billy thought about Garrett, the tighter his muscles got—around his stomach, along the sides of his eyes, at the back of his neck. A dull pain began to push through his head, and all his plans seemed to fall away, replaced by the memory of the place that Garrett had put him: the big corner room in the Murphy & Dolan building. Sitting in the rocker, looking out the window, waiting for the hanging.

Billy pushed himself away from the adobe wall. He paced across the ranch house porch. The time had come, he told himself. He would leave now and be in Fort Sumner town before nightfall. Maybe there'd be a *baile* where he could kick up his heels and get this sheep ranch out of his blood. And Paulita would be there—he could stand a little of that too. And if one of Pat's deputies was trying to nose around in town, that would make it perfect.

He went into the house and told Juanita he was on his way.

She stood staring at him, her hands coated with cornmeal, her black eyes gleaming with anger, seeming too big for her thin face. Billy could feel his smile giving up under the strain. He picked his jacket up off the bench and fumbled with it as he faced her. After a while he decided he couldn't say anything more, and he turned to leave. Her sob stopped him short.

"Oh, Billito," she said. "What is it? What's wrong?"

"What do you mean, Juanita? Nothing's wrong. I just got to go is all."

"But why can't you stay here? Have I done something? What is it?"

"Oh, don't even say that. You're just about the finest girl I know." He turned back now and kissed her and said, "Just stay good till I come back, you hear?" He smiled at her again. He couldn't understand why she shoved him away.

"Get out," she said. "Go on if you're going to leave." She managed to hold on to her angry look for just a moment more before she turned away. Billy knew what was coming. He had too much on his mind to consider soothing a crying woman now, so he walked out the door and saddled his horse.

He was still thinking of Juanita as he rode east, away from the ranch. There was just no way to explain it to her—that was the real problem. How was a man supposed to keep his mind on her when there was a girl like Paulita so close at hand? Poor Juanita, the Kid mused, it's not her fault she's not quite pretty enough, even if she's so nice and willing.

After the killing of Brock there was no trouble convincing Tip McKinney to come along. The three of them—Garrett, Poe, and McKinney—rode up the Pecos toward Fort Sumner and reached the sand hills outside of town by evening. They camped just long enough to eat some stale sourdough biscuits before Pat gave the order to move on.

Nothing was said during the last leg of the ride. No plans had been discussed concerning their course of action once they reached town, but neither Poe nor McKinney ventured to ask the sheriff what he had in mind. Garrett was drawn tight, as if only a word were needed to make him snap. The two deputies were content to wait and see.

They reached a peach orchard short of the plaza as dusk was tinting the town with gray light. Still not saying anything, Pat dismounted, led his horse behind a tree, and motioned to his deputies to follow suit. When they were all crouched behind cover, Pat said, "We'll wait for dark."

The night came soon, and it was nearly pitch-black, the only illumination coming from a sliver of moon. Pat gazed across the grove toward the adobe building that had once been the army post's quartermaster store. He gave his eyes time to pick up sharper outlines among the dark shapes before him.

"That's Celsa Taveras's house over there," he said quietly. "If her husband's not around, the Kid could be with her. Or he could be on his way there. We'll wait here a while to see if we can see him coming or going."

"And after that?" asked Poe. "What if we don't see him? What do we try next?"

"If we see him here we won't have to try anything else."

Tip McKinney let out a grunt of a laugh. "You're not worryin' too much about the future, are you, Pat?"

"I'll tell you one thing I'm planning on," answered Garrett. "If we get seen by anyone, I'm planning on trouble. If Billy's in town, you can bet he's got things going his way around here. Anyone who sees us is either going to tell Billy or take a crack at us himself. Your job is to watch my back. You can plan on that."

Tip glanced at Poe, then faced the sheriff again. "Fair enough," he said. "We're here to pitch in, Pat."

Garrett led the way forward to find cover that was closer to the house. A sound made him come to a sudden stop.

He wasn't sure what it was. It might have been a rustling of branches, or perhaps a faint footfall. Whatever it was, it had made McKinney and Poe stop also. All three men were frozen in place, glancing from side to side, waiting for the next sound that would tell them what they had heard. They listened for several minutes, but there was only silence.

They huddled behind a tree some fifty feet from the Taveras house. On this still, hot night, the orchard was as silent as it was dark, the quiet broken only by an occasional thin voice from the plaza. The silence was so complete at times that it made Pat hold his breath, as if exhaling would be a raucous disturbance. They waited and watched for half an hour without seeing anything. Presently, the voices from the plaza got louder and soon there was music coming from one of the houses nearby. Now that the *baile* would drown out any telltale sounds in the grove, Pat strained to see deeper into the black night-shadows beneath the trees.

The watch continued for another hour.

Garrett began to wonder about Poe's question. *Where will we look next? Do we take a chance going into the plaza? If we don't, we take the chance of not finding the Kid. And how long do we wait here before I make that decision?*

A figure rose on the other side of the orchard.

It looked like a man wearing a wide sombrero, though it was nothing more than a dimly outlined silhouette without any discernible features. Pat figured the man must have been on the ground the whole time he and his deputies had been here; he was sure no one could have slipped into the grove without his noticing. But then again, in this darkness, it was difficult to be absolutely certain.

Pat could feel his deputies stirring beside him. They were looking his way. The sombrero made Pat think that the figure was not Billy, because the Kid ordinarily wore a slouch hat. Pat knew he didn't have much room for error. If he chased the wrong man, he could betray his presence in town and come up empty at the same time. The whole night would be lost. Pat hesitated, but then something told him he couldn't just let this man go by.

"I'm going to try to get a closer look at him," he whispered to Poe and McKinney. Pulling out his Colt .44–.40, he crept away from the tree.

36

Billy hadn't expected her to come with him into the orchard, but once Paulita agreed, he figured his time had come. All of which made things so confusing later on.

For a while, all they did was lie side by side at the edge of the grove. Neither of them said anything; they just stared at the star-filled sky. The heat had made Billy lazy all day, and the night air was soothing even if it was only slightly cooler. Lying around was all he cared to do for now, and besides, he didn't really have to do anything. Paulita was his tonight—he was sure of it. He would have known better, though, if he had been able to get a good look at her face, veiled now in darkness. There was apprehension in her fine blue eyes.

The *baile* music broke the orchard's lazy spell and prodded Billy into sitting up. Paulita sat up too, moving abruptly, the Kid thought. He figured it was just a well-bred girl's natural skittishness, and didn't pay much attention to the way she angled slightly away from him. He leaned closer.

"You like that music, don't you, Paulita?"

She nodded. "They're playing it at the Garcia house. We could go there now. Wouldn't you like to dance?"

"Sure. I always like to dance. You know me. Except for those times when there's something better to do." Billy held his head to the side to take a long look at her graceful, rounded features. "You're a beauty, Paulita. You surely are." He put his arm around her before she had a chance to turn away, and he pulled her close. He laughed, then kissed her. Paulita's lips were pressed tightly together. Not letting up, Billy soon felt her soften in his grip, but when he pressed her back toward the ground, she quickly swung an arm behind her to keep herself in place.

"Aw, c'mon, Paulita," he murmured. He laughed again to put her at ease. It didn't work. She wrenched to the side and struggled against his hold until he finally let go.

Billy watched her prop herself up, her back still partly turned to him; he narrowed his eyes as he tried to figure out what had just happened. A moment later, she broke the silence.

"I can't marry you, Billy," she said.

The Kid's face was blank. Never having asked her to marry him, he thought this was one of the stupidest things he had ever heard. But he had enough sense not to say that.

"My brother spoke to me today," she continued.

"He told me what would happen if I went away with you. I suppose I should've known all along, but he would make life terrible for us, any way he could. I just can't marry you."

Billy knew he had to shake this idea out of her before it got too far along. He grabbed her by the shoulders; Paulita didn't try to get away, but she barely looked at him. "A woman's got to do other things for a fella other than marry him," he said. "I'm a hunted man—you know that, Paulita. And when a man's under the gun the way I am, he's got to have a woman who'll do anything for him, to keep him strong. And with all I've got to do, standin' up for everybody against the likes of Chisum and Garrett—well, you can't expect to do all that without a real woman. A man can do only so much by himself."

She looked up at him, then lowered her eyes again and started shaking her head. "Billy, you're not doing anything."

The Kid opened his mouth but nothing came out. He looked at her, puzzled. "What the hell does that mean?" he finally said with a laugh.

"You're not doing anything. You're just running. That's all."

It didn't take long for Billy to decide he was wasting his time. Pretty as she was, she wasn't the only woman in this world, he thought, and she sure didn't know much about anything worth knowing. He pulled away from her, giving her a look that was full of pity.

"You've got to become a full-grown woman sometime," he said. "It's just my luck it isn't tonight." He picked up the sombrero he had borrowed from

Garcia, planted it on his head, and walked toward the plaza.

The shadowy figure had already gotten too far ahead.

Pat might have been able to get close, but only if he broke into a run, and that would have made too much noise, alerting both the man in the sombrero and anyone else who might be about. And besides, Pat thought, it might not even be the Kid after all.

Garrett stopped behind a tree. He'd watch the man long enough to see where he was headed just to get a clearer picture of what was going on at this end of town. He told himself to be satisfied with that. His mind was so intent upon the silhouette figure heading toward the plaza that he nearly jumped when the footfall reached him from the side.

He pressed himself against the tree. He snapped the Colt up. His thumb was on the hammer, ready to cock and fire as he saw the second dark figure emerge into a gap between the trees, twenty feet away. Still undetected, Pat moved the gun to keep the figure in his sights, his index finger applying the slightest pressure to the trigger. He told himself that the revolver was only a tool, one that had to be used. He then saw the outline of the figure as it stepped in front of the light background of an adobe house beyond the grove. It was a woman.

Garrett stayed put as the woman left the grove and entered the plaza; and then he found himself remaining there even after she was gone. Sensations rushed through him, bringing a tremor to his fingers.

Soon Pat crept back to his deputies. "We're going to take a closer look at the Taveras house," he told them. "If we can't see anything, we'll find a way into the plaza."

A fandango was just the thing to get Billy's spirits up once more. Letting loose a howl, he took a turn in the center of the Garcias' floor, and he stomped and clapped and pranced while the rest of the *baile* crowd cheered him on. His shirt was drenched in sweat when he was done, but he was flying high. He didn't even mind that Paulita hadn't been there to see him take over the dance floor.

He stayed at the *baile* until eleven o'clock. As much as he had put Paulita behind him, he still couldn't quite shake part of what she had said, and he decided he should leave the dance to prove her wrong. *I'm not doing anything?* he thought. *We'll just see about that.*

Billy had to admit he still hadn't found someone to get the message to Garrett that he was in Fort Sumner, but that could be corrected soon enough. He walked along the east side of the plaza to clear his head and let him sort through the possibilities. While passing the Bowdre home, he idly noticed someone standing at the corner up ahead smoking a cigarette. At first he was too preoccupied to pay the man much notice, but then something suddenly registered with him, and it sent an icy feeling through his stomach.

Backing up against the front of the old post hospital, he assured himself that the deep shadow beneath the overhang had probably been enough to keep him concealed on this dark night. If the figure standing near the end of the south side of the square had noticed him, Billy couldn't see any sign of it. He studied the figure.

The man was tall—very tall—and lean too. That was what had struck the alarm within Billy. The man stood behind a spring wagon, facing slightly away from the Kid, the red pinpoint at the end of the cigarette moving up and down as the man took his puffs. It occurred to Billy that it might not be a cigarette at all. It could be a cigar—just like Pat Garrett smoked. Billy couldn't make out any details, but the figure's height told him that the man just might be the genuine long-legged bastard.

Billy moved slowly along the porch, staying close to the adobe wall, placing each step with care. The long man didn't move as Billy got closer and showed no sign of noticing the Kid's approach. *Take that extra moment,* Billy cautioned himself. The Kid flexed his fingers around the double-action Colt. At the end of the porch, he sprang to the side and set himself. Turning quickly toward the sound, the tall figure took a startled intake of breath that reddened the tip of the cigarette in his mouth and cast a faint orange light across his face. That was what saved him.

"Damn," Billy said. He lowered the gun.

The cigarette in Juan Gallegos's mouth dropped to the porch as his mouth hung open.

Juan was tall for a Mexican, but not much taller than Billy. The Kid could see now what had tricked his eyes. Standing behind the wagon, Juan's legs had been concealed; Billy hadn't been able to see that the Mexican was standing on the boardwalk built six inches above the ground. Billy cursed himself for being too nervous and too jittery to have realized this.

"Billy," Juan now managed to sputter, "what are you doing? I haven't told anybody about you. Not nobody."

"Shut up," the Kid snapped at him. He was still jumpy. Holstering his gun, he stepped closer to Juan. He glared at the Mexican, then looked around the plaza until he managed to put his thoughts back in order.

The first thing to do, he told himself, *is make sure some people know what's expected of them. Can't take on Garrett until I'm damn sure I'll get the word when he comes in. I can't go around throwing down on everybody in town.*

Billy got close enough to Juan to poke him in the chest. "If you're going to stand around all night, you make sure you keep your eyes open," he said. "You hear me?"

Juan nodded quickly.

"If I hear Garrett or any of his damn deputies gets by you I'm going to throw down on you for real." The expression on Juan's face told Billy he didn't have to say any more. He wheeled and headed back along the east side of the plaza.

Billy was satisfied with himself for making the best of a bad incident. *There are times,* he told himself, *when a man's got to push.* Paulita couldn't say he wasn't doing anything now, that was for sure. *She'll see how wrong she is before too long,* he thought.

As he headed back toward the Garcias' *baile,* he noticed something that made him slow down and put a smile on his face: a light shone in Celsa

Taveras's window. He decided there was more than one way to put Paulita out of mind.

The possibility that Celsa's husband might be home tonight didn't bother him. He could always jolly Taveras along and pretend he had come to share a jug of whiskey with him; after an hour or so he would leave, biding his time till Taveras was not around. For that reason, Billy strolled in through the front door instead of taking the back way. Because of that he didn't see the three men leaving the yard at the rear of the house.

37

The *baile* made it impossible to find out what was going on inside the adobe. Pat and his deputies crouched beneath the Taveras's rear window to try to hear if anyone was talking inside, but the guitar and fiddle music and the hooting of the dancers ruined that idea. Pat and McKinney then tried to get a look through a window on the other side, but as soon as they would get into position they would have to drop back behind cover as people on their way to the dance passed dangerously close. Giving up, the three-man posse retreated to the edge of the peach orchard.

From behind a tree, Pat could see Beaver Smith headed toward the Garcia *baile* with Bob Campbell. Smith clapped his friend on the back and tilted his head back to let out a big, drunken laugh. *He's back on Billy's side of the fence again these days,* Garrett brooded.

"How will we get to the plaza?" Poe asked. "Over to the church?"

Garrett gave this some thought. "Don't think so," he answered. "I figure we still might have one person we can talk to in this town. Come on. We'll circle around this way." Pat moved low to the ground, angling to the right, toward the blackness behind the Garcia house.

He was confident that he was striking a course that was far enough away from the *baile,* so confident that his step quickened and he started to pull away from his deputies. He was glancing at the swirling dancers through the back window of the Garcia house when he stumbled into the man with the liquor jug.

The broad-shouldered Mexican's eyes were hooded and lazy from the tequila he had been drinking, but once he had regained his footing, those eyes flashed in recognition. Jose Valdez immediately dropped the jug. With a practiced sweep of his hand, he then whipped a hunting knife from his boot and swung it at Pat's face. Even in the darkness, the blade seemed to gleam as it rushed toward Garrett's eyes, just as Pat jerked his head back, out of the knife's way. Valdez didn't bother with a second swipe. He bolted for the plaza.

For a moment, Pat was dazed by the sudden attack, but he then lunged forward to chase the Mexican racing toward the lights of the town. *He's going to Billy* was Garrett's only thought.

Valdez had the head start. Pat, though, had the long legs. He came within a few feet of him, grabbed the back of Valdez's shirt, and in one motion, came to a stop and swung the Mexican to the side. The knife flashed toward Pat again. Dodging to the left and dropping to a crouch, he grasped Valdez's arm from below. He rose quickly and smashed the arm against his upraised knee. He heard something snap.

McKinney and Poe arrived in time to pick the whimpering Mexican up off the ground and hustle him away from the plaza. Dropping him behind a boulder, the deputies tied his feet together, gagged him, and tied his good arm to his body. They jogged back to meet Pat behind the Maxwell house.

Pat took one more long breath to try to settle his jangling nerves.

McKinney said, "We're ready to watch your back, but we can't do a hell of a lot about your front, Pat, if you get too far ahead of us."

Garrett didn't seem to hear him. He jabbed a thumb toward the near corner of the long rectangular building to his rear. "Pete's our best bet," he said. "His bedroom's off the plaza. So we'll have to go around to the other side."

They had to move slowly to make sure they were concealed by the night shadows that clung to the sides of the house. When they reached the porch bordering the plaza, John Poe crouched along the edge of the splintery boardwalk, positioning himself behind an upright; McKinney knelt just a few feet away, his eyes on the plaza. Pat stepped through the open doorway.

The room was even darker than the covered porch. Pat stood just inside and waited for his eyes to adjust. The doorway allowed only the faintest square of light to reach the threshold floor; the window in the wall to the right was just as dim. Soon Pat's ears picked up the sound of regular breathing. When he determined the source of the sound, he moved in that direction and, along the far right wall, found the bed. The darkness made Pete Maxwell's black-haired head nearly indistinguishable from the white pillow underneath it. Sitting on the edge of the bed, Pat reached out and shook Maxwell's shoulder.

"Pete," he said quietly, "get up."

Maxwell turned quickly, waking with a start. He squinted at Pat and tried to get his bearings.

"I know the Kid's in town," Pat said. "Where is he, Pete?"

Maxwell tried to shake himself awake. "Hasn't been here," he said. "Not in this house." Maxwell's words were slurred with grogginess. Garrett figured the man wasn't thinking clearly either.

"He wasn't here at all?" Pat prompted him.

"This afternoon. Yeah. But not since then. I haven't seen him since."

"You got to tell me more, Pete. You're the only one I can talk to here."

Billy had no reason to hurry. Taveras had left for Las Vegas that morning and the rest of the night was ahead of him. He pulled off his sweaty shirt, took off his boots and gunbelt, and stretched out on the bed, as much at home here as he was anywhere. He grabbed Celsa when she passed him on her way to pull the curtains. Holding her on his lap, he kissed her neck and playfully wrestled with her when she pretended that she wanted to get away. As tempting as she was, he was still willing to put it off. He let her go.

He eyed her full figure as she walked away and relished the anticipation. Leaning back, the Kid patted his bare stomach. He said, "I'm awful hungry, Celsa. What can you feed me?"

She pulled the curtains together. "Nothing here, Billito."

"Well, what's a man supposed to do? Starve to death for his best lady? You ask an awful lot of a man, Celsa. No wonder Taveras went to Las Vegas."

She smiled at him. Billito always had something funny to say; not like her plodding husband. "There's some beef hanging outside Maxwell's place. A whole quarter. Should I get some for you?"

"Don't you bother yourself. Just bring me something to carve with. I'll bring back enough for the two of us."

Putting his gun into his waistband, Billy took the carving knife that Celsa brought him and walked barefooted out onto the plaza.

The *baile* was winding down now; only a melancholy guitar tune carried through the windows of the Garcia house and across the town. Walking leisurely in time to the music, Billy thought the song was sad in a way that made a body feel good sometimes, like when the day's work was done and a man could think about times gone by and hard things that had had to be done. The Kid was humming along when he stepped onto the south porch of the Maxwell place.

He stopped just before the open doorway. He thought he saw someone move just a few feet away, along the edge of the porch. He peered through the blackness beneath the overhang. Someone was there all right, crouching behind the post. Billy pulled out his gun.

"*Quien es?*" he demanded.

As soon as the words were out, a bootheel scraped against wood. Billy turned to see a second figure, a few feet beyond the first, coming to his feet. There was a metallic chink that sounded like a spur getting caught in wood. Briefly, the figure staggered.

Billy bounded back against the front of the adobe house. "Who is it?" he asked again.

On the other side of the wall, in Maxwell's bedroom, Garrett could hear the voice. At first he thought it might've been Poe or McKinney. Both Pat and Maxwell sat perfectly still.

On the porch, the three men were just as still. For a suspended moment, the two deputies stared at the man by the door, and the Kid watched the two figures at the edge of the porch. No one could make out any clear details.

Billy thought the two men might be friends of Maxwell, but he wasn't going to expose himself any more than he already had. He backed into Pete's bedroom.

To Garrett's eyes, Billy's figure was dimly outlined as he stepped through the doorway. But only for a moment. Then it merged with the room's deeper darkness. Pat couldn't see who the man was, though the sound of the voice had already triggered suspicion, enough to start his blood racing.

"Pete," said the Kid, "who's outside?"

The voice was now much closer than it had been when the man had spoken on the porch. It made Garrett certain.

Billy took another step toward the bed. Pat could

hear that the Kid was closer, but he couldn't see him clearly. He reached for his gun.

It wasn't on his hip.

Groping quickly, he found that it had shifted around toward his back when he had sat down. The sheriff's movement caught Billy's attention, and Pat heard him take a step back.

"Pete, who is it? Who's there?" The incident with Juan Gallegos came to Billy's mind. This man could be another friend, he told himself.

Garrett tried to think if there was some way to keep Maxwell quiet. He realized there was nothing he could do. If he tried to cover the man's mouth, he would be placing himself in front of the window, making a target of himself. And if Pat said anything, Billy would know who was on the bed. The shooting would start before Pat could get his gun clear.

But Maxwell kept quiet on his own.

Pat now wrapped his fingers around the handle of his Colt. He had to twist his hand around his back to ease the gun silently out of the sheath. Billy would already have his gun up, Pat thought, and he would only have to squeeze the double-action revolver's trigger to set it off. Garrett hadn't seen a gun in the Kid's hand, but he knew it had to be there.

Billy moved back again, almost next to the door. "Who is it?" he demanded once more. "Pete, who is it?"

Pat lifted his gun clear of the holster.

"Who's there?" the Kid shouted.

"Just an old woman, Kid."

Garrett's voice coming out of the dark made Billy lurch one step to the side, into the fringe of the doorway's square of light. Pat could now see the Kid swing his gun arm around as he snapped his own gun up to shoulder level. Pat jacked the hammer back. He pulled the trigger. The Colt .44–.40 roared across the adobe room, and the slug crashed through Billy's chest and spun him away from the door. For an instant, Pat saw the Kid's face, half-lit, frozen in a grimace, his buckteeth bared. Then, still driven off balance by the force of the shot, Billy backpedaled to the far wall.

Pat heard a groan.

He fired again, aiming as best as he could in the dark. He had no idea if he hit his target, but he heard the soft thud of the Kid hitting the wall, then a moment later, a long, rattling wheeze.

Garrett was frozen in place. He sat listening until he was sure there was nothing more to hear.

EPILOGUE

The rider appeared in the middle distance as he rounded the sharply cut shoulder of a low ridge and entered the bunchgrass flat. From the window, Pat studied him until he recognized the man by his barrel-chested build. Garrett moved quickly toward the door, then cautioned himself to keep his expectations in check. He stopped to tell Wilcox to look after things and took an extra moment to pull a cigar from his vest pocket before stepping outside.

Leaning against the ranch house, he pulled in long drags of cigar smoke, but agitation soon got the better of him again. He tossed the cigar aside and walked through the cool autumn air to cut down the distance that much quicker. John Poe had dismounted and was leading his horse when Garrett reached him.

"You're a little early," Pat said. "I didn't figure you to reach here until nightfall."

John Poe nodded, trying not to show anything on his square-jawed face, but his eyes revealed enough.

"No reward," Garrett said quickly, as if some of the edge would be taken off if he managed to say it before his deputy could give him the news.

"At least not for now," said Poe. "I don't know what to tell you, Pat. I gave them my deposition, but it hardly seemed to matter at all. If it isn't one excuse, then it's another one on the way."

"What about your deposition? The governor can't say it wasn't really the Kid we caught up to when he's got your statement right in front of him."

"That's what I mean, Pat. He acted as if he was convinced the Kid was dead all along. Like he didn't have to see my statement to think so. And then he ups and says that the five hundred dollars was offered by Wallace. Ritch says it was Wallace's offer—not his."

"Well, Ritch is the governor just like Wallace was. What's the difference?"

Poe let out a long breath and shook his head. He looked like he was as weary of these complications as he was of the long ride from Santa Fe. "Ritch says it was Wallace's *personal* offer. Those are the words he used—personal offer. Wallace put up the money as a private citizen. That's what Ritch is saying now, anyway."

"Wallace signed that offer as the governor. Ritch can't deny that. What kind of cheating bastard is he?"

Poe fiddled with the reins and shrugged his shoulders.

Garrett held back his anger, realizing it was time to leave the subject alone, at least for now. He had made it worth his deputy's while to ride up to Santa Fe by promising him a part of the reward money, so he knew the man had done everything he could. And as much as he wanted to sound off, Pat could see that the last thing his deputy wanted to do now was rehash all the infuriating arguments. Then Poe surprised him.

"You got any idea why the governor's doing this?" the deputy asked.

"Maybe it just goes with the job," Pat said, attempting a wry smile. "Come on in, John. There's some food for you back in the house."

Wilcox's boy Pablo came out of the ranch house carrying Elizabeth when Pat and his deputy drew near. Pat took his daughter and stood her on the ground.

"She can get from here to there by walking, you know," Garrett said.

"Sorry, sheriff," the boy said, worried that he'd done something wrong. "I just figured she'd want to see you . . . want to be with you," he quickly corrected himself.

Garrett patted him on the shoulder. "You did a good job, Pablo. I just get real determined about some things."

Taking his daughter by the hand, Pat led her to the buckboard and let her climb up on her own. Her hands felt their way efficiently on her way up to the seat. Pat only had to offer a hand for the last leg of the climb, a part that required more arm strength than the two-and-a-half-year-old had.

"Tell your father to take care of John here," Garrett

told Pablo as he got into the seat next to his daughter. He loosened the reins and noticed Poe standing a few feet away from Elizabeth, studying her with a curious look. The deputy had met Elizabeth only once before and wasn't quite sure what to do with himself around a blind child.

"Man is there," Elizabeth said. "Man is there."

"Yeah, he's still standing there," said Pat.

John Poe smiled self-consciously. "Taking the girl for a ride, eh Pat?" His tone made it clear he had no idea why Garrett would be doing that.

"Yeah, I try to give her a chance to take in some country from time to time. I've got some business in town so I thought I'd bring her along." Pat smiled. "Apolinaria's probably having kittens just thinking about it. You can say goodbye to her, John. She hears just like everybody else. Probably a little better."

Along the road to town, Pat tried not to think how he'd get by the next few months without the reward money. At times he was able to put it out of mind, but feeling Elizabeth sleeping against his side brought the worries back again. *The fight's not over yet,* he told himself. Chisum might be able to help, and maybe some other big men too. *Hell,* he thought, *Boskett should be willing to put in a word for me with what I know.*

It was early evening when they reached Fort Sumner. Bypassing the plaza, Pat drove the buckboard directly to the cemetery and saw that the stories he had heard were correct. He was about to do something about it, but Elizabeth started clamoring to come along.

"Not this time," he said. "I've got to do something, then I'll be back. You stay here."

He held her hand in a way that told her that he wasn't going to tolerate any trouble. She puckered her lips as if she might cry, then nodded her head and did as she was told. Leaving the buckboard at the edge of the cemetery plot, Pat headed toward the table set up beneath the cottonwood on the other side.

In front of the table was a freighter's wagon; the wagon's teamster was talking to the small, fine-featured man standing on the other side and was putting something into the man's palm. By the time Pat approached, the freighter was already on his way, and the small man was covering a jar with a burlap sack. The jar next to it was already covered.

The man greeted Garrett with a smile as he hooked his thumbs into the lapels of his plaid coat, a coat that was just a tad too small. Pat stood quietly next to the table, letting the other man have the first word.

"You're lucky, friend," he said. "I was just about to pull up stakes for the day. Well, to be honest, not just for the day. I'll be moving on tomorrow for Puerto de Luna, so unless you come from Puerto de Luna yourself, this here may be your last chance for a while. Not that Puerto de Luna's my last stop, not by a long ways, not with the interest these days in interesting specimens. It's just that . . . you know, a fella's got to keep on the move. So, all in all, you might be luckier than you think."

"What's in the jars?" Pat asked.

"Well, you see, that's the part that'll require a small payment. Not for myself now, just as a sort of contribution to keep the exhibit going, you might say."

"How much?"

"Now that really depends. One specimen seems to be of more interest than the other and as a result is a bit more dear. This jar over here contains William Bonney's left ear, which is good for ten cents, but the other contains his trigger finger, which naturally is more interesting and costs fifteen cents a look. All specimens are perfectly preserved, of course."

"Show me both of them."

"Sir?"

Pat took the badge out of his jacket pocket and showed it to him. "Take the sacks off. Now."

The small man moved quickly. "Why certainly, sir. No problem. Sheriff Garrett, isn't it? I can understand your concern, sheriff. Some rascals'd pass off a counterfeit specimen as the genuine article and it's only right that you examine them to see for yourself. You see? Here they are. Exactly what I said they would be, right?"

The folded ear and the yellow, wrinkled finger hung suspended in liquid in their respective jars. Pat was willing to guess they were genuinely human, and in that respect were less of a sham than other exhibits he had come across. He picked up one jar at a time and threw them both to the side, smashing them against a nearby rock. Then he kicked the table onto its side.

The small man in the plaid coat made a good show of looking surprised, which just made Pat angrier. He grabbed him by the lapels and hoisted him up onto his toes. "Get the hell going and stay the hell out of Lincoln County. Get going, you little shit." He shoved him away. The man almost lost his balance, then straightened up and, looking suddenly indignant, went over to the rock and picked up the ear and the finger. He stuffed them in a pocket.

"My property," he announced to Garrett. He started walking away, then stopped to face Pat again. "I suppose if you ever catch me again you'd shoot me the dark. Isn't that the way?" He didn't wait for an answer. He turned quickly and strode toward the plaza, breaking into a run after the first few steps.

Pat watched him briefly, then wheeled back toward the buckboard. He stopped himself short and picked up the table and heaved it further away from the cemetery before he walked back across the plot.

His agitated place slackened when he was some thirty feet short of his wagon. He stopped next to Billy's grave.

On either side, the graves of Tom O'Folliard and Charley Bowdre were still marked by crudely made crosses, bearing the names and dates of death carved into the crosspieces. The Kid's wooden headboard, though, had been knocked over, and it was easy to see what had caused the damage. Pat counted six bullet holes in the rotting board. He thought about the men who had fired those bullets. *Where were they when the Kid was alive and I was raising posses to run him down?* he wondered.

There wasn't much left of the headboard, but Pat couldn't see anything nearby that would serve as a substitute, so he dug a fresh hole for it out of the crusty soil and set it back in place as best he could. He continued to crouch by the three mounds for some time, the twilight bringing a deeper stillness to the place that he had no desire to leave for now. He was thankful that he was alone this time. The last time he had come, a pregnant woman came into the cemetery, took one look at him and started to rail at him. "You son-of-a-bitch," she screamed. "You murdering son-of-a-bitch." She tried hitting him in the face, but he grabbed her wrists and restrained her. Only when she finally walked away and got aboard a wagon manned by Damaso Lopez did Pat recognize her as Lopez's daughter.

Pat was now suddenly aware that it was getting dark. He rose to his feet and went back to the buckboard.

"Pappa was angry," Elizabeth said when he sat next to her. He was in no mood to talk. He slapped the reins across the backs of the team and turned the buckboard around.

"Pappa was angry," she said again, looking worried. Pat knew he wouldn't be able to ignore her.

"Yeah, I was angry," he said. "Some fella was doing something over there that I didn't much care for. I wanted to make sure he didn't do it around here. Some boys I used to know are buried here."

"What?" she said—her perennial question. She repeated it when Garrett didn't answer right away.

She would have no idea what he was talking about, but he thought her questions might stop if he said something. "Those boys buried back there—I just don't want buzzards hanging around them. Those boys were friends once, before they went too far wrong."

If Elizabeth had anything more to ask, she quickly forgot it; she wore that pensive look that appeared when things became far too puzzling. She found she was much more interested in the night sounds along the river road back to Roswell. After a while, the rocking of the wagon had its effect, and Pat saw her eyelids droop and her head start to list. Gathering her up, he drove with her sleeping on his lap.

Left alone now, he thought about the three graves and couldn't help but feel that some kind of prayer should be said. The problem was that he had nothing to pray to. Just the same, he hoped there was another life, for the sake of Charley, Tom, and Billy. After ruining themselves the first time, they could use the second chance.

WE HOPE YOU HAVE ENJOYED THIS KNIGHTSBRIDGE BOOK.

WE LOVE GOOD BOOKS JUST AS YOU DO, SO YOU CAN BE ASSURED THAT THE KNIGHT ON THE HORSE STANDS FOR GOOD READING, EVERY TIME.